MW00389448

The Slave Yards

Middle East Literature in Translation
Michael Beard *and* Adnan Haydar, *Series Editors*

For a full list of titles in this series, visit
https://press.syr.edu/supressbook-series
/middle-east-literature-in-translation/.

The
Slave
Yards

A Novel

Najwa Bin Shatwan

Translated from the Arabic by
Nancy Roberts

SYRACUSE UNIVERSITY PRESS

This book was originally published in Arabic as *Zarāyib al-Abid* (Beirut: Dar al-Saqi, 2016).

Copyright © 2020 by Najwa Bin Shatwan
Syracuse University Press
Syracuse, New York 13244-5290

All Rights Reserved

First Edition 2020
20 21 22 23 24 25   6 5 4 3 2 1

∞ The paper used in this publication meets the minimum requirements of the American National Standard for Information Sciences—Permanence of Paper for Printed Library Materials, ANSI Z39.48-1992.

For a listing of books published and distributed by Syracuse University Press, visit https://press.syr.edu.

ISBN: 978-0-8156-1125-7 (paperback)
        978-0-8156-5509-1 (e-book)

Library of Congress Cataloging-in-Publication Data
Names: Ibn Shatwān, Najwá, author. | Roberts, Nancy N., translator.
Title: The slave yards : a novel / Najwa Bin Shatwan ; translated from the Arabic by Nancy Roberts.
Other titles: Zarāyib al-ʿabīd. English
Description: First edition. | Syracuse, New York : Syracuse University Press, 2020. | Series: Middle East literature in translation | "This book was originally published in Arabic as Zarayib al-Abid (Beirut: Dar al-Saqi, 2016)"—Title page verso. | Summary: "Set in nineteenth-century Ottoman North Africa, The Slave Yards is a heartrending and unexpected love story whose riveting events draw readers into a matrix of social, political, sexual and religious themes that open a window for us into a dark, untold chapter of Libyan history"—Provided by publisher.
Identifiers: LCCN 2020004524 (print) | LCCN 2020004525 (ebook) | ISBN 9780815611257 (paperback ; alk. paper) | ISBN 9780815655091 (ebook)
Classification: LCC PJ7936.S53 Z3713 2020 (print) | LCC PJ7936.S53 (ebook) | DDC 892.7/37—dc23
LC record available at https://lccn.loc.gov/2020004524
LC ebook record available at https://lccn.loc.gov/2020004525

Manufactured in the United States of America

O wayfarer, your footprints alone are the path.
O wayfarer, there is no path.
Or rather, the path comes into existence as one goes,
As one goes, the path comes into existence.
And when we look back,
We see the road that
We can never travel again.
O wayfarer, there is no path,
But, rather, footprints inscribed on the sea.

—Antonio Machado

Contents

The Slave Yards

Fate Unites and Divides

A LONG NARROW dirt road was flanked on either side by rows of houses. Apart from their irregular heights, all of them looked more or less alike, their faded white paint peeling off in large chunks. The homes were interspersed with a number of small shops, most of them owned by neighborhood residents. At a spot where the road intersected with another thoroughfare stood a tiny pharmacy with no sign in front. The only pharmacy around, it was known as "Giuseppe's Shop." The owner didn't like the name Giuseppe, but that's what people called him when he wasn't around.

In one of the houses a little boy said to his mother, "There's an old man at the door who wants to talk to you."

It struck the mother as odd that a man her son didn't know had come to their house. Patients and strangers always went to her husband's shop. It was a Sunday morning and she was busy in the kitchen, while her husband sat on the patio smoking his pipe and reading a book. From time to time he would put the book aside and play with a dark-skinned little girl who looked as though she must be his granddaughter.

Bypassing his father, the boy went straight to his mother to tell her about the visitor at the door.

"The man wants to see you," the boy said. "He asked for you, not Baba."

Wiping her hands on a cooking rag, she went out and told her husband about it. They were both surprised that somebody would come asking for the lady of the house rather than the man.

"Anyway," her husband said, "go see what he wants. Maybe he was sent by the clinic or the mission."

More bewildered than hesitant, she approached the front door, her head full of questions and her two children in tow. She peeked out from behind the curtain on the door to see who was there. A tall man dressed in a clean *jard* stood facing the street, his hands clasped behind his back.[1]

When she saw how nicely groomed the visitor was, she thought: *He must have come specially to see me. There's no way his jard would be so white if it were the one he wears every day.*

"Yes?" she said, his back still turned to her. "What can I do for you, sir?"

"Good day, ma'am," the man replied, spinning quickly around.

As soon as he greeted her, he averted his gaze.

She returned the greeting, anxious to know who this was and what had brought him to her doorstep. It was hard for him to catch his breath or think of what to say. He couldn't let himself look at her for very long, though at the same time he wanted to take her in. In those brief moments of encounter, he felt the need to rearrange his words again. He wanted to make sure they were persuasive enough that she wouldn't shut the door in his face and refuse to talk to him. But what made him think she would do a thing like that? Her voice had been gentle and kind. Maybe he should quit speculating and just get on with things.

It wouldn't be appropriate to say, "I've come to speak with Atiga, daughter of Tawida, servant to Hajj Imuhammad Bin Abd al-Kabir Bin Ali Bin Shatwan." No, no, that wouldn't do at all. He should avoid mentioning the word *servant*. On the other hand, he didn't really have any other way of identifying Tawida—the reason for his

---

1. A *jard* is a toga-like men's garment, a traditional part of Libyan dress, and is usually white or off-white. The fabric is knotted in front of the left shoulder, from which it falls freely, with a large swathe draped over the right shoulder, and sometimes over the head.

visit and the person he'd come to talk about. After all, nobody had given this servant woman a name or description other than what slavery had made of her. He'd never known her in any other capacity, and he didn't know exactly what to say to her daughter. He stood in opposition to the slave culture that had left its imprint on his whole society, and the challenge before him was to speak of a slave woman simply as a human being, without any reference to her lowly station.

So how was he supposed to go about this?

When she asked him who he was, the visitor replied that he wanted to speak with her in private. After all, he was going to be speaking with a woman he didn't know and had never seen before, while she would be listening to a stranger who was about to introduce himself as her relative and offer to tell her things she didn't know about herself and her mother, who'd been a servant of his family's.

It was as though they had just been dispatched from another life in which they'd been something quite different from what they were now. What if she preferred to close her door, retreat to her kitchen, and go on with her life without hearing what he had to tell her? What if she wasn't interested in knowing what had happened?

Part of him cringed at this possibility. But another part of him—the liberated, optimistic part—imagined him sitting in her house as an esteemed guest. Her hand on the doorknob, and the voice that had spoken a few brief words to him, were all he had experienced of her.

What would he say? How would he answer her when she asked, "Who are you and what have you come for?" Would she recognize his name, or would she never have heard of him before?

He adjusted his jard over his shoulder and fixed his eyes on the door. The words coming out of his throat in staccato fashion, he announced, "I'd like to speak to Atiga, daughter of Tawida."

"And who might you be?"

The anticipated question had come. After a slight pause, he replied, "I'm Ali Bin Shatwan."

"Who?" she asked somewhat shrilly, her tone a mixture of confusion and astonishment.

"Yes, ma'am. I'm Ali Bin Shatwan."

"And what can I do for you?"

"Well, I've come to tell you something, but it can't be discussed in the street. Might I come in?"

As if she suspected who he might be, she replied, "I don't know you, and I don't need to talk to you. It looks as though you're the one who needs this conversation, not me. So leave me alone, and don't cause me any more worries than I already have. Whatever you've got to say won't do any good."

"Please listen to me."

"No."

She pulled the child standing between them on the doorstep into the house and hurriedly closed the door.

For a few moments he stood frozen in place, not knowing what to do. Then he took a few steps forward and started to speak as though she were still behind the door and watching him through the cracks.

He said, "If you can hear me, I work in Al Funduq Al Baladi marketplace. If you decide you'd like to talk to me, send a servant there, and he'll find me easily. Everybody there knows me. I'm going to put your birth certificate on the doorstep now, and you can take it even if you decide not to meet with me or talk to me. I had it written up specially for you. For your children's sake, I just ask you to hear me out. Please."

Out of a pocket in his *farmala* he brought a document that had been rolled up and tied with a string.[2] Slipping it under the door, he said, "God's peace be with you, Atiga Bint Muhammad Bin Imuhammad Bin Abd al-Kabir Bin Ali Bin Shatwan. Your right has been restored to you. Please don't refuse it."

His eyes still fixed on the door, he stepped away.

Deep inside her were things Atiga didn't know how to describe. Without a word, her almond eyes summed up the story of a wretched slave woman's love for her master. With these eyes she had retreated

---

2. A *farmala* is an ornate traditional Libyan vest.

into her work as the mission doctor's assistant, most of her patients women and children. She rarely spoke with anyone. However, her outer silence was paralleled by an extended inner dialogue with herself about who she was, about the struggle to craft an identity out of two colors. What was she supposed to do with dark skin and almond eyes, and with a grief that belonged to no particular race or blood line?

Why are you reopening my wounds now, Hajj Ali? Why should stories surface when it's too late to do anything about them? To correct their details? To apologize for their painful parts? Atiga wasn't one to reveal her perspective to a stranger, even if he'd shown up in person at her house to acknowledge her identity and her long overdue rights. So she closed the door on him, content to keep her distance.

Like her mother, Atiga was long-suffering and silent, like a boulder that endures the pounding of the salty waves year in and year out without being eroded away. Even so, she gave in at last to the insistent urging of the dignified, elegant Ali, who stood apart from the family that had spurned both her appearance and her person. She told him stories and he listened. On the other side of blood and pedigree, he acknowledged her suffering, allowing her to voice her pain in his presence to the extent that she was able. He opened the doors that had been closed to her for so long, letting her choose where to situate herself in place, time, and perception. He embraced her life with all its complications, all its winding roads. He loved experiencing Muhammad through her. In her he saw Muhammad's eyes, and a bit of the gap between his teeth when she smiled.

He loved and commiserated with her proud, dignified sorrow. He drew near to her without revealing his own secret. He came close to her through a silent embrace, realizing that there was no use in resisting fate. However much he wished he could reach out and touch her spirit, he knew he mustn't try to come closer than the distance between them would allow.

Don't Close a Door
God Has Opened

AS A GENTLE BREEZE BLEW, Atiga and old Yousef lay together one evening under the lemon tree outside their humble abode, her head resting on his arm. They talked at first about the paint on the window grates, which was wearing off from the humid seaside air. Atiga liked her house clean and well maintained, and took care of it down to the last detail. Yousef promised to talk to Basyuni the painter. They'd agree on his wages and when the work would begin.

She fed him a date with an almond inside it, saying mischievously, "Since you're an old man, you understand right away what your wife wants without getting into a long argument. So she's going to keep on feeding you dates with almonds inside them the way you like her to!"

He gave a soft chuckle.

"Have the children gone to sleep, my lady with the almond grove in her eyes?"

"Yes, except for the oldest, the one that taught the rest of them to be troublemakers!"

"He's still awake because he wants to go to sleep under the stars next to his little moon."

"Lucky me!" she said, giving him a playful nudge. "I've got an old man who's always selling me sweet talk, who shares my love for my humble Arab abode and for sleeping under Benghazi's starry sky!"

"But I wasn't old when I sold you my first word."

"Oh yes you were! You were a grownup and I was still just a kid. That's why I believed you!"

They laughed together as they thought back on the days before friendship turned to love, then to a family and a shared destiny.

"I'm the lucky one—I love home, and I love my work too! When I'm at the pharmacy, I keep my eye on the clock until the last customer's gone so I can close up and come home right on time. And I keep my eye on my wristwatch the same way until my nurse comes home from work in the evening."

"You've always been like clockwork, old man!"

"Don't say 'old man.'"

"All right, then, you Negro that I love!"

"Ah, that's more like it! Now snuggle up closer and tell me about your day."

"Well," she began with a sigh, "we treated patients from the suburbs today. I helped Sisters Maria and Francesca. They were little children who needed to be quarantined. It wasn't easy, since their mothers were from outside Benghazi and didn't have any place to stay nearby, so we had to put them up in another room of the clinic."

"Well done, my dove. Well done."

She passed her hand over his face and took off his glasses.

"I'm not your dove."

"Oh, really? What are you, then?"

"I'm your moon. Isn't that what you told me a little while ago? Or do you change your story all the time the way other men do?"

"Oooh, oooh, my little one, I'm so sorry! Now give me my glasses back so I can see right. That way I'll be able to tell whether you're my dove or my moon!"

They burst out laughing again the way they did whenever they were together. Then they gazed at the stars without saying a word. After a while he said, "Go talk to him if that will make you feel better. You might find out something you didn't know before. Anything you learn might be nice."

"How did you know I was thinking about him?"

"I knew it because I know you so well. I'm not just making things up."

"I've actually been thinking about him ever since he came that day."

"Go, then. Maybe it will bring you some relief. You've got nothing to lose, anyway. Give him and yourself the chance. Don't close the door from the very start."

"Is that really what you think?"

"Yes. I don't think you should miss this opportunity. He seems like an honest man to me. Otherwise, why would he have gone to the trouble of getting you an official birth certificate stamped by the Islamic court, and come all this way looking for you? I don't think he's some greedy lout, or somebody with an ulterior motive."

"But I can't figure out why he would come now."

"No matter when he came you would have said the same thing: Why did he come now? It's the will of God. God's the one who chooses the timing of things, and maybe there's some blessing in it for you."

"So what did you think of him?"

"I don't want to put thoughts in your head. But what we're talking about here is your roots, your origins, and you don't cut out a root by closing a door. If I were in your shoes, I'd think about my children. It's better for them to have a past to look back to than not to know anything. In the end, though, the choice is yours. I won't push you into something you don't want to do."

After a brief silence, he asked, "Have you talked to Miftah?"

"Yes, we've spoken."

"And what did he say?"

"You know how important family is to him. He's said more than once that even if your family is nothing but a dog or a cat, you should never give it up."

She giggled.

Then she went on, "He's encouraged me to talk to the man and to invite him to the house. He's even offered to go to the marketplace with me once I'm sure that's what I'm supposed to do. He's happy for me."

Her husband made no comment. After an extended pause, he asked, "Have you gone to sleep?"

"No," she said. "I was thinking about what you said."

"Go to bed now, and never mind what the old Negro has to say."

"The old Negro is my friend and my sweetheart, like that star way up in the sky. Do you see it?"

"Which one?"

"That one."

"Ah. What about it?"

"I can see it more clearly than the millions of other stars out there. It twinkles in the sky and lights up my precious home, not just now, but all the time. And it goes on shining and doesn't leave until I've fallen asleep."

"Oooh, you trickster you!"

You Tell Me the Story

CROWDED AS USUAL, the Jarid Market was bustling with merchants, their male customers, and slaves of both sexes. It was considered improper for a free woman to go there. Even so, Atiga hazarded the venture with Miftah. After delivering her to her destination, he told her he would be nearby when she was ready for him to escort her home.

Clad in European attire that set her apart from the local women, she went in search of a merchant by the name of Ali Bin Shatwan. When he was informed that there was a woman asking for him, he dropped what he was doing and came running. He knew it had to be her. He looked different to her than he had the first time. Unlike the day he'd come to her house, he wasn't wearing a jard. The most attractive thing about him was his gray-flecked hair, along with his towering height, his slender build, and his fair skin. He had handsome features, and his Arab attire was spotless. He had the look of the quintessential merchant.

When he saw her, he greeted her, but without extending his hand. Her coming to the market had made him a bit uncomfortable, since as far as he was concerned, it wasn't a place fit for women of standing.

"Why did you come by yourself?" he asked. "Why didn't you send for me?"

With a sardonic smile, she replied, "Don't worry about what people will say. I'm not important enough for anybody else to care what I do. Nobody knows who I am. I'm hardly even recognized as 'Atiga the nurse!'"

"Now don't talk about yourself that way!" he chided solicitously.

He walked awkwardly ahead of her, clearing the way before her so that she could pass unhindered. He hadn't wanted their relationship to start out with this glaring difference in status, a difference he was doing his best to conceal, and whose consequences he wanted to be rid of. After dismissing some laborers who had been organizing merchandise, he set a chair in the doorway to indicate that the store was closed.

He avoided having her sit across from the entrance so that she wouldn't be visible to passersby.

He was happy to see her, and happy that she'd come. It was the first time he'd been able to get a more complete picture of her, and she was different from what he'd imagined her to be. Wanting to make their first visit as pleasant as possible, he ordered tea for her and opened the conversation by asking her general questions about her life. But when he noticed her curt replies and the long silences between them—as if she hadn't come to talk, after all—he went silent too. As she checked out the shop with her eyes, he took the opportunity to get a good look at her. She was tall and slender, with a darkish complexion. She was pretty, too. In contrast to his general idea about women, she didn't wear Arab dress, and worked outside the home in an institution.

Anxious to break the silence, he said, "This is my grandfather's original store, where our business first got started."

She nodded without saying anything.

"Your father worked here. But he didn't sit behind the counter."

"What? Where?" Atiga replied, as if she'd been thinking about something else.

"He used to sit right where you're sitting now," he said, pointing to her.

"Am I keeping you from some work you're supposed to be doing?" she asked suddenly.

"No, no. You're welcome here! I'm happy you came. You might not believe it, but I really am."

A smile flickered on her lips, as though she were laughing to herself at the senselessness of what was going on around her. Then suddenly her features took on a serious look again.

"So, tell me . . . ," she said.

After some hesitation, he asked, "What do you want me to tell you?"

Just then he had a sudden coughing spell. He went red in the face and his eyes teared up. She waited for him to catch his breath.

"Are you ill?" she asked.

"No, no! Don't worry about me. You tell me a story."

"What story? I don't have any stories to tell."

"Then tell me what you'd like to know. Or anything . . ."

"Why did you come looking for me?"

Her question seemed to surprise him.

"Well," he said, "I had to look for you before I died."

"Are you going to die soon?"

"We're all going to die. Death is close to all of us. It could come at any moment. So please, help me set right whatever I can. I want to make you happy, to communicate with you. You're my roots."

At this point his tone of voice changed, and he really did seem like a sick man. She fixed her gaze on him as he spoke, as though he'd finally hit a tender spot in her heart.

"You might not believe me, of course. You might say, 'So where have you been all these years?' And my answer would be, 'Unless I tell you things you don't know, you won't be able to picture what came before you.' Even if you'd refused to see me again and this were the last time you came, I'd be happy I'd finally been able to meet you, and that I'd restored as much as I could of what's due you and your mother. I've managed to establish your name and your lineage. And now that I've proved that you're Muhammad's daughter, I'm fighting for your inheritance rights too. You don't realize what I've been doing for you in these distant parts of the family domain!"

"Thank you. But why do you talk about death so much? Don't you think I've suffered enough losses already?"

"Because I really am sick."

He sensed that, deep down, she sympathized with him.

"But I didn't come to talk about an inheritance," she clarified. "I came out of curiosity. I want to know what happened, and how it happened. In this crazy world I want to know my own story, the story that belongs to Atiga Bint Tawida. After all, my story is part of my ancestry. It's an inheritance nobody can contest my right to."

"That's right," Ali concurred, holding a handkerchief to his mouth. Then, as if in reconfirmation, he added, "That's right. You're the daughter of Tawida and Muhammad Bin Imuhammad Bin Abd al-Kabir Bin Shatwan—and my cousin!"

"Will you come to my house someday?" As she spoke, she hurriedly got up out of her chair.

"I'd be honored to know your family. I hear your husband is an educated, thoughtful man. And that you have children."

When he said the word *children*, he smiled.

He went on, "I want to get to know them, and for them to know me as an uncle. I'll definitely visit you. And I'll keep coming around for as long as I live."

At the Mission

SOMETIMES YOU WAKE UP to find yourself in a new place, with new people, and starting a new life without knowing how any of it happened. The only explanation you can offer is that it's the will of God—destiny. Both of them—the will of God and destiny—are forces nobody's ever been able to understand completely. We don't know how they operate, so all we can do is accept our lot, since we have no other choice.

In my case, I found myself under the care of nuns at the Josephite Mission in the Fuwayhat neighborhood of Benghazi. They took care of me until I was good as new. One day when I was lying in bed, one of the senior nuns came and sat down beside me. She started talking to me about things relating to my stay in the mission clinic and how I found the place. Then she asked me if I knew how to read and write, and if I'd been to school.

At first I didn't understand what she was talking about, and she had to explain what she meant. I told her I didn't even know what a school was. Aunt Sabriya had told me she was saving up to send me to the literacy school run by Bint Flayfila. She said that if I got an education, I could have a better future than if I just stayed all my life in the Slave Yards.[1]

---

1. A reference to the encampments outside Benghazi where, during the historical period in which this story's events took place, most of Libya's slaves and former slaves lived out their primitive existence.

She kept talking to me about the idea, especially when we'd go into the city to serve some family having a wedding celebration. She told me that this job of mine was only temporary, and that she was looking for permanent work in somebody's home so that she could send me to the girls' school and pay my tuition.

The person who arranged for me to go on being taken care by the nuns after I got out of the clinic was Yousef. In those days this sort of thing was easy to arrange. The mission took in lots of orphans, both black and white. The nuns taught them reading, writing, and proper etiquette. They erased some things and put other, more refined and civilized things, in their place. The children really took to what they learned at the mission, so that there was an obvious difference between somebody who'd been brought up by the nuns, and somebody who'd grown up in a poor home with lots of brothers and sisters, and in an environment that lacked pretty much everything. Children in the latter category didn't learn anything other than how to beg, work in the markets, or be domestic servants. If they were distant relatives of the mayor, they'd wait till they were given jobs as street sweepers. The city was so full of them that if you swept the streets in the daytime, some relative of yours was probably sweeping them at night!

At the mission I learned to read and write Italian. I learned other things too, like knitting, and I discovered that there are things in the world that can make life happy and fun. I learned that by mastering a skill, people could escape the life of abject poverty in the Slave Yards. When the girls at the mission reached puberty, they were trained to be seamstresses, nurses, or teachers. Since I had a knack for making people feel better, I joined the nurses. I enjoyed this kind of work, especially with little children.

After Aunt Sabriya died, I was given new mothers that I loved and learned from and got attached to.

The love I received from Yousef Giuseppe was the most wonderful thing I could have imagined. When he came into my life, I started moving away from the world of the Yards and into a different sort of world. My new world was broader than the one I'd known before. It was based on human connections—not on race, or color, or whether you were somebody's relative. I can't belong to a society where everything's dictated by blood relations. I have a mind and a heart, which is all you need to be a member of the human family.

The people closest to me in this world were Miftah, Yousef, Aunt Aida, Jaballah, and Durma, who came to see me whenever they could. Aunt Aida would check on me and give me advice just the way Aunt Sabriya used to do, while Durma would come to lighten my load with a different way of looking at things. Miftah's smile, his sympathy, and his caring broke through the cloud of sorrow and loneliness that hung over me. As for Yousef, words fail to describe his mysterious presence, which turned later into a total partnership of body and spirit.

My special bond with Yousef, who was quite a bit older than I was, started developing when we would sit on the grounds of the clinic together. He showed interest in the things I was learning, and he encouraged me to read and write. Yousef was in a class of his own. Other men of his generation considered it improper to have women around them in their daily lives, and most girls my age were housebound. But Yousef insisted that I go out, get an education, and work. Every time he came to visit, he'd bring a newspaper or a book, and on Saturdays and Sundays he'd sit beside me and have me read to him.

Little by little, I opened up to the man in him. I felt him close to my heart, and his image would stay with me after he'd left. His spirit would surround me during the day and visit me at night. When the nuns locked the doors at night and I went to sleep by myself on my side of the mission, I didn't feel alone.

Little by little, I started missing him whenever he was gone. I would write him letters and wait for the mailman to come to the mission, either to collect what I'd written to him or deliver what he'd written to me. Then, when it came time to see him off, I cried my heart out. He was leaving to go study in Italy with a recommendation from the church, and there was a possibility that he'd stay there permanently.

Years went by. Miftah would come see me when he didn't have work, and his visits always lifted my spirits. I would run to meet him with open arms whenever they told me he'd come. He'd been settled for years in a single job, which he loved so much, it seemed he'd been made for it. His new mother had helped him get the job with a relative of hers who ran a bakery that specialized in a kind of fried bread we called *sifiniz*. Miftah was honest, clean, conscientious, and helpful, and the shop owner thought so highly of him that he put him in charge of making the sifiniz. When he came to visit, he would bring some for me and the nuns, and tell the sisters to take good care of me.

He used to tease me and call me "Little Blackie." So I started calling him "the sifiniz man."

"Good going, brother!" I told him. "In just a few years you went from being flour to being a nice brown pancake!"[2]

I started working full-time at the mission clinic, where I did the same jobs as the nuns. I lived a public sort of life, which left no room for anything private apart from my occasional exchanges of letters with Yousef and chats about the future with Miftah.

Then one day the mailman brought a special letter from Giuseppe— the name Yousef had taken on in Italy. He told me he was coming home to Benghazi. In a PS he wrote, "Benghazi means Atiga." I could hardly wait to see him, and I was counting the minutes and the seconds till he got home. I talked with the nuns about his homecoming and how I wanted to plan a little party for him. When Miftah noticed how excited I was about Yousef's return, he made a pastry especially for the occasion and called it "Little Blackie and the Slave"! It was a kind of raisin cake topped with roasted nuts and honey.

Yousef came back more grown-up, citified, and educated than before. I could see that he'd changed, and he could see that I had too. The thirteen-year-old girl with tight braids and white ribbons in her hair was now a woman.

In the days that followed we met regularly outside the mission. One day we'd been studying together, when suddenly the topic of conversation shifted, and he kissed me. This was followed by a dreamy night like none I'd ever experienced before. Early the next morning he

2. Miftah's last name, Daqiq, means "flour" in Arabic.

came to my quarters, and I realized he was going to tell me he loved me. The sisters had noticed the succession of changes in our relationship, and Sister Maria said, "The fact that he rushed out here on a cold winter morning like this must mean he's going to propose!"

And in fact, he asked for my hand, in spite of the age difference between us.

He didn't go on for a long time about it. He just said he wanted us to get married, and then talk about everything. He said he didn't have any set vision of our life together, but that we could imagine everything and work to achieve it.

We laughed later about the way he'd proposed, and when we saw how fast our first child came.

He used to say that if he'd gone on dragging his feet, our baby would never have been born. If, on the other hand, he'd lost his head, or if, after going along with his amorous expressions up to a point, I hadn't disappeared for a day at a time out of embarrassment, especially with him being a grown man and me just a girl still, he might have been born before his time!

Little Muhammad's birth was the start of another life for me. He gave new meaning to my existence.

That's Me in the Picture

I DON'T SHOW UP in this picture, but I'm there—I'm hiding beside Aunt Aida and her son Baraka. Aunt Sabriya had left me with them that day and gone to the city. It was blazing hot, with lots of flies, and we spent all day sifting sand.

I'd sit around the sand sieve from morning to night with other neighborhood kids. Our job was to sift sand from the seashore for the construction workers. We'd talk and argue, and sometimes we'd get so loud that the old Negro assigned to keep an eye on us would start cussing us out in some weird language we couldn't understand. He'd bop anybody he could reach with his stick, even if they hadn't had any part in the fracas.

A group of Negroes, some of them women, took turns overseeing the little sand sifters. They would pass by to examine our work, then disappear into their huts to get out of the heat. Sometimes they'd prod us to work harder and, as a way of getting everybody moving, they'd smack some of us with the palm leaves they used to shoo away flies.

I didn't like it when the women supervised us, since we couldn't pull the wool over their eyes! They caught onto our tricks right away, and wouldn't let us get away with the lies we'd tell them, since they'd heard them all before.

I liked to stay away from the supervisors, which was why I was always tucked away in a corner somewhere. I'd squeeze in between boys and girls who were bigger and stronger than I was so nobody could find me and hurt me.

One time after we'd finished sifting, I told my friend Durma that I wanted a mirror, and I asked her to help me find even just a little piece of one. She asked me what I wanted it for, of course, and I told her I wanted to see my face in it. After that she didn't ask me any more questions. She told me she knew a Sudanese girl in the Yards who had one, and that we could go see her.

Some time passed after we'd agreed on our idea. I'd decided to wait until I knew Aunt Sabriya would be gone for a day or two. Then that mysterious servant came on camel back the way he'd done before, had her get on behind him, and rode away with her somewhere. Once I'd seen her leave, I went with Durma to see the Sudanese girl, but she said we'd have to pay her for the service. We didn't have anything to give her, and promised to bring her something later. But she wouldn't have it. Wiping some taffy off her mouth with the sleeve of her dress, she said, "You'll get it when you bring the payment."

I didn't have the guts to challenge her. She looked like a bully who was in the habit of getting into fistfights, and who was good at using her fingernails on her enemies' faces. She was big and strong, her face covered with scratches. If I said another word, she might push me to the ground and sit on top of me until she squeezed the life out of me, or punch me in the nose so hard that I'd end up blind.

I grabbed Durma by her dress and signaled to her with my eyes to try to soften the girl up. Durma was a slick bargainer, and I figured if she gave it another try, the girl would give in.

Standing a few steps away from the other two girls, I could hear their exchange while staying safely out of range in case the *bouri* exploded in the Sudanese girl's brain and she started spewing it all over us. (*Bouri* was a name we used to describe a wild rage that black slaves were known for.) Well, she didn't blow up, but she didn't give in, either. She said she couldn't show us the mirror until we'd paid up. Then she whispered something to Durma that I couldn't hear from where I stood. Durma nodded without saying anything, and we went home again to get ready for another try the following day.

The next day I got up from the sieve and went with Durma, who cleaned some of the dust off me. She blew on my face and wiped it with her hands until my features were visible again. She looked for some water, and when she couldn't find any, she spit into her palms and wiped my face with her hands again to see what I looked like without the dust mask left by the sifting. Looking at me as if she were seeing me for the first time, she said, "That's good. You can see your face now. Let's go."

Even so, I asked her if we could go down to the sea first so that I could wash up. She showed me her dirty bare feet and said, "Well, your face is cleaner than my feet at least!"

On our way there, we saw people sprawled out under their huts to get away from the heat and the flies. They didn't do anything most of the time. There was nothing to do to pass the time but shoo away flies, talk, or sleep.

We went to the hut where the Sudanese girl lived. It was a little bigger than the tinplate shack I shared with Aunt Sabriya and Miftah, but it wasn't as clean. There were pieces of watermelon rind along the edges of it. Big green flies were buzzing around, and it smelled like a latrine, since it was close to the small sewage canals that had been dug between the slaves' encampments and that emptied into a big trench leading down to the sea.

The girl was lying on the floor with one arm under her head when she was informed of our arrival by one of the dozens of children darting in and out. When we came in, she sat up and started scratching her hair with both hands while she talked to Durma about something she'd asked her for.

"I haven't forgotten about it," Durma told her. "But leave it till the *danga* season.[1] It's right around the corner."

"All right, all right," she muttered.

Turning to the reason for our visit, Durma said, "We've come for the mirror."

---

1. Slaves used to put on a yearly carnival known as the *danga*, and part of the celebration involved making the rounds of the city in dance performed to the beating of drums.

"My mama took it with her this morning," the girl said.

"Where did she take it?" Durma asked, taken aback. "Didn't I tell you we were coming?"

"I swear to God, I couldn't keep it here. My mother took it today to fix the whores' hair." She was talking about the prostitutes, known in our parts as *kuwayyisat*.

She went on scratching her scalp, irritated by something in her hair and talking about "the *kuwayyisat*." She didn't seem to notice how shocked I was by the word, even when I clapped my hand over my mouth. Durma pinched my thigh to make me settle down. From then on I left all the talking to Durma, who didn't bat an eyelid at any of the nasty words the girl used as she scratched her butt and her head.

"So where's the other piece you're always hiding?" Durma asked.

The girl seemed surprised that Durma knew about the spare mirror, which was only brought out on special occasions.

"Come on," Durma coaxed. "Show it to us, and I'll show you what I brought for you."

The girl didn't say anything for quite a while. Then she jumped up in such a hurry that she stirred up the sand around us. She said something to the little kids in a language I didn't understand. Within seconds they were gone, together with the flies, and we had the place to ourselves. The girl had facial hair on either end of her upper lip. She was fat and dirty, and gave off a stench that penetrated my nostrils as she bent over to search through a pile of sacks. When she turned around to face us, we were both staring at her. Holding something behind her back, she said to Durma, "So where's the payment?"

Right away Durma pulled a small package out of her neck opening and handed it to the girl.

"Here," she said. "The cigarettes are from me, and the can is from her."

As the girl handed over the mirror fragment, she gleefully grabbed the bundle out of Durma's hand. Durma looked into the mirror before I did as the girl busied herself scrutinizing the gift. Sidling up to Durma, I squeezed my head in between her and the mirror to get a look. She breathed onto its surface and wiped it with her hand, making it a little cleaner than it had been before. I saw Durma's reflection, though it was a little distorted. We took turns grabbing the mirror away from each other until finally Durma let me keep it.

So the first time I encountered myself was in the hut of a smelly Sudanese girl. I was nearly speechless when I saw the girl that was me. At the same time, I was so taken by the whole idea of a mirror that lets people see themselves that I practically forgot about my face, which was the whole reason I'd wanted the mirror to start with.

I looked hurriedly for the thing that made people stare at me, and when I saw it, I was taken by it just like everybody else. It was something about my eyes. But before long I'd noticed something else, too. Even though my hair was sort of kinky, it had a softness about it, and a wine-red tint that you never saw in Negroes' hair. So from the time I left that Sudanese girl's house, I wanted to know who had passed these things on to me, and why he'd never looked for me.

When her tobacco- and food-induced euphoria had worn off, the Sudanese girl spun around, announced that our time was up, and grabbed the mirror out of my hand so quickly that she cut both herself and me.

"That's enough," she said. "Somebody will catch me with it. Now get out of here."

Not giving us a chance to ask for more time, she hid the mirror fragment among the piles of stuff in the corner of the hut. Then she stuffed the cigarettes into her bosom and the can into her trouser pocket. She seemed to sense exactly how long it would take the flock of children to make their way back to the hut, because just as she withdrew her now empty hand from her bosom, they started clattering in. By the time she reached back to scratch her butt and her scalp, all the children were back—they and the flies.

The Hot Pepper

IN THE SLAVE YARDS, nothing ever stayed a secret. Anything and everything that was done or said—even a sneeze, or the movement of cats and dogs, or my seeing my face in the mirror after a day of sifting—was bound to get out.

I don't know how Aunt Sabriya found out that I'd gone with Durma to see the Sudanese girl. But she punished me by throwing me on the floor and sitting on top of me. At least it was more bearable than it would have been to have a hot pepper stuffed into my mouth or my private parts.

It wasn't long before I'd confessed, hoping to God that Aunt Sabriya would get off my back. I was scared of being tortured with one of the hot peppers that hung in a bundle from a post in our shack.

I told her it was Durma, not me, who'd brought the pack of cigarettes. She asked me how Durma had done it. Had she grabbed or begged it off a police officer? Had she filched it from one of the boys? I swore I didn't know. I thought she believed me, since she got up off of me, and my spirit started gradually coming back into my body. But when my spirit was halfway home, she grabbed me by the hand and pulled me over in front of the stove, which consisted of three rocks. After sticking the iron poker in the fire, she told me to listen up. She'd turned downright evil. The bouri had gotten into her, and her eyes were gleaming red. Crying and shaking in fear of that hot poker, I promised to do everything she told me.

"By the soil on my mother's grave, that's the last time!" I told her, cringing. "I swear by God and the Prophet, I won't do it again, Auntie!"

An ominous look in her eyes, she said, "So you're back to hanging around with that rotten girl, are you?"

"By the holiness of the Prophet David, I promise I'll never hang around with her again!"

It came as a shock to be told that Durma was "rotten," as my aunt put it. But before I could take it in completely, she started yelling.

"Don't swear!" she scolded me angrily. "The Prophet David was a holy man, but we won't have his blessing as long as that monster's around!"

Still shaking, I hurried to correct myself. "Right, right. Forgive me, Master David! Forgive me, all you prophets, by the holiness of Master Mu'min!"

Threatening me with the hot poker again, she said, "And don't swear by Master Mu'min, either!"

"Okay, okay. I won't swear by anybody! There—I've stopped!"

I clapped both hands over my mouth, tears streaming down my face.

"Durma isn't a good girl. That's all there is to it. Don't get together with her ever again."

Then she brought the poker up close to me till I could feel its heat. I started to scream, thinking she was going to roast me with it.

"That's enough, by my aunt's life!" I pleaded. "I won't do it again!"

My face was drenched with tears as if the sea off the Slave Yards had poured itself into my eyes till they overflowed. I begged Aunt Sabriya's forgiveness by the soil of my mother's grave. Then I saw the instrument of torture retreat. She put the poker back in the fire and got up, leaving me a wreck. I didn't really think the soil on dead people's graves could save me from anything. If I had, I would have prayed for it to bury me quick, before the hot peppers went into me and their infernal blaze tortured me to death. I knew some girls were punished by having hot peppers shoved into their vaginas, since we would see them running like mad toward the sea, screaming hysterically. Even so, everybody was determined to have the "locking ceremony"[1] performed on their daughters before a man had touched them, even if the hot peppers had had their desired effect.

Afraid to cry too close to the poker that had been trembling in my aunt's hands not long before, I went out behind the shack to be by myself. I cried off and on as the hours dragged by. I would sob for a while, then stop when children chasing cats and dogs ran past. Then I'd start to hurt again and go back to crying. I stayed behind the shack until evening, at which point the heat that had roasted our bodies during the daytime gave way to a deadly, damp chill. I was afraid my aunt might leave me there until morning, the way she'd done one other time when she was mad at me. I was honestly afraid I might freeze to death. So I buried my legs in the warm sand to take the edge off the chill. However, the cold had me completely surrounded. It was above me, underneath me, and on either side. I curled up and cried some more until I started to fall asleep. Only then, when she noticed that I'd stopped crying, did my aunt come out. Nudging me with the poker, which had shrunk from the cold the way I had, she said, "Come on in now, you little shit, before you freeze to death."

It had been a tough price to pay for getting to see my face in the mirror. Even so, I slept well that night, since now I knew what it was that always caught people's attention, what it was that made me different from other dark-skinned people. I knew now that it was in my eyes. I also knew it would never change, and that for as long as I lived it would make people do a double take the first time they saw me.

It was an identity that couldn't be falsified by anything I said or did, a select gift from a free man from Misrata, whose people "are as white and red as the Germans," as the saying goes. It was the color I'd seen in the mirror, the color of eyes the likes of which you wouldn't

1. Also known as armoring (*al-taṣfīḥ*), the locking ceremony (*qafl al-banāt*) was an ancient ritual whose purpose was to protect girls from being raped. Unlike female circumcision (*khitān al-banāt*), it involved no physical mutilation.

find in the Slave Yards, and it was inextricably tied to my fate. Thanks to this color, my eyes were legendary stars in the sky that stretched out between uptown Benghazi and the ghetto where the slaves made their home.

I'm a String and He's a Wall

A BIG FAT GREEN FLY—the kind that likes rotten smells—was buzzing near my nose. I shooed it away with my hand and pressed my face to the hole in the hollowed-out clay wall so that I wouldn't miss anything. It wasn't the same fly that had been buzzing a little while earlier. I'd already killed that one. There were lots of flies here, and they hovered around you for no reason.

Of course, the fact that we were right next to Lallahum's privy was reason enough. There was nothing separating us from it but a sack that hung over its entranceway. The sack was so short and high off the ground, you could see the feet of whoever was using it when she squatted over the raised hole in the dirt floor to relieve herself.

A group of women sat chatting in the courtyard of the old Arab-style house. As we waited our turn to go in and see Lallahum, they were too busy talking about this and that to pay attention to the young girls they'd brought with them. So was Aunt Sabriya, which was all right with me.

Ever so slowly, I scooted over to the mud-brick wall of the old woman's room and peeked through the little hole in it. A bit of dim light came through the hole, along with a slight cool draft that relieved the dryness in my throat and took the edge off my thirst. It's easy to bore little peepholes in walls like those. The eyes of nameless onlookers compromised people's personal spaces with their unannounced, nosy presence. But nobody bothered to close up the holes as long as they didn't notice that their privacy was being violated.

The peephole had smooth edges, and although it was so small that you could hardly see it, it had been skillfully bored from the outside in such a way that it provided a view of the entire room. The old woman was sure not to have noticed it, since if she had, she would have rushed to plug it with thick mud, or stuffed it with a rag or piece of paper. Even though Rabiha was a tall girl, I could see her from head to toe as she jumped off the solemn wooden tick-tock chest—so-called because the rattling of the key in its lock sounded like the ticking of a clock—and swallowed the fifth of the seven dates required to close her up. She had two more dates waiting for her on the wicker plate next to the old woman and, once they were gone, the operation would be over.

Like the girl before her, Rabiha had gotten flustered and made a mistake as she repeated the magic formula. But the old woman didn't notice, since otherwise she would have stuck her fingers in the girl's thighs, and she would have looked smaller through the hole as she shrank in pain.

The wooden chest Rabiha was standing on was locked seven times, once for every time she jumped off it. Every time she jumped she had to say, "I'm a wall and he's a string" as the old woman spanked her behind with her wrinkled hand. The reason she used her hand was that Rabiha hadn't brought one of her father's shoes for this purpose. She didn't have a single one, much less a complete pair. From the day he was born till the day he left this world for the Great Beyond, his feet had never known the companionship of a pair of shoes or sandals.

When her little womb had been duly locked, Rabiha smothered the old woman's hand with kisses. The girl's mother had instructed her to thank Lallahum and seek her approval, and she'd done everything she was told. She was thrilled at the thought of something that would cause her to be viewed as a "little woman" among women. Her locking ceremony was over now, and the women who had witnessed it would advertise her as an eligible bride when the time came. The big transition in her life was complete, and from the moment she presented her bottom to be smacked she'd felt the joyful anticipation of being able to look for a husband.

For a long time the bony old woman, who spoke an odd mix of the local eastern dialect and that of the western region, had been locking the wombs of young girls and unlocking those of new brides for their rightful husbands. Lallahum, who did what she did in keeping with the prevailing customs, provided protection for growing wombs against a danger faced by males and females alike—the danger posed by their sexual urges. Males tended to view these urges as a point of pride, whereas females would live the rest of their lives in shame if they answered Satan's call to satisfy them beyond the bounds of the licit.

The purpose of the locking ceremony was to ward off Satan's temptations before marriage. As for his temptations after marriage, they can't be detected, which is why married women who give in to them aren't in danger of being recognized and harassed. They waged war on Satan's whispers, or the pull of instinctual desires, by thwarting them before they'd been translated into action.

Sex is forbidden to women outside of marriage, whereas it's permitted to men whether they're married or not. Tradition makes an exception for girls and women of unknown parentage, who can be enslaved and exploited for others' sexual amusement and entertainment, whereas this can't be done to free women.

The locking ceremony is a kind of magic spell that prevents a fornicating or adulterous man from having an erection and deprives the fornicating or adulterous women of sexual pleasure. It places an invisible "something" between the penis and the vagina, keeping them apart and frustrating any attempt at union or enjoyment unsanctioned by matrimony.

So when they resorted to these spells, what was it that they hid in these little girls' wombs? Actually, the spell consisted of nothing but some mysterious words, a key in a lock, and seven dates. Lallahum would feed dates from Mecca and Medina to prepubescent girls and hit their bottoms as they jumped off the tick-tock chest, which she locked and reopened seven times for each girl in turn.

Girls who were orphans, who had poor lineages, or whose fathers were unknown were left to the last, while priority was given to girls whose families were well-placed materially and socially. In other words, a man's social status would influence how his daughter was classified. Daughters of notables, merchants, policemen, and military officers would be given the operation first, before Lallahum began getting tired and bored, while girls of lesser status had to wait until she had turned into a surly old hag who had no compunctions about vilifying a girl's reputation, insulting her family, verbally abusing those within ear range, and complaining about how her cruel lot in life had landed her in what she referred to as a nasty, miserable profession.

An important part of the locking ceremony involved spanking a girl whose father was dead or absent. It was thought of as a way of bringing blessing, and of completing the blessing if it wasn't complete already. The girl had to be spanked barehanded if her father had had no shoes. Some girls reported that the old woman's hand, which was as wrinkled as her face, came down hot and hard. They were sure that the shoes and sandals other girls' fathers had worn across barren desert expanses would have been gentle and kind by comparison with that wizened extremity of hers. When a shoe was used, only a small part of it would actually make contact with a young girl's soft little behind, whereas Lallahum's hand was notorious for the stinging smacks it could deliver.

Aunt Sabriya held onto me as we stood at the end of the line of girls waiting their turn to go in. I was getting restless as the scorching noonday sun came closer and closer to our heads, threatening to strike us down if we and the others waiting with us didn't go away. I fidgeted terribly until, even though she knew how uncomfortable I was, my aunt signaled for me to stop it and not press my luck. She even pinched my thigh a couple of times to make me sit still. But when I whispered to her that I wanted to "go" somewhere other than Lallahum's privy—which was full of poop, pee, and flies—she was kind and understanding. I thought at first that our jaunt outside the courtyard would take us back to the Slave Yards, and that Lallahum would give us an appointment on some other day. Then again, by the time the other appointment rolled around, I might have reached puberty or been touched by someone.

After a lull in the chatter—though so many conversations were going on at the same time that I didn't know which one the lull belonged to—my aunt asked, "Do you need to pee or poop?"

"I think I just need to pee," I said, pressing on my front part with my palm.

Adjusting her shawl over her head, she took me by the hand and asked a gaunt-looking Negro woman to hold our place for us. The woman agreed, and we left Lallahum's courtyard for the open area outside it. My aunt looked around in search of a private spot where I could take care of business. We didn't see anybody coming our way. There was actually nothing in that wide expanse that would have drawn people, apart from the service Lallahum offered in her house, and that was only for women and girls.

We moved our feet slightly out of the way. Then my aunt held out her shawl to hide me, and told me to make it quick. So I peed as fast as I could, but I was in such a hurry that I got the edges of my underpants wet. Observing me from over the top of the shawl she'd walled me in with, she said, "Pull your caftan up high and spread your legs wide."

My aunt guarded me from one side with her shawl. However, I was so nervous thinking my bare bottom might show from the other side and that somebody might come from that direction, I wet my caftan and my trousers. To my relief, I knew the wind would erase the effects of the accident, since it was the hottest, driest part of the summer, and nothing wet could hold out against Mother Nature's fans. The fact was, the precautions we'd taken hadn't been necessary in that untrodden region, since there wasn't a soul for miles around.

As I looked up from watching the urine soak into the ground, my aunt said, "Finish up now. Our turn's coming up, and we don't want to miss it."

"Okay," I said in a raspy voice that came from deep inside. Then, my voice clearer than before, I asked her, "Why do some of the women go in before us even though they got here after we did? We've been sitting out here roasting all day long!"

She huffed irritably, the way she did when she was bothered by the heat. Then she looked this way and that, saying, "Those women are free. They're not like us, and we're not like them."

All my mind could take in was that free people had white skin. They weren't like us even when they were like us. I wasn't bitter toward them for being different from us in their color, what they ate, what they wore, where they lived, the way they made their living, and their overall fortunes in life. In fact, my admiration for their nice clean clothes, their pretty houses, and the charity they gave us made me want to do everything I could to be like them. At the same time, I couldn't figure out why they were the masters and we were the servants, why they were raised a degree higher, and we were several degrees lower.

It wasn't blackness that stood between us, but whiteness. I could see that without anybody explaining it to me. White people's light skin couldn't come close to us and cancel out the distance. In fact, it was a basic part of the distance.

As I was trying to get rid of the effects of my accident, my aunt took a little bundle out from under her clothes. It contained four eggs, a small bunch of mint, and an almond-shaped stick for painting your lips. She'd brought them to give the old woman in return for "locking" my uterus against men's lusts. Like all good mothers, sponsors, and caregivers, my aunt wanted to predetermine my uterus's attitude toward any attempt to lead it astray. Otherwise, why would she have brought me out on that sweltering, desert-dry day to wait from the early morning hours?

My aunt set the bundle aside. Maybe she'd been bothered by it; maybe she was afraid it would come untied while she was holding her shawl around me. She'd collected the four eggs over a period of time so that she'd have enough to pay for this or that. However, even four eggs wouldn't have been enough if they weren't accompanied by the requisite half-piaster. Maybe she'd hidden it in the special handkerchief she kept under one of her breasts and was going to get it out when it was needed. It was no easy matter for a Negro to announce that he or she had money beyond what they'd been paid for their labor. It had cost a lot of Negroes their lives. But there were a number of chores a slave woman might have performed in order to have a half-piaster in her possession: she might have sifted wheat for a whole day at Al Funduq Al Baladi marketplace, washed woolen bags or bundles of clothes, chopped a lot of firewood, worked a long stint in the salt mountains, delivered several pots of drinking water to people's houses, shoveled manure out of the cattle pens, peddled boiled broad beans and chickpeas in the market, or spent the day getting prostitutes ready for their customers.

Half a piaster was what Aunt Sabriya would get paid for carrying four huge clay jugs of water on her head from the *shayshama*—which is what we called the public spigot—to a Benghazi household some distance away. From her I learned how to work hard for what I earned, hoping that someone would reward my effort with some charity on top of my wages. When I first started out, I had to go four times to the *shayshama* in the Shabi District to supply a household with water, and ten times to the sweet spring in Zurayriʻiya, on the outskirts of Benghazi, to fill a giant jug sitting on a nearby wagon. It was obvious from the fact that my clothes were constantly wet and that my hair was falling out at the spot where the water jug rubbed up against my head that I'd earned my few piasters by the sweat of my black brow.

After I'd relieved myself, I pulled my trousers back up to the sound of my aunt's sighs. She brought her shawl over her head and let it fall loosely over her back without gathering it in front. Then, taking me by the hand, she led me back to Lallahum's house. When we walked in, we were met by a huge commotion. Not knowing what was going on, we stood aside at first, but it didn't take long to figure out what had happened. A woman by the name of Akhwira had brought her daughter, Maghliya, for the locking ceremony, but she'd given Lallahum a shoe belonging to a man who wasn't Maghliya's real father. When Lallahum discovered what the woman had done, she'd thrown her out for cheating. After being shamed in front of all the other women, Akhwira and her daughter had left in disgrace.

I felt horrible for poor Maghliya. I knew what had just happened would haunt her for the rest of her life.

A number of men had passed in succession through Akhwira's bedchamber, and any of them could conceivably have laid claim to this girl's paternity. The mother vehemently denied this, and attributed Maghliya to her most recent husband. An older man with standing and prestige in the community, he'd been swept off his feet by the gorgeous, youthful Akhwira. However, by the time he had relations with her, she was already pregnant with Maghliya. This was the man whose shoe Lallahum had summarily rejected, and no matter how many piasters Maghliya's mother slipped into the old woman's hand, she refused to perform the locking ceremony for the girl. Lallahum would have had no objection to taking the piasters, of course. However, she was a close acquaintance of the man whose shoe had been brought to her and, wanting to get back at him for a festering grievance, she sent Akhwira away in tears, knowing this would be hard for him to take.

Standing in the doorway to her room, Lallahum delivered a homily of sorts to the women and young girls gathered around her. She said that cheating wouldn't get this woman anywhere. She added that she'd known Akhwira's husband, Yadam, since he was a young man, and that he was a womanizer who'd never been able to have any children. So how, she asked, could he have fathered this girl, especially so late in his life?

Lallahum's sermon was met with approval by some of the women. But others started whispering among themselves about the woman and the girl. As for Aunt Sabriya, she didn't say a word. She showed no interest in the controversy, as if her senses weren't taking in what was happening, or as if none of it made any difference to her.

I overheard a couple of women talking in hushed tones about Lallahum's connection to the scandal.

"God knows, sister," one of them whispered. "But word has it that when Lallahum was young, she was his lover. Otherwise, how would she know he's barren?"

The other woman widened the neck opening to her caftan and spat into it. Then, smacking herself gently on the rear several times, she exclaimed, "Say it, sister!"

Not long afterward, the gathering was hailed by a stout woman whose twin daughters had lost their father some years before. She'd kept one of her late husband's shoes in a special chest so that, when her girls were about to reach puberty, she'd have something to bring Lallahum for the locking ceremony. The women seemed impressed with the shoe, if not with the person who'd brought it. But then one of them raised a question—namely, whether a shoe that hadn't been used for so long, and had been hidden away among people's clothes for the whole eight years since its owner died, could perform the magical function that such shoes were expected to perform in the locking ceremony.

"Besides," the woman remarked, "the odor and body heat from the owner's foot would have faded after all this time. So what sort of magical power would the shoe have left?"

The crafty woman who had posed the question was backed up by an even craftier one, who took the inquiry a step further, saying, "So where does the power lie: in the shoe itself, or in the scent of the man who wore it?"

However, what Lallahum accepted or rejected, what she would and wouldn't use in her rituals, was nobody's business but hers. She had the final word when it came to deciding whether something was effective or not.

There was a lot of talk among the mothers sitting in Lallahum's waiting room that day about the merits of the locking ceremony, with only a few reserved comments from women who said it had let people down. For the most part, opinion favored the rattle of the key in the lock, which announced that the door to a girl's womb had now been closed to the dark forces of human beings and spirits alike.

Rabiha, a tall, hyperactive white girl, came out of Lallahum's inner room with a story to tell. Smacking her lips as she recalled the taste of the dates, she started telling other girls proudly about what had happened to her behind Lallahum's closed doors. Before long, ten young girls had gathered around her, dying to hear what else she had to say, and watching her mouth in rapt fascination. I was the only dark-skinned girl there. Consequently, several girls shoved me out of the circle so that I ended up at the back of the group. I'd been looking forward to seeing Rabiha and hearing her talk about the room, the old lady, and the things she'd seen. I craned my neck, trying to get a look at her. Finally, by standing on the tips of my dirty, urine-spattered toes, I managed a glimpse of long-legged Rabiha's chatterbox mouth as she sowed her story like seeds in a field.

One girl had been terrified that when the old woman spanked her, she would hit a swollen boil on her behind. Trying to keep her fears in check, she'd gotten in line, her thoughts scattered every which way. When she got in the room, she was still mixed up and instead of saying, "I'm a wall and he's a string," she stammered, "I'm a string and he's a wall."

Later on, after men's desires had been kept at bay for some time thanks to the effects of heavy tick-tock chests of aromatic *kumari* wood, she got pregnant, even though her husband, Najib ad-Dallal, was infertile. When he discovered she was pregnant, he began to think maybe he wasn't infertile after all, or that she was just exceptionally fertile herself. In any case, they ended up with a chubby, fair-skinned baby boy who, as time went by, looked more and more like a peddler who came around on donkey back to sell his wares to the neighborhood women.

Nobody knew exactly how the white Maltese sperm had managed to penetrate the barrier that had been set up by the tick-tock chest. However, the penetration had been torrential, daring, and successful. It shattered the myth of the seven magical turns of the key and gave Najib ad-Dallal a beautiful, fair-skinned son behind the back of the tick-tock chest, and behind Najib ad-Dallal's back too. The same thing had also happened to other husbands, whose wives might have recited the protective formulas incorrectly when they were little girls because of some flawed connection between their uvulas, tongues, and teeth. Or maybe the ritual hadn't worked because of the bad dates!

Rabiha related what she'd heard about the incident in the "locking" room. Wiping her mouth with the sleeve of her caftan, she continued, "The tall *shushana* who serves Lallahum, the one with big boobs and scratches on her face . . ."[1]

"Yeah, we know who you're talking about. Go on . . ."

"She's the one who opened up Mar'i Sharwi's bride on their wedding night. Mar'i's wife had been 'locked,' and he couldn't do anything!"

The girls burst into giggles, clapping their hands over their mouths to keep the women from hearing them.

According to Rabiha, there would have been a scandal if that particular shushana hadn't been a tambourine player at the wedding. When the uproar started, she stepped in to solve the problem, and nobody tried to stop her. She examined the bride and discovered that she really had been "locked."

"That's right," Rabiha added. "She'd been locked just the way I was a little while ago!"

The bride's mother had had her daughter locked before they moved from Bani Walid to Benghazi. Then the mother died suddenly during a bed beating from her drunkard husband. Nobody bothered to ask her if she'd gone through the ceremony until, one day while she was out playing in the street, her relatives decided to marry her off. They took her away from her playmates, brought her inside, and rushed to get her washed up. Then they dressed her in a white caftan that made her look older than she was and combed her hair down around her face. The women of the family told her to be quiet, so she didn't say a word. Given how young she was, and the rift between her father's and mother's sides of the family, she'd forgotten to tell her maternal aunts about the locking ceremony. She didn't even completely understand that she was getting married, and her maternal aunts didn't attend her wedding because of what her father had done to her mother. When

---

1. The term *shushana* (masculine, *shushan*) refers to a slave who had been born to slave parents.

she finally realized what was happening, the little bride struck herself on the face, begging the women gathered around her for mercy. But instead of listening to her, they lit into her with cruel words: blaming her, ripping her reputation to shreds, and cursing her wedding night, saying that it was as black as she was.

"I've been locked!" she cried. "My mother, God rest her soul, had it done to me in Zliten."

But those vicious, busy-body old ladies were convinced that she was lying to them the way a lot of girls do when they can't prove they're virgins on their promised night.

"God damn your mother!" they hissed. "Black women are liars, and they're hot in bed! Isn't that right? That's the plain truth about slave women!"

Even with all her begging and pleading, nobody believed her. After all, it was a strange thing for a Negro girl to have been locked.

But Lallahum's shushana, who was there at the wedding to play the tambourine and the darabukka, did believe her, and she delivered her from a death sentence that would have been carried out by a rifle the minute the door opened. Intervening without anybody asking her to, the darabukka player made her way through the crowd of women, pushed the door open, and slammed it shut behind her. The *bouri* had a grip on her, that was for sure. Once inside the room, she shoved the bride onto the bed without giving her a chance to do a thing or even say a word. Then she spread the girl's legs and fixed her gaze on her crotch. Embarrassed and terrified, the girl screamed and covered the spot with her hands. The woman would have none of it. She struck the girl on her hands and forced them away from the spot. By this time the poor thing was in shock, shaking like a leaf.

That shushana must have had a good heart, though. Otherwise, why would she have gotten herself mixed up in the situation? Without a word, she shattered the dresser mirror with her bare fist and tore the bride's clothes off as if the matter was her personal concern. She had a steely confidence that she'd find proof of the bride's virginity. But not once did she look the girl in the eye, even when she'd uncovered her private parts.

"Stand over the piece of mirror and open your legs wide. Then look at the cat's head in the mirror," she commanded.

Confused, the girl asked her what she meant by "the cat's head," and where to find it.

The girl's question spiked the level of bouri in the shushana's veins, and her blood boiled hotter than ever. She grabbed the girl by the crotch and squeezed. The girl moaned. She knew now what the "cat's head" was.

"This is it. You get me now?"

The girl stood there petrified, covering her chest with one hand and her crotch with the other. The darabukka player said to her, "Take a good look at it. Take your hand away and look at it in the mirror."

Hesitant, the weeping girl looked where the older woman had directed her. "Do you see it?" she asked her.

"Yes, yes," she replied, brightening.

"Did you take a good look at it?" she asked again.

"Yes, yes."

She then instructed the girl to put on her bridal tunic without the underpants, and to sit calmly on the edge of the bed without imagining the rifle. She went and opened the door to the men and women gathered outside. Then, shoving the rifle-bearer out of the way, she called the groom to come in and prove his virility, assuring him that his bride had been chaste. There must have been some good-hearted men there too, since otherwise they wouldn't have sent the groom in, and the poor girl would have been a goner.

Escorted by a number of his brothers and angry male relatives, the groom came up looking shell-shocked, cap in hand. The shushana didn't make eye contact with the other men. In fact, she acted as though she hadn't even noticed them.

"Are you the sultan?" she asked the groom.

"I was," he replied.

"Well, you still are," she assured him confidently. "Go in to your bride. She's a virgin."

The other men didn't believe her. They thought she was playing a trick on them. Grabbing the poor groom by the collar with her powerful fist, the shushana said imperiously, "Put on your cap, and take what's been given you in trust. Be a man!"

With no chance to think and no choice but to do as he'd been told, the young man walked timorously into the bridal chamber. It wasn't long before he reemerged, holding the good news in a white handkerchief. He came out a man vindicated, his index finger red with the blood of the little hymen. The men and women alike scrutinized his forefinger to verify that he hadn't cut himself to patch up the situation. Yes, it really was her blood. One of his cousins told him not to wash it off till the next day. Too overjoyed and relieved for words, the groom received people's congratulations on his wife's blood. If it hadn't been for that good-hearted, level-headed darabukka player— who also happened to be the shushana now standing next to Lallahum—the wedding might well have turned into a funeral.

As Rabiha finished telling the story she'd heard in the inner room with the mud-brick walls and the peephole, I could feel my heart sinking into my stomach. I was so scared, and my feet hurt from having had to stand on tiptoe the whole time she was talking. Staring in the direction of the room, I thought about that slave woman and the brave thing she had done. I felt as though she was sharing her strength and patient endurance with me, even though she still bore the marks of her slavery. For all I knew, she might have lost her virginity in some barbaric way, like so many young Negro girls did. But in spite of it all, she fed dates to young white girls to prolong their virginity, and filled the palm leaf tray again whenever they ran out. She brought the old woman tea, water, and snuff, and didn't grumble or complain about having to stand for long stretches. The women who came to see Lallahum brought her all sorts of things in return for the locking ceremony, and this servant woman would collect them in a big sack without coveting any of them for herself, content with whatever her mistress saw fit to give her.

I squatted on the ground and started talking with a girl whose mother had brought her to be locked. After a while the women waiting nearby asked the girl and me to go play. They didn't want us to hear what they were saying. So we went wandering around among the circles of little girls. Sometimes we'd play, sometimes we'd talk, and sometimes we'd get into fistfights. Then we'd get a tanning from the slave woman who worked in Lallahum's kitchen. She came out at us with her blackened bread paddle—which she used to resolve most of the contentions that arose in our little-girl world—and smacked whichever of us she could reach with it. This was followed by a temporary lull in the racket.

After Rabiha left, the crowd thinned and the fearsome kitchen worker disappeared. To my amazement, I found myself standing in the old woman's room, where the fragrance of a cherry tree helped slightly to cover up the smell of dried urine coming from me. When I started to approach Lallahum, she said something to Aunt Sabriya in an angry tone of voice while I stood halfway between them.

"Who told you a servant girl could be locked??" she demanded.

Aunt Sabriya furrowed her brow, then softened it again. "But her father's known," she objected.

"Who's her master? And who are you?" Lallahum asked sharply. "You're going to make problems for me if the masters find out I'm locking their servant girls."

Sounding fearful, Aunt Sabriya said, "She doesn't have a master. She's free."

"What?" the old woman scoffed angrily, tugging on the urine-stained edge of my caftan. "That's ridiculous! A servant girl who's free? Since when has that been possible?"

I looked back and forth between the two women, not knowing which of them was telling the truth. The old woman refused to lock me because I was a slave, a servant—in other words, a Negro. My aunt told her that my father was a free man from Misrata, where they're "as red and white as the Germans."

"You all say the same thing!" the old woman retorted. "You'll have to provide a guarantee from a known individual if her father is dead, or not around, or refuses to acknowledge her."

"Please," my aunt pleaded. "She has a birth certificate. Her father is a free man from Misrata, and her mother was a relative of mine."

The old woman said nothing, her thoughts busy with a theory she was forming. Then, as if she had no choice in the matter, she asked, "Who's your master?"

"My master . . . my master," my aunt replied uneasily, "my master is Imuhammad Bin Shatwan."

"How long have you been with him?"

"Since I was a child."

"And the girl, who's her father?"

"Master Imuhammad Bin Shatwan's son, Muhammad."

"In that case, go now and get me a certificate from him to prove it."

So we left the clay room with the wooden ceiling. I was being haunted by my dark skin, which was shunned by the nonblacks of Benghazi. Even people who were darker than they were light were entitled to reject our blackness, which was alien to the white seacoast. What the old woman had said about my skin color made my body feel darker than ever, so dark that I was lightless outside and in. Then the blackness continued its journey until it filled my milky little heart and settled there as a gloomy feeling over something I hadn't done to myself and which I wasn't the cause for at all, at all.

Now empty, the old Arab house's spacious courtyard was calm, and the voices that had filled it until shortly before the noun prayer had died away. Even lanky Rabiha's raucous, gleeful voice had stopped relating stories she'd picked up in this room or that. As for our story, it had come from some other place, and it was one that no Rabiha would be telling.

Aunt Sabriya and I were both speechless, our hearts heavy. I turned to look at her, and saw her gathering her skirts in preparation to leave. In her agitation, she stumbled and fell on her way out. She'd tripped on the raised doorstep. Weak as I was, I tried to help her. But then I saw her collapse, weeping, in Lallahum's courtyard. I was terrified by her tears, which poured like rain down her black cheeks. It seemed like the first time I'd realized that her face had been black ever since it had come into the world, and that it had never been any other color. I was so traumatized, I started crying along with her. She reached out to me, her hands parched and cracked from gathering salt, shelling peanuts, washing clothes, attending women and animals in labor, and everything, everything. She hung on my neck and sobbed.

My tender-hearted, compassionate, strong aunt—the one who found a solution to every problem in our lives, who was tight-lipped even with women who were colored like her, who always kept her feelings to herself and came to other people's rescue—was crying her heart out like a motherless child in the Slave Yards. Whatever it was that had brought this on, it had to be something so huge that she couldn't push it away, a wound so deep it couldn't be treated.

"Come here, you two."

Standing with one foot outside the old woman's room and one foot inside, Lallahum's servant woman was calling out to us. She was a Negro like us, and the face that peered out from atop her ponderous black frame had seen many a day on Earth. But it recognized us and understood us even if we didn't speak. And why should we speak when we could see that her complexion understood our complexion, and felt what we felt? She might have come from Abuja, Darfur, Wadi ad-Dum, or some other place. She'd either been given out of hunger and deprivation—as so many young children had been—to the chief of their tribe so that he could sell her to feed his children and his wives, or stolen by Libyan caravans, sold in Kafra, Waddai, or Fezzan, and raped by her abductors as their "rightful possession." Or maybe her family had fled from famines and tribal wars to countries whose people offered no resistance to invaders, where slaves converted to Islam and were treated in accordance with Islamic practices, whereby Negro women and girls were turned into concubines and "rightful possessions" who lived in the shadows until they died. Maybe she'd been born to a white Libyan master who'd refused to give her his name so that she wouldn't be able to inherit from him along with his free children. Maybe she'd been taken captive in her home country by a hostile tribe that had sold her to a Libyan caravan that took Negro children and placed them in military camps to make them into slaves, eunuchs, "gifts," and fighters, knowing they could make a fortune off them as they multiplied.

Whatever the story's particulars, it had happened long before, so long as to have been forgotten. Many were the slaves who had forgotten the story of their enslavement and had integrated gladly into the life of those owned by Muslim masters. As for those who married other members of their own race and, in some cases, won emancipation, they were delivered from hunger to hunger, and from poverty to poverty. Apart from a few details here and there, we were like her, and she was like us.

I was the first one to hear the woman calling as Aunt Sabriya lay curled up in her cloak.

"Come here, you two," the woman called again. As she spoke, she pointed to me with her large, knotty hand. I thought I saw a silver ring gleaming in her pug nose as she looked back and forth between us and the elderly woman inside the room. She was still standing in the doorway.

With one hand my aunt took hold of me and, with the other, steadied herself against the ground to get up. As she rose, her shawl slipped off her head and she grabbed it quickly. Then we headed back to the room together. For some reason or other, the servant had taken an interest in us, and Lallahum had taken pity on my aunt or me.

When we came back into the room, Lallahum was leaning on her right arm, yawning, and wiping the remains of some snuff off her nose. Without looking either of us in the eye, she said, "For Asgawa's sake, I'll lock the girl. This is the first time I've locked a servant in all my life."

"God bless you and protect you, both you and Asgawa!" my aunt said gratefully. "The girl is an orphan, and you'll be rewarded for helping her!"

My aunt covered Lallahum's hand and head wrap with kisses.

Lallahum made no comment. However, letting her hand glide easily over to my aunt's full lips, she said to the ponderous Asgawa, "Bring some dates if we have any left."

Then, with her eye on my aunt, she cautioned. "You make sure nobody hears about this now! The masters will punish me if they find out I've been performing the locking ritual for servants."

Lallahum's servant whispered something to my aunt. I gathered it was supposed to be kept a secret from her mistress.

But all I picked up was: "Don't you dare tell anybody."

"Don't worry. Nobody will hear a word about it," my aunt assured her. As we were being sworn to secrecy, my aunt slipped the bundle out from under her clothes. Lallahum pretended not to see the present until it had been placed beside her. Then she ran her hands over it and called out, "Asgawa! Tell Mabrouka to make us *shakshouka* for lunch!"

The shushana shuffled heavily back and forth over the mat. Lallahum told me to come closer, and I inched toward her. My aunt slipped her hand under one of her breasts in search of a hard-earned half-piaster.

Handing me a date, Lallahum set me on top of a chest that sat perched on the mat in the dimly lit room. After turning the key in the chest's lock, she told me to repeat after her: "I'm a wall and he's a string."

"I'm a wall and he's a string," I intoned.

I had no idea, of course, who it was that Aunt Sabriya was trying to keep away from me, and who was going to be turned into a string at the hands of this half-blind old woman. Nor did I know on whose account Lallahum had rejected us, and who had made my aunt and me cry before the servant Asgawa intervened on our behalf. Who was suspected of threatening my virginity, and on whose account was I held suspect until I'd married? Once you were married, nobody cared about protecting or repairing your honor.

My aunt drew her hand out from under one breast and thrust it under the other. She was dripping with sweat, her upper lip trembling. Lallahum pinched my upper thigh. I stifled a scream. Maybe the old woman had heard me recite her magic formula full of strings and walls in the wrong order. Or maybe she'd pinched me as a way of scaring me so that I wouldn't mix things up. In any case, she called me a dirty name and told me to correct myself, while the kind-hearted shushana standing nearby told her I'd said it right.

"Come on now, that's a good girl," she murmured encouragingly.

As for my aunt, she was ecstatic. It was as if she'd already forgotten all about what had happened a little earlier. Either that, or she considered it a small price to pay for what she now saw happening before her very eyes. The dates, some wormy ones included, made their way in succession to my mouth, while the walls and strings between me and the world of urges and desires grew successively louder and longer. As I swallowed wormy dates, I pictured Mjawir, who'd gone after me and fondled my bottom even though I was his youngest daughter's age. He loomed before me with his white teeth, his coal black skin, and his fleshy lips trying to come between me and the towering walls. As I repeated after the old woman, I was dealing Mjawir the death blow with my lips. He surged before me like the waves of the sea beside the Slave Yards, and the tempestuous blackness that had shattered my childhood and blasted my innocent illusion that grown men aren't interested in girls who are young enough to be their daughters imprinted itself inside me.

"I'm a wall and he's a string."
A wormy date.
Click, click in a rusty lock.
"I'm a wall and he's a string."
A wormy date.
Click, click, click, click.

Rust and worms . . . walls . . . strings . . . clicks . . . dates . . . slaps on the bottom . . .

Seven times I was stalked by Mjawir's face. The fifth, sixth and seventh times, his black, inflated beast—the one he'd flashed at me at the well one hot afternoon at Zurayri'iya—chased me like mad. I jumped off the chest, fleeing from his face the way I'd jumped away from the swollen thing dangling from between his legs that afternoon. I wore out the chest and the key and the lock, and I emptied Lallahum's containers of their rotten dates. My bottom had nearly turned into a drum from all the times it was beaten that day. But I didn't mind. It was all right with me for Lallahum's faithful servant, companion, and confidante to be rewarded at my behind's expense. Thanks to this reward, my cat's head would escape from Mjawir's black beast, and from other men's beasts as well, the way it had escaped that sweltering afternoon thanks to another Negro man who'd shown up all of a sudden and starting pooping in the garbage. Mjawir was so scared when he saw the guy, he'd taken off running to the seashore.

Two black figures—Lallahum's shushana and the man who'd crapped in the garbage—framed Mjawir's face and his dangling black organ in my imagination, and drove him away. And as I'd panted that day in the field near the Slave Yards, I panted today in Lallahum's house on the tick-tock chest.

My aunt finally came across the half-piaster hidden under her fleshy breast. She handed it, still moist with her perspiration, to Lallahum, who grabbed it and thrust it hurriedly into her brassiere, whereupon it set out on a new journey with a new breast, waiting to team up with its other half to make a whole piaster.

Her footsteps heavy and loud on the mat, Lallahum's shushana went over and dragged out the sack of gifts for Lallahum to look through. At this point, the two women seemed to forget we even existed. I'll never forget that old woman's face as she rummaged through her sack that day. My cat's head will never forget it either. It was a thin, wizened face whose sole functioning eye had been assigned the task of protecting our tiny, vulnerable wombs. This eye was anxious to dump the bag's contents on the floor and sift through them with childish delight. As for the other, it was lifeless and still, its gaze frozen in a state of shock.

As we left, Lallahum was holding the gifts up to her real eye to get a good look at them. She did this with everything except the eggs, which she recognized by how they felt to the touch.

Date Pits between the Toes

AUNT SABRIYA and I were walking home along a foot-worn dirt path under a merciless noonday sun when all of a sudden we heard footsteps behind us. When we turned to see who it was, we saw Lallahum's kitchen servant Mabrouka—the one who'd smacked me with the bread shovel—running to catch up with us. Out of breath, she kept looking behind her, as if she were afraid somebody would see her. She held one hand on her head to keep her bandanna in place, and the other on her chest to keep her big boobs from jiggling up and down.

When we saw her approaching, she stopped in her tracks. Her bare feet, visible from under her caftan, were covered with dirt.

"Lord have mercy," Aunt Sabriya murmured when she saw the girl. The farms we were walking past were surrounded by tall hedges of prickly pear cactuses. We stopped to wait for her in the latticework shadows cast by the towering plants on either side of the path. The girl came up to us, out of breath, saying, "T . . . a . . . k . . . e . . . t . . . h . . . i . . . s!"

As she spoke, she reached out and placed an egg in Aunt Sabriya's hand.

"What's this all about?" my aunt asked, bewildered.

"I don't know," the girl said. "Asgawa just told me to give it to you."

"Why?"

"She said it could be the little girl's lunch."

As she said "the little girl," she looked at me.

"Does Lallahum know about this?" my aunt inquired.

Seeming afraid, she didn't answer.

"I'm late," she stammered. "The *shakshouka*'s going to burn, and Lallahum will notice I'm gone."

Realizing that the girl would be punished if the old woman took notice of her absence, and knowing what a tight spot Asgawa would be in if that happened, my aunt said to her, "You'd better get right back then."

The servant girl looked hard at me. Then she turned and headed back.

As she scurried away, my aunt called after her, "Give my best to Asgawa!" Which was another way of saying, "Tell her thank you for me!"

From what I could see, Asgawa had returned to us one of our eggs behind the old woman's back. Maybe she figured four eggs were too many for Lallahum, and that considering our miserable lot in life, we deserved that fourth egg more than she did. Besides, since she only had one eye, she wouldn't be able to tell that anything was missing when she had lunch that day, since all the eggs would be beaten together to make the *shakshouka*. After what happened, I concluded that Asgawa really did have a good heart, and that she and the kitchen servant were probably in the habit of pulling the wool over the old woman's eyes together.

We started off again without a word, my aunt clutching the egg in one hand and holding onto me with the other. A few moments later, I looked back to see the kitchen servant, but all I saw was the cloud of dust she'd stirred up with her bare feet. She'd disappeared as quickly as she'd appeared. A wistful silence had come over my aunt, and when I spoke to her, she didn't say anything. We'd been walking for a while by now, and it seemed like we'd never make it back to the Slave Yards. My aunt let go of my hand, since we were sweating so much that we couldn't hold on to each other anymore. The last half of the way home we just kept our eyes on our feet, trying to find some saliva in our mouths. When the Yards with their huts finally appeared in the distance, they looked like heaven to me. Meanwhile, the sea breeze broke the heat, freshening the air.

When they didn't have any work to do, the people who lived in the Slave Yards didn't go anywhere or do anything. They just spent their time talking and shooing away the flies that swarmed all over the place when it got hot. As they waited to be summoned for this job or that, they would chase the cats and dogs—of which there were more than there were people—patch their worn-out clothes, weave floor mats, boil broad beans and chickpeas to sell in the streets, and brew bad booze. The women and girls would bring water from nearby wells and sweep out the huts with brooms made from dry palm leaves. When they didn't have any clothes to wash or meals to cook, the women might get together and gossip. Meanwhile, the hungry children, who were as numerous as the flies, would gather around the soldiers who came to inspect the ghetto from time to time, begging for food or waiting for the scraps the soldiers would leave behind for them.

Mounds and mounds of garbage lay piled up along the highway leading to the Slave Yards. The sides of the road were strewn with liquor bottles and remains of things that were no longer recognizable—ruined boats, empty food cans, and lard and oil tins that were usually picked up by Yard residents to finish off their huts with, or to put to some other use in their wretched lives. I'd seen tins like that turned into utensils for cooking, eating, laundering, or water transport. I'd also seen them filled with sand and lined up or stacked to wall in rooms and entire houses.

Tired and hungry, my aunt and I were walking as fast as we could to get out of the hot sand. We passed some little kids who were rummaging through the garbage for something to eat. Poverty made it a normal thing to visit garbage heaps. But Aunt Sabriya didn't like me mixing with those children. She would take me with her to the sea to wash up several times a week. She'd scrub the fleas off me and pick the lice and nits out of my hair. As for Miftah, she'd shave his head so close you would have thought he'd never sprouted a hair in his life. We got dirty fast, and there was nothing to keep the filth off us except for the clothes other people had thrown away because they were no good anymore, or because they had so many they didn't need them. We would patch them and put them on, and it wouldn't even occur to us to change them until they'd started wearing off our bodies. It wasn't unusual to see girls wearing pants they'd gotten from soldiers at Baw-wabat as-Sur under their dirty caftans, or for women to go around in threadbare army fatigues that soldiers had left along the roadside. As for the men, they would wear tattered uniforms and army boots that had been nabbed from their owners while they were drunk or dying, then altered to fit Negroes' lean, lank bodies, and protect them from the hot sands.

There was an elderly Negro man by the name of Tazay who had made himself a reputation as a good clothes patcher-upper. As a young man he'd been a slave in the orchards of Ghadames. Then, at the age of sixty, he'd been freed by a notable of the region to atone for a sexual sin he'd committed. Islam grants its adherents the chance to atone for certain sins by freeing slaves, although many people would indulge in sins without bothering to atone for them. Either that, or someone would free a slave who wasn't very important. So one person was granted freedom in return for somebody else's sin—this was a religious principle. But it meant, ironically, that a single sin by one person was equal to another person's whole life!

Tazay was known for his ability to alter shoes in such a way that they were unrecognizable to their original owners—that is to say, to the people they'd been stolen from. He'd done it so many times that he'd become quite good at it. With his rusty awls and needles, Tazay could work wonders with a piece of leather. One time my aunt took me to him to alter some shoes that were too big for me. They'd been given to me by a nice lady I'd worked for in Souq Al Hashish. I don't know what he did to them, but when he was finished they were the same shoes, only a little smaller.

Tazay would patch old rags together and turn them into weird-looking outfits that protected Slave Yards residents from the cold and the heat but which, for some reason, were even uglier than they'd been before. In any case, he was good about not throwing anything away, including his incomprehensible African jibber-jabber sprinkled with words from the local dialect.

As he sat in front of his hut in what was left of an old pair of trousers, Tazay looked to me like an old man without a color. His skin was so dry and cracked that it was hard for him to move around, so his bony wife would bring him the things he needed for fear that his skin would peel right off.

Tazay was good at other things too, such as building huts that looked like the ones in residents' home villages. The abundance of palm branches everywhere helped him to create the similarity. He and others would climb the palm trees, strip off the dry fronds, and spread them in the sun. Then they would knead them together with straw, dry grass, and sea spume and fill metal tins with the mixture to make the roofs and walls.

Out of a hundred huts inhabited by around a thousand Negroes, Tazay had built sixty-five huts in this way. They were surrounded on the outside by additional walls, and the space in between the inner and outer walls was used for cooking and housing chickens, animals, or homeless Negroes.

Not far from Tazay's hut, a woman by the name of Sadina came up to my aunt and started talking to her. As the two women stood chatting, Tazay's scrawny wife watched him patiently, weaving away without a word. She didn't budge unless he asked her for help. As for me, I felt as worn-out as Tazay's skin, and I was dying to get back to our shack and rest.

My aunt, who'd been carrying her shoes under her arm, set them on the ground and put them on again. I did the same. As for Sadina, who had her feet stuffed into an old pair of army boots, she seemed determined to go on chattering in the hot sun. Unlike me, my aunt didn't seem to mind despite how exhausted she was, so she didn't try to cut the conversation short. Maybe they were talking about something that was important to her.

Some hens scurried across the narrow paths that ran between the huts nearby. A young man passed through after the hens, pounding softly on a drum, as if he were getting ready to play for a wedding or some all-night celebration, or maybe in anticipation of the big danga season coming up.

Sadina asked the young man a question, but I couldn't hear what it was, since her voice was muffled by the sound of his drum. It had a beautiful, vibrant rhythm and a black skin that was drawn taut like ours. As he mumbled something to the woman, he kept the drumstick moving deftly and delicately over the drum's surface. Then Sadina turned back to my aunt, who told her she'd come in the late afternoon for them to wash the mats belonging to the Ridwan family in Benghazi. The income it brought them would be a welcome reward after a grueling day.

Sadina remarked, "The family wants servants for their son's wedding party. He's getting married to a Jewish girl. They weren't going to agree to it, but Ridwan's so crazy in love he threatened to convert to Judaism. Well, that gave them a scare! It would have been the disaster of the century. The family would never have been able to live it down. The fact that it's going to be such a big event means they'll need lots of mats to seat the guests. We can make a few piasters off it and get ourselves some food, too. After all, it isn't every day that a Muslim marries a Jew. Just think: Ridwan Khalifa Ridwan gets hitched to Khamisa, the daughter of Sihoun the scrap metal merchant, or, as folks around here call him, 'the sweeper'! The Jews of Benghazi will be hopping mad about it, and so will the Muslims. Nobody saw it coming, that's for sure. In any case, Ridwan's family will insist that Khamisa declare herself a Muslim in front of some big gathering of notables with a Muslim sheikh in attendance. That's the only way they can ensure that the marriage will be recognized as legitimate and keep people from giving them a hard time over it. As for the Jews, they'll be so disgraced that they'll shut themselves up in the synagogue on Qazzar Street and weep and wail for days. Khamisa's mother is an observant Jew, you know. Seeing the daughter she's dedicated to the service of Yahweh marry a Muslim man isn't going to sit well with her.

She and Khamisa's two hardline sisters, Sisi and Mazala, are going to put on a funeral, not a wedding."

My aunt was so wrapped up in what Sadina was saying that she'd stopped feeling tired and sad, and when I looked at her face, I didn't see the woman who'd taken me to be locked earlier that day.

"Come on, come on. I'm hungry!" I whined, tugging at the hem of her dress.

"I know, I know," she said, putting me off gently. "We'll go in just a bit."

She didn't see how desperately I'd been trying to keep from peeing on myself: squeezing my thighs together, writhing and dancing around so that I wouldn't leak in front of anybody. But finally, when I couldn't hold it any longer, I let the pee come rushing out between my legs like the *shayshama*. Hot, humiliating, and copious, it dug a rivulet in the sand underneath me and got my caftan and my bloomers wet all over again. But the loud splatter at least forced the chatterbox Sadina to notice I was there.

Instead of paying attention to the distress I was in, however, Sadina went from talking about the Jewish girl to talking about how I couldn't control my bladder. Then she started telling my aunt to "treat" me by putting a date pit that had been heated in the fire between my big toe and the toe next to it. Apparently she didn't think there was enough torture already in the Yards, since otherwise she wouldn't have volunteered her unwanted advice when she could see us roasting on the hot sand.

Realizing her mistake, my aunt bowed her head without a word and took my hand. Then, interrupting Sadina's sermon, she led me away with my hand in hers and we headed back to our tinplate shack, our little heaven.

She said to me, "We'll have something to eat and rest for a while. In the evening when Miftah comes, we'll have supper together and then go wash the Ridwan family's mats and clean ourselves up after that."

What a day it had been. It was the day when my virginity had been walled in—a day of stinky urine, exclusion, hunger, searing heat, tiredness, and sadness. It had started with wormy dates and ended with somebody advising my aunt to torture me by sticking a hot date pit between my toes!

Whoever had thought up ideas like that must have been schooled by the accursed Satan himself, before God decided to ease life's cruelty and create the angels.

My Brother in God's Book

MIFTAH HAD FAIR SKIN and blue eyes, I had dark skin and almond eyes, and Aunt Sabriya was a Negro. But we lived together under the same tinplate roof, and we felt like family.

Miftah had been my playmate in the Slave Yards for as long as I could remember. When I got tired, he'd pick me up and give me a piggyback ride. He was so attached to Aunt Sabriya that he tagged along wherever she went. He used to help her with things, and sometimes he even gave her advice. Miftah was lanky and handsome, and there was almost always a smile on his face. He did everything fast, he had a loud, hearty laugh, and there was a blue vein in his forehead that would stick out when he got mad. He was brave too, and from the time he was a little boy he guarded our humble little shack as if it were a palace. Famine and drought struck when he was little, so from a young age he went to work in the salt flats. Like other kids in those days, he wasn't free to choose the life he wanted. It was basically a choice between homelessness, thievery, and death, or the most menial, grueling jobs you could think of to keep yourself alive.

Miftah would bring us something to eat on his way home from the salt flats. He'd take what he'd earned slaving away from dawn to dusk and buy a watermelon, or a couple of tomatoes and a loaf of bread. When he got home, he'd collapse exhausted at the door to our shack. The minute he put his head down he'd fall fast asleep, and bugs would go crawling all over him without his feeling a thing. I used to step on his legs while he was sleeping, but instead of blowing up at me he'd just grumble groggily, "You'd better cut it out, Little Blackie."

Whenever Aunt Sabriya had time, she'd massage his feet, stroke his head, and sing him old ditties. She loved Miftah and worried about him as if he were her son from some white man who'd taken off and left her. When he fell asleep in front of the shack, she would pull him inside, lay him down on the bed, and put a pillow under his head so that he could get a good night's rest.

It wasn't unusual for children to work, and since he wouldn't be able to go to school, Aunt Sabriya had to help him find a job. He had to get ready to face life early by learning a trade. Children who start working from a young age develop a sense of responsibility, and they grow up before their time. Their mental age outstrips their chronological age, and before you know it they're fully formed human beings.

Miftah knew how much I loved watermelon. So on summer days when he had the money, he'd buy a little watermelon, stuff it under his clothes, and bring it home to the Yards. He'd come rushing back and, while he was still some distance away, he'd call out to me, "I bought you a red watermelon! Come help me bury it in the sand next to the shore!" That was what people did back then to chill their watermelons. We were on top of the world, knowing we had a "refrigerator" that half the residents of the Slave Yards didn't have.

Aunt Sabriya taught me to thank him by kissing him on the head, so I did it even though I didn't think a brother should tease his sister by calling her "Little Blackie."

"Don't call me 'Little Blackie,' Fattouha!" I scolded.

"All right," he'd say with a laugh. "I'll call you Farina, then, and you call me Ubaidi!"[1]

And that's what we started to do after a while: he'd call me Farina and I'd call him Ubaidi. He laughed at most of the things I did, especially when I played dress-up with myself. I'd put this on and take that

---

1. *Farina* being Italian for "flour," and *Ubaidi* Arabic for "my little slave."

off. I'd borrow my aunt's belts and dresses and arrange them in a way that suited me.

"Farina's lost her marbles!" Miftah would tell my aunt with a giggle.

Then, as if he hadn't made enough fun of me already, he'd go out looking for something to "complete my look," as he put it. He might bring me the black poker from the oven and say, "Hold it in your hand the way a queen holds her scepter." Or he might pull some stripped palm branches out of a broom and say, "Put these on your head—they'll make your hair look softer by comparison!"

I'd get all mad and tell Aunt Sabriya to make him leave me alone. But all she'd do was smile and say something in his defense—either that, or pretend to make him stop.

Never once did Miftah disobey Aunt Sabriya or give her any trouble. He loved her so much that he'd get sick himself if she came down with pneumonia, and he wouldn't go to the salt flats. She didn't ask much of him. All she ever wanted him to do was to keep an eye on me. Whenever she asked him to watch me, he'd just say, "Yes, ma'am," and stay on the job till she got back. Then he'd take off to play with the other boys. Miftah was older than me, but not by a lot. When we lay down on the seashore on hot summer evenings and looked up at the sky, he would ask Aunt Sabriya serious questions, as if he were thinking about his identity. He'd ask her to tell him about his family—what they'd been like, who he looked like, and lots of other things. No matter how naïve or incredible her answers sounded to us later, she always made sure to answer all his questions, as if she didn't want to let a single one go on worrying him.

When Miftah asked about his origins, Aunt Sabriya told him his family had been from the outlying desert region of eastern Libya, and that like most other people, they'd run away because they couldn't pay the taxes they owed the wali, or Ottoman governor. Fleeing with their little boy from cruel punishment and from the spread of hunger and disease, they disappeared into the Yards, where it would be hard for the wali's tax collectors to go after them. Hiding hadn't been difficult since Miftah's family was small: two sisters, his father, his mother, and him. But he'd lost them all when, during a certain high-tide season, the sea had rushed into the Yards in the dark of the night and inundated it, sparing only a few souls who'd been destined to survive. Their dog had drowned, and so had their only milk goat. A small group of survivors later rebuilt the Yards, and Miftah had been among them.

When Miftah asked about the flood, he'd found people who could confirm the story. It was an actual event that had left a huge death toll.

"But how did I make it out alive?" he wanted to know.

"Well," Aunt Sabriya explained, "what happened was that, as the waters were rising, your mother lifted you on top of her head and cried for help. We were neighbors, and I heard her screaming. So, since I knew how to swim, I went and got you from her. Then I put you on my head and swam with you until I found a wooden plank to set you on. Then you and I kept on going till dry land appeared."

"And where was Atiga then?"

"She hadn't been born yet."

"Was I older, or were my sisters?"

"You were the youngest."

"What were their names?"

"Your mother's name was Fatima and your father's name was Muhammad. Your sisters' names were Salima and Maryouma."

"And why is my last name Daqiq—'Flour'?"

"It might have been passed down in your family from earlier generations. Maybe one of your ancestors used to load flour onto carts for transport. Or maybe he was as white as flour—like you!"

Then, to make her hypothesis more convincing, she added, "You know, the Al Sifiniz family name comes from the fact that one of their ancestors used to make sifiniz—or he really liked it, at least, and the family name Al Huwwat, which means 'fisherman,' comes from the fact that one of their ancestors used to catch or sell fish, or that he just ate a lot of fish. So, as you can probably guess, the family name Al Iyat, which means 'crying,' comes from the fact that somebody in the family used to cry a lot!" Then we tried out the same idea with the family names Farina and Ubaidi, and we laughed till we cried.

Then the two of us would get really quiet. Aunt Sabriya would yawn and, muttering a prayer for God to forgive her, say to Miftah, "Ask God to have mercy on them. A lot of people died the year of the flood."

So, lying wearily on his back after slaving away all day in the salt flats, he'd lift his hands heavenward, intoning reverently, "Oh Lord, have mercy on them, and make Heaven their resting place!"

His curiosity satisfied, Miftah would ask Aunt Sabriya to tell us a story.

"What story do you want to hear?" she'd ask.

"Anything make-believe."

Then Aunt Sabriya's stories would take us away to another world that little children love.

When she started telling the story of Umm Basisi, Miftah would sneakily walk his hand over in my direction and brush my arm as if it were a crab. I'd scream and nearly jump out of my skin. When his dastardly deed had been exposed, Aunt Sabriya would tweak his ear and say, "If you spook her, you'll make God angry, and the stars will get sad! A real man doesn't scare his sister—he protects her and sticks up for her!"

Miftah was friends with Aunt Aida's kids, and with Yousef too. When Aunt Sabriya and Aunt Aida got together to talk, they'd say things like, "God's the one who's raised Miftah."

The only times Miftah would leave us were when he had to go work in the salt flats. But then, one day, some lady from a notable Benghazi family came to the Yards. It seemed she'd come looking for Aunt Sabriya so that she could buy Miftah from her. It came as a huge shock to me. Never in the world would I have expected Aunt Sabriya to sell her own son, the son she loved and had raised herself! She insisted that she hadn't sold him to anybody, and that she was just going to leave him at the lady's house to work as a servant there. She said domestic work would be a lot easier on him than salt extraction had been. But I'd seen the woman give Aunt Sabriya some money. When I asked her about it, she told me she'd hired him out to the lady.

I was devastated over what she'd done, and I secretly hated her for it.

Miftah didn't want to go with the lady, but he didn't object, either. He didn't say anything. As Aunt Sabriya worked to persuade him of the idea, his eyes showed how he really felt. He was a good actor, and he pretended to be convinced just to please her, but in his heart of hearts, going to that woman's house was the last thing in the world he would have wanted.

I didn't like what Aunt Sabriya had done one bit. I was furious with her. I told her that from then on I wasn't going to love her too much, just in case there came a day when she sold me off the way she'd done to Miftah!

Even so, I think she suffered as much as I did on Miftah's first night away. I cried and talked about how much I missed him, while she just hung her head and made no reply to my reproaches.

When she did finally say something, she reassured me that we'd go on being one family and facing life's trials together. She told me Miftah would come back to live with us when we had a little money and could afford to buy a house in the city. In fact, she went on, if she lived long enough and saved up enough, she was going to have him bring his wife and children to live with us in one room of the house, and she'd go with him on the pilgrimage to Mecca.

I could tell from the way her voice sounded that she wanted to cry, but she wouldn't let herself break down in front of me. Her talk of a house, a family, children, and the pilgrimage comforted me temporarily, and I gave myself over to her big dreams, surrendering to the magical vision of what time would bring once Miftah had become a man.

Miftah ran away from the lady's house a few times and came to stay with us. He said she was nice, and that she loved him and treated him like her own son, but that he liked his life with us in the Yards more. He said he didn't know anybody there. Everybody was always looking him over and asking rude questions like, "Where did this orphan come from? What a shame that a boy like him would lose his family!"

Knowing full well that he could hear her, a certain old lady with penetrating eyes asked, "So did he lose his parents or was he a foundling?"

Some people made fun of his name. "So," they'd ask with a snicker, "is he *daqiq qamh* (wheat flour), or *daqiq sha'ir* (barley flour)?"

Sighing in resignation, Aunt Sabriya would console him with the thought that when people got used to him, things would get better.

"Don't you pay any attention to what people say!" she told him. "You're all that matters! Life is hard, and you'll have to learn a trade to support yourself. Once you've done that, everything will change, and you'll have a craft that wins people's respect."

She didn't tell him the other half of the truth—namely, that when people keep doing obnoxious things, you get used to them, and they turn familiar and ordinary.

To our surprise, the lady who had taken Miftah to live with her came after him when he left her house. She promised Aunt Sabriya that nothing would ever happen to upset him again. She said she'd spoken with a relative of hers who was a coffeehouse owner who would hire Miftah as his assistant in the evenings, and that she thought the job would suit him. I was trying to figure out why this woman was so determined to keep Miftah at her house, so I asked Aunt Sabriya about it. But instead of offering me an explanation, she put me off, saying, "Hard times lead people to accept things they couldn't accept before."

My big mistake wasn't in my understanding of the overall situation—that is, the fact that Miftah gradually got used to growing up in that family—taking on their customs and getting comfortable with their acquaintances and relatives and the kinds of things they did. Rather, my mistake lay in the angle I took on things because of my lack of experience with life and people. There are realities that, in order for us to understand them, time has to pass, not so that the realities can grow up the way we do but rather so that we can grow up to the point where our heads are on their level. And Miftah—my brother and my dear soulmate—was one of them.

We're All Looking
for a Lost Key

AUNT SABRIYA told me about a time when a storm blew up over the Slave Yards and sent huts flying. It was the season of wild winds, and the more they blew, the more fragile the things in their path became. The motto you had to live by in the Yards was: only trust in the bad things, since they're the ones most likely to come true.

People got busy fixing their huts, repairing what had been broken or torn away, and tacking down the rest. They did what they could to help each other prepare for the worst if the winds proved as destructive as the water had done twice before, turning the Yards into a floating mass of wooden planks, bulrushes, corpses, and debris.

People stayed put, prepared for the onslaught. Their previous experiences with Nature's storms hadn't been happy ones. One winter, the sea had overflowed and gobbled up all sorts of things. Before coming to its senses, it had scraped the place clean with deadly force within the space of just two days.

Whether hot or cold, the wind was another enemy of the poor in those parts. When people sensed danger, they would pack up their clothes and whatever else they could carry into bundles so that they could be on their way if the storm didn't die down. After the storm had passed, the sun would come out with a kind of unruffled neutrality. Then, with the help of the sea salt and the air, its heat would disinfect the place, clearing out the pockets of disease that had formed here and there. Otherwise, this sickly piece of Benghazi would have rotted through and through.

During one bout of crazed weather, the three of us were huddled together in our hut for a whole day and a night: a baby girl still nursing, a little white boy, and a black woman. Miftah told Aunt Sabriya that he wouldn't go to sleep and leave her and his sister to listen to the storm alone. "Instead," he said, "we can overcome our fear and defeat the winds by talking to each other."

Not letting on how distressed she was, Aunt Sabriya smiled, held him close, and sang him something about the family's little hero:

> I'm crazy about my little gazelle
> He's as fine as fine can be.
> He means the world, and more, to me
> I'd give him my eyes if he couldn't see!

Wondering why he didn't say anything about food even though he hadn't eaten since the day before, she asked, "Are you hungry, Miftah?"

"No, no," he replied stoically.

She squinted at him skeptically. What he'd said wasn't true, of course. He was starving, and if there'd been a handful of *zummaita* in front of him, he would have gobbled it right down.[1] But he was patient and stoical by nature.

Bracing himself against his hunger, Miftah stuck out his tongue, saying, "See? My mouth isn't even dry!"

Wanting to lighten the atmosphere, Aunt Sabriya told him playfully that as soon as the winds died down, she'd go to the city and do some work there so she could feed her favorite boy. And if she didn't find any work to do, she'd go to her friend Aida and borrow something from her house—like some *zummaita* and dates or some barley flour.

---

1. A traditional Libyan treat, *zummaita* is made by kneading a mixture of ground roasted wheat (or barley) and cumin with water and oil, then dipping it in sugar.

"No, no!" he broke in. "Not barley flour! I don't like it! Bring us a little couscous from her house. Then I'll go with Uncle Mustafa Al Huwwat and help him fish. We'll catch a fish that'll stretch from one end of our shack to the other. You can make couscous with it, and we'll give some to the neighbors."

To add to the fun, she said, "But couscous calls for onions, oil, tomatoes, and green vegetables!"

"Don't worry about that!" little Miftah said reassuringly, determined to keep his dream alive. "I'll bring you whatever you need!"

"But how will you do that, my little gazelle? And where will you get it?"

"Let me see," he said pensively. "I know! I'll get it from God. Don't you always tell me God will give us whatever we need? I might go ask Bouga how to do it, and she'll tell me. Bouga's a nice old lady, and she knows all about God."

Amid the whistling of the wind and the rattling of the huts, a neighbor called to Aunt Sabriya from outside her shack, saying, "There's somebody looking for you!" Surprised that anybody would be looking for her in such stormy weather, she braced herself for the worst.

Pulling back the flap that covered the shack entrance, she peeked out and saw a neat, impeccably groomed white woman.

When she saw Aunt Sabriya peek out, she said, "Peace be upon you. I'm looking for Tawida."

Sabriya remained silent as Tawida thought back on the past.

After a pause, the woman said, "That's all right. All that matters is that you know the story behind this piece of cloth, and the pink towel a certain baby was wrapped in once upon a time."

This said, she reached under her *farrashiya* and brought out a piece of fabric that matched the one that had been tied around Miftah's wrist on the night he was born.[2] Tawida felt undone. However,

---

2. A *farrashiya* is a traditional white Libyan robe worn by women in public. Its shape and design generally reflect its owner's economic status.

Aunt Sabriya replied calmly on her behalf that the two women would have to go inside so that they could speak in private.

Miftah was eyeing the stranger who'd come to visit, and she him. To get him out of ear range, Tawida said to him, "Go to Bouga and ask her how we can get some onions and oil to make couscous."

The woman squeezed his hand as he left, saying, "Do you need onions and oil? And would you like some sweets too?"

With a confident, slightly stern air the child replied, "We don't need sweets right now, Auntie. My mother and I just want to eat, and I want milk for my little sister."

"No worries," the woman said with a smile. "I've brought you all a basket that's got the things you've mentioned in it."

"And how did you know we needed food?"

"Sidi Abdussalam Al Asmar sent me to you.[3] Hasn't your mother told you about visitors the saints send to people when they need something? They usually come when it's windy and rainy!"

Miftah had heard all sorts of "once upon a time" stories about saints and their magical emissaries.

"So has the fairy come to see us?" the little boy asked.

"That's right," Sabriya replied with a nervous smile. "But you still need to go ask Bouga about the onions and the oil. Tell her your mama says hello, and that she also needs some *shidd ma jak*."[4]

"What's *shidd ma jak*?" he asked curiously.

Ready with a quick reply, Sabriya told him, "It's a medicine they give to little children to help them sleep and not be afraid of the wind. Tell her we need it for your little sister Atiga."

So off he went.

3. Sidi Abdussalam (1455–1575) was a renowned Muslim ascetic and mystic known for having performed numerous miracles on others' behalf. He was born and died in the Libyan town of Zliten, where his grave was a place of visitation until 2012, when it was destroyed at the hands of Muslim fundamentalists on the pretext that Islam forbids the veneration of saints and their tombs.

4. An expression that means "keep the person who's come to you at your house."

Smiling sadly, the woman asked Sabriya, "Is that really my son? You've raised him so well!"

"God's the one who's raised Miftah."

"So his name is Miftah—Key?"

"That's right. He has a way of opening things up, both for himself and for others."

Then she added, "You're late, by the way. I expected you to come for him when he was a baby!"

"*Allah ghaleb*," the woman said, bursting into tears.[5]

❧

They say the woman hankered after Miftah so much that when she got pregnant again, she had two babies who looked just like him. They also say that when a pregnant woman looks often at something she either hates or loves, it will affect the child she's carrying. If she's been looking at a person, the baby will look like that person. If she craves a certain kind of fruit that's out of season, the shape or color of the fruit will be imprinted somewhere on the baby's body, and when that fruit is in season, the birthmark will glow. If she looks often at somebody she loves during her pregnancy, and if she drinks water over this person's head while he's sitting down without his realizing it, the baby will be identical to the person concerned.

Like religious doctrines, superstitions work to conceal things that people aren't allowed to talk about, or speaking of which might bring someone harm. So we need superstitions to keep painful realities hidden away. When Miftah went to serve in that woman's house, he was actually going there to be near his real mother, who'd been forced to give him up in order to avoid a scandal. So when Sabriya agreed to give him to her, she was simply giving him back to his birth mother. In his new home he would be living with his own flesh and blood, but as a servant. Sabriya had no wish to deprive this woman of her own

---

5. Meaning "God is victor"—in other words, "God is the one who decides everything," the expression *Allah ghaleb* is used to express resignation in the face of circumstances beyond one's control.

son or to punish her for a fleeting rush of passion. What good would it have done to keep him away from her or expose her to ridicule? She had no authority to do such a thing and, even if she had, it would have been unthinkable to her.

Since other people didn't know the real story behind her relationship to Miftah, Sabriya had to put up with their criticism for having allegedly abandoned a bright, obedient, well-mannered boy who had come to her as a gift from Heaven. She couldn't tell people she was just giving back to others what was rightfully theirs. Some people would have found the truth offensive. It would have been as devastating as the storm winds that used to rage through the Yards, and people would have hated it, no matter what hidden blessing it might have brought.

Besides, what good would it have done for her to tell anyone? Nobody would have stopped hurling accusations. They would just have shifted the blame from Sabriya to Miftah's mother, and the pain and condemnation would have gone on. Besides, if the truth had come out it would have spelled a far worse catastrophe for Miftah's mother, and for Miftah especially, than it would have for Sabriya.

So the only thing Sabriya could say was that she hadn't "sold" Miftah, as rumor had it, but that she had just sent him to serve at the lady's house, and that the money and food the lady had given her weren't "payment" for her priceless Miftah.

Lest her heart shatter under the weight of people's suspicions, Sabriya asked Miftah's mother not to send her anything that could be seen by hateful, envious folks in the Yards, who were sure to use them as an excuse to gossip about her. She was more than willing to sacrifice for Miftah's sake, but she couldn't bear to hear other people saying she had sold an innocent child that she had raised as her own son. If rumors like that got around, Miftah was sure to get wind of them sooner or later, and she didn't want to hurt him. Instead of sending Sabriya things, the mother could help her find work that would enable Sabriya to endure hunger, drought, and poverty, and, at the same time, allow her to stay closer to Miftah.

Sabriya, Bouga, Aida, and Jaballah knew whose son Miftah Daqiq really was, but they didn't let on to anybody. After all, he'd been flourishing so beautifully, none of them could bear to think of doing anything that would spoil his growth and keep him from finding happiness. Life is cruel enough as it is without our making it that much crueler!

Hunger hadn't dampened Miftah's hopeful spirit, nor had the hardship of life in the Yards taken away his smile. He was a white boy growing up in a black community, he was poor and served in people's homes as a white slave, and he did backbreaking labor breaking up and gathering salt on the seashore. But none of that could break his determination. Nothing could diminish his conviction that everything is foreordained by God and that life is a precious gift that deserves to be lived.

Miftah adored Sabriya, who'd raised him as if she were his own mother, and he believed the things she told him about his family and his origins. It was through her words that he'd come to love his family, a family he thought had died. He dreamed of being able to make the pilgrimage to Mecca not just once, but twice—once for himself, and once for his mother, his father, and his two sisters. The distant future—the only time when it seems hopes can be realized—always holds out the promise of happiness.

He told her, "When I grow up and get married, I'm going to name my daughters after my mother and my sisters. And if God gives me a boy, I'll name him after my father. But the first girl has to be called Sabriya. That way I can get back what the sea took away from me. But I have to love the oldest girl in a special way, the way I love you. Then you'll be both my mother and my daughter!"

Touched by his childlike transparency, Sabriya burst out laughing. She gathered him in her arms and, between one kiss and the next, said, "God bring you joy, my little one!"

She didn't make fun of his dreams. On the contrary, she believed in them herself. She went along with even the impossible ones, saying, "Of course, some people will tell you the name Sabriya is old-fashioned. So forget about using that one. What matters is for you to have a family of your own and to live a happy life."

Sabriya always came to Miftah's defense and would do anything to spare him disappointment or humiliation. She would rather have died than have him discover that he'd been an illegitimate child, conceived out of nothing but somebody's greed for pleasure, that he'd been born to a girl who'd surrendered herself to the man she loved only to have him abandon her when she was pregnant with his child, doomed to endure her brokenness alone. Fortunately for her, her family had dealt honorably with the situation. If they hadn't, she could never have married and lived a life of ease. But as it was, no one outside her family ever knew she'd borne a child out of wedlock and had to leave him at the door of a mosque. And when an older man came and asked for her hand, the family guarded her honor by telling him that when she was a little girl she'd been playing among some trees when she fell on a sharp stick, perforating her hymen.

If a girl's parents confess to her suitor that she isn't a virgin, it's viewed as a sign of their honesty and integrity. Consequently, the man married her and treated her well. She bore her husband a daughter and they lived comfortably together until, one day, she told him she wanted to hire a male servant. Her husband was the jealous type, and he would obviously have objected to having another man in his house. But when she told him that the servant she had in mind was a young boy who'd been recommended to her by a trusted friend, he agreed to her request. Her husband worked for the national patrol and traveled frequently. So, knowing that a male was present in his household, he could rest assured that his wife and daughter would be well looked after. As for the person she had chosen to fill the post, it was none other than Miftah Daqiq.

Miftah met all the woman's purported conditions, and went to work for her convinced of the reasons his mother Sabriya had given him. She'd said, "Your sister and I need to eat, and you need to work to make us a living. The country's being destroyed by famine and drought, and people are having to choose between staying here and dying or emigrating to survive. The work God has given you at this lady's house will be a lot easier than breaking up blocks of salt with a sledgehammer and gathering them in. I've got pneumonia most of the time so I can't work very much, but I've got to be strong and hold out. What else can we do?"

Miftah would have done anything for Aunt Sabriya. So he accepted everything she said and shouldered this new responsibility for his multihued family like a little man. Who could have helped but love him?

A Steed of Wind

SPREADING OUT the mat on the beach, Aunt Sabriya piled sand on one end of it to keep it from being washed away by the waves. She stood looking at me, ankle-deep in the water, her black-and-white striped dress being buffeted by the wind. She gripped the corner of it in her mouth, making it into a sail that billowed in the wind but without taking her anywhere.

I liked the feel of the air and the water against my spindly frame as my wet clothes clung to my skin. Aunt Aida's son had brought a donkey to transport the mats after they'd been washed, and a bunch of boys were amusing themselves jumping on and off its back. Exasperated, Aida's son pushed them away with his feet. Then, turning the humble mount into a mighty steed, he barked in his gravelly little voice, "Giddyup, horsey, giddyup, horsey, giddyup!"

Abandoning the mat I'd been working on, I went over and started playing with the boys on the donkey. I'd been away so much, helping my aunt serve in people's houses or sifting sand for the construction workers, I think I must have really missed playing.

"That's enough," Aunt Aida scolded. "You're going to kill the poor thing. Leave him alone now!"

Using the little donkey as their point of reference, the children started needling each other.

One of them said, "It hasn't turned into a big fat ass like you yet, Nani!"

"You mean like *you*, Baraka!" Nani retorted.

"No, like *you*, Magawi!"

"Like *you*, Masouda," Tijani chimed in.

"No, like you, Barnawi!" echoed Arabiya.

Aunt Aida shooed the children away from the squat little pack animal and we loaded the clean mats onto its back. Baraka led the donkey along and I walked beside him, my hand on its back to keep its load from slipping off. We headed for a big empty lot that served both as a dumping ground for everybody's old stuff and as a border zone that divided the Yards into two different neighborhoods. Whenever we washed the mats for some household, we would spread them to dry on the palm tree stumps there. The place was littered with empty tin cans, rocks, charred palm tree stumps, garbage, driftwood, and various and sundry pieces of junk. Many items came from houses in the city and had been dumped outside the city gates by municipality workers. Residents would pick them up and take them home, thinking they might come in handy for one thing or another.

The empty lot provided a space for playing ball and tug-of-war, and for social gatherings. At night it was occupied by the men, who would get together to drink and shoot the breeze. It was also the place where dance events were held and where stray animals would spend the night.

As the night progressed, the Yards would gradually get quieter and quieter. Some people would get drunk and collapse on the ground like war casualties, and the ones who had no wives or mothers to take them back to their huts would sleep where they were till morning. In fact, there were some who would spend the night out in the open even though they had mothers and wives, since they were so stone drunk that it would have been too hard to drag them home through the sand. At one point we had to step over a man who lay sprawled motionless across the narrow path. Dogs would come by and sniff him, and ants and other small insects were crawling up his nostrils.

As we passed Durma's shack, I had the urge to go in and talk to her but I didn't want my aunt to know about it. So I said to Baraka, "You go ahead of me to the empty lot and I'll catch up with you. But don't go back to the beach without me."

He led the donkey away while I stood in the dark looking at the shack. I tried to push the tinplate door open, but it was locked. I had the distinct feeling that Durma was inside. After all, where else would she be at that hour?

My bare feet were sinking into the sand, so I got down on all fours and started crawling back and forth in search of a crack in the hut wall so that I could see what was going on inside. Durma had plugged a lot of the cracks with pieces of old clothes, some so recently that they still smelled like sweat. I was quietly unplugging one of the cracks when I heard a rustling sound come from inside. I brought my ear up close to the tinplate wall, being careful not to touch it for fear of making a noise. At the same time, I steered clear of the shack's foundations, which she had surrounded with barbed wire to keep busybodies from peeping in at her. I listened closely, wanting to make sure what I'd heard was actually coming from inside and that I hadn't just imagined it. It sounded like murmuring mingled with a low moan. I was itching to know more about what was happening to Durma. Did she have a fever? It was a possibility, since Durma lived alone and had no family. Besides, she had asthma.

Or was she groaning from the taste of that nasty-smelling liquid? I'd noticed it in a wooden cup when I went once to take her some donkey milk that she could use to treat her asthma. Aunt Sabriya had sent it with me that day in a motor oil can. Durma had been lying on the mat inside and coughing like mad. She'd even put a pot beside her in case she needed to throw up, and she was moaning and groaning.

Whatever the cause, Durma's shack with racked with fever, with the heat of something I'd never encountered before. The place was completely dark. But it was a nice sort of darkness. It was delicious like curiosity, and warm like the sea on a summer morning. Whatever was happening, I wasn't the one experiencing it. Durma was. She had a direct knowledge of it that I didn't have. The moaning was coming from her, while the murmuring was coming from somebody else, whose pleading voice seemed to be coming from between her legs.

I felt drawn toward the feverish whatever it was in the darkened shack. At the same time, I was worried about taking too long to get back to Aunt Sabriya. Baraka hadn't come back for me, so I knew he might have gone back to the beach by himself to tell Aunt Aida and Aunt Sabriya where he'd left me. I jumped up, wanting to get my ear away from that tinplate wall, and to stop thinking about Durma being sick, but I was haunted by the murmuring and moaning I'd heard. As I tore through the sand on my way back to the seashore, my clothes billowed in the wind and started to dry. But the closer I got to the beach, the more scared I felt of what Aunt Sabriya might do to me.

When I got back, I found her and Aunt Aida washing some clothes. Aunt Sabriya had finished the bundle she'd brought from somebody's house and was helping Aunt Aida wash her dresses. The two of them were sitting and talking as they did the laundry. Not far away there sat some elderly women who weren't doing anything. A few young men were swimming, but they weren't paying any attention to the evening laundry gatherings since they didn't include any girls. A little group of puppies in search of food ran around barking here and there, while the moon lit up the evening hours for one and all.

Aunt Sabriya saw me coming. I couldn't tell at first how she was feeling, so I tried to read the expression in her eyes. But I could see right away that Aunt Aida was hopping mad. Baraka must have come back and told them that he'd unloaded the mats by himself, which meant that I'd spent longer at Durma's wall than I'd thought I had, and that my sprint through the sand had been for nothing. I hated Baraka now, and I cursed that nappy hair of his that hadn't been combed since the day he was born. By this time he'd disappeared with his father's donkey. I expected Aunt Sabriya to hit me, but she was uncharacteristically calm, and didn't even make a move in my direction. Instead, she beckoned me over to where she was. Then she slipped her hand inside my clothes and, digging her fingers into my flesh, gave me a hard pinch somewhere not far from my private parts. I yelped. It smarts like all get-out to have somebody pinch you right there of all places, and my aunt's fingers found their way to the spot without any help from her eyes. The fact that there was a pair of underpants between her fingers and my skin did nothing to mitigate the sting, and Aunt Aida did nothing to defend me. Gritting her teeth, Aunt Sabriya hissed, "Haven't I told you not to go to see Durma or even talk to her?"

The only thing I could think of to deliver my thigh from those pinches was to confess, beg and plead, and make promises.

"Ouch!" I yelled. "That's the last time, Auntie, I swear! I swear by the dirt on my mother's grave!" And maybe it really was the dirt on my mother's grave that delivered me from her that day. The only thing I'd ever been told about my mother was that she'd died. In any case, I decided to try swearing by the dirt on her grave more often, since my aunt wasn't going to stop disciplining me with pinches no matter how old I got, and I was bound to need it in some other crises along the way too.

I finally broke loose from her grip and threw myself in the water to cool myself off. I rubbed my thigh, moaning in pain, while the two women looked over at me and called Durma bad names. I could feel the water cooling the spot where I'd been pinched, and putting out the fire that had been lit inside me by the tinplate shack. It also helped me recall what I imagined to have happened there. Deep down I supported Durma, who had mounted her own peculiar steed, determined to follow the path she'd chosen for herself now that Heaven had turned on her red faucet and her master's lips had given her fruit wine to drink. The people of the Yards had nearly eaten her alive with their gossiping, envious tongues on account of the things that had started showing up in her shack. They were things they could never have dreamed of owning themselves: clean food, new clothes, a pair of good leather shoes cobbled especially for her long feet, a silver bangle instead of the bead bracelets servant girls wore and, most important of all, money stashed under her newly budding breasts.

So whose lips had Durma been kissing that night in her shack, and whose lips had been kissing her?

After cooling the blaze of the punishment I'd endured on account of Durma and the one who'd been pleasuring her, I looked into the sky and wiped the saltwater out of my eyes. Then I squatted submissively beside my aunt as she poured more prohibitions and threats into my ears. I stole a glance over at Aunt Aida, who had put the angry words in Aunt Sabriya's mouth.

I wanted to be gutsy like Durma, brazen like the prostitutes whose ranks she had joined. I felt like telling my Aunt Aida, "You just hate Durma because she's turned into a first-rate drummer. Have you forgotten that one of your own kids robbed her shack one time? And now you're working to stir up everybody in the Yards against her because she figured out who the thief was by noticing what you were wearing around your neck! She exposed him in front of everybody. As for you, you got so riled up defending your boy that bouri was oozing out of your pores!"

As the two of them went on with their laundry, they talked about the Ridwan wedding.

"Did she sing yesterday?" Aunt Sabriya wondered aloud.

"Yes, she did," Aunt Aida replied. "They say Khalifa was stone drunk, and that he swore not to let anybody leave. So the party went on all night. No doubt she was drunk too, and didn't make it back. I'll bet somebody took her to his house and she spent the night there."

Aunt Sabriya offered no comment. Aida started singing something Durma had performed at recent weddings. The youthful new singer, tall and slender, who'd swept out of the Slave Yards on a steed of wind, not only had a beautiful voice but she could spend all night dancing, singing, and playing her drums without getting tired, and her songs had spread like wildfire all over the city. According to the men who'd slept with her, she had a warmth about her that they'd never found anywhere else—and they'd tried out their share of women. So this might have been another of her distinctive features.

As she scrubbed Jaballah's trousers with both hands in a big cooking pot, Aida started singing a song of Durma's that she was good at imitating:

> I went to hunt the gazelle on my own,
> But my shotgun let me down!

I don't know who or what she was singing that song for: for herself or for Jaballah's trousers, which never came out of the cooking pot.

But she kept it up the whole time she was doing the laundry. And who was the gazelle, I wondered? As for who had brought guns to Benghazi, the Maltese merchants who'd settled there would have known the answer to that question.

The two of them laughed together, and then Aunt Sabriya sang another one:

> They've kept me from my beloved, near though he be,
> I'm thirsty even though the water's right in front of me
> When you come to the well you need a long rope.
> But mine's too short and I've lost all hope!

Aunt Halima quickly joined in along with another group of women who had been drawn by the night, the sea, and the singing, which went on until the last piece of laundry had been done. After I'd finished fetching water, I squatted in the sand looking out at the waves of the sea, dreaming of mounting a steed of lightning, thunder, and wind.

From that time on I started to perceive something new and mysterious that nobody else could see.

Misjudged Good Folks

I HADN'T SEEN DURMA for a long time, and I missed her. After I promised my aunt not to see her or talk to her anymore, Durma sold her tinplate shack in the Slave Yards and moved to town to live in an Arab-style house with a group of darabukka players. The day she left to start her new life beyond the high wall that separated us from half of humanity, I hadn't gotten to tell her good-bye, and I regretted it like mad.

Durma had learned to sing from an elderly slave woman from Fezzan who, seeing that she'd happened upon a rare talent who could perform *marskawi*, started depending on Durma to perform at weddings and other social occasions.[1] Of course, singing was a comfortable job compared to the forced labor slaves had to do. In fact, no matter how good or bad they happened to be at it, everybody in the Yards resorted to singing to help themselves get through their grueling lives. At night after people's work was done and they headed back to the Yards, somebody would start to sing. Then somebody else would join in, and somebody else, and somebody else. Before you knew it, the gathering had expanded to include a growing number of performers,

1. *Marskawi* is a kind of traditional music that traces its origins to the city of Murzuk in southern Libya. Marskawi combines Bedouin Arabic poetic lyricism and elements of the Amazigh (Berber) heritage. Most of the artists best known for the performance of marskawi are from Benghazi and Bayda, Libya, such as Warda al-Libiya, Shadi Al Jabal, and Ramadan Wanis.

clappers and dancers, and the whole neighborhood would be bursting with raucous circles of song and dance. Tunes were something to be celebrated, and song was a healing balm. People who'd had too much to drink would often reel and totter around, losing themselves in the ecstasy of the marskawi. Song and drink were medicine for the afflicted soul, a remedy for the suffering born of exile, degradation, and the frightening unknown.

When Yagouta, the daughter of Ubaydallah and Makhzouma, married a slave boy from the Yards, Durma's gift to them was to come and perform at their wedding celebration. When she came, she received a huge welcome. After all, even though she'd left for the big city, she hadn't forgotten the folks back home, and she never stopped helping the needy among them with what she earned from her gigs, which went on till the wee hours of the morning, and sometimes for days.

It was only to be expected, of course, that some men would end up inviting her to bed. After all, a passionate black singer like her would let a man discover his wild side, and liberate him from the alien "other" self that controlled him when he was part of a herd.

Musically induced rapture is inseparable from the quest for love. Female singers were thirsty and their thirst was quenched. They gave to drink, and were given to drink. The world wasn't fair, and it didn't give the Negro woman a house, a breadwinner, and children, since no man would marry a singer even if he was black like her. The singing profession turned a woman into a whore who was available on demand. So even though Benghazi households vied for the chance to have her perform at their social functions, their respect for her didn't go beyond the hand that beat the darabukka, the throat that crooned the songs, and the body that writhed as skillfully in bed as it did on the stage.

By the time Yagouta's wedding was over, more than one man had proposed to let his daughter work with Durma.

Fortunately for life here, there were people who took a different view of things and people generally classified as "bad." I personally loved Durma inside and out. I loved everything about her, and all that she was. So when I missed her, I made no distinction between one part of her and another. I didn't pick and choose which parts of her I wanted and which ones I didn't. One of the signs of love is that you love what you love without asking yourself why it is that you love it.

In with Sassi,
Out with Asgawa

EVEN THOUGH the Slave Yards were close to the seashore, the heat there was unbearable. On the day folks went to work gathering empty tins and filling them with sand and pebbles to build a hut for Asgawa, the air was so hot it would have dried up your bones, and the sun's rays beat down mercilessly on everything in sight. Even the shade was sweltering, since people's homes had been constructed from iron, wood, sand, and anything they'd happened to find lying around. However, it was a matter of urgency to build Asgawa a place to live, so everybody in the Yards pitched in to get it done. Asgawa had no family, and she was one of us now. Most of the other folks in the Yards were in the same situation, so, separated in both place and time from their roots in a black, multiethnic south, they'd banded together to form a community of their own.

The people who first established the community had settled on an empty, deserted patch of coastline that nobody else was interested in. They hadn't chosen the place so much as they had been led to it by circumstances. No whites objected to their being far away, of course, since they weren't wanted by the white community, and no white would have been willing to live there in the first place. On the contrary, whites saw the Yards' location as perfectly suited to the inferior color of its residents. Over time the black community came to have its own population center as well as borders that established a further distance between blacks and their white overlords. Yet it was a distance that always served the whites' interests and reinforced their sense of superiority.

Now that Asgawa had grown up, it wasn't considered fitting for her to go on living with the elderly Sadina. Besides, Sadina had a son, Sassi, who was coming from Tarhuna to live with her. Sassi's father—Sadina's master—had passed away, and his light-skinned siblings weren't willing to feed the boy or keep a roof over his head anymore, so they'd arranged a one-way trip for him to Benghazi.

Before Sassi came to live with his mother, Asgawa had her first menstrual period. The unannounced, gooey visitor from down below scared her out of her wits. Terrified, she ran to ask the old woman what had happened to her, and why her caftan was all bloody.

"So then," the old woman muttered unhappily, "it's menstruation."

She taught Asgawa how to take precautions against the deluge during the first few days when the flow was heaviest. She searched among her things for a black dress, tore it into strips, and made them into rags to collect Asgawa's crimson rain. Cautioning the girl to wrap that part of her body in the black rags when the visitor arrived every month, she brought her a large tin of seawater to wash with. Then she put her to bed and waited on her hand and foot. She prepared her some herbs for the pain, massaged her back and the area under her navel with aged olive oil, and fastened the rags in place with a belt around her waist. She told Asgawa blood was an enemy that would weaken her health as she got older and that, as she would see for herself, it would make her fall ill more and more over time until, eventually, medicinal herbs wouldn't help with the pain anymore, and she would just have to put up with it all night long.

"Why's that?" Asgawa wanted to know.

Sighing, the old woman crushed some dried chamomile and mint stems between her rough hands. Then, in a faint, raspy voice she replied, "When you're young, you feel so strong, you take your health for granted."

As the old woman placed the crushed herbs in a pot of water that was boiling on the stove, Asgawa cast her a puzzled look, still wondering why this thing hurt so much and would go on hurting. Her face careworn and drawn from the weight of life's burdens, the old woman peered at the young girl's forehead. Now that she'd gotten her first period, the way was being prepared for events that were bound to leave their mark on her heart and her features alike.

Asgawa was a tall, slender girl, and her ebony skin had a peculiar sheen to it that was admired by everyone in the Yards. She had wide eyes and a pug nose with a silver ring in it, and, like the other poor girls of the Yards, she wore clothes that had been pieced together from a hodgepodge of old scraps.

One day, as she was fetching water from a nearby well to load it onto Mjawir's wagon, water splashed out of the bucket balanced on top of her head. After drenching her sleeves, the water trickled down in a zigzag line from her armpits to her feet. As she and the other young girls wearily loaded jugs of water onto the wagon, Mjawir leaned up against the wagon, watching them. When it was Asgawa's turn to come under Mjawir's scrutiny, she saw him eyeing her armpits, then following the water as it dripped down between her feet. Her clothes clung alluringly to her youthful body and, as Mjawir made a show of helping her pour water into the large jug, he made a furtive comment to her about how he envied her new dress. Noticing the strange effect this man was having on her, she looked down shyly and ran away. She was so discombobulated by the flirtation that she forgot to take her pail with her when she fled, so one of the other girls followed her to the well with it.

As they waited for their turn at the well, Asgawa whispered to one of her older companions about how Mjawir's comment had made her wet from the inside. Giving a wicked giggle, the girl broadcast the news to the whole flock of water carriers. Mortified by all the embarrassing comments, Asgawa regretted saying anything. The news spread all over the Yards, and when she went to the beach that evening to help wash mats, she could hear even the waves repeating Mjawir's sultry words. After finishing her work, she swam out until the water was up to her shoulders.

As the lamp light flickered against the hut ceiling that night, Asgawa's thoughts flickered every which way. Borne on the night breezes, the voices of other Yard residents wafted softly in her direction. Some of them were roasting peanuts over hot coals, and she figured they must also be having some tea, which some Yard dwellers had as an occasional treat.

The old woman stepped out to dump the chamomile dregs in front of the hut, turning her head from side to side as though she were trying to confirm something she'd detected in an easterly direction. She stepped into the hut to get her wrap, then came out again. Asgawa asked her where she was going. "I won't be gone long," she replied, draping the wrap over her head. "Don't go to sleep before I get back."

Asgawa stayed in bed, alternately resting against the shack's metal wall and stealing furtive glances through the spaces between the unevenly stacked tins. Looking out, she could see a bit of dim light coming from a distance as well as another light that was recognizable as the lighthouse. She heard footsteps passing by outside and scattered bursts of laughter. Life in the Yards was a bleak, bland existence brightened by diversion, song, the beating of tambourines, the strumming of the tambour,[1] and by anything and everything after nightfall.

She heard footsteps approaching their hut which, from the distinctive gait and the sound of soft humming, she recognized as Durma's. Her heart leapt for joy, especially given that the old woman, who couldn't stand Durma, wasn't back from her errand yet, and suddenly she forgot the pain that had been racking her insides and her back. Durma stood outside calling.

"Come in, come in, Durma!" Asgawa answered. "The old lady isn't here."

Durma came in, nearly stumbling over herself as she cleaned the sand off her long feet.

"Where did she go?" she asked. "Hope she never comes back!"

"Never mind her for now. I need help tomorrow from you and the girls. I need everybody to get a tin and bring it over."

---

1. A long-necked, stringed instrument resembling the mandolin.

She was planning to build her own hut.

Fiddling with the black garter around her skinny leg, Durma asked Asgawa how much pain she was in. Asgawa told her that the chamomile the old lady had made her had helped some, though the flow was still heavy. Durma laughed out loud, teasing Asgawa with some obscenities. Worried that the old woman might be lurking nearby and listening in on their conversation, or that somebody might tell her what they'd been saying, Asgawa peeked out through the cracks in the hut wall. People always stopped to eavesdrop whenever they heard a conversation going on, and whatever a person heard would get passed on to everybody else in the ghetto. That was why in the Yards, slaves might enjoy freedom from whites, but they suffered an even worse subordination to members of their own race.

"Get out of here quick, before the old lady comes back," Asgawa cautioned. "And don't forget to come early tomorrow, before the sun gets too hot."

"I don't have to fetch water tomorrow."

"So what do you want to do? Are you going to sleep all day and party all night?"

"I can do whatever I want," Durma replied, her tone defiant. "I don't care what anybody says. Whoever doesn't like Durma can go jump in the deep blue sea. It's right over there!"

Durma looked down, stealing a glance over at her friend, who regretted telling her that she'd been warned not to spend time with her.

Coming over to Durma and kissing her on the head, Asgawa said, "Don't be mad at me now!"

"No, no! I just don't want to spend my life fetching water for people and having my hair fall out from carrying tins on top of my head!"

Asgawa started with alarm. "Really?!" she asked, "So where are you going to get enough to eat? People are already about to eat each other alive!"

Durma hesitated. Then, twisting her garter nervously, she mumbled something indistinct.

"You don't have to worry about me," she added nonchalantly. "Oh, and by the way, how's Mjawir getting along with your dress these days?"

"What??" Asgawa retorted in a fright. "You be quiet, damn you! He's an old man!"

"Ha! And can't he do what men do?"

"No, no! For shame!"

"Oh, right—for shame!"

Their conversation was interrupted by the sudden entry of the old woman.

"Good evening, Auntie," Durma said in greeting, her head bowed.

Obviously not pleased to see Durma with Asgawa, the elderly woman grudgingly returned the greeting, her voice barely audible, as she busied herself with something in her hand. "Good? Good?" she muttered. "Do you even know what *good* means?"

Knowing herself to be unwelcome, Durma got up to leave. "Have a good night," she said as she walked out.

Only Asgawa reciprocated the well wishes. Meanwhile, she braced herself for a lecture on why she shouldn't spend time with Durma, whose profession had earned her a bad reputation among the residents of the Yards.

Handing Asgawa a rag with something warm wrapped inside it, the old woman said, "Haven't I warned you not to go around with that girl? You're like a daughter to me. So when will you start listening to what I say?"

Intent on opening the small bundle in her hand, Asgawa pretended not to hear anything. It contained warm roasted peanuts. Delighted, she asked the old woman where she'd gotten them.

"From Mjawir's house."

Asgawa's heart skipped a beat, and her hands trembled as she brought the peanuts to her mouth.

She stopped chewing. "From Mjawir's house?"

"Yes. His wife, Iljiya, is a nice lady. When I asked her to send a few back for you, she gave me these."

"And he's as nice as she is," the old woman added with a sigh. "He's a real gentleman."

Then, turning from the subject of the nice family, she said, "Haven't I told you to drop that nasty girl? Being friends with her will lead to no good."

Asgawa munched on the peanuts from Mjawir's house with the old woman's warnings ringing in her ears, the taste of the peanuts in her mouth mingling with the taste of Mjawir in her body. After the old woman had gone to sleep, Asgawa's thoughts turned to the subject of the men in the Slave Yards.

The pain in her belly was so acute, and the fragrance of the man in her body so intense, that she couldn't get to sleep. She brought to mind all the boys in the Slave Yards who'd recently become men. She reviewed them one after another in the darkness of the hut, like soldiers under her command. She searched among them for her ideal and, as dawn approached, she still hadn't made up her mind which one it was. But in the end there was only one who suited her fancy: the one whose hands had roasted the peanuts she'd eaten the evening before, and who had placed some for her in his palm. She knew that Mjawir's own hand had touched those peanuts before she'd placed them in her mouth, mixed them with her saliva, and crushed them with her teeth. Yes, he had touched them. And he was the one who, at that very moment, was touching her virginal places. What a feeling, and what a lovelier than lovely coincidence it was that the old woman had turned her nose to the source of the aroma and, having realized where it was coming from, had gotten up and brought her something to satisfy her craving.

As Asgawa opened her dreamy eyes in the darkness, she heard the barking of dogs in the distance, and she liked the sound when she imagined Mjawir's dogs among them. She heard the buzzing of some flying insects and the snoring of the old woman who slept nearby. She also picked up on strange sounds coming from something hidden between her ribs. It asked her about her mother and father, her brothers and sisters. It asked her whether she had a family like Mjawir's. It asked her about her first childhood, whose features she didn't recall clearly. Where had it been? How had she ended up in the Slave Yards, whereas her sister had ended up in Tripoli, where she performed with a *zimzama* who was popular with the city's dignitaries?[2]

She had a feeling that once Durma had taught her to play the darabukka, she might get herself a job in her sister's band, and they could be together again.

One thought led to another until, one day, she conceived by Mjawir.

2. *Zimzama* is a colloquial Libyan term referring to a female wedding singer, usually of color, who is assumed to smoke, drink, lead a promiscuous life, and have a foul mouth. The term thus carries a derogatory undertone. A zimzama has no real social status, although hiring one is a sign of such status.

A Horse, a Carriage, and a Disappearance

IT WAS THE FIRST of many days when Aunt Sabriya would mysteriously disappear from the Slave Yards without my knowing where she
had gone. The disappearances always followed the arrival of a Negro
slave that nobody recognized. He never said a word to anyone and no
one knew anything about him. Nobody knew where he came from
or why he came specifically for Aunt Sabriya and nobody else. As for
Aunt Sabriya, she never acted surprised or confused when the man
came around. On the contrary, there would be a joy and excitement in
her eyes that I rarely saw at any other time. So, did the mystery man
come of his own accord, or had somebody sent him?

The disappearances started occurring on a regular basis and,
whenever one happened, it would end as mysteriously as it had begun.
In the meantime, questions would swirl around me, getting bigger
and bigger. Then they'd sink unanswered over the horizon like the
Yards' sun.

All I could gather about the man with my childlike intuition was
that he wasn't some ordinary, wretched slave. Nor was he some fugitive who'd escaped from his masters and fled to Benghazi from this
direction or that. He knew the city well, and he knew just where to
find us: near the wells in Zurayri'iya where we washed Benghazi families' clothes for hire.

One day I was helping my aunt with the laundry along with a few other women. She was hunched over a metal laundry tub, busily scrubbing away, and drenched to her shoulders with water and sweat. Then along came a carriage, driven by a Negro slave we'd never seen before, drawn by a beautiful horse. At first my aunt didn't know what he wanted. Then, little by little, the carriage drew up closer to our little group, and she realized he had come for her. She gathered herself up and ran toward him. The man said something to her without getting out of the carriage. Then she ran back in our direction while he waited. She started gathering up her batch of clothes, both the clean ones and the ones that hadn't been washed yet, and gestured for me to come with her. But she didn't say a thing to the women she'd been chatting with. The women seated around their laundry basins stared at her, murmuring things I couldn't make out, while she tied the wet clothes into a separate bundle and put the dirty ones back in the burlap bag. I searched her face for some sign of what she was feeling. I saw no indication of resistance or distress. In fact, she was in such a hurry to be on her way with the mysterious carriage driver that she forgot—or neglected—to say good-bye to her little group of laundry companions. A faint smile flickered across the wet, down-turned corners of her mouth, and her hurried movements took on an air of happy anticipation.

The driver got down and wordlessly helped us to lift the bundles of laundry onto the carriage before we got in the back. I wished he would say something, since that way I might get some answers to the questions running through my head. A silence had fallen over my aunt as well. As we rode along, she sat with one arm over the other, craning her neck forward as if she was trying to see what lay at the end of the road. When we got to the Yards, I expected the slave to drive past it. However, my aunt asked him to stop at the gate and wait for her there. Nodding his big shaven head, he helped us out of the carriage and unloaded the bundles of laundry. When Yousef saw us, he came and took the bundles from the carriage driver. My aunt asked Yousef if he'd seen Aida anywhere. He replied that he'd just come from her hut, where she was cooking *asida* for her children.[1] Aunt Sabriya instructed Yousef to tell Aida to meet us at our shack right away. And to make sure she knew she could trust that the message was from her and from no one else, she added, "Tell her to grab her right thumb two times, the way we agreed!"

Yousef disappeared in a flash down the shortest of the winding paths that led to Aida's hut. We brought everything inside, and my aunt urged me to work with her so that we could finish as quickly as possible. When Aunt Aida came rushing in, Aunt Sabriya was hunched over another bundle, looking for something that belonged to her. I stood at the shack entrance, watching the two women and trying to hear what they were muttering to each other. Then suddenly Aunt Sabriya stopped looking through the pile of colorful fabric as though she'd found what she was looking for. But instead of acting happy, she ordered me outside, her voice shrill as though she'd suddenly lost what she'd found.

I heard the rattling of the laundry tub as Aida helped Sabriya finish washing the clothes. Aunt Sabriya hurriedly closed up the shack and the side pen, while Aunt Aida hoisted the bundle of laundered clothes and the ones still in the gunnysack onto her back. Then she looked around for Yousef to help her take them back to her hut. I looked into my aunt's face, lost in a spinning orbit of questions. It was as distant as the black lands that give their unborn children to the lands of the whites. It had wandered off toward an unknown destination, where it could escape its present miserable reality and lose itself in rapturous joy.

"Now don't give your aunt Aida a hard time while I'm gone!" she said to me.

"And when will you be back?" I asked, looking up at her quizzically.

---

1. *Asida* is a traditional sweet, sometimes eaten as a main dish, made on top of the stove from flour, salt, and water. It is then coated with butter and garnished with date syrup.

Aunt Sabriya didn't seem sad about the idea of being away from me and Miftah for a couple of days. In fact, she seemed about to burst with excitement. Aunt Aida must have known where her friend was going, since she wasn't asking any questions. In fact, she wasn't saying anything at all. It was as if she'd already asked all her questions and gotten all the answers she needed.

When I asked Aunt Aida where Aunt Sabriya had gone, she replied, "She's gone to serve in somebody's household, and she'll be back."

And she said no more.

"Why didn't she take me with her?" I pressed.

Turning her back to me, Aunt Aida replied, "The family that called for her didn't want any children to come along. That was one of their stipulations."

Then suddenly she said, "Why don't you go fetch water with Baraka?"

Water. I can't remember how many times conversations were cut short with the word *water*. It was a ready, convincing excuse not to talk about something. Aunt Sabriya's absences meant having to stay for a couple of days or more in Aunt Aida's hut. I would watch people around me in silence, and instead of playing with the other children, I spent most of my time alone. Sometimes I would go fetch water with the women and the older girls. It was usually Aunt Aida who assigned the task, and she rarely did anything for me. When there was no water to fetch, I would sit in the shade of the hut watching whoever and whatever passed by: children dragging things from the garbage dump to their huts; hens pecking for food; cats chasing shade for a comfortable place to sleep; dogs wagging their tails and lolling their tongues to cool themselves off; poverty-stricken women rushing to and fro, and talking, and talking; and Miftah, whose visits to the Yards had grown fewer and farther between since he started working at the bakery. Bakery duty meant spending his nights at the lady's house, since he worked till a late hour and had to start again early in the morning.

Noticing how glum and withdrawn I was, Yousef tried to draw me out of my shell. One day he took me to play with Aida's children on the beach. Once he'd gotten us there, he divided us into two teams for a swimming race. I didn't really feel like it, but I participated anyway. When I was about to get ahead of one of the boys on the other team, he grabbed me and pulled me down, and I nearly went under. Yousef, who'd been standing on a boulder watching us, saw what the boy had done.

He jumped in and swam over to me in the twinkling of an eye.

"You nearly drowned, girl," he told me as he pulled me sputtering out of the water. "But we won the round!"

After punching the boy in the nose in front of everybody, Yousef disqualified him from the race for cheating. Before I knew it, I was surrounded by children cheering for my having made it out alive. But I wasn't thinking about the fact that I'd nearly died. As far as I was concerned, living meant being with the woman who was far away from me now. Without her, no matter where I was, I had no life. The absence of the sad face that I loved, and the tender hand always holding mine, meant that I'd already died.

When one of Aunt Aida's children rushed off to tell her I'd drowned, she came running, and found me in the middle of the cheering crowd of boys and girls. Shaken, she took me in her arms, her lower lip quivering, and examined me all over.

"What happened to you?? What happened to you??" she repeated over and over.

When Yousef told her the details, she was furious with him for taking us to the beach when the sea was choppy. He'd nearly killed me, she said. Yousef didn't say a word. After warning him not to let anything like this happen again, she marched me back to her hut and sat me in the sun to get my clothes dry, since she didn't have anything else to put on me. I got the feeling she was still mad at Yousef, since she kept warning me not to go anywhere with him without telling her first.

"Is my aunt home yet?" I asked.

"She'll be back today, *insha'allah*," she replied without looking at me.

By this time I missed her like crazy. I missed the shack we shared together. And I missed Miftah, whose most recent absence had been especially long. I waited for her all afternoon and into the evening, and when she didn't come back that day either I felt like a hostage in Aida's hut. I witnessed all her battles with her children, who squabbled over food and who got to sleep where. I started crying and wouldn't eat. Yousef looked on as Aunt Aida worked on getting me to take some food. Feeling sad for me, he apologized to Aunt Aida, but she didn't forgive him and wouldn't let him talk to me or even come near me.

Early on the morning of Aunt Sabriya's third day away, I sneaked out of Aunt Aida's hut without her noticing. I crawled over her sleeping children and went back to our shack. It was cold, and the light was just starting to break through the darkness as the sun rose over the huts. The only sounds you could hear were roosters crowing in the distance, dogs barking, and an occasional snore here or there. I was determined to get home, since I figured she might have gotten back the night before but hadn't come to get me because it had gotten too late. To my disappointment, I found the shack empty. I sat down in front of it and started to cry, begging her in my heart not to leave me with anybody else again.

As day broke, the residents of the Yards began stirring. When Aunt Aida discovered I was gone, she and her children came looking for me, although Yousef had beaten them to it. When he found me, he patted me on the shoulder and asked me why I was crying. Was I hungry? Afraid? I told him I wanted my aunt and didn't know where she'd gone.

"Don't you know when she's coming back?" he asked me.

"No."

"Come along with me, then," he coaxed. "And don't cry."

"Leave me alone," I snapped.

He sat down next to me. "Listen," he said reassuringly. "We're your family—me, Aunt Aida's children, and the other kids too, even the naughty ones. If any of them hits you, you tell me about it. Then just wait and see what I do to him! Remember how I punched the boy who tried to keep you from getting ahead of him in the race?"

"Nobody's ever hit me or stolen anything from me."

"Good," he conceded. "But have you gone all around the Yards and found out everything there is to know about it?"

"No."

By this time I'd decided to go back with Yousef, and as we made our way down the narrow paths that wound their way between the shacks and huts, I asked him, "Do you have a mom and dad?"

"No," he said, "I've got no family. I was raised by the streets. The person who took care of me when I first came here was Old Lady Bouga. She taught me to take pride in my color. She also taught me how to treat people with herbs so that I could make that my profession instead of having to steal or be a slave. All I know about my mother is that she was a servant woman who died of a contagious disease."

Interrupting his narrative all of a sudden, Yousef said, "Let's pass by Aunt Aida's so that I can let her know you're with me."

"So do you call her Aunt Aida too?" I asked, surprised.

"Yeah," he replied. "All the women here are my aunts, and all the men are my uncles. I love everybody in the Yards—they're my family. I love even the thieves and the drunkards and the criminals. I've got nothing against any of them."

When we got to Aunt Aida's hut, she refused to let me go anywhere with Yousef. In fact, she kicked him out and threatened to beat him with the oven paddle if he came near me again. Yousef didn't say a thing. He just made himself scarce. Then she handed me a bowl of rice that she'd boiled with some turmeric. She'd cooked it along with the little worms that infest rice when it gets old.

When the dead worms floated to the surface, she said, "Stir the rice with your hand to make them sink, then eat them. They won't hurt you."

And she meant what she said. She stuck her hand into the bowl in front of me and demonstrated, saying, "Stir it like this to make them disappear."

And sure enough, they disappeared, just like Yousef. As he took off down the narrow path, he hummed a tune I'd heard before in one of the Benghazi households we'd served in. It was a house with high walls, and the people who lived in it were as white and red as the Germans. Their menfolk learned the Qur'an, traded in slaves, and did things to turn their male slaves into eunuchs.

A Horse, a Carriage, and a Disappearance • 97

I squatted behind the hut, holding the bowl of rice. Before taking the first bite, I swished my hand around in it until the worms had sunk to the bottom. Then little bites started going down one after another. As I ate, I thought about Aunt Sabriya, wondering where she was and what she was doing.

As my thoughts drifted away from the Yards, my eyes drifted away from the bowl and its contents the way Yousef's voice had faded away with his sad song:

> My tears flow like drops of blood,
> So deep are my longings and fears.
> I spend the long night bleeding,
> Shedding the blood of my tears!

Descended from Diggers
of Underground Canals

AUNT AIDA left early one morning to cook for a wedding in the city, taking her two oldest girls with her to help. That way they could learn a skill that would earn them a living. Baraka and I finished drawing water from the well and filling Mjawir's jugs. Mjawir was always on the lookout for a chance to pinch me when we were at the well alone. But whenever he was about to do it, I'd edge away from him and stand right behind Baraka.

On our way back to the Slave Yards, we ran into Yousef. We were walking as fast as we could to keep the hot sand from blistering our feet, and shading ourselves from the blazing sun with the water tins on our heads. My hair was a mess and I was dirty. In fact, I hadn't washed for a couple of days. Most of the water in my tin had spilled on my head and my dress.

"How long has it been since you washed last?" he asked as he took the tin from me.

"Since Aunt Sabriya left the Yards," I replied.

"Come on," he urged. "Let's all go wash up in the sea."

Baraka said he wanted to bring their dog, Khilafo, to wash the ticks off of him. Yousef went to his hut and got a tin for washing and a piece of old esparto rope, which he unraveled to make it into a homemade loofah. As we were walking to the beach, I saw him closing his right fist over something so that Baraka couldn't see it. When I asked him what it was, he said, "It's a piece of soap." It was smooth and white, with a nice smell, and it was chipped on one end. So, this was the soap I'd heard about but had never seen before!

He assured me he hadn't stolen it from anybody. "Nobody in the Yards would have any soap to begin with," he said. It had been given to him, along with some dried rations, by a Sicilian sailor named Francesco. Francesco had wanted to explore the Yards and had asked Yousef to escort him. Besides interpreting for him, Yousef had protected Francesco from thieves. He also protected him from the Bedouin boys who had fled to the Yards from famine and tribal wars over pasture land, and who would stalk foreigners and hound them for money. Yousef was a good interpreter and explained to Francesco whatever he wanted to know about, especially the conditions of the people fleeing to the Yards from places in Barqa where fighting was going on.

"Here," he said, handing me the soap. "It's yours. But don't show it to anybody. And only use well water with it. It won't work with saltwater."

It was the custom for the residents of the Yards to go to the sea to relieve themselves, bathe, and wash their utensils and clothes. The dogs would come along with them, and there were always chickens roaming up and down the shore, picking up crumbs and looking for whatever else there was to eat.

One day, some women from the Yards who were doing laundry and bathing asked me why Aunt Sabriya wasn't with me. Yousef told them she was serving some people who didn't want black children to come along. Yousef was quick on his feet, and managed to extinguish their curiosity before I'd said a word. Maybe he was good at talking to people because he was so much older than I was. He was poor, but mild-tempered and gentle, and he didn't have a dirty mind like the other boys and girls around. He told me he had friends who served in the Italian church, but that he didn't go to them to beg the way most of the homeless children did. Instead, he told me, he would sell them broad beans and chickpeas and sometimes sifiniz from Miftah's bakery, and that in return he got to learn how to read and write. He told me his friends from the church liked him so much that they'd started reading him the letters they received from their families and friends. With a shy laugh, he told me he wanted to become a translator like some other black men had done. Either that, or he wanted to work with the police, so that he could help other Negroes who were needy.

The water that day was as warm as Yousef's words and presence. I took off my dirty dress and left my pants on, then got into the water with the esparto loofah Yousef had made. Yousef sat on the shore and scrubbed my threadbare dress for me with sand and sea spume. Then he wrung it out and spread it on a boulder to dry, pulling it taut and holding it in place with small rocks. I washed myself with gusto, and he watched over me the way he would have done for a little sister. I was puny and weak, and I didn't know how to stand up for myself when mean kids hit me or shoved me away from the well, then dumped the water out of my tin to make fun of me.

That's how I met Durma, in fact. One morning we were standing in line at the well when a couple of girls pushed me from behind after I'd finished filling my tin. I fell on the tin and it split my forehead open, and all the water spilled out of it. Durma, who was thirteen years old and tall for her age, had been standing behind me with her tin. When she saw what had happened, she came up and slugged both girls. Then she drenched them with the tin that belonged to the boy who'd taken his turn right before us. One of the girls ran away, but the other one stood her ground. Durma stuffed dirt into the mouth of the one that hadn't run away and threatened to pee on the other one's head when she got hold of her. Durma was crazy, and if she had a fit of bouri you were best advised to watch out! That was the last time any of the other kids harassed me at the well. From then on, nobody would have dared hit me for fear of getting a mouthful of dirt and a head covered with pee.

Durma was several years older than me, and I loved her like a big sister. The same thing was happening now with Yousef. I was always the puny little underdog who needed somebody older to stick up for me and take care of me, except that the only brothers and sisters I had were my brothers and sisters in God—namely, Miftah, Durma,

Yousef, Aida's kids, and the other kids in the Yards who hadn't turned into bullies.

After washing up, I sat on the rocks while my body and clothes dried out. That was nothing unusual in the Yards, and boys and girls did it all the time. What *was* unusual was for somebody to take his shirt off to give it to somebody else. That's what Yousef did for me.

As we talked, Yousef started looking at my hair. He commented that it didn't look like other Negro girls' hair. Mine was shiny and flowing, with a hint of chestnut in it. Like my eyes, my hair didn't quite seem to belong. It still had plenty of lice in it, though! Going through it strand by strand, he pulled out a big louse and showed it to me. I told him I'd gotten lice from Aunt Aida's kids, and that Aunt Sabriya always picked them out for me. He promised to bring some kerosene and wash my head with it. He said he'd ask Francesco to put a little for him in a bottle. Kerosene would get rid of the lice for good, he said, so there wouldn't be any more need to sit around picking them out one by one the way the women in the Yards were always doing. Yousef told me he could treat me with kerosene when he got hold of some, and I consented with a nod of my bug-infested head.

Yousef told me things I'd never heard before. His ancestors, who had been enslaved a hundred years earlier, had been skilled at locating water in the desert.

He said, "After leaving the Sudan they settled in what came to be known as the Kingdom of Fezzan, where they were enslaved. Their masters kept them in slavery so that they would reproduce in captivity, especially given how useful they were in digging and maintaining underground canals called *fijarat*."

"What were they like?" I asked.

He picked a stick up off the ground and dug a little depression with it. Then he used it to draw a sketch, saying, "The *fijarat* were subterranean canals in sloped areas or foothills that brought water to the surface through tunnels that were slightly curved. It would take more than a hundred slaves to dig just one of them, and some of those slaves were my ancestors. Maintaining a single canal required that hundreds of thousands of buckets of sand and other debris be removed from it every year."

"How did your ancestors know how to find water in the desert?"

"They used a type of limestone known as travertine. The presence of this stone meant that there was water nearby."

"Is that why you always keep a piece of limestone with you?" I asked.

Bending his right leg with his hand, he looked into the distance and said, "It's my own special amulet."

"And is that why you're always clean?"

He chuckled and said I was a smart girl who ought to learn how to read and write and knit like the nuns on Santa Barbara Street and Via Torino.

"So," I asked, my curiosity piqued, "what do you know about the Christian nuns?"

"I'll take you to see them someday," he said as he helped me put my dress back on. "But first you've got to meet Bouga."

Here was another mysterious part of the Slave Yards that I'd never known about even though I'd lived there all my life. How could my world have been confined to nothing but fetching water, hovering around Aunt Sabriya, and hiding behind Baraka?

With Yousef I was always finding out new things and learning to see the world in different ways: watching the stars sink into the sea at night and trying to swim out and catch them as they fell; taking in the moment when the moon was half-immersed in the water; fishing in the dark. But the strangest thing of all had to do with a Negro soothsayer who used to come out to the sea in the middle of the night with an elderly white woman. He would carry her on his back from a long way away to help her recover a granddaughter of hers who had drowned in the sea. When the moon was aligned with other heavenly bodies, he would look up in the sky, recite incantations, and perform some mysterious calculation. He would do this in the presence of the old woman, who was convinced that a beautiful, innocent child should never have died such a senseless death.

She clung to the belief that her granddaughter had actually survived and that she was living in the depths of the sea with other innocent creatures, but wouldn't be able to return to the terrestrial world without supernatural assistance. Just as, according to Muslim belief, Jesus Christ didn't really die on the cross but was taken up alive to Heaven, where he lives to this day, this woman believed her granddaughter had been taken alive to the bottom of the sea.

Nobody tried to stop them from engaging in these rituals of theirs. Instead, they would think about the story of Isaila, a beautiful girl who'd been kidnapped and taken away to Italy, then miraculously rescued and brought back to Libya by Sidi Abdussalam Al Asmar.

So people knew what the soothsayer and the old woman were doing but they paid no attention. Maybe they understood that he was giving her a hope she couldn't live without. Both he and she knew she didn't have many more years to live. But how much more merciful it would be for her to die still hoping to find her granddaughter alive under the sea than for her life to be cut short by grief and despair!

One night Yousef and I sneaked down to the beach and hid behind a sand dune to watch the rituals it was hoped would bring the girl back. We saw black birds soaring about in the dark as the old woman, facing the sea, knelt in a lengthy prayer. As she prayed, the ponderous soothsayer burned sticks of sweet-smelling incense and beat rhythmically on a frame drum, calling the names of strange entities in the other world who were known to no one but him.

His long rosary dangled from his fingers and sometimes he would strike the back of the drum with it, altering the sound it made as the strange nocturnal birds circled around him.

"What's he saying?" I whispered to Yousef.

"He's calling the names of certain jinn kings. He's summoning them to help," he whispered back.

"Will they come?" I asked, more curious than ever.

He told me to keep quiet, saying that if the jinns knew people were watching and listening in, they wouldn't show up.

The old soothsayer was performing the rites necessary to summon the jinns to our world, but for some reason they were slow to appear. I fell asleep on the sand dune that night as I waited for a glimpse of the drowned child being resurrected from the sea.

When the first rays of the next morning's sun woke me to my actual world, I wondered why I'd been so captivated by that girl's story that I'd been willing to spend the night waiting for her to come back with the same anticipation as her bereaved grandmother, if not more. Oh place, wherever you are, oh sea, oh sky, oh time, she and I both call out to you! One of us has been sleeping for years in the water, the other on land. One of us is white, the other is black. One drowned, though her grandmother never believed she'd died; the other had a grandmother who would have liked to bury her alive and be rid of her forever!

Oh, My Aching Heart!

JINNS MIGHT BE MUSLIM, or belong to some other religion. They might have no religion at all, or be a mixture of religions. They might be any color. They might be made from fire, or earth, or water, from all of them together, or from none of them at all.

Because of these mysterious qualities, the jinns that had accompanied Bouga for most of her life hadn't been affected by the seventy-odd years they'd spent under her coal-black, parched skin and the lashings it had endured. They'd moved like slaves from Ghat, to Fezzan, to Hun, then to Tawergha, then Benghazi, from one black community to another across the land of sea and desert. So, just as they listened to the stories she told, they'd also helped to create them.

Bouga was a tireless storyteller, and she told tales in vivid detail about implacable Libyan caravans that had penetrated deep into Africa and brought slaves back from the Niger River basin, the Sudan, Chad, Mali, and wherever they found black people who were hungry and destitute, victims of tribal wars and sultans' insatiable greed.

The longer Bouga lived, the longer the stories got in her head and, with her, they settled in the Slave Yards. It was as if she had only traveled all those distances and lived all those years in order to put down roots at last on the Sabri beaches, which, like the watering holes in Africa's parched expanses, were congested with the miserable dwellings of the hungry and needy who had fled from life in the desert, the cruelty of slavery, pain, and disappointed love. It was said that slaves in

Benghazi were treated better than they were elsewhere. So, drawn by the echo of story after story, dismal concentrations of black humanity multiplied along the periphery of the Mediterranean where they created a story of their own.

It was far from being a perfect life, but at least people were released somewhat from the iron grip that had held them elsewhere.

When Aunt Sabriya left me for a day or two at a stretch, I'd tag along wherever the other kids went. One day I was with a flock of kids who had nothing to do. We went wandering around the Yards like a bunch of stray, tick-infested animals, and that was when I found out that the Yards actually came to an end, and that on its far edge there was a big, wide world of sand dunes, sunbeams, and fresh air.

That same day Bouga was meandering around with a long stick in her hand. Like us, she'd been just passing the time, and she stopped to talk to us. She had a custom of gathering orphans, most of whom were descended from African tribes, and helping them reconnect with their roots. She had what you might call a shamanic muse that could penetrate barriers of time and space. Through this muse she was able to travel back through history and over long distances, and it would give her a description of these children's families of origin and their ancestors: the villages they came from and what their lives had been like before the slave hunters and their caravans set foot on their lands and carried them forcibly away.

"So would they sell them?" we asked her.

"Yes. But first they'd hunt them down. And sometimes they'd steal them."

"And would they enslave them?"

"Yes."

Bouga grouped the children into blocs based on the regions out of which their ancestors had been enslaved. Accordingly, she gave them names like the Bagramawis, the Waddawis, the Sallamis, the Rashidis, the Sudanis, the Barnawis, the Dijawis, the Sarawis, the Farawis, the Hijrawis, the Bandawis, and so on. In this way she established black identities in a country where you couldn't be acknowledged unless you were associated with this or that clan or community.

Bouga might have asked for help in determining the children's origins from the jinns that possessed her, or from the afreets that told her things. It was said that she had worked with Muslim jinns to find out about the children's families and their histories. She would take a child and give him or her a long, intense, weird sort of look. Then she would close her eyes and hold the child's head while she recited mysterious shamanic incantations. Sometimes her upper body would bend this way or that, sometimes her lower body, so the sight of her would have scared anybody out of their wits. But in the end she would start to talk. She would say, for example, that the boy or girl was from such and such a tribe in west Sudan, for example, or from French Sudan, or from Chad, or Niger. Or if the mother was black but the father wasn't, she might say the child was descended from such and such a clan.

Word got around that Bouga had consorted with the jinn, and that this was why she had never slept with a man. It was said that a certain jinni had fallen in love with her and reserved her for himself, and that she had another family from the world of the spirits. When whites heard about all this, they would refuse to buy her, so she'd ended up living as a beggar.

Even though Bouga had been left to herself, both white Arabs and Negroes started seeking her out to help solve their problems. Her fellow Negroes might have been trying to help her make a living by drawing their masters' attention to her supernatural powers, and in fact they turned out to be useful both to her and to them. Bouga had come to the Yards when the first hut was built there, and she resisted the nuns when they came to take the orphaned children to the Josephite Mission center to, as they put it, "give them an education and save them from homelessness and even death."

Bouga often talked about a caravan that had captured a little girl from Borno, and described people that nobody around her knew anything about and who might not even have been alive anymore. One of these people was an ugly black merchant from the Zuwayya tribe who'd raped a five-year-old girl. He was the commander of a caravan that transported slaves, ivory, and spices. When the caravan stopped to rest, he'd taken the little girl by the hand, and was friendly to her in a desert that was anything but friendly. She had nothing to wear, and was so hungry she'd begun eating the grasses along the way. She was sick as well, and had been stricken with diarrhea for an entire day. He rubbed her belly with olive oil as if to treat her for her stomach pain, but no sooner had he done her this supposed kindness than he showed his true colors and took violent hold of her. She screamed and tried to push him away. Paying no attention to her pleadings in a language he didn't understand, he overpowered her until she felt something heavy and hard that he'd kept hidden under his cloak. When she started screaming again, he gripped her mouth between his teeth. Besides, who would have heard her but the vast desert expanse and the mighty Living One who sees but isn't seen, and who hears but isn't heard?

Behind the man's shoulders, she saw the sky slowly vanish between the sand dunes. Then his unnamed "thing" vanished inside her as the stars and the sky vanished from sight. For days she was absent from the world, rocked to and fro on the back of a camel as other girls in the caravan attended to her needs.

The caravan's slave driver came up, wiped some *bazeen* broth off his mouth, and flogged his captives to make them get up and march.[1] The young men among them were in shackles, while the children stumbled along barefoot in ragtag groups. He beat many of them, eliciting even more screams and cries. Those who couldn't take another step were left to their fate as the caravan continued oblivious on its way.

The last thing the sky saw of them was the gleam in their eyes, which wandered lost in spirits withering away without succor. If only it had poured down rain, moistening their parched tongues one last time before they departed, thirsty, to meet their Lord.

1. *Bazeen* is a North African dish consisting of stewed meat and potatoes seasoned with onion, tomato, fenugreek, turmeric, salt, and pepper, which are arranged in a circle with hard-boiled eggs and hot chili peppers around a large dumpling of sorts known as asida, made from barley and wheat flour.

Forced to travel on foot from their countries of origin to the land of those who had enslaved them in pursuit of filthy lucre, they walked through the desert for months on end. However, so merciless were the hunger, thirst, and exposure that many of them succumbed easily to death. After countless floggings intended to hasten them to Tripoli, their spirits exited their bodies through their flayed skin and escaped to freedom.

Tripoli? Tripoli was nowhere in sight, but the afterlife lay just a step or two away!

Bouga wept for days over children in the caravan who had been left to die alone in the desert after helping to dig in search of a well that had been filled in by desert sandstorms. As a little girl she had cried for her brother, who had expired just moments before they hit water. He had dug with them in search of that well with his tiny, frail hands, his one hope being to taste a sip of water.

Hungry crows, cawing, hovered overhead. After all, they needed to eat, and they'd found their day's fare. Indeed, God would provide them with sustenance whence they knew not. The children had marched from the Niger River basin to Tibesti just to become tasty morsels for them. Otherwise, what purpose would their brief existence have served? Not once in centuries had a caravan waited for anyone, nor had a crow gone hungry. No wonder desert fowl thrive in such abundance.

When Bouga turned to look back at her brother, she saw the crows rowdily lighting on his head and pecking at his live flesh as the caravan went on its way. A black girl from another tribe closed Bouga's eyes to keep her from seeing the ones who were dying, even though others were bound to meet the same fate as the journey wore on. This was one of their rituals of consolation.

As an adult, Bouga would break down every time she heard a marskawi singer extolling God's power to provide for His creatures:

> Oh you who grant the bird its portion,
> grant me the beauty of the peregrine's eye!
> Oh you who grant the bird its paths,

grant that the one I hold dear will draw nigh!
Oh you who grant the bird its wings,
grant me to be wherever my love may lie!

When Durma performed, Bouga would walk in after everyone else and squat in a far corner, as if she'd come to receive her share of musical healing balm. She would cry thinking back on a little boy who, like so many others down the centuries, had been food for the birds in the Libyan Desert. When Durma looked into Bouga's eyes and felt the old woman's tears, she decided to stop performing songs like this one anymore.

Instead, she would sing:

Oh you who've patiently endured as I have,
you've endured forever and a day.
You've borne up beyond the limits of the bearable,
you'll endure your sorrows away!
Oh, my aching heart, my aching heart!

This was the consolation Durma offered the old woman's spirit with her rich, mournful voice.

The Maharisiti

"GIVE THE WOMAN SOME WATER," said Seena, the slave driver, to the *maharisiti*.[1] She's crying for help."

The maharisiti just stood there, stone-still and arrogant, unmoved by the woman's cries. Her moans grew louder. Afraid she would give up the ghost just when they were about to reach Murzuk, the slave driver pressed the maharisiti. "She's going to die of thirst," he said. "Give her a sip!"

"I'm not giving my last drop to anybody," the maharisiti replied coldly. "She'll have to bear it. Water in the desert is precious, and saliva's worth more than gold."

Then, with a wicked laugh, he added, "I could give her some of my saliva if you want!"

"You wish!" scoffed the slave driver. "If she dies, we'll have lost a head we paid money for. You know the overlords won't pay for the loss out of their share. It'll be taken out of ours. Don't forget the agreement, and don't forget that the girls we've got with us aren't virgins anymore. We're the ones who'll have to pay the fine on them, and if this one dies we'll be so deep in debt we'll never take another caravan out. You get me?"

---

1. The term *maharisiti* refers to a Tuareg man who is skilled at riding a mehari camel, the mehari being a breed of camel prized for its exceptional speed and used in racing.

The maharisiti, who'd been gazing at the horizon with his back to the slave driver, spun around angrily.

"What did you say?" he demanded. "Do you mean to tell me there isn't a single virgin left in this caravan?"

"No."

"So between Ghat and Murzuk you spoiled the last one?! Damn the lot of you! Didn't I warn you?"

His neck in the maharisiti's iron grip now, the slave driver wheezed fearfully, "We ask you every night, and you always say yes."

"Don't you realize that when you ask me that question, my head's thick with hashish?" the maharisiti growled.

"But from the time you took that young one for yourself, you haven't shared her with any of us."

"So, then, because I didn't give you any, you took some for yourselves! Just wait till we get to Murzuk. You'll get what's coming to you."

"How were we supposed to hold out in this harsh desert when there were girls right there in front of us?"

"And which of your overlords will go near any of them now? Tell me that! You know as well as I do that the slave owners and the sheikhs who head the *zawiyas* won't touch a 'rightful possession'[2] unless she's a virgin. You took what belonged to somebody else, and you're not getting away with it. So take your choice now, you sissy. Which will it be: me or my bosses?"

With that, the maharisiti snatched the whip out of the slave driver's hand and started to flog him with it, alternately talking to him and lashing him. He fled behind a sand dune. The maharisiti ran after him.

"They stipulated in the purchase agreement that they wanted them virgins, you stupid asshole!"

---

2. *Mulk yamīn*—literally, "the possession of one's right hand"—is derived from the Qur'anic phrase *mā malakat aymānuhum* ("what their right hands possess") in reference to female war captives and slaves (see, for example, Q. 4:24, 23:6, and 70:30).

"All right, all right, then!" the slave driver relented, cowering. Once we get there, the guards and I will give you the money. Just write on the bill of lading that we found them this way."

"There's no way any of them will believe me if I say that, you idiot, and that'll be the last time I head a caravan. Do you expect us to deliver pregnant slaves to the sheikhs at the zawiya?"

"All right, all right, then. We'll give you whatever you want for them and you can replace them with some good-looking young ones who were born in Fezzan. Nobody'll ever know."

"I want a hundred gold coins."

"That's too much. You wouldn't pay that for free women, much less slaves!"

"Listen. You trespassed on my bosses' property. And if they find out about this, they'll either kill you or turn you into slaves yourselves."

Looking at the part of the slave driver's chest that was visible through his neck opening, the maharisiti went on, "They'll flay that sunbaked hide of yours till you're no different than one of these slaves here."

Terrified by the maharisiti's threat, the slave driver thought back on what had happened to a man who'd once led a slave caravan that stayed in the desert for an especially long time. By the time the caravan reached its destination, all the female captives were pregnant and, in response to a complaint filed by the European merchant who had funded the caravan, the *qa'imaqam* had the caravan commander thrown in prison.[3] After this the merchant bribed the prison guards to let him into the caravan commander's cell, and he raped him repeatedly. It was said that over a period of days, he assaulted him twice for every pregnant slave woman the caravan had delivered. Then he appealed to the qa'imaqam to have the commander released, and from then on the two of them went around like bosom buddies!

Whoever can't take the demands of the slave trade is better off staying away from it, since it'll cost a man either his life or his honor.

---

3. A *qa'imaqam* is an Ottoman official who oversees an administrative district, or *qada'*.

Tuffaha's Street

AS A MATTER of politeness and respect, people often address their elders as "Uncle" and "Auntie." In the case of black people, however, they're expected to address all whites in this way, regardless of how old or young they happen to be, and whether the white person concerned is their owner or someone who's hired them for pay. So you can imagine how many "uncles" and "aunties" I've had in my life!

Auntie Sadina used to cook on special occasions for the big families of Benghazi. Her food was out of this world. When word got around about what a wonderful cook she was, well-to-do families started to seek her out to prepare feasts at weddings, pilgrimage homecoming celebrations, circumcision parties, and that sort of thing. She was always sitting in front of her hut with a metal tray in her lap, picking tiny pebbles, sticks, and pieces of dirt out of aromatic herbs that she would crush and prepare for the next big meal she was getting ready to make.

One morning while Auntie Sadina was preparing spices and crushing ginger and coriander in a tall iron mortar, she told Aunt Sabriya that the people she was going to be cooking for over the coming several weeks had asked her to find somebody to wait on the bride for the week of the wedding. My aunt, who had just come back to the Slave Yards a couple of days before, agreed straightaway.

That afternoon, Mjawir took us into the city to meet the lady we'd be working for so that she could explain her terms and tell us what we'd need to do for the bride. He hit the donkey every now and then to give his riders the illusion that he was a good driver, but his wagon was so wobbly that we nearly fell out a few times. Meanwhile, he tried to break into the conversation Aunt Sabriya and Aunt Sadina were having about the details of the trip. He loved butting into other people's business, so they both tried to avoid him.

As we got out of the wagon, I held on tight to Aunt Sabriya's dress. I was determined to keep myself out of Mjawir's reach in case he tried to pinch me somewhere, and I knew I had to be on my guard. Keeping an eye on his hands, I moved away without turning my back to him, clutching my aunt's dress from the back. When he climbed back on the wagon, he deftly held the hem of his *jallabiya* in his mouth to keep from tripping over it. I guess that was his way of showing off in front of the women and girls he chauffeured. Then, once he'd made sure nobody was around but the two women, who were too distracted with each other to notice, he flashed the huge blackened thing between his legs at me.

Of course, he wasn't the only one who did that sort of thing. In fact, it seemed to be an established tradition among men around there, though none of them would have admitted to doing it himself. They all did it in secret, but they'd blast anybody who got caught doing it in public!

The house of the family we'd come to see was on a narrow, well-kept alleyway paved with dirt that had been moistened and packed down hard. The houses were so close together, they looked as though they were holding each other up. Even though the street was clean, police officers and military patrols avoided coming there alone for fear of being mugged, either by locals or by Bedouins from the country-side. Along the same alley, however, there was a well-known house of prostitution that they frequented in groups. There were conflicting accounts about its owner who, apart from police officers and military personnel, rarely received any visitors, with the possible exception of an elderly woman who was an expert on herbal medicine.

The prostitute in question, known as Tuffaha, was a pretty girl of Bedouin origins whose family had died in an outbreak of the plague. Her village had nearly been wiped out, and she was among a small number of villagers who'd been taken to quarantine and had managed to survive. But after being released from quarantine, Tuffaha hadn't had anywhere to go. Hunger and poverty were ravishing the countryside, and all people thought about was how to save their own skins. When some men from her village talked to her about Benghazi, she agreed to go there with them, and in return they started to coming to her for sexual favors. As time went on, she made a profession of entertaining men just to survive. But Tuffaha was no prostitute at heart. In fact, she was the kindest soul in the world. Warm and welcoming, she shared her earnings with her neighbors and only kept a little for herself. One time she seduced a high-ranking Turkish officer so that destitute members of her clan could rob him of his money and his weapon. Tuffaha wasn't alone, either. In fact, there were lots of "Tuffahas" in similar circumstances who sacrificed their personal comfort and honor for others.

At the end of Tuffaha's street there lived an expert Jewish seamstress by the name of Manita who made holiday outfits for Arab customers as well as uniforms and other clothes for soldiers stationed at the garrison. One day my aunt decided to take me to this woman's house to have a dress made for me—quite a luxury for a little black girl from the Slave Yards! In preparation for the outing, Aunt Sabriya wrapped a heavy shawl securely around her head and upper torso. As for me, she had me wear the same dress I always wore, but she tied a small scarf around my head to hide my hair—or maybe to hide me! When my girlfriends in the Slave Yards saw the scarf on my head, they said, "Where are you going, Atiga? You look like you're getting ready for a trip!" They knew, of course, that nobody in the Slave Yards traveled anywhere. The farthest we ever went was downtown Benghazi, where we served in people's houses for a living.

As a way of keeping me on his wagon for as long as possible, Mjawir took his time getting us to our destination. I was feeling excited, and every now and then my heart would skip a beat. My aunt seemed excited too, and as we rode along she sat taking in the city streets as if it were the first time she'd ever seen them. Or maybe she was just thinking back on things she remembered seeing before.

As we rode along, my hair started to frizz up and peek out the back of my scarf in a little tail. My thick lower lip drooped even more than usual as I gaped at the sights in the city. I'd always thought everybody everywhere was poor like us and dressed the way we did. I figured they all walked around barefoot for most of their lives, lugging water from wells and doing all sorts of other exhausting menial tasks. But I saw now that this wasn't true after all.

A short distance from Tuffaha's street, I saw a woman who was all dolled up and dressed in a wedding gown even though there was no wedding going on. She stood inside a large archway that had a smaller door in the center of it, chewing gum and showing herself off to everybody who walked by. At the alleyway entrance, a little girl stood staring at the woman in a kind of fearful fascination. The woman tried to lure the girl over to her by waving a piece of colorful *bambila* candy in the air.[1]

Suddenly a hairy hand reached out and grabbed the girl. The hand belonged to a young man—her big brother, apparently—who started beating her mercilessly with a shoe, screaming, "You little bitch!" The girl cried out in pain, but no one intervened to rescue her even though there were people everywhere. Writhing in agony, she begged him to stop, telling him how sorry she was and calling on the Prophet, God's righteous saints, and the local Sufi adepts as her witnesses. I had no idea what she'd done wrong. After all, she'd just been standing in the street watching! Even so, the shoe kept coming down on her little body as violently as ever, without the righteous saints' being moved one iota.

Terrified, I held on tight to Aunt Sabriya, who didn't seem the least bit shocked, or even surprised. Neither did the people walking down the street, or even Mjawir's donkey, which got bonked with the shoe as it sailed past the fleeing girl. To them it was a completely ordinary scene, but it wasn't to me. As far as they were concerned, this

1. Also known as *halwa az-zawiya*, or "zawiya candy," *bambila* was a kind of sweet often distributed at religious retreat centers.

was just a "little man" disciplining his sister. In fact, to them it was admirable that he was so "manly," and keen to preserve his "honor." I concluded that if anybody else there had been in the boy's place, he would have done the very same thing, with or without the help of a shoe.

In the end, the floozie stormed back into her house and slammed the door behind her, and we continued on our way to Manita's house. When we got there, we found a heavy woman stretched out on her belly in the middle of her inner courtyard. She had her head pillowed on one arm, while another woman, equally heavy, sat next to her checking her head for lice as the two of them chatted. As we walked in, Aunt Sabriya murmured, *"Bismillah al-rahman al-rahim"* ("In the name of God, most merciful, most compassionate") before greeting the seamstress, who paid no attention to us at first. Summoning the protection of the Prophet and our master David, Aunt Sabriya added under her breath, *"Ya Rasul Allah, ya Sayyidi Dawoud, al-baraka lana wassukhtu lil-yahoud!"* ("Oh messenger of God, Oh Master David, send blessings on us and curses on the Jews!").

Raising herself up on her side, the woman asked us what we wanted.

"We've come to have a dress made for the little girl," my aunt replied.

She looked me harshly up and down, clearly contemptuous of my color and my scruffy appearance. After asking my aunt who we were and what relation she was to me, she told the other woman to bring her the measuring rod and the scissors. When she asked what kind of fabric she'd brought, my aunt said, "Rose chiffon."

Shaking her head in disdain, the seamstress broke into a popular song: "Rose chiffon, rose chiffon, take a rose and give me one!"

My aunt took out the piece of cloth she'd brought, and Manita told me to come up closer so that she could measure my chest, neck, and arms. That's as "tailored" as clothes were back then. I was apprehensive, and I felt her eyes going straight through me. For all I knew, she didn't believe a black girl like me was good enough to wear fabrics that were usually reserved for free folks' daughters. The woman might not actually have been thinking this, of course, but it's what was going through my head.

As Manita was taking my measurements, there was a commotion outside. We heard the woman who'd been checking Manita's head for lice talking in a loud voice. Then she came back in crying. Manita dropped what she was doing and went out to the roofed-in area at the front of the house. The other woman told her in a language I didn't understand about something going on in the street. At first I thought the boy we'd seen earlier had gone back to beating his sister, or that the dolled-up lady had come back out to her doorway and caused somebody else to get a beating they didn't deserve. But something in the two women's demeanor had changed, and they began beating their left shoulders and chanting an agonized Jewish lament: *Woooh, woooh! Hamiyu jiranu ras bila tagiya, sadr bila suriya!* Part of it had to do with somebody going around with a bare head and chest, but I couldn't make out the rest of it.

The longer the refrain went on, the more upset I felt. I didn't like this place, and I didn't like what was going on. Manita's body gave off an acrid smell, and I could hardly stand the sight of the bushy hair on her legs. She also had a slight mustache along her upper lip, which I didn't like, either. It seemed these things were only true of Jewish women, since no Muslim woman I'd ever seen, black or white, had had whiskers or hair on her arms and legs.

My feelings were all mixed up, and it seemed that something catastrophic was happening. I wriggled up as close as I could to Aunt Sabriya and held onto her tight. I told her I was scared.

"Don't worry," she replied calmly. "I'm right here."

Despite the visible questions in my eyes, and whatever it was that had people rushing out into the street, I was reassured by Aunt Sabriya. Nothing seemed to scare her, as if she knew ahead of time everything that would happen in this world.

When we left the seamstress's house and I caught a glimpse of Mjawir's wagon, I raced over to it as fast as I could, not because I was anxious to see Mjawir again, and especially not that thing that dangled between his legs, but because I couldn't wait to get away from this weird, scary world with its strange people and strange-looking clothes. The sight of the wagon meant going home to the Slave Yards.

As things quieted down in the street, I realized that the uproar had been over a Jewish man's funeral procession that had been passing by. Egged on by some adults, a number of street children had lobbed clods of manure at the bier. This had made the funeral goers angry, of course, since now they would have to wash the dead man's body all over again before they could bury him. This used to happen whenever a Jewish funeral procession passed a bunch of troublemakers, who got a kick out of mean pranks like this.

After that we went to see the family hosting the wedding. We sat in an open, roofed-in area adjoined to their house, where there was a long discussion of the agreement relating to the service we were required to provide for the bride. I didn't understand most of what was said. I did understand, though, that I would have to stay near the bride night and day so that I could bring her whatever she asked for and make sure she was comfortable and happy.

One term of the agreement was that I'd have to wear a dress that was suitable for a wedding, which was why Aunt Sabriya had taken me to the Jewish seamstress's house. I would also have to bring the bride a basin of water and wash her feet, clear away her food when she'd finished eating, bring her whatever she needed to wash her hands with, and pour her used bath water into the street whenever she performed the ritual washing required after having sex. I'd be expected to do all these things wearing my new dress! And this two-week celebration was all on account of the mere fact that a woman was getting together with a man for the first time!

Dakakin Hamid

IN THOSE DAYS women used to crush grains and herbs in empty mortar shells that were referred to as *bombs*. Because they were long and hollow, they were ideal for this purpose since they didn't allow the dust produced by the grinding process to fly every which way. We used them to crush the cloves that went into cosmetic preparations, as well as into the mixture that was applied to brides' hair before their weddings. The job I'd been assigned in Fattouma's wedding preparations was to carry bombs to wherever they were needed. Libya had been the target of plenty of bombs over the years, which was why we had so many of them around. But as time went by, they'd proved so useful for purposes that had nothing to do with war that we tended to forget the horrors they'd brought on us and our country.

Outside the room where Fattouma's hair would be done there sat a bomb and, next to it, a long iron pestle stood propped against the clay wall. We were waiting for all the hairdressers to show up, as well as the bride's maternal aunt, whose job was to bring the distilled oil, crush the cloves, and prepare the beauty mask. Once she arrived, the rituals involved in getting the bride ready could officially begin.

The aunt in question was a grouchy old woman who could keep the bride in line whenever she objected to having the lice picked out of her hair, being smeared with cloves, and being depilated and rubbed with distilled oil in preparation for her first encounter with a man. The marriage contract, which had been signed in the presence of several witnesses, contained a stipulation next to Hammad's and Fattouma's names that he would give her three sheep. However, only one of the three sheep would actually be slaughtered for the occasion. The other two would be cared for by the bride's father in hopes of selling them as Eid al-Adha approached.

Fattouma was less than two years past puberty when some neighbors asked for her hand in marriage to their eldest son, Hammad. Hammad himself wasn't even twenty years old yet when he found out that he was engaged to the girl next door. After finishing a term of service in the salt flats, he'd come home to spend the holiday with his mother and father. The minute he walked in, his mother started to weep and trill, and his father wrapped him in an emotional embrace, wiping his tears with the edge of his robe. Thinking that some relative must have died while he was away, Hammad took his mother into his arms and burst into loud sobs.

"Who is it, Mama? Who is it?" he repeated over and over.

When the neighbors heard the weeping and wailing, they started pouring into the house. With the taste of the couscous from the engagement feast still in their mouths, they set about trying to calm the situation.

"Don't worry, Hammad," they reassured the young man. "Nobody's died! It's just that your family's found you a bride, and they're happy for you!"

Smitten with a sudden awkwardness, Hammad stopped crying. Imagine that! His parents were happy, not grief-stricken. And they'd found him a suitable wife at an affordable price!

Adjusting to this new realization, Hammad was careful not to say a word about the chosen bride. He asked no questions about who she was or how they'd located her. By keeping quiet, he opened the way for his mother to tell him about the bride of her own accord. Being a woman herself, she would know how to say everything that needed to be said, and in the way it needed to be said. By playing this traditional mother's role, she would spare her son the risk of broaching some overly sensitive topic, posing a question that might turn out to be embarrassing or inappropriate, or asking for information she didn't have.

His mother set out the glasses and the utensils she'd need to prepare the tea, invited her son to sit next to her, and handed him an extra cushion to lean on as she warmed to her topic. Before saying more about the prospective bride, she asked him about his work in the salt flats and how much he'd been earning, and he assured her that he had a good income.

"Wonderful!" she said. "That will make it easier for us to marry you to Fattouma, Hajj Abdullah Abd Rabbuh's daughter!"

Aha! So now Hammad knew who his children's maternal uncles would be.

As she prepared the foam on top of the tea, his mother talked on and on about how nice their neighbors were, how easy they were to get along with, and how good they were at keeping feisty women in their place. She said Sakita, the neighbor girl's mother, was as docile as they came. She was the sort of woman who'd believe whatever you said to her and do whatever you told her to do, and she'd raised her daughters so strictly that people used to describe her as a man. (They meant it as a compliment, the mother remarked, but Sakita used to take it as an insult!)

Hammad cleared his throat slightly, signaling his mother to get back to talking about the bride. Taking the hint, she drew her wrap demurely around her head so that he couldn't see her face, and resumed talking about Fattouma. She described her in glowing terms, saying she was sure she'd have beautiful children, keep a clean house, be a wonderful mother and hostess, fatten up the livestock, and take good care of his blind, invalid grandmother, not to mention being a good seamstress who could bring in a generous income for the family.

Satisfied with his parents' choice, Hammad figured Fattouma's trousseau would include a sewing machine. But if he wanted to make sure he won her, he would have to face a test of virility that he didn't dare fail.

He'd only seen Fattouma's face a few times in the days before she was shut up in the house and forbidden to go with her father to the marketplace, and the only thing he could remember about her was her frizzy, wiry hair. But now his imagination went beyond this memory in search of some mysterious essence that a man looks for in a woman. As he convinced himself that he'd found his heart's desire in his Fattouma, he suddenly realized how different his life would be with a woman in it. After all, once he'd been able to "sow" his new bride, he'd be a father even before he turned twenty years old, and that would prove his virility to his buddies and the other men and boys in the neighborhood.

That night, just as his dreams were beckoning him to bed, Hammad heard his father calling, so he got up to see what he needed. He found his father in the stable. In keeping with custom, father and son lowered their glances out of mutual respect.

"Son," the father began, "why don't you choose the best ram in our stable and take it as a holiday gift to your fiancée's family? It would be a way of showing your goodwill toward your future in-laws. They've waived their request for one of the sheep the bride's representative stipulated as part of her dowry, which was really nice of them, don't you think?"

The next day, Hammad went out to the stable before the sundown prayer and looked around to see which of the rams would best suit Fattouma. He wanted one that was virile and fertile, the way he wanted her to see her husband-to-be. His glance fell on a reddish ram with curved horns that had been chasing a couple of ewes and had them trapped in a corner. After several unsuccessful forays across the stable, Hammad caught hold of the ram. The chase left him out of breath, his pores dilated, his knee bruised. When his father came in to take a look at his son's animal of choice he said, "Not the red one, son."

"Why's that, Baba?" Hammad wanted to know.

"That's the one I'm planning to slaughter for the holy day. I've already spoken to the butcher about him."

"Take another one to the butcher."

Trying to persuade his son, the elderly man said, "The red one would be too much for us. I realize it's the only time we'll be expected to give your in-laws a present like this. But don't forget—the wedding will involve other expenses."

Convinced by his father's reasoning, Hammad started back into the stable to replace the red ram with another animal. After finding a white ram that would fill the bill, he lifted it onto his back and headed for their neighbors' house.

He rapped on the door with his feet. "Who is it?" he heard a young woman's voice ask. Hammad's heart, which was already working overtime from chasing down his catch and from the suspicion that Fattouma was nearby, nearly pounded out of his chest. Disturbed by the sound of Hammad's panting, the sheep began bleating so loudly that it drowned out his uncertain, quavering voice.

Through one of the numerous holes in the neighbor's tinplate door, he caught a glimpse of an eye staring out at him, though he pretended not to have seen it. Stricken with a sudden fit of desert-boy shyness, he looked away, saying, "My father's sent a sheep to Hajj Abdullah Abd Rabbuh."

The girl replied that the Hajj was at the mosque and that there were no men at home to receive it.

"Well," he suggested, "if you crack the door just a bit, I can put it inside."

The door opened just enough to allow him to deliver the gift. He lowered the sheep off his back and nudged it through the narrow gap. As he did so, he glimpsed the girl's feet and a bit of her dress. He realized she was probably his fiancée herself, and her nicely rounded leg mitigated the effect of thinking about her wiry hair. As he raised his head after setting the sheep down, he came eye to eye with the girl inside. Flustered now, he felt a warm rush sweep over him. But then, as if a bucket of cold water had suddenly been dumped on his head, he started with fright and took off running back to his house.

It was a hot, sticky night, and Hammad reeked of sheep urine. He went to the privy to wash up and, seeing that the water had run out, headed for the well, filled a pail, and took it to the kitchen to heat the water over the stove. As he waited for his water to get hot, he found a washcloth that made him think of the dress he'd seen Fattouma wearing. He held it to his nose, thinking it must have been made out of the same fabric. He figured she must have given the leftover cloth to his mother so that she could use it in her kitchen. With this thought, he sniffed himself into a state of ecstasy, despite the fact that the odor brought him closer to the vegetable market than it did to the girl next door.

He carried the pail to the outhouse, lowered the long gunnysack that served as its door, and started scrubbing himself down. Seeing a shadow moving against the house's mud wall, his father wanted to go out to make sure the night visitor wasn't a thief who was about to make off with some of their livestock. Certain that the shadow belonged to their son, his mother persuaded her husband to stay inside. All it took was a simple statement: "Your son's become a man!"[1]

After hearing his wife's comment, the old man was quiet for a bit. Suddenly he flung himself in a heat of enthusiasm atop the nightie-clad figure beside him in a reminder that he wasn't as old as he might seem, and that the wick still had plenty of oil left in it even though the years had passed and his son had "become a man."

In the quiet hours of that sultry night, Hammad lay in bed trying to recall everything he knew about women so that he could be at his best with Fattouma. He fantasized about the plump thigh he'd seen, the curious gaze, and the tensely held breaths. But when his imagination reached her hair, he felt a twinge of aversion. His boyhood memories of that hair of hers weren't pleasant ones. Truth be told, Fattouma had the worst hair of any girl in the neighborhood. It didn't fall nicely over her shoulders the way his mother's did. Not even her bangs would lie down flat. He concluded that he might have to set aside a special budget from his hard-earned pay to buy oil to treat his wife's hair with. But the fact was, you could have poured the contents of all the olive oil presses in Zliten on her head and it wouldn't have made a bit of difference.

1. According to Islamic teachings, bodily secretions relating to sexual functions require both men and women to bathe in order to maintain the ritual purity required for the performance of the five daily prayers. The fact that Hammad was taking a bath at night was taken by his mother as a sign that he had had a seminal emission, which would mean he had "become a man."

So what was he to do? Could he overlook Fattouma's top half for the sake of what other parts of her provided? He asked himself if he'd be able to settle for the "other" things as a consolation prize of sorts, though he had no choice but to answer in the affirmative. After all, it wouldn't be right to go against the word his father had given in the presence of the neighborhood elders. Besides, why give up the chance to be related by marriage to Hajj Abdullah Abd Rabbuh on account of some hair his bride-to-be had inherited from her father's whiskers through no fault of her own?

Hammad remembered the goodwill sheep and what it had done to his knee. It hurt to bend it now, and he groaned as he lay in bed trying to get some rest. Then again, his reward was the luscious thigh that would be the stuff of his dreams for nights to come. Holding the kitchen rag to his nose, he slept for the first time since learning of his engagement.

The next morning, Hammad tried to get his mother to tell him more about his wife-to-be. Holding the rag in his hand, he asked her if she liked the cloth it was made of as much as he did. If she did, he said, he would go to the market and buy some for her to make a dress for Fattouma.

Drawing her hand out of the bowl of bread dough in front of her and wiping it on the piece of cloth he'd been holding in his hand all night, she replied, "No, son, no need for that. It wouldn't be proper for a mother and daughter to wear the same type of fabric!"

Clove Girl

HAMMAD PLANTED his right foot inside the dimly lit room where Fattouma sat waiting for him. Trembling, he leaned for support on his cousin, who, after giving him a pep talk that would have been enough to prepare for him for a hundred Fattoumas, nudged him the rest of the way in. Slightly bowlegged, Hammad was lanky, fair-skinned, and handsome, with a muscular physique that he'd acquired from years of working on the salt flats.

Fattouma, who had escaped having her hair done with ground cloves and distilled oil after having declared ferocious mutiny on the bomb and its contents, sat perched on a canopy bed, waiting for Hammad's other foot to appear. Seeing how much her rebellion had upset her mother and her ladies-in-waiting, her father had carried out a behind-the-scenes intervention.

"Tell her to do her hair with those cloves," he whispered sternly in her mother's ear, "or I'll come in and smack her. If it weren't for cloves, she wouldn't even be around!"

Maybe Fattouma wanted to forget what the scent of cloves did to people, and that if it weren't for its magical effects, nothing would have happened between her father and mother and she would never have even existed! She wanted to forge a new path with a different fragrance, which was why she had rebelled against the clove treatment in the first place.

As for Hammad, he would have to undergo repeated tests of his strength and endurance over the course of his seven-day wedding festivities. The family had sent for a *tighi*, or professional wrestler, from the Matrouh borders, and Hammad had to meet him in hand-to-hand combat several nights in a row. After battling for some time with batons, they started to wrestle, each of them trying to bring the other down. As the first round progressed, Hammad's cousin started to worry that the wrestler might come out the victor, so when nobody was looking, he bribed him by doubling his wages in return for letting Hammad win. When Hammad found out that his victory had been rigged, he was furious. But then one of his more level-headed cousins took him aside and said, "Calm down now. Do you think you're the first one this has happened to—or the second, or the fourth, or the fourteenth, for that matter? It happens all the time!"

When at last it was time for him to be with his bride, Hammad took off his cloak to reveal a snow-white tunic. Over it he wore a jacket with silk-embroidered sleeves made in Damanhur. When Fattouma saw her man, she couldn't believe her luck. *Is this really all mine?* she wondered. When he sat down beside her and took off his cap, she nearly fainted. Hammad had silky, blondish hair that couldn't have been more different than hers!

Hammad consummated his marriage to Fattouma the Islamic way. That is to say, he didn't use his forefinger to puncture her hymen as local custom dictated. Fattouma's uncle and Hammad's cousin were standing a short distance from the room where the couple's awkward first encounter was taking place. Every now and then the uncle would furrow his brow and mutter, "The boy's taking an awful long time in there. God have mercy . . . God have mercy!"

Wanting to calm the impatient uncle, the cousin complimented him on the rifle he had slung over his shoulder as he paced back and forth across the outdoor enclosure. When that brought no response, he asked him what he thought about the arms market, and the rising prices of contraband being smuggled across the border with Egypt. But Fattouma's uncle was clearly in no mood to chat about the state of the arms market, or about anything else for that matter. He was too preoccupied to be distracted by such secondary matters.

So he closed the door to further conversation with a curt "the arms market's no concern of mine. That's God's business!!"

All he could think about was his brother's daughter, who was being touched by a strange man, now her husband, who bore the burden of testifying to whether she was a virgin or not.

After what felt like an eternity dotted with pleas for divine protection, the door to their room made a loud creak and out came a shell-shocked-looking Hammad. Without a word, he handed the bride's uncle a blood-spattered white sheet. The uncle hastily hid the sheet in the folds of his flowing wrap and took it out to a group of men gathered in front of the house. This done, he gleefully set about emptying the contents of his shotgun into the air. This was his way of sharing the good news with his brothers and cousins and the bride's maternal uncles, who sat waiting behind the house for the white sheet to emerge no longer white. The uncle hurriedly unfurled it like a victory banner, the battle of innocence now won, and the effectiveness of the tick-tock chest in protecting the family's honor duly proven. Now that the bloodied sheet had appeared in the distance, they could hold their heads high in the knowledge that their honor was intact.

This precious piece of cloth would stand until Judgment Day as evidence that Hammad was the first male Fattouma had ever had contact with. As such, it would close the door to any lies that might circulate in the future if, God forbid, Hammad got it into his head to divorce her someday and rob her of her dowry by claiming that he hadn't found her a virgin on their wedding night. This was the outcome of a mutual collective deception for which a woman's virginity had been chosen as the playing field!

As the proof of Fattouma's purity lay concealed once more in the folds of her uncle's farmala, and as the smoke from the gunfire dissipated into the sky, the women's trills rang out, and they sang the praises of Fattouma's unsullied honor. Their crooning was true music to the ears of the men, who were intoxicated from this victory in the onerous test of honor:

Oh Fattouma, God preserved you,
    and your uncle is proud as a pasha today!
Oh Maryouma, best of mothers,
    your prudence and wisdom kept harm at bay!

I had a close-up view of the contest between Hammad and the tighi, and during the first night's round, Hammad did his best to prove himself to Fattouma, although he didn't quite manage. I'd attended other matches as well, and I'd only seen a few real cocks, whereas the rest had been nothing but hens in disguise strutting around the barnyard.

Nobody seemed to notice that there was something wrong with the custom of having the groom use his hand on the wedding night to determine whether his bride was a virgin. On the contrary, even the women thought it was perfectly normal. It had never occurred to them that it was just a way of covering up for a man's possible impotence.

Women had been lulled to sleep for centuries before they learned to read and go in search of what they lacked in worlds not governed by the specifications of local male authority figures. Only then did they realize their own right to pleasure, and that what they had missed, they had missed due to nothing but a pack of lies.

As a child who served couples from the upper class, I witnessed a lot of things in the private world of men and women who were encountering each other for the first time for the simple reason that they had gotten married. Since, as far as they were concerned, I was nothing but a naïve little girl who couldn't possibly understand what I was seeing, they had no reason to worry that I would spread their secrets. Besides, I was black, which meant I only had a quarter of a brain!

I would hear the women crying and the men beating them, calling them names, and threatening to divorce them or claim that they hadn't been virgins on their wedding nights. In the end, the women would quiet down, resigned to their fates, and keep their pain bottled up inside. Then the children would come, love would fade—if there'd been any to start with—and the whole sky would cloud over with sorrows.

The *Jard* and the
Birth Certificate

AUNT SABRIYA had gone into the city on some errands, but when she came back on that ill-fated day she found the Slave Yards completely different from the way she'd left it. It was going up in flames! Crazed by the sight, she dropped the broad beans and chickpeas she'd brought for us and came running.

What was happening? There was no explanation ready at hand. We were so shocked and confused at first, all we could do was take things in with our eyes. Then word got around that the government authorities were trying to stamp out the plague that had been ravaging the country, and their way of going about it was to set fire to entire neighborhoods where the disease had broken out. Death was on a rampage, and unless they took drastic measures, it threatened to destroy their colony.

It wasn't water or wind this time, but fire that was destroying everything in its path. The blacks of the Yards met the situation with a river of tears as wide and deep as the sea. As for Benghazi, it absorbed the smoke from behind its towering wall in a stony, grave silence.

People were swarming like ants around the entrances to the Yards, none of them taking any notice of my aunt. In an apocalyptic scene like that one, you'll hardly notice yourself. Undaunted by the soldiers stationed around the ghetto, Aunt Sabriya shoved them back, screaming, "Let me in, damn you! I've got to get the jard and the birth certificate!"

With an agonized wail, she tore past the soldiers, and all we could see of her was her dusty bare feet and her gray wrap fluttering behind her. When Giuseppe tried to run after her, the head of the mission held him back, reminding him that the people inside were afflicted with the plague.

"Don't pour kerosene on the entrances!" Aunt Aida screamed at the soldiers. "She's coming back out!"

She pleaded with a high-ranking army officer and a doctor with a Red Cross badge on his arm. But the doctor just shook his head as if to say, "There's nothing I can do!" and lowered her hands off him with a sorrowful look. As for the officer, he refused to withdraw his orders, and they were carried out by a soldier standing nearby with a tin of kerosene in his hand. Pouring the fuel along the entrance, he prepared to close off the last remaining section of the Yards with a wall of fire. That was when I realized I was losing Aunt Sabriya in this blazing inferno. In a wild panic, I started scattering dirt over the ground in an attempt to keep it from bursting into flames. Giuseppe rushed over and started heaping dirt with me on top of the kerosene that had been poured out on the ground. Aunt Aida and other Negroes did the same, while others made a rush to start scooping water out of the sea with whatever containers they could find in a desperate, doomed attempt to save their homes. Yard residents poured in from all directions to put out the blaze. We worked ourselves to exhaustion, but the fire kept on as strong as ever. Giuseppe took hold of my arm and started pulling me back, his hands stiff and hard, my body heavy as a corpse.

Aunt Aida went on fighting the soldiers, screaming at both them and a black interpreter who worked for the plague-extermination campaign. As they pushed her away, she told the interpreter to tell them that the woman who had pushed past them into the Yards was healthy, and hadn't been stricken with the plague.

"Tell them she's gone in to get her savings and that she'll be right back! Please, just give her a few more minutes—don't burn her alive!!"

But nobody paid any attention to her. They just started herding the exhausted people onto wagons like disease-infested livestock, threatening to shoot them if they refused to go into quarantine in Jalyana. We felt more desperate and hopeless than ever now. Letting out what sounded like a primal scream, Aida started beating her breast and tearing her clothes. The things happening around her were driving her mad. Even so, she had the presence of mind to look around for me, and when she found me she had a terrifying gleam in her eye. Grabbing me hard by my shoulder, she wrenched me out of the mental vacuum I was in and, grapping me away from Giuseppe, headed me back toward the Yards while everybody else was going in the opposite direction. I couldn't believe Aunt Sabriya had actually been trapped in the flames, and I was delirious too. My eyes darted back and forth in the thick smoke, hoping against hope for some miracle that would bring her back to me. All I could see anymore was a giant inferno that was devouring everything in sight, and I had a feeling her lungs, which were weak to begin with, would give out before the flames reached her.

In that moment, when it seemed that everything and everybody was burning up, I came to a realization that turned my life upside down. Aunt Aida was in as much shock as I was. Then suddenly she blurted out, "Cry for the woman who'll never come back. Cry for your mother. Cry for your mother!"

Giuseppe had run after us and was trying to rescue me from her grip.

"Sabriya is your mother, not your aunt!" she screamed. "She's your mother, not your aunt! And her real name is Tawida!"

Some soldiers beat her with the butts of their rifles, warning her to get away, since she was hindering their mission to exterminate the plague. Desperate now, Giuseppe pulled me away again and hid my face in his chest to keep me from seeing any more. So now I really was an orphan. I'd lost my foundation in life at the very moment when I'd discovered what and who it was. It wasn't until I lost my mother that I found out she'd been by my side all along. She'd hidden herself in order to hide me, to spare me harm and protect me from the evil that people might do to me. It was my own mother who had braved so many fires for my sake, the last of which she'd walked into in order to rescue my father's written acknowledgment that I was his daughter. The statement had been backed up by his jard—his traditional Libyan cloak, and a symbol of his honor and integrity. As I wept and wailed, Giuseppe held me in his arms, agonizing with me over my loss, in shock like me over what Aida had just said. He told the head of the medical mission that he was going to take me to the wagon he'd be riding in.

As I called out to my mother for the first time just as I was losing her, my misery was beyond description. The very thing I'd come to know I didn't really know at all, or at least I didn't understand it.

Was this the work of human beings or divine foreordainment?

Whatever it was, Giuseppe didn't leave my side. As we got into the wagon, he explained, "They're going to take us to a place where we all have to take baths and be disinfected, and they'll get rid of all our clothes and things."

At first he cried along with me, but then he got hold of himself. As he laid my head on his shoulder, I felt a crazy person leaving my body and running back to the Yards.

As if he could see what was happening, he shouted, "Don't look! Don't look!"

I was reliving the legacy of my mother's ancestors, who'd been enslaved by my ancestors on the other side. I shut my eyes tight so I wouldn't have to see others die, which would have killed me too.

That was the day I cried, "*Yamma*! Mama!" for the first time in my life. "Mama, don't leave me! Mama, come back! Mama, don't go!"

The last thing I saw of the Yards' tragedy was thick black smoke that obscured both earth and sky. The air was filled with the stench of humans and animals being roasted alive. The spirit of my mother, who hadn't been afflicted with the plague, was suffocating. Like the others who had been imprisoned by the flames, she'd been alive when the authorities poured kerosene over the huts and set them alight with everything and everyone in them. Like them, she'd been created from blackness, and to blackness she had returned.

As I clung in tears to the remains of the vision, I saw my mother floating into the sky. She stepped among the straw huts and tinplate shacks, heading for the sea to do laundry and scrub down floor mats. Then she disappeared, the way little girls would disappear with mysterious beings and never be seen again. That was the first and last time I uttered the word *Yamma*, but my mother—or "Aunt Sabriya," as she'd always had me call her as a way of protecting both of us—didn't hear it. There are no words to express the sorrow and regret I felt at that moment!

At the Josephite Mission Center, some nuns injected me with a tranquilizer. I think I slept for days from the shock of my loss. Every now and then I'd lift my head for a moment, then go straight back into my coma. That might have been the best thing for me, since it gave me a rest from the pain. When I'd open my eyes and see the white nuns in their spotless habits flitting about me, I knew I was breathing, but no more than that. They would smile kindly, hold my hand, and talk to me, as though the only reason for me to open my eyes was to receive those smiles. Then I'd drift back into my extended swoon.

I knew Giuseppe was with me. He made a point of checking on the people he'd known from the Yards, though most of them weren't alive anymore. He looked for Aunt Aida to find out more about the things she'd kept hidden from me. He told me that after people's grief had subsided, they were planning to go back to the Yards to pray over their dead and give their remains a proper Islamic burial. After that, he said, the Italian government was going to build them a new camp.

The Yards were gone, but they still lived inside us.

Giuseppe told them he'd go with them. He wanted to try to figure out where our tinplate shack had been so that he could bring me anything he found of it. Realizing what a useless question it was, he asked me hesitantly, "What would you like me to bring you from there?"

The Yards had been my life. It could never disappear. It could never burn up. So what could Giuseppe bring me from there that I didn't already have inside me?

When he saw me start to cry and wipe my tears, he hung his head. I was lying on a tidy bed in a room painted with white lime. Apart from the bed, the room contained nothing but a small table and a big cross that hung on the opposite wall. I saw the faces of three Italian nuns who were all talking with Giuseppe. I'd never seen a place like it before. I could hear them talking about me, but the only part of me that seemed to be present was my poor little body that had grown up in a Negro slum. I was young, and an orphan, and I'd lost everything, so my life was going to be especially difficult from here on out.

"Where will she go after she comes out of her coma?" I heard somebody ask.

That question, which I heard over and over as the nuns talked beside me, whether among themselves or with Giuseppe, kept echoing in my head, lurking in a distant corner of my spirit, or running like a hungry animal toward its prey whenever the pain of loss came over me again.

"Poor thing! No mother, no father, no family!"

It wasn't just the loss of my aunt, who'd actually been my mother, but the Yards and all it had meant to me: my childhood, my work, my aunts, my girlfriends, the sea, the giant sand sieve, love, song and dance, tears, the slave who used to tell us our fortunes and reveal what was approaching from afar, and the one-of-a-kind Bouga. After Bouga died and her body was examined by an Italian autopsy specialist who sold corpses to the Faculty of Medicine in Rome, he said, "This heart, my friend, which looks as though it belonged to a sheep, came out of a legendary human being!"

At first I thought Miftah had been spared the sight of what happened on that black day. And in fact, he hadn't seen it with his own eyes. But he wasn't spared the grief it brought in its wake. He would guess where our tinplate shack had been and go to that spot. He would sit there alone, glued to the ground, and cry, not wanting anybody to comfort him.

On the morning of his wedding day, Miftah disappeared. Figuring where I could probably find him, I got in the wagon with Giuseppe and we took off for the seaside. I glimpsed him in the distance, dressed in the traditional costume Libyan men wear on their wedding day. He was sitting with his head between his knees, and when we came up closer, I heard him telling my mother he was about to get married and that he'd miss her at his wedding. He told her he'd do everything he'd promised he would: that he'd name his first daughter after her, make the pilgrimage to Mecca on her behalf, and never abandon me.

As we came closer, I could hear him crying. When I came up and hugged him, he burst into sobs. With tears streaming down his face, he said, "I miss her, sister! I miss her!!"

I am the legacy of those who didn't look at their dead, who closed their eyes so that they wouldn't see death's cruelty, leaving them open just enough to let their tears escape.

I'm the plant that was watered by those tears.

The Burn

MUMBLING TO HIMSELF, he staggered past the enclosure where the servants and the livestock slept. Then Tawida heard him fall to the ground with a thud.

"It's Master Muhammad Junior," she said to the deaf woman sleeping across from her.

The woman, who lay curled up in her bed, muttered something unintelligible, then turned over on her other side and went back to sleep.

Even if she'd heard what Tawida said, she wouldn't have had the energy to care. She was exhausted, having spent all day in the kitchen preparing the winter provisions of *usban al-shams* and jerky.[1] She'd spent an eternity filling one clay jar after another, marking them to show which ones contained just jerky, which ones contains jerky mixed with lard, and which ones contained lard alone.

Wrapping herself in the other woman's scarf, Tawida went out to help the master inside. She was afraid that if she didn't, he might call for Jaballah or Aida, only to have them not come in spite of the racket he was making. They were the servants he always called on if he wanted something. Tawida took him by the hand and helped him

---

1. *Usban al-shams* is a Libyan dish made from sheep's stomach stuffed with salted, dried sheep's lung, heart, and muscle meat finely chopped and seasoned with salt, hot pepper, dried mint, caraway, and coriander. The stuffed tripe is held together with strings made from strips of the sheep's intestines, dried in the sun, and fried.

up, and he readily accepted her help. Then she moved him away from the eaves gutter, which was overflowing and dripping on everything below it.

Running his hand over the cap on his head, he grumbled, "What's wrong with the sky? Something must have poked a hole in it!"

"Yes, it must have, Master," she said agreeably.

"What did it?"

"I don't know, Master. But whatever it was, winter seems to have come early this year."

His wet body was right up next to hers as she lifted him, and as she placed her hands on his shoulders, he noticed her face.

"Who are you?" he asked suddenly.

"I'm your servant, Master," she said, flustered.

"Aida?"

"No, Master. I'm Tawida."

"Aah. So, Tawida, how long have you been here?"

"For a long time, Master."

"Why have I never seen you before, then?"

"I don't know, Master. I live in this house, and I see you all the time."

"Really?"

"I'm the one you poured the tureen of hot soup onto at Master Siddig's stag party."

"Oooh! Wasn't that Aida?"

"No, it was me, Master."

He slapped himself on the forehead with the palm of his hand as if the pot of soup had spilled right then and there.

"I am so sorry! Really, I am! Were you hurt?"

As he repeated his apology, Tawida escorted him to the door without a word, supporting him from behind.

"That was a long time ago, Master. Don't you worry about it. Come in now. You're getting cold."

"Tell me the truth. Don't be afraid. You can ask me for any compensation you want. You can even ask for your freedom."

"I don't want anything, Master."

"No. I'm not going in until you tell me what happened."

"My leg got burned. That's all."

"You mean, I burned you?"

"Don't be angry with me, Master. Please."

"You mean I burned you, and I caused you pain? Shame on you for not saying anything!"

"It wasn't you that burned me, Master," she corrected. "It was the soup."

"Show me your leg," he commanded.

"No, Master, I couldn't do that."

"So, then, you're lying to me! I wouldn't hurt a flea—ask anybody you like, and they'll tell you! Now I'm going to punish you for lying."

"I would never lie to you, Master," she insisted, terrified. "You didn't hurt me at all. So please don't hurt me now!"

"Show me your leg."

"No, Master."

"Why don't you want to show it to me?"

Hesitating, she said, "It's my upper leg, Master."

"Just lift your dress, then," he said, "and nobody will see but me."

She was still reluctant to uncover her thigh to reveal the burn. Nevertheless, she did as she'd been told, feeling all the while that her master held her in contempt, especially when he said, "I can't see anything. It's pitch dark."

She thought to herself: *That's just the way you'd expect a white master to treat a black slave woman who's been in his house forever without his even knowing she exists!* He reached out and ran his hand over the burn.

"Here?" he asked.

"Somewhere around there, Master."

"Here?"

"Yes, yes, there."

"Does it hurt, my little one?"

"No, not anymore."

"What's your name?"

"Tawida, Master."

He was sitting on the pallet where she normally slept. He could barely keep his eyes open enough to look at her. Then, looking nauseous, he shut his eyelids and went silent. She stood there speechless for a few moments, shocked to see her master, usually so powerful and dignified, in this state of imbalance. Like everyone else in the household, she'd carried an entirely different image of him in her mind: the image of the invincible sovereign who speaks little and whose command is never disobeyed. Under normal circumstances, nothing made him more furious than to have to repeat himself. That, by the way, was what had happened at the lunch banquet that had been hosted for his cousin Siddig's stag party, so he'd lost his temper and flung the soup tureen at her.

Muhammad Junior was answerable for all the family's affairs to his father, Master Imuhammad, who had delegated more powers to him than he had to any of his brothers, both older and younger. Unlike his brothers, Muhammad had nothing to do with the slaves, and wasn't inclined to sleep with the black slave women that filled their household as white masters generally did with "what their right hands possessed." His personal preference was for white prostitutes. But when he did go to them, he was circumspect about it. Never once had anyone seen him in a state of debauchery or indecency.

Knowing that Jaballah and Aida were together in the livestock pen, Tawida wasn't sure what to do. She was determined not to ruin the two lovers' happiness, even though she knew somebody might come looking for the master and find him in her room.

She crouched next to the door in her soggy dress. The situation was so novel and unprecedented, she hardly realized her clothes were sopping wet. She stared at him in the lamplight, incredulous that this was the same harsh, stern Master Muhammad that people told such frightful stories about. What would she say to him when he woke up and found himself in his servant's lowly bed? What would she say to Lalla Uwayshina the next day if she asked her where Jaballah and Aida had been?

When she realized that the master's burnoose was wet, she jumped up. Then she crept apprehensively over to the pallet where he lay, but hesitated at first to take it off him. At last, however, she bent over him and began removing it ever so slowly and deliberately. It was heavy, and it smelled of a fragrant local brew known as Nazli Durna.[2] Emboldened by the fact that he was too drowsy to realize what was happening, she took a good look at his face, studying it one bit at a time: broad eyelids closed over a pair of almond-colored beads; a lovely nose with just a hint of pugness; a raised moustache and a red beard with a soft sheen that lay down flat over his cheeks; thick, silky hair and a pearly white neck; long fingers covered with thick hair; and an engraved ring set with a small blue stone on his right ring finger.

She removed his shoes and set them aside to reveal a pair of clean, oval-shaped feet with long, slender toes. He was the first man she'd ever had the chance to see at such close range. And he was white, not black. She devoured him with her eyes, memorizing his appearance down to the last detail so that, if what had happened on this night never repeated itself, she could recall it later. Here was a man who was neither a slave nor an ordinary freeman. He was someone she would never have imagined herself having a conversation with. How much more unimaginable would it have been, then, for him to sleep in her bed after his body had leaned on hers as she lifted him up from under the eaves gutter? From now on, that eaves gutter would be one of her favorite things. She would even love the rain, and never again would she hang the sieve under the gutter to keep it from dripping into the atrium. After all, the rain was what had brought this most lovely of coincidences into her life—the loveliest coincidence, she felt certain, that any slave woman in all of Benghazi had ever experienced. So how would she tell Aida about it? What would she say?

Her heart started to pound again under the influence of a shock she hoped never to recover from. She was the black slave girl no man had ever wanted, whether slave or free. Unlike all the other slave girls and women she'd known, she'd never even been touched. Never yet

2. A locally made alcoholic beverage known for its refreshing fragrance.

had she experienced the thing she'd heard about and waited for so long. Nobody in the household or in the market had ever fondled her or flirted with her, so she'd concluded that she must be so ugly that no man would ever want to come near her. That special membrane she'd been born with was still intact. Aida, by contrast, had had relations with a number of men before Jaballah—some white, others black.

Then there was Ahbara, a thirteen-year-old the family's oldest son had slept with, and who had gotten pregnant in less than a week. Looking over at the deaf Negro woman asleep in the same room, Tawida thought out loud, "Even this woman, who's over forty, has a man who comes to be with her. All the servants know about him, too. And of all people, it's Master Muhammad's cousin Siddig, who got married not long ago!" Siddig was a young white man, but he had a thing for older Negro women. He was so wild over them, in fact, that he wasn't satisfied with the ones in his household, and would go after them wherever he could.

Tawida went quietly back to her spot next to the door, absorbing herself till daybreak in thoughts about the earthquake that had struck inside her. She didn't sleep. How could sleep have graced her eyes when her soul echoed with the realization that a man who held sway over countless people had lifted her dress and, with his creamy white hands, had touched the place that had been burned by that pot of soup? He'd touched the very place where he had wounded her!

In the early hours of the morning, the master woke to find himself in the servant woman's bed. He had no idea how he'd gotten there, and when he saw her slender silhouette huddled at the door as though she'd been waiting for him to wake up, he was stupefied. She came and knelt in front of him. Moments passed without him knowing what to say to her. He might have thought that when he got drunk the night before, he'd slept with her, which worried him.

"What happened last night?" he asked her at last.

"Nothing, Master," she reassured him. "You fell in the rain, and I brought you in."

He hung his head in silence.

"And where did you sleep?" he wanted to know.

"I didn't sleep."

"Why not?"

"I sat at the door all night."

"And why's that?"

"Because you were sleeping in my place."

He fell silent again, trying to think of something to say.

"Who are you?"

"Your servant."

"And what's your name?"

"Tawida, Master."

"How long have you been here?"

"I've been here for a long time, Master."

"So why haven't I seen you before?"

"I've been in this household for a long time, and I always see you."

"But I don't recognize you."

"I'm the one you poured the tureen of hot soup onto the day of Master Siddig's stag party."

"Whoa!" he exclaimed after a short pause. "Wasn't that Aida?"

"No, Master. It was me."

He got up off the pallet and she handed him his cap. Then she bent down to put his shoes back on him. He didn't speak. His usual surliness had been softened somewhat by this act of self-abnegating obedience on the part of a servant he had belittled by not recognizing her, and who had even been the victim of one of his angry outbursts. *What's happening?* he wondered to himself. He touched her hands as she handed him his burnoose.

"Your hands are freezing," he noted with concern. "Keep yourself warm!"

She didn't say a word. As he passed her on his way out, her heart sank at the realization that this night, in which she had enjoyed his presence near her, was over, and wouldn't be followed by another. As he headed back to the house, he could smell himself. He'd picked up the scent that was unique to slave women. He sniffed himself all over. The scent had clung to him so powerfully, it was as though he'd spent the night in her arms, not just in her bed, as though she hadn't spent the night huddling at the door, but bathing him in kisses.

In order to get rid of the odor, he would have to take a full bath. He filled the large bathtub, immersed himself, and closed his eyes, his features somber. Then he repeatedly scrubbed and sniffed himself to make sure the smell was gone. As he did so, he recalled all the things Siddig had told him about black women and the sweetness of having sex with them. He himself had never tried a single one, and no matter how much he thought about it, he didn't feel inclined to. On the contrary, he had doubts about his cousin's taste, and suspected that he was exaggerating his descriptions. When he came out of the bathroom, he felt like a new man, or like someone who's grown an extra organ of perception. He'd recovered his ability to feel certain things, although he still held them in contempt. He saw such urges as a kind of youthful vanity that caused some men to get carried away before coming to their senses again.

A few days after his encounter with the fragrance that had taken him over so unexpectedly, his common sense starting coming back into operation, and he spent more time thinking about that tureen of hot soup than he did about the details of the slave woman's face.

As he and Siddig stood measuring out barley and wheat, he turned to his cousin.

"Siddig?" he began.

"Yes?"

"What makes you go after older black women when you're married to one of your most beautiful cousins?"

Taken by surprise, Siddig put his measure down.

"And why do you ask about things that don't concern you? Haven't you always told me I've got rotten taste?"

Muhammad turned his head away before looking slowly back at Siddig.

"Come on now, cousin," he chided. "Forget about the joking we used to do. I'm asking you a question man-to-man."

"So, the lily white Muhammad has started asking about Negro women! What's the story?"

Siddig added with a chuckle, "What would you know about that warm feeling a man gets when he's in a black woman's arms? It gives you a high so sweet you wish you never had to let her go."

Muhammad pursed his lips and shook his head as if he didn't get the point of his cousin's hyperbole.

"So that's how it is!" he said flatly.

Sticking by his claim, Siddig affirmed, "Yeah, that's how it is, and more! Just ask Mahdi, Sharef, and Hamza. They believed me when I told them about it and gave it a try, and they've never regretted it. You're the only holdout. I don't know what you've got locked inside that head of yours. What are you waiting for?"

"Well, since you're an expert on these things, I'll tell you about something weird that happened to me a few days ago with one of the slave women. She's one of our most miserable slaves. But what happened really got to me."

"So, did you sleep with one of your own slave women, or somebody else's?"

"You know the only women I go for are short, petite, and white. But when I got drunk the other night, I found myself with a servant woman of ours that I'd never even noticed before. Who knows what back corner she'd been hiding in."

"Describe her to me. I'm a connoisseur of black beauty and I know things you don't."

"She's an ordinary-looking girl. In fact, she's in a hard way—kind of wretched."

Siddig rolled his eyes. "Wretched, you say? Ha! What you don't know is that that wretchedness can turn into a deadly boldness when the time is right. Believe me, cousin, you're the one who's wretched!"

His curiosity piqued by his cousin's story, Siddig concluded secretly that this was a new treasure he'd have to check out for himself at the earliest opportunity.

Meanwhile, Muhammad went on, "She pulled me out from under the eaves gutter, brought me inside, and had me sleep on her pallet. Then she kept vigil by the door all night in the cold."

"Did that surprise you?"

"Yes, especially after I found out that I'd hurt her at your wedding. I threw the soup tureen at her and burned her upper thighs. So why was she so good to me even though I'd maimed her like that?"

"That's how servants and slaves are. They're extremely good-hearted, patient, and devoted."

"She's been on my mind ever since that morning. Maybe I sensed how degraded and humiliated she felt. It's the first time I've ever thought about a black person this way. You know my only dealings with them are as master to slave."

"Go try her out," Siddig whispered to his cousin. "You'll be forever in my debt!"

Muhammad frowned haughtily. "I'm not like you," he retorted. "You brush up against them so much your skin's nearly turned black. Look! Your hair's even started to get kinky like theirs!"

"So then," Siddig said with a mischievous grin, "do I have your permission to take her from you?"

"Don't you dare, Siddig," Muhammad replied ominously. "When it comes to things like this, I'm dead serious."

Hearing his cousin's sudden change of tone, Siddig said, "Hey, what's with you? You trash something, then you begrudge it to me!"

Muhammad furrowed his brow slightly. Then he got a strange gleam in his eye as he made up his mind to act with a rashness he would never have expected of himself.

"Don't you dare, Siddig," he repeated. "When it comes to things like this, I'm dead serious."

Enraged by Siddig's request, Muhammad had said what he did in the full certainty that the girl he had encountered that night—who, for all he knew, was married to one of their slaves—would never give herself to anyone as a joke or an "experiment."

As the two men finished measuring out the grain, they discussed the merchandise and how to transport it to the storehouses. On his way home, Muhammad passed by the spice merchant's shop. For the first time in his life, he stopped to observe the female slaves in the market as they bought and sold herbs and spices. He watched them turn them over in their hands and test them with their noses and mouths, and listened as they babbled away in a language that only slaves understood. The market was teaming with blacks shopping, selling, working, and begging. He paid close attention to the women, as though he were out to discover what it was that gave them their secret allure. The scent of the black girl whose pallet he'd spent the night on, which had clung to his spirit even though he hadn't slept with her, came wafting over to him again. Reminiscent of the scent of the spice merchants' shops in the Jarid Market, it brought to mind what Siddig had said about the sweetness of slave women and the keys to ecstasy God had given them. With this thought he felt upset again, as he suspected that his cousin would try to get to the slave girl with the burned thighs. He felt like an idiot for having told Siddig about her, since now the word was out.

By the time he got to the end of the street, Muhammad's paranoid ruminations about Siddig had reached a fever's pitch, since he was sure to spare no effort to get to her. Siddig might even ask the elder Imuhammad to send her over to do some chores at his house so that he could be alone with her. And who would bat an eyelid at something that happened all the time? As Siddig's image impressed itself on his mind, he turned back in the direction of the spice merchant's shop. When he got to the door, he hesitated, but then he firmed his resolve to go in.

As he walked into the shop, Muhammad greeted the shopkeeper. Then, as the shopkeeper was asking about Muhammad's father and his cousins, he surprised him by requesting perfumes that women used as aphrodisiacs for their men, something to prolong an erection, and something that would make a man more lovable to a woman. After making his purchase, he hid it in his pocket and proceeded hurriedly to his destination.

Good Evening,
Good Morning

IT WAS LUNCHTIME in Master Imuhammad's household, and the slaves had set two tables side by side, one for the women and one for the men. Two slave girls were serving the food, busily going back and forth attending to the people having their meal.

Noticing his interest in one of the two girls, Muhammad's mother gestured to her husband with a wink to look over at his son. He wasn't taking part in the conversation, as if his only concern was the girl in question. He would stare at her when she wasn't looking, but avert his gaze if she looked his way. Similarly, he would lower his gaze as she passed, then pursue her with his eyes as she walked away.

Then, as everyone was eating and the two servant girls were standing nearby ready to receive orders, he spilled some soup on his farmala and jumped to his feet. Tawida ran up to him with a napkin, preparing to treat the spot. As he took it off and handed it to her, she saw him direct his eyes meaningfully to a certain part of the garment. She rushed to the kitchen with the farmala and her speculations and filled a tub with water to remove the spots. When Aida brought Tawida the salt, she leaned over and, with an impish grin, whispered, "Smell it first."

As she brought the garment gingerly to her nose, she remembered the fragrance she'd taken in throughout the long night he'd spent in her room. She remembered how enraptured she'd been by the scent, which she'd never smelled on a man before. So, then, her suspicions had been correct: the master who had once poured hot soup on her in a fit of rage now wanted her in a state of tranquility. The master who had touched her in a state of drunkenness wanted her now in a state of full awareness, to enjoy her and be enjoyed.

As she was about to immerse the farmala in the water, she felt something in its pocket. She took it out and what should she find but a small bundle containing a chunk of musk, some frankincense, a *miswak*, and a piece of hard candy as well as one other thing that she didn't recognize.

Realizing instinctively what was to come, she hurriedly concealed it in her bosom, then tied the neck opening to her dress securely closed. She was so excited she nearly floated off the ground.

What's happening, Oh merciful God? Could a man that handsome really want a simple servant girl like her?

After lunch he wanted to go to the kitchen, where the servants spent most of their day. He had no reason or excuse to do so, though, since the servants were having their own lunch now. So he retreated and lay down on a rug under the grape trellis. He placed his hand on his forehead and closed his eyes. As he and the other masters of the household took their afternoon naps, the servants went about their business in hushed tones. Sensing what he was feeling, Tawida began gathering up some carpets and rearranging them near where he lay. When he heard someone stirring close by, he lifted his arm off his face and, finding that it was she, took her hand briefly without a word before letting her go her way.

That evening she sat in her room with a couple of friends in a state of hopeful anticipation. One of them said he wouldn't come, while the other one said he might. As for her, she was listening to the voice of her heart and clinging to what stirred there. As she'd said to Aida, "I bet he'll come!"

Then what should she hear but the sound of soft, leisurely foot-steps. Her heart started to race. It was him. He *had* come. There was a knock on the door. Having prepared herself enthusiastically for this eventuality, she opened the door and came out wearing something notably different than what she wore during the day. She'd uncovered her hair, lined her eyes with kohl, perfumed herself with the musk, and cleaned her gums and teeth with the miswak he had given her. And in her bosom she carried the other thing that she hadn't recognized.

"Good evening," he said to her.

"Good evening," she replied.

They stood there for a while in silence. Then he took her gently by the hand, and she followed, her heart and her body open to whatever the evening would bring.

Neither of them could find anything to say to the other. Instead they shared a silence that breathed back and forth between them. They began by discovering each other's worlds, which were so strange and different, with their eyes. Then their hands reached out to discover more and more until, when morning came, her head was pillowed on one of his hands, while with the other, he held her hand on his chest. Not a word was spoken until he said, "Good morning."

"Good morning, Master," she replied.

Gazing at her tranquilly he said, "You smell good."

She smiled bashfully.

"Did you like the gift?" he asked, stroking her neck.

"Yes, Master," she replied, nodding. "God keep you."

"And do you like me?"

Without a word, she squeezed the hand that held hers.

"Do you know how to apply henna?" he asked suddenly.

"Yes, I do!" came the enthusiastic reply.

"So, then," he said, "I'll bring you a bagful. But don't tell anybody about what's happened."

He got dressed and left her wrapped in the blanket with his fragrance, with joy, and with the memory of things she could hardly believe had happened.

Then she went about her day thinking about the henna and what would follow it.

The Homecoming

IN KEEPING with his parents' desire to forge marital ties within the family, which had lived on the same street for generations on end, Muhammad's brother Amin was soon to wed a relative's daughter. The occasion would also include circumcision ceremonies for Sadeg's and Isma'il's little boys, and everyone on the block was busy getting ready for the upcoming festivities. Muhammad's caravan was bringing a number of elder uncles from Misrata, and the travelers were expected to arrive a few days before the wedding. It had been agreed to postpone the celebration until after Muhammad had returned safely from a commercial voyage. It had been an arduous, months-long journey, and there were times when there had been no news of him at all. During his absence there had been a new outbreak of the plague in and around Fezzan, which had worried his parents and other relatives, and left Tawida's heart crushed and sick with longing. Everyone, young and old, was increasingly anxious to have him home again. His absence was mourned openly by his mother, and in secret by Tawida, who by this time was passionately in love with him and thought about him her every waking minute. She often confided in Aida about him, venting her longings, desires, and worries.

Once she told her, "I've stopped feeling like a slave woman who's just giving pleasure to her master without getting anything in return. I receive pleasure from him too and, as far as I'm concerned, we're equals. We're one. In love, he's even more my slave than an ordinary slave would be. When he's with me, Muhammad is a different man than the one people see on the outside. He's not my master. He's my sweetheart."

Muhammad was in love with Tawida too. In her he had found what he would never have expected to find in a slave woman. With every passing encounter she excited his passions more. She made love to his very heart, where she'd come to embody womanhood itself. Not surprisingly, his fondness for her had aroused envy and rage in various quarters. However, his parents figured that whatever had developed between their son and a slave woman was nothing but a passing fancy, and that as familiarity and boredom set in, its flame would gradually die out. As for his wife, her fears had turned to resentment and complaints. After all, who was a lowly, wretched slave woman to compete with her for her husband's affections? Her fears were being fueled and intensified by her husband's sister Halima, who lived in Derna.

In short, Muhammad and Tawida had become everybody's business, and nary was there a gathering in which they weren't the topic of conversation.

When at last the traveling party arrived from distant Misrata, trills of joy filled the air, slaves sprinkled the entryway with rosewater, and sweets were passed around. Muhammad's nephew Ali was ecstatic to see his uncle, his father, and the friends who had traveled with them. Embracing his uncle joyfully, he started chattering nonstop.

"The Shatwan clan isn't worth a lick without you!" he said breathlessly.

"Be quiet, boy," Muhammad replied with a grin. "People are going to get so jealous our uncles will cart us back to Misrata!"

With Aida by her side, Tawida stood watching the scene from a distance while his mother, his wife, his sisters, and his daughters crowded around the door to meet him.

"I can't believe I'm actually seeing him again. He was gone so long, and not having any news about him made it seem all the longer and more excruciating."

"So," Aida bantered gently, "if I pinch you, will you believe it?"

The two slave women, who had left the kitchen to watch Master Muhammad being received by the women of the family, were being watched themselves. While everyone else was busy with the reception, certain individuals had their eyes on Tawida. She followed Aida's advice and kept her feelings under control when she saw the long-lost beloved whose seed was growing inside her with every passing day.

As she watched him from her remote observatory, Tawida was moved as deeply as she had been the first time they confessed their love for each other. She thought back on their last encounter, the night before he left. He'd been bowled over by her forwardness. Yet it was a forwardness he loved. In fact, it was something he'd long dreamed of. In his surprise and delight, he'd wondered to himself how he could have been so oblivious to the love that waited so near him for all that time, and how he could have failed to see that his real life lay hidden on the far, neglected side of his household!

He didn't see Tawida among the women clustered around him. However, as he told her later, he'd begun watching for a chance to see her as the crowd began to thin. As he sat among his sisters, his mother, his maternal aunts, the wives of his paternal uncles, and all his other female relatives, his sister Fatima said, "The servants have requested permission to greet you and welcome you home."

"Have them come in," he said. A long line of slaves then filed into the room. But it didn't include Tawida, who had slipped back into the kitchen alone, fighting back the tears. When she heard footsteps approaching the kitchen, she busied herself with the pots and pans. Aida had come to report the latest news to her the way Ahbara reported the latest kitchen news to her mistress, Lalla Uwayshina.

"We were the last ones to welcome him home," Aida told her. "The women were shocked out of their minds when he asked Fatima where you were!"

Tawida's heart practically fell into the soup pot. But she revived again when, to her amazement, the master came into the kitchen to say hello to her. He was thin, his beard had grown out, and his eyes were full of longing. Tawida didn't utter a word. She froze in place, her eyes brimming with all the love she had reserved for him alone, and with the yearning borne of separation. Ahbara stood at the door watching them, preparing to relay what she'd seen to her mistress.

Fed up with the girl's obnoxious skulking, Aida tried to get rid of her.

"You get out of here!" she barked. "What do you think you're doing, hovering around us like a damned fly?"

When, that evening, Lalla Uwayshina learned from her spies that Muhammad had been asking about Tawida, she issued instructions to keep Tawida working late into the night. However, her plan was foiled when her son sent Aida to her with the words, "Master Muhammad has sent asking for Tawida. What shall I tell him?"

Hearing what Aida had whispered in her mother's ear, Fatima suggested, also in a whisper, that it would be wise not to make problems in front of the guests, who had come from near and far to congratulate them on her son's safe return and to attend another son's wedding. After all, she added, they wouldn't want to give busybodies a reason to gossip.

Lalla Uwayshina sat in silence for some time, pondering her daughter's advice. At last she nodded her agreement.

The minute she'd been given the word, Aida rushed to get her friend out of the kitchen, telling her to go take a bath right away because the master had called for her and was waiting for her in his cousin Siddig's men's reception area. Tawida was ecstatic. No one made any objection to the arrangement, since Muhammad had just come back that same day.

In the wee hours of the morning, Muhammad's mother said to his father, "He sent for the slave woman that's robbed him of his senses and driven him to neglect his wife. It's a total disaster! I swear by the soil over my father's grave, she's bewitched him. Only a piece of trash would do this to him! And how can he be so reckless? That boy's going to give me a heart attack one of these days!"

The father didn't like what was going on any more than his wife did, but he was so overjoyed to have his son back again, he hesitated to say very much. After urging his wife to calm down and leave their son to his own affairs, he added, "Let him be this one night. Then I'll take care of it myself."

Undeterred, the wife went on, "Without a second thought he replaces his beautiful wife with a black woman descended from his grandfather's slaves. Isn't he even embarrassed by the fact that she's pregnant? I swear, she's put a hoax on him to drive him mad and rob him of his money. And it's working!"

"Your son isn't some little boy that could be duped by a slave woman. He's just taken her as a concubine, that's all. After a while he'll get bored with her and brush her aside."

"I'm curious to know what he finds in her that he couldn't find in some other woman. I mean, why is he so attached to her?"

"Let's leave off thinking about him tonight," the husband urged. "We've got more important things to attend to now."

"Well, alright," the wife conceded grudgingly. "But only for tonight," she added, raising her freshly hennaed index finger in her husband's face.

"Only for tonight," he repeated after her, sensing a plot in the air.

Rose Petals

THE TWO FRIENDS rested on their pallet in Aida's shack in the wee
hours of the morning, rain tapping gently on the tinplate roof, while
the small stove sent out gentle waves of heat along with the sweet fragrance of a handful of incense that Aida had fed it before going to bed.

Tawida told Aida about a magical, romance-filled night in which
her master had charmed her in every imaginable way. The tryst had
taken place in his cousin's Siddig's nearby residence to the sound of
music and drumbeats coming from a wedding celebration in a neigh-
boring house. The music was supplied by Mariana, a well-known
singer in those days. Muhammad had prepared for their encounter
by making sure none of the house's residents were home when he
summoned her. Jaballah escorted her there and let her in through the
servants' back entrance, and when she entered she found him eagerly
awaiting her. At the sight of her he grinned from ear to ear, revealing
the gap between his two front teeth. On her way in he wrapped her in
a welcoming embrace, saying, "Hi, good-looking!"

For the first hour he did nothing but kiss her and take in her scent
as Mariana's voice wafted through the room with a beauty that enraptured the stag partygoers. It was as though she were singing to all the
lovers in the world. Whenever she came to the refrain "oh, my aching
heart!" Muhammad would laugh and say, "Listen to the way a black
singer can tug at the heartstrings of a group of straitlaced white men!
And you can see for yourself how a black enchantress has stolen her
lovesick white master's heart!"

He had brought her gifts, including a red satin dress.

"Come over here so that I can put it on you," he said.

They both laughed when she said, "Do you want to dress me, or touch me? Just remember that you might have trouble getting it on me, since there's a little pooch in my tummy!"

"Ahh!" he said, delighted by the news he'd just received. "So, then, this is a perfect night for drinking, dancing, singing, and love-making till the sun comes up. Now wrap this sash around your hips and dance for me!"

"I can't."

"He folded his arms around her, then went down on his knees, asking, "How old is it?"

"It happened the night before you traveled. Do you want it, or shall I abort it?"

"Nobody's going to abort *my* seed!" he replied quickly. "Don't you dare do anything without my permission."

"In that case, promise me you'll give the child your name and that you'll never sell him or let anybody in the family buy him or take him away from me."

"Don't worry. He's my son! When he comes I'll carry him to the mosque in my arms so that the whole world will know he belongs to me and to my lady, whose wish is my command!"

As he said this, he knelt down and kissed her navel, and love's wine swept them away from everything once more.

Taken by her friend's confessions, Aida asked, "Would a master kneel before his slave unless he really loved her?"

"He told me he wanted me to come to the shop this morning," Tawida continued. "He said he wouldn't be coming home for lunch and that I had to be the one to bring him his food. When I got there, he closed up the shop, took me by the hand, and led me back to the storeroom. He'd covered the floor with rose petals, and when I asked him, 'What is this, Master?' he told me they were part of their merchandise. He said they sell them to women who use them for decoration and perfuming, and that he was going to have me roll around in them to give them some of my blackness before they were touched by any of the women of Cyrenaica. After I did that, he made love to me with the rose petals all around us. He went wild over me, and I went wild over him. Oh God, I love him so much! I'm sure the only reason God made my heart was for me to give it to him!"

After a pause, Tawida leaned back against the hut wall with a sigh.

"What's wrong?" Aida asked.

"I'm afraid of Mistress Lalla Uwayshina and Master Imuhammad. I have a feeling they know about my relationship with their son, and that they're plotting a way to separate us."

"Love is a wonderful thing, Tawida. Live it for all it's worth and don't waste time being afraid. Nothing can happen to us unless God's destined it to."

Then she began to sing:

> You've known so much pride and joy, oh my soul,
> so very much have you known.
> The beloved you pined for
> at last is yours alone!

Finishing the stanza, Tawida joined in with the words:

> The love between you and the radiant one
> Has the power to console.
> Pride and joy are yours now—
> Yours alone, oh my soul!

Then the two friends went on singing back and forth until they drifted off to sleep.

Water from Heaven

WOMEN PREPARED for bath day the way they would for a rec-
reational outing. It was a special day that brought together friends,
relatives close and distant, and women who never saw each other anywhere else. The bathhouse was a place women liked to go not just
to bathe, but to relax and socialize. Servants also looked forward to
going there, since, after tending their mistresses, they got their turn
to bathe as well. The hours would fly by, and everyone would come
home spic and span until the next time around.

A few days beforehand, the servant women would prepare the
clothes, perfumes, and soap for the occasion, and the slave that served
as the coachman would get ready to take them to the bathhouse and
bring them back by coordinating his comings and goings between the
market and the men's businesses with the women's requirements for
the day.

As preparations were being made for bath day, Lalla Uwayshina
spoke with her daughter Fatima about the changes evident in Tawida.
She was visibly pregnant by now, although she was trying to hide
it, since the father of the child belonged to the slave-owning family.
She'd been seen vomiting next to the bread oven. Hoping to dissuade
her mother from what she intended to do, Fatima said, "Even if what
you say about Muhammad being the child's father is true, please leave
her be!"

"No!" her mother retorted angrily. "I won't stand for such a thing.
The child's mother is a slave woman who was born into slavery, and

Muhammad has a wife who's pretty as a picture. Just as she's borne him daughters, she can bear him sons."

"I beg you, Mother, by Grandpa and Grandma's graves, don't give her the potion! We're dying to have a male to carry on the family name. Who knows? She might be pregnant with a boy. So leave her alone."

"No black slave woman's son will ever carry this family's name! That's something we'll never allow. Let him make love to her all he wants. That kind of thing is bound to happen. But have children by her? Over my dead body!"

That night, Lalla Uwayshina prepared the mixture of herbs that her friend Manani had brought. Once it was finished, the two of them would divide the potion between themselves, since Manani also had a couple of slave women she wanted to abort. One of them was a concubine of her husband's; the other, her son's. As a group of women sat in the courtyard talking, Fatima sat in silence. Lalla Uwayshina called Tawida, gave her a cup of the mixture, and told her to drink it. She'd been laundering clothes, and was tired from leaning over the washtub. After drinking a little of it, she stopped, revolted by the taste.

"It's bitter, Auntie," she said. "And it burns my tongue."

"Keep drinking, keep drinking," Lalla Uwayshina insisted. "It won't hurt you. In fact, it will make you strong and lively, even in bed, and it'll make your sweat smell nice."

To keep Tawida from suspecting her mistress's intention, the other women sitting there emptied their own glasses. However, theirs contained nothing but plain water. Lalla Uwayshina winked at Manani and Saada, their cackles filling the courtyard. Tawida closed her eyes and downed as much of the vile liquid as she could. Leaving the dregs, she wiped her mouth with her sleeve, a look of disgust on her face.

"That's enough, Auntie," she said. "I can't drink any more."

"Fine, go finish the laundry now. Then come have supper with the girls. Hajja Manani's cooked something for you all as a charitable gift on behalf of her deceased relatives, and all of it has to be eaten or the dead won't receive the merit it brings."

Unsuspecting, Tawida bent down and kissed the old woman's hand, saying, "May God accept your gift, have mercy on your loved ones, and cause you to meet them in Paradise."

At Manani's house, her two servants were given the pure "water from Heaven"—a potent, cathartic mixture of expensive herbs—to drink in the same way as Lalla Uwayshina's had. Then they were given the rest of the potion in the form of food.

She told them, "Lalla Uwayshina has cooked something for you as a charitable gift on behalf of her deceased relatives, and all of it has to be eaten or the dead won't receive the merit it brings. When you see her tomorrow, don't embarrass me by forgetting to thank her. I wouldn't want it to be said that the girls that live in Manani's house don't know their manners!"

The two servant women replied dutifully, "May God accept her gift, have mercy on her loved ones, and cause her to meet them in Paradise."

That evening Tawida got up from the washtub, sweating profusely. Instead of subsiding, however, the sweating got even worse, and she had a hard time going to sleep. Was it the hot weather or was it just her? She tossed and turned, at the same time feeling strangely limp all over.

"Go to sleep," her friend said to her, "and stop thrashing around like that."

"I can't," Tawida replied. "I feel as though my whole body's gone limp."

"Oh, really? Is that so, or do you just miss him? Be honest!"

"I don't know," Tawida replied after a pause. "Maybe it's both."

"Go to sleep, go to sleep. Tomorrow's bath day and it will be really nice. We'll see the girls and chat and laugh and get out of our misery for a while."

"Yeah, you're right. It will be a special day."

Aida Belongs to Jaballah, and Tawida Belongs to Salem

JABALLAH HAD BEEN on the lookout for a moment when his master was especially pleased with him, such as when he was carrying him home on his back from one of his wild nights out. On one such occasion, he hinted at his wish to marry his fellow slave Aida.

"So," the master wanted to know, "do slaves get married?"

Craning his thick neck to look back at his master, the slave replied, "Yes, they do, Master."

"You mean they really get married?"

"Yes, yes, they really do, Master."

"So they have feelings the way we do?"

When Jaballah made no reply, the master gave him a gentle slap on the face. "Answer me, you good-for-nothing slave!" he snapped impatiently.

"God forbid, Master," Jaballah replied at last.

At this, the master gave a guffaw so loud that he nearly fell off Jaballah's back. Holding the master's cane and hat in his hand, Jaballah slipped the drunk man's shoes into the pocket of his farmala.

"Ha!" the master continued. "Do you think I don't know what tricks you're up to?!"

"Pardon me, Master—what tricks?"

"So are you saying you like slave women, too?"

"We're home, Master," Jaballah said, evading the question. "I'll have to set you down while I get the key to the courtyard gate."

"Aha! So you're learning how to think, are you? You're the slave that's dearest to my heart. Did you know that?"

"Yes, I do, Master—may God grant you a long life. That's a blessing to me."

"You're a kindhearted, gallant man. I'm nothing like you."

To avoid being seen, the slave let his master in through the back entrance, which wasn't visible from the street where the market was located.

"Don't you dare let Auntie know I was at Fatima Turilli's house."

"Of course not, Master. When have you ever heard me say anything to her or anybody else?"

The slave women were awake when the master arrived home. When they heard Jaballah bringing him in, they helped him bring the master's pallet and lay him on it. Then they carried him with Jaballah to his bedroom. Jaballah was always the one who put the master to bed when he was drunk. After telling Jaballah to lock the door behind him, Lalla Uwayshina grilled him about where his master had been.

"Just like always, Auntie, he was with friends at Hajj Mousa's house," Jaballah replied, his head bowed.

"Were there any singers there?" she asked, turning slightly and fixing her eyes on Jaballah.

"Oh, no, ma'am. I didn't see any at all."

"Tell me the truth now, Jaballah."

"I am telling you the truth, Auntie. I saw Abdul Jalil, Sharef, Saheli, Hajj Mousa, and Sayyala, and they were talking and joking."

"Do they drink?"

"Well, Sharef does, but Hajj Mousa doesn't."

"All right, you can go now."

Jaballah had expected his mistress to ask him which wagon they'd ridden in so that she could guess where they had come from. When she didn't, he lumbered hurriedly away, locking the doors behind him before she could think of some other question to ask him and call him back. When he passed the women's quarters, he called to Aida in a whisper. She'd been waiting for him. She had changed her clothes, perfumed herself, and taken the kerchief out of her hair. Jaballah loved to see Aida this way: with her nappy hair wild and free, and her ebony skin exposed to his touch. He loved to take in her scent and listen to her furtive whispers.

He told her he had spoken to his master about her because he couldn't bear to live without her anymore. With a glint in his eye and his heart racing, Jaballah reached out and touched Aida, and when she didn't push him away, he invited her to the livestock pen. She accepted, and they were there till daybreak.

As his wife was helping him put on his farmala the next morning, Master Imuhammad remarked, "If I'm not mistaken, Jaballah talked to me about Aida recently!"

"Aida?" she asked, surprised. "When? And what does he want from her?"

"When, you ask? Yesterday! As for what he wants from her, let me think . . ."

"Yesterday!" his wife exclaimed.

His wife suspected that her husband had been so drunk the night before that he only imagined hearing the question he'd just reported. Angered by his wife's suspicions, which might lead to an interrogation about where he had been, and with whom, he suddenly changed his tone.

"Well," he retorted with a note of finality, "even if I did just imagine it, Jaballah's going to marry Aida. And that's that!"

Then he left the room shouting at the top of his lungs, "Aida! Aida! Aida!"

Abandoning the dough she'd been preparing, Aida came running, alarmed by the urgency in her master's voice. Lalla Uwayshina stood next to her husband under the grape trellis, not knowing what he was going to do.

"Yes, master," Aida said breathlessly.

"What day is today?" the master asked, his cane under his arm.

"It's Thursday, Master."

"All right, then. Next Thursday I'm going to marry you to Jaballah. So prepare yourself. I'll inform him as well."

That said, he looked over at his wife, tapping the end of his cane as if to tell her before he left that Master Imuhammad's wish was reality's command!

Taking advantage of the situation, Lalla Uwayshina rushed to add, "That's right! You'll belong to Jaballah and Tawida will belong to Salem. Let's celebrate both weddings at the same time!"

Perhaps what moved Master Imuhammad to insist on marrying Aida and Jaballah over his wife's objections was his desire to ensure a steady supply of new slaves for the family through the children that would be produced by their union. This, at least, was how Aida explained why the master had consented so readily to Jaballah's request. What he didn't know was that these two servants had already exchanged more than a few furtive glances and conversations, and had even professed their passionate devotion to each other.

After filching some peanuts from Master Imuhammad during one of his nights out carousing, Jaballah hid them for Aida in his farmala pocket. As for her, she set aside some of the asida she had made for her mistress and her friends for the celebration of the Prophet's birthday. Then she placed it on a tray and hid it for him in the manger so that none of the other slave women would see it and snitch on her.

The asida was warm and smothered in date syrup and homemade ghee, its delicious aroma announcing its presence in the stable the moment he walked in. Aida looked around cautiously as she handed Jaballah the tray. Her eyelids heavy with arousal, it was clear that she had thought about him as she prepared it, and that she had been anxious to give it to him. Delighted by her gesture, he dipped her rough black fingers into the dish and licked them. Then he licked them some more, and some more, and some more. From that day onward, their physical affection needed no occasion but love alone. Aida went back to the kitchen trembling, wiping the smell of the ghee and the date syrup off her hands with the hem of her dress. She wanted to get rid of the smell of the food, but not of the effects of the licking, which lingered in her body and her memory. When she saw Tawida, she told her she was ready to give Jaballah her heart. Tawida hugged her, rejoicing in the love that had found its way to them even in their stifling prison of an existence.

When Aida heard Master Imuhammad's announcement, she was bowled over by the surprise. Just the day before, the foundations of a new closeness to Jaballah had been laid after they'd been apart for some time, and now the door was being opened for her to enter this new life without fear. After Master Imuhammad left the house—luckily without being interrogated—Aida stood in a daze until Lalla Uwayshina jolted her out of her trance.

"Hey, girl," she said. "What's happened to you?"

Aida wiped her hands on her dress in disbelief, still without saying a word. Then she bowed her head before her mistress, who didn't really care about the answer to her question. Lalla Uwayshina saw the wisdom in her husband's decision to have the two slaves wed, since they stood to gain a generous supply of slaves this way. Marriages of this sort would save his family the expense of buying and training new slaves when the parent slaves grew old and weak.

Aida didn't let on to Lalla Uwayshina why she was agreeing to the marriage, and Lalla Uwayshina likewise concealed what was going through her mind. However, she did ask Aida duplicitously, "Do you like Jaballah, or would you rather have Salem instead?"

Caught off guard by the question, Aida replied, "That's up to my master. This is what he thought best, and we mustn't go against his wishes."

With a bawdy laugh, the mistress winked at her and said, "Come on, now. I know you like him. In fact, it's obvious that you've tried him out! Now get out of here, you naughty girl!"

Again Aida bowed her head before her mistress, who issued instructions for a small party to be arranged. Food would be served to the poor and they'd try out a new darabukka player. It would also be a bloodless way of getting rid of Tawida.

Lalla Uwayshina was a big fan of marskawi music performed by black women with their throaty, melodious voices, and she would invent excuses to bring them to her house.

Thursday came all too slowly for Aida and Jaballah, the secret lovers longing to be united. But come it did, with a celebration complete with masterful marskawi performances:

> Servant girl, I'm sending you out
> To bring news of my love long gone.
> With your eyes so black and your earrings so round.
> I send you with this sad song:
>
> My heart is heavy when you're not here,
> I'm too weak to bear my own weight.
> Longing burns hot in my breast
> As your tidings I anxiously await.
>
> Neighbor girl, I'm sending you forth,
> With my heart sore aflame.
> Such pain do I suffer from his absence
> that I hardly remember my name!
>
> Like a thunderbolt the news of his leaving
> descended upon my soul.
> The blaze in my heart will never be quenched
> till his presence makes me whole.
>
> They say he's sick and tired,
> so my heart knows no rest.
> Servant girl, I'm sending you out
> To bring me news of the best!

Hidden Destinies

"GO GET SALEM FOR ME," Muhammad instructed Jaballah.

Resting his elbow on the sales counter, Ali said, "Listen, Uncle, don't pressure him, since then he might turn against us. After all, he's her rightful husband."

"Don't worry. I know how to deal with him."

"I'm afraid . . ."

"Shush," Muhammad broke in, waving a small cleaver in his left hand. "You'll see."

Shortly thereafter, Salem arrived and Jaballah left. Muhammad set a chair in the shop entrance to indicate that it was closed. Then he brought another chair, turned it around, and sat down facing Salem. His brow furrowed, he spoke to the slave without looking his way.

"So," Muhammad began tensely, "I hear you're getting married this Thursday."

"Yes," the slave replied, oblivious as to why the master had called for him. "That's what Master Imuhammad wants."

"And you—what do you want?"

The slave made no reply.

Muhammad repeated the question.

"Tell me, and don't be afraid of anything."

"There isn't anything I want."

"And your master's orders?"

"There's no questioning them."

"How about my orders?"

"There's no questioning them, either."

"Good. So, then, put your hand on the table."

"Which hand, Master?"

"The one you need the most."

At first the slave just gave him a sharp look and didn't move. Then he placed his left hand on the table without batting an eyelid. Ali's eyes darted suspiciously back and forth between his uncle and the slave.

The uncle said ominously, "If you lay a hand on Tawida, I'll cut them both off."

Then, with lightning speed, he brought the cleaver out from under the table and drew it across the slave's hand, leaving a slight gash. The slave looked fearfully at his blood on the cleaver, not comprehending his master's threat. He was still for a moment, leaving his hand where it was.

At last he said, "Yes, sir."

"And don't you dare speak to anyone about what happened here today. If you do, you'll have no one but yourself to blame."

"Understood, sir," the slave replied with certainty.

"You can go now."

Ali turned and pulled the chair away from the shop entrance so that the slave could leave. As he made his exit, he pressed on the wound with his other hand. As Ali lazily straddled the doorway with his arms raised high, he and his uncle exchanged a look of mischievous satisfaction. They laughed out loud at this sly preventive measure.

Then, succumbing to a sudden urge to be contrary, Ali said flippantly, "What you did might work. But who knows? Maybe he'll find Tawida so irresistible that he'll decide to try his luck!"

Incensed, Muhammad grabbed the boy by the collar.

"Ali," he growled menacingly, "don't make me lose my temper. Otherwise I might go after him and slit his throat. That way I'll be rid of both him and your speculations!"

"Since you can't face the people higher up, you pressure people who are under you. Just be careful not to wrong an innocent man."

Shaken, Muhammad let go of the boy, but made no reply. Then he picked up a small bag that he had prepared ahead of time and left the shop, trampling with his white shoes on the viscous drops of blood that had dripped from the slave's hand as he made his exit.

The master had left in a rage, but the servant had left content. Some measures serve not their intended purpose, but hidden destinies!

He Sneezes and Coughs!

THE FAMILY had married Aida to Jaballah and Tawida to Salem, giving each couple a tinplate shack of their own in the annex that served as a livestock enclosure. Most slaves were happy to have achieved such a standard of living under their masters' protection and were relieved to experience this degree of stability in their lives. They would settle down together and have lots of children. And if they left their tinplate shack, they would only leave it for some more spacious shack, or for the afterlife, which was the most spacious of all, of course.

Lalla Uwayshina was delighted to have rid herself of Tawida and gotten her out of her niece's—and daughter-in-law's—way. With this arrangement in place, it would be easier to fulfill the long-awaited dream of the male heir. Now they awaited her son's return to his nest, and the arrival of a grandson.

One night, as Lalla Uwayshina and her husband were alone in their bedroom, she remarked, "Muhammad hasn't said a word about that slave woman's getting married. He wouldn't talk about it even when Fatima brought it up in front of him."

"May God guide him aright. Hasn't Rugaya said anything?"

"Poor Rugaya. She's being so patient, the way a good wife always is! She's shy around me and doesn't open up to me about her private life."

Sighing sadly, Lalla Uwayshina added, "But I know things haven't changed. He sleeps in his own bed now, but he doesn't go near her."

"Sooner or later he'll need her and then he will," the father said confidently.

"One time Fatima asked Rugaya why she wasn't having any more children. 'Well,' Rugaya said, 'they aren't going to fall out of the sky, or come from me alone!' Fatima was surprised at what her sister-in-law had said. So, to avoid embarrassment, she flipped her shoes over. In answer to Fatima's unspoken question, Rugaya turned the shoes over again, saying, 'Neither.'"[1]

"Do you think he doesn't want her anymore?" the father suggested.

"Why would he stop wanting her now for Heaven's sake? After she's given him three girls? She got pregnant with their first daughter within weeks of their wedding. I swear to God, that rotten slave girl's cast a spell on him! I know what I'm talking about, or I'm not Aisha Bint ash-Shakka, and before long you'll be saying the same thing: Muhammad's been bewitched!"

That Thursday night after the wedding ceremony, Muhammad went in to be with Tawida while Salem made himself scarce, allowing other people to think he was with his wife. When Muhammad went in, he found her adorned as a bride, decked out in a new dress, her hands and feet freshly hennaed. He took her hand and looked admiringly at the henna. Confident that his preventive measures would forestall a family dispute that would have led to no good, he closed his eyes and, without a word, held his nostrils to her right cheek. His trysts with Tawida became a nightly occurrence, after which he would come home late, if he came at all, while Salem slept in some corner of the livestock enclosure. As for Salem, he never voiced any objection to this arrangement and didn't even seem upset.

After some time, Lalla Uwayshina asked Salem how things were between him and Tawida, but all she got in response was a curt, "Praise be to God!"

Whenever she asked him anything more specific and tried to get him to talk, he just nodded. One night, after another of her abortive

---

1. By turning her shoes over, Fatima was asking her sister-in-law if her husband was having anal intercourse with her. By flipping the shoes back over, Rugaya was saying her husband wasn't having any kind of sexual relations with her at all.

interrogations, Lalla Uwayshina gave Salem a glass of milk and a plate of dates.

"Take these to your wife," she said. "They're a newlyweds' present from me, and you should both have some."

As a matter of fact, she had spiked them with some magic love potion meant to ensure that the couple would never part.

The slave nodded and thanked her, saying, "God bless you, Auntie."

Then he went to the tinplate shack that he shared with his wife and tapped lightly on the door with his fingers. When Tawida opened the door, he handed her the milk and dates, head bowed, and said, "This is for you from the mistress."

Things went on this way for some time, the love between master and slave blossoming and growing by the day. Then one evening, out of curiosity, Muhammad went to check on the abandoned corner of the livestock enclosure into which Salem disappeared every evening and from which he would only emerge in the predawn hours to clean out the pen and take care of the livestock, wordless and content.

Muhammad trod softly around the place, which was as dark as a vermin-infested underground cellar. It was as if he hadn't known anything about this side of their household before. He paused for a moment in the darkness, his ears pricked at the sound of a soft rustling, like the sound made by insects or cats moving through the hay. Before long, however, he heard something else. There was a murmuring coming from behind the haystacks. He paused again, listening intently. It sounded like human breaths coming in rapid, yet cautious succession. At first he thought it must be a male slave having a tryst with one of the slave women. All the more curious now, he crept slowly forward. In the near-total darkness behind the haystacks, he discerned a pair of shadowy human figures. What looked like a two-headed mass moved up and down, up and down. All the more determined now to know who these creatures of the ruins were, he stepped behind the haystacks and came suddenly upon them, interrupting them in the midst of their ecstasy.

"Who's there?" he asked.

The bodies quickly separated into two distinct forms, one of which was visibly smaller than the other.

"Who's there?" the master repeated in an imperious tone.

Head bowed, one of the two figures said in a trembling voice, "Please don't expose me, sir."

"Come closer," Muhammad commanded. "Who are you and who do you have with you?"

The figure remained where it was, still as a stone, while the other one hid, slipping as best it could into the hay.

"Come out or I'll kill you," the master bellowed.

So out he came, pleading again not to be exposed. What followed came as a complete and utter shock. Never in his life would the master have imagined the sorts of things that went on behind their house without his awareness or knowledge. The blood rushed to his head when he saw their slave naked, his black skin glistening as though it had been greased in preparation to be sold at auction. He was trying to pull his loincloth on and hide his private parts.

Grabbing the slave's head, the master demanded, "Who's with you?"

The slave said nothing.

"Tell me who's with you!"

Again, the slave made no reply. For a moment Muhammad fell silent himself. He understood now what the silence meant.

"So, do you sneeze and cough, you good-for-nothing slave?"[2]

"I beg you, Master, please don't tell anybody about me. Please! Nobody knows my secret."

"And the other one—who is he?"

After some hesitation, the slave replied, "It's Master Hussein, al-Figgi's son, sir."

Hussein!! The shock of the surprise couldn't have been greater. So Hussein sneezed and coughed too?

"Come out, Hussein."

2. A Libyan euphemism for homosexuality.

Fearful and naked, the young man stepped forward and, like his companion, begged for his secret not to be exposed. Before he could finish speaking, Muhammad knocked him to the ground with a slap on his face. He didn't dare say anything in objection. As for Salem, he came to Hussein's defense.

"Beat me, not him!" he pleaded. "I'm the one who deserves it!"

Then both men started receiving the kicks and the slaps together. They submitted in silence to the beating. Salem kept his composure, but tears streamed down Hussein's face.

Once he'd battered them to his satisfaction, Muhammad drove Hussein out naked.

"Get out of here, you scum! If I see you again, I'll kill you, wherever it happens to be."

Enraged, Muhammad turned to a terrified Salem. "Who else is there?" he asked.

"Nobody, sir," the distraught slave replied. "I swear. Master Hussein's the only one."

"Master Hussein's the only one, you scum?"

Twisting the slave's jaw in his hands, he repeated over and over, "Talk! Tell me! Tell me!"

"I swear! I swear!"

"Tomorrow you come to the shop and you divorce Tawida."

"Yes, sir."

"*Tfu 'alayk*. I could spit on you!"

Once the battle was over, Salem disappeared, trying to catch up with Hussein before he got to the street corner. Blood dripping from his mouth, he kept going until he found Hussein, who was sobbing in a low voice and walking close to a wall in an attempt to conceal himself. Without uttering a word, Salem took off his clothes and put them on Hussein, hot tears welling up in his eyes. After all, the well-bred slave was expected to sacrifice himself for a free person.

As the boy was about to make his way home, Salem took Hussein's head in his thick hands and said, "Keep hold of yourself now."

Love's Wine

AS SHE AND HER MASTER were making love one night, Tawida
said suddenly, "When I heard you were coming, I got distracted and
forgot to hang up the meat."

"What meat?"

"The meat for Master al-Figgi's banquet tomorrow. It'll get eaten
up by the cats that come into the kitchen."

"Don't go off and leave me now!" Muhammad objected.

"But the cats are going to eat it, and then Auntie will get really
angry with me and punish me."

"Tell her it was some other servant that forgot to hang it up."

"I can't do that. She asked me specifically, and gave other girls
other jobs to do."

"But I'm telling you not to leave me, and to hell with the meat and
al-Figgi. Come over here . . ."

Subdued by her master's irritation, Tawida said no more. Even so,
the matter of the meat kept bothering her, and she found herself hoping Aida would notice it and hang it up for her. As if to humor her,
he whispered in her ear, "If the cats eat the meat, I'll get some more
tomorrow. Don't worry, sweetheart. Just think about me and nothing
else right now."

"Please let me go take care of it. I promise not to be long!"

"Your master's leaving on a journey tomorrow, and you're wasting
time talking about silly things like cats and meat and al-Figgi's banquet. Curses on them all, I say!"

"Please don't get mad at me, Master."

"Drink this if you love me."

"It'll be a disaster for me," she said, pushing the glass gently away. "It makes me throw up."

"Come on now. Nothing will happen to you!"

"No. Please spare me, Master, and I'll do whatever you ask me to."

"But I'm commanding you. Are you going to disobey your master who calls you his sweetheart? Drink it for me, or I'll drink it for you."

"I'll be dizzy all night the way I was that other time."

"But that was your first time. This time you won't get dizzy or throw up. Come on now."

"All right, then, you drink it for me."

"No. You drink it for me."

"Okay, then. You take a sip and then I'll take one."

"How luscious you are, and how luscious it is to be drunk on you, Tawida, your master's beloved!"

She took a second sip, then a third, and before long she was drunk in her master's arms. He rolled her over on top of him, laughing out loud, wooing her with total abandon. "My sultaness, my royal highness!"

In her confusion and delirium, she went back to talking about the meat she'd forgotten to hang up. Then he spanked her till it hurt, and she called him names. He cursed her. She bit him. He snarled from the pain. Aroused all the more, she started to lick him. He flung her down, and she did the same in return. Then he dangled her off the bed, and their excitement intensified. When she climaxed before he did, he murmured again, "My sultaness, my royal highness!" His white neck made a delectable meal for a stray black cat which, driven wild with hunger, hardly recognized herself.

The Sin

LEANING HIS ELBOW on the counter, Muhammad said to Ali after a pause, "I found them on top of the shipment of gunpowder that we'd stashed under the haystacks."

As the two men waited for al-Figgi to arrive, Ali looked over the accounts ledger.

"If I were you," he said, "I'd kill the both of them."

"Better to choke a dog than to kill it. I'll use him to get a stranglehold on his father."

"Good idea. The bastard's got way too much power over Grandpa, and a tongue smoother than the devil's."

As they spoke, Yousef and Ahmed Bin Shatwan—cousins of Ali's—came wanting to speak in private with their uncle.

A steamship laden with gunpowder, fabrics, glassware, and copper was due to arrive from Malta within fifteen days at the most if the sea was calm, and the cargo would need to be unloaded well out of sight.

"It will be coming in at night," the men said. "It'll have to be unloaded quickly, and we'll need a couple of porters we can trust. We also need to make sure the spies that work for the Jews, the Italians, and the Maltesians are far from port while the new shipment's being loaded."

The men finished their business quickly and left.

"Do you remember when we brought Salem here and warned him not to touch Tawida?"

"Yeah."

"He wasn't interested in her in the first place, and that's why the threat didn't have any effect on him."

"He duped us to save his own skin, since he didn't want anybody to know he wasn't a real man. We've got no need for him anymore, the bastard."

"He's afraid of being sold. And for good reason. Anyway, I've sent for al-Figgi, and we'll reach an understanding man-to-man."

"And what if Grandpa finds out?"

"How would he? Like, who would tell him? Al-Figgi will keep quiet about it on his own."

Ali chuckled and closed the accounts ledger. "Don't you go crazy now!"

"I've never been saner."

When al-Figgi arrived, he was about to blow his top. He started talking from the shop's doorway without even bothering to say hello.

"Why did you beat the boy?" he demanded. "What had he done to you?"

Without inviting him in or even looking up at him, Muhammad replied, "Didn't he tell you himself?"

"You think it makes you a man to go picking on a young kid?"

"Lower your voice, Hajj."

"It seems you've got no shame anymore."

"You're the one who's got no respect for anybody."

"Some nerve you've got, talking this way to somebody who's old enough to be your father!"

"Bring him a chair, Ali. Let the self-important sheikh sit down so that I can explain things to him. And close the door behind you."

Without further ado, Muhammad dropped the bomb on al-Figgi.

"For your information, Sheikh," he said, "your esteemed son Hussein is a faggot. That's why I beat him. I caught him in the act with one of our slaves in our livestock enclosure. The slave's inside if you'd like to speak with him yourself."

Shocked and incredulous, al-Figgi went silent for a few moments. Then he gulped and, in a tone of alarm, said, "That's ridiculous! What you're saying can't be true! You've just got a grudge against me. That's why you're saying things like this."

"I do hate you—I can't deny that. But I'm not using Hussein. I found your son on our property, so I beat him. It's not as if I'd seen him on the street and assaulted him for no reason."

As if overcome by a temporary death, al-Figgi froze in place, his eyes bugging out. Then he took off his cap and wiped the sweat off his brow.

"Good God, good God," he muttered. "Oh Lord, protect me in my time of trial. Oh Lord, protect me in my time of trial! I can hardly believe it. Hussein's memorized the Qur'an. He prays all his prayers. He's shy and respectful to everybody. And now this?!"

"For a long time I've been telling his mother that we should marry him off young to keep him from learning things that might take him off track. But she's been stubborn about it. She says things like, 'The boy's still too young.' So this is all her fault. It's her sin."

"Maybe his mother suspects something and has been waiting for things to become clear to her. Either way, she's more sensible than you are. At least she comes to her son's defense and doesn't want him to be exposed."

Muhammad and Ali exchanged glances, realizing what a shock this was to the father's heart. Handing him a glass of water, Ali said gently, "Drink this, Sheikh, and calm yourself."

Al-Figgi downed the water as though it were medicine. Then he sank to the floor in tears.

"This is a disaster. My boy! God forbid, God forbid! He's my only son and I've been counting on him. I'll kill him myself and bury my shame."

Grabbing hold of him together, Muhammad and Ali pleaded, "Don't do it, Sheikh. Haven't you seen how people cover up for their children? Keep his secret hidden and let God take care of the rest. What would you gain by exposing him?"

Tripping over his jard as he got up, al-Figgi said, "Let me go. Good God, good God!"

Ali winked at his uncle to let the man be on his way, and not to compound his suffering. He'd already been dealt enough blows to make his heart stop.

However, Muhammad said, "Before you go, Sheikh, I want you to write up a divorce certificate for Salem and Tawida and put your stamp on it. And remember: we've still got more to discuss in connection with your son's desecration of our house."

Once al-Figgi was gone, Muhammad heaved a sigh of relief. Kissing the divorce certificate, he said, "Tawida is mine, and I won't share her with anybody. She's my plant, and no one but I can water her, give her shade, or taste her fruit."

Looking at him warily, Ali said, "You're starting to scare me. Why don't we just close al-Figgi's account once and for all and be done with it?"

"No," Muhammad replied, stroking the tip of his mustache. Not yet."

≈

Several weeks later, al-Figgi came and, in a state of total collapse, prostrated himself servilely before Muhammad.

"Sell me the slave," he begged. "Hussein's my only son. Shame on you. Ever since that night, the boy hasn't eaten or drunk. He's sick in bed and won't talk to anybody. His mother's so upset over him, she's about to perish. I took him to a Sufi *hadra*, but it didn't help. I even took him to the graves of Sidi Abdul Jaleel and Sidi Ruwayfi al-Ansari and that didn't help either. But if he sees that slave again and they can talk together, maybe he'll come out of his grief and misery. Sell him to me, God keep you!"

"No."

Muhammad's reply was final.

"Cancel all my father's debts and sign the capital from the Tunisia trade over to him."

"You're lording it over me now."

"I know. But this is an appropriate settlement in view of the sin your son committed against our household."

Then, ending the conversation with a warning, Muhammad said, "Don't you dare go to my father behind my back and ask him to sell you the slave."

The price Salem was fetching that evening was higher than even he could ever have imagined. As the two men negotiated over Salem, he was negotiating a crazy idea of his own. Inspired by the idea, he sneaked over to al-Figgi's house for the first time—and in broad daylight. He and Hussein hadn't seen each other for months. He stood at Hussein's bedside until at last Hussein became aware of a presence next to him. He opened his eyes and saw Salem. Bending down without a word, Salem lifted Hussein onto his back and headed for the sea. When he reached the water's edge, he waded in deeper and deeper until the water engulfed them and they vanished into the waves.

The Platform

THERE'S NOTHING EASIER than getting rid of an obnoxious slave girl. Just sell her at market, or give her to someone whose favor you hope to curry, or to somebody you want to hurt!

One day as Hajj Imuhammad and al-Figgi sat chatting in the mosque after prayer about the state of the market and the city, Hajj Imuhammad confessed suddenly, "I've got a problem in my household, Sheikh."

"What's going on?"

"My son Muhammad is in love with a slave woman of his, and he's neglecting his wife."

"It won't last. He's young and fickle, and pretty soon he'll get over her and come to his senses. Have a talk with him."

"We've done that, but it didn't help. His wife's complained about him to his mother. They're living together like brother and sister."

"Doesn't he do anything?"

"No."

"Nothing at all?"

"Nothing at all, Sheikh."

Al-Figgi just sat staring at the ceiling at first, while Hajj Imuhammad fiddled with his prayer beads waiting for al-Figgi to say something.

After some time he said, "Maybe he just wants to make his wife jealous."

"I know my son, Sheikh, and I don't think he'd do that. In any case, he's being stubborn, and I'm tired of hearing his mother complain about him. He's married to my wife's niece, and her family are influential merchants in Misrata who'll make things hard for us if they hear how our son is treating her. His infatuation with this slave woman is just making problems for us."

"Ah, I get it now! So it's a matter of business and family ties."

Adjusting his sitting position and stroking his beard, al-Figgi went on, "The best solution would be to sell the slave girl as soon as he goes on another business trip."

"Where's he going to go when he just came back from a trip that took him away for several months?"

"It doesn't have to be a caravan trip. Ships are coming and going all the time to and from Malta. Malta isn't far from Benghazi, and it's an easy, short trip."

"How's that?" queried Hajj Imuhammad, a glint in his eye.

"There's a steamer leaving in two days with a shipment of wool and barley. You can send him out on that. Captain Ali Rayyani told me about it the day before yesterday. If your son goes to Malta, he'll see things that will make him forget all about that servant girl!"

"But Rayyani and I aren't on good terms. There's a problem between us that goes way back."

"Well, give it some thought, and leave Rayyani to me."

Hajj Imuhammad cleared his throat and shifted in his seat. Then he said, "But I haven't got enough money for a mission like this now."

"I'll lend you whatever you need."

"No, no," he protested uneasily. "That'll just put me deeper in debt. I haven't even paid back the loan you gave me for the Tunisia trade yet. Do you think I'm going to go piling another debt on top of that one?"

"Don't worry," al-Figgi said reassuringly, squeezing his friend's shoulder. "My money's your money, and yours is mine. Besides, don't you think it's better to spend your time worrying about a debt than to be upset over a disobedient son? Our children are precious. So if they're sick or unhappy, we have to sacrifice for their sake. We owe it to them."

Hajj Imuhammad went home and reported on his conversation with al-Figgi to Lalla Uwayshina. She approved of the plan, and even devoted a whole prayer session to calling down blessing on al-Figgi. Then she told Aida to prepare tea for her and her husband in the house's inner courtyard. She instructed her to set out her special embroidered cushions and perfume them with *oud al-gmari* incense,[1] to put a few drops of rosewater in the hajj's clay water jug, and to light the kerosene lamp and hang it in the tree. It was a perfect evening for some intimate exchange.

As Aida came and went with this and that, she caught snippets of the conversation between the husband and wife.

At one point Lalla Uwayshina asked the hajj, "So when will the market open?"

"A new slave caravan will be arriving from Jalu tomorrow, and the sales will start right away."

"How much are you going to ask for them?"

"I've told the middleman to sell the mute slave woman at the market price. For Tawida, I'm asking 130 gold coins. As for Masoud, I plan to barter him for another slave. He's been coughing for months now and he can't take the chaff dust anymore, so he wouldn't sell well. But I might trade him for a mute or lame slave who could work bagging merchandise."

Then, as if he'd just thought of it, he snapped his fingers and said, "Maybe I could repay some of my debt to al-Figgi with what I make on the deal."

As she poured the tea, Lalla Uwayshina asked, "How could you repay a debt by just selling a couple of slave women?"

"Well," the hajj replied, "I'm not going to use the new slave myself. I'm planning to hire him out to grain merchants, and I figure he can make me a fairly good income."

Pleased with her husband's plans, Lalla Uwayshina took a handful of peanuts and added them to his glass of tea. Then she whispered

---

1. *Oud al-gmari* is combined with other types of wood to produce the traditional Libyan incense, or *bukhur*, used to ward off the evil eye.

something in his ear. He smiled and bowed his head, embarrassed at the thought that somebody in the house might see them flirting.

"Shshsh . . . ," he whispered back. "Now isn't the time for such talk."

With a bawdy laugh, she whispered, "You've been promising me a new pair of hoop earrings. Are you planning to buy one for me soon?"

Aida rushed to tell Tawida what she'd heard. The minute she heard Aida's report, her heart sank. She had no idea what to do. She wept the way slaves always weep when they learn they're to be sold. They weep as though it were their first day in slavery. They weep because they know things will be different under a new master, with new work, and new companions. Despite their nameless existence, they still fear the unknown—the nameless future. They know things might be somewhat better, of course. On the other hand, they might be a lot worse. Either way, they weep over the loss of the familiar which, miserable though it is, is still less frightening than being placed at the mercy of some new master.

In short, no one wants change for fear that the new will be harder than the old.

Muhammad had set sail for Malta several days earlier with a shipment of hides and salt. It was said that Rayyis Rayyani had been slow to grant the ship permission to sail, which was why Muhammad hadn't been informed of his departure until the last minute. Consequently, he had bidden Tawida a hasty farewell, saying, "I'll sell my goods and come right back."

Knowing there was nothing she could do to save herself, Tawida shed bitter tears, hoping against hope.

A few hours after sunrise, the city began awakening to its usual hustle and bustle. The market opened its doors, and the auctioneer began putting young slaves on display in the market's main square. They were naked, barefoot, and malnourished, their bones about to pop through whatever skin they had left. Nevertheless, their freshly greased bodies gave off a sheen that was certain to entice potential buyers. When the slaves who had come on the Jalu caravan encountered those who had arrived from Fezzan, they exchanged looks of recognition, as though they were bound by an ancient tie. The slaves who had come from households in Benghazi were visibly better off than both those who had been brought from Jalu and those who had crossed the desert on foot, and who had been whipped, starved, and deprived of proper clothing. The three slaves who were led away to the market from Master Imuhammad's household knew where they were headed. Grief hung in the air, and Tawida couldn't stop crying. Her last night with Muhammad had been just days before, and now she was bound for a destination unknown. Would she ever see him again? Or, as she mounted the platform half-naked to commence her new sojourn in slavery, had everything between them come to an end?

She was approached immediately by a Bedouin who had been sitting on the ground next to his donkey and devouring a piece of bread. Still chewing on the bread, he grabbed her breasts so hard that his thick mustache quivered. He tugged on them twice, not with any intention of buying her, but just for the fun of it. She realized that most of the men who grabbed her breasts did it for the same reason. After all, slave women for sale were a source of entertainment for anybody who came to the market to look around. The Bedouin was followed by a foul-smelling old man. Scrutinizing her, he lifted her robe and ran his hand over her private parts. He hovered around her for such a long time, she thought he was going to buy her. However, he had apparently been more interested in touching her than he was in making a purchase. When the auctioneer asked him why he'd changed his mind, he said her hips were disfigured, and he described her vagina with a word so vulgar that even the crudest of plebeians wouldn't have used it unless they had been in the middle of a brawl. Calling him every name in the book, the auctioneer drove the old man away for fear that what he had said might ruin his chances of selling her.

Other men behaved in similar ways, and never once in the course of all their inspections did anyone take notice of the tears trickling down her cheeks. They all squeezed her breasts and touched her pubic hair. Meanwhile, the women to her right and the men to her left endured the same humiliations. While the women were being pinched, squeezed, and tugged on, the men were having their testicles handled, and if they'd been castrated, they were punched in the nose. This was potential buyers' way of determining how much strength a slave had stored up in his or her blood. It was thought that the slave whose eyes got teary and red was a "purebred," born to a Negro mother and father. Otherwise, or so it was thought, he wouldn't be suited for strenuous labor, since it was only the pure, unadulterated Negro blood that made a slave as strong as an ox and as tough as a mule.

It would hardly have occurred to anybody that when a slave's eyes got red and teary, this wasn't some reflex reaction that proved the purity of his or her Negro lineage but rather a sign of an urge to weep in a normal human response to pain and humiliation. No one race or lineage has a monopoly on tears. But when they come from a slave, no human value is attached to them.

In front of a small shop not far from the slave bazaar, an elderly black woman sat on the ground sifting barley, her face covered entirely with dust except for a few creases here and there. As she sifted, she sang:

> Don't shed many tears, no purpose will they serve,
> No good from them will you glean.
> Be patient in trouble, 'tis the will of God,
> The future remains to be seen.
> Your tears won't help you, there's nothing we can do,
> Our lot is ours to bear.
> What you've got no hand in, endure no matter,
> God's deliverance is near.

The Market

WHEN ALI BOUGHT BACK the families' slaves, he was only seventeen years old. He was an orphan who had been raised by his grandfather, whom he'd never disobeyed in his life. So when he came forward to buy back the slaves his grandfather was offering for sale, it was an act of defiance the patriarch would never have expected from a grandchild he had taken in as his own son.

He bought Tawida not because she was pregnant again, but for the sake of the absent Muhammad. In fact, neither he nor Muhammad was even aware of her pregnancy. He had heard that she had lost two children—one at the bathhouse after being forced to drink the herbal potion that caused miscarriages and one when she fell off a ladder as she was cleaning the roofed enclosure.

As soon as he heard what was happening, Ali rushed to the market place, his throat tight at the realization of the plot that had been hatched against Muhammad. He felt sure his grandfather must have lost his mind. As he ran toward the market, he racked his brain for possible explanations for what his grandfather had done. Why would they have tricked Muhammad into going away and then sold off his beloved along with other slaves?

Ali knew how in love Muhammad was with Tawida, and he couldn't bear the thought of his being in torment when he came home and didn't find her. Nobody seemed willing to understand that love erases the boundaries between master and slave, white and black, Arab and Negro. Such boundaries didn't exist in the realm of concubinage, which was a practice no one objected to. But the minute things went beyond mere pleasure-seeking to a love that joined two souls on an equal footing, these human distinctions would rear their heads once more, looming like mountains on the horizon. When this happened, the distinctions themselves became the reason to wage all-out war on the love that had come into being. What bizarre things happen to the human soul!

That night, Ali was banished from his grandfather's house, which had been his home. His grandfather was hurt by what he had done: he had publicly gone against his word and challenged his authority by buying back the slaves he had said were to be sold. He'd stood up among the vendors in the market and shouted, "My ancestors' slaves aren't for sale, and if anybody comes near them, I'll slit his throat with this knife!" Who did this boy think he was, anyway? The fact was, Ali hadn't been defending the slaves or his ancestors' legacy. He'd been defending his uncle Muhammad, who'd been deceived and dealt a treacherous blow to his very heart, and who had been whisked away to Malta to get him out of the way.

Standing with a group of merchants on a platform that was slightly elevated above the level of the crowd, his jard wrapped about him, Ali's grandfather stared at him in stunned silence. Meanwhile, other men were asking, "What's your grandson doing here? How dare a young boy keep his grandfather's word from being carried out in front of the whole world? Besides, why are you coming here to sell slaves if you're just going to buy them back again?"

It was at best an impropriety, at worst an ignominy and a show of outright disloyalty!

Men were swarming around Tawida and other slave women on the display platform when suddenly Ali stepped briskly forward, yanked someone's jard off him, and covered her with it. So enraged that he was hardly aware of what he was doing, he shrieked, "Enough! The market's closing! Now get out of here!"

A spiteful merchant in the crowd—a crony of his grandfather's— shouted, "How much did you pay for her, boy?"

Looking at his grandfather, Ali replied, "I'll be surety for what-ever my grandfather is asking for them. I owe him many a blessing."

The person speaking wasn't some teenager still wet behind the ears, but a grown man. Thinking perhaps, like others there, that Ali wanted the slave women to himself, the grandfather bellowed, "Go back to your shop now. Go!"

"I'm not leaving before they do," the grandson replied evenly.

Ali had his grandfather over a barrel now. Left with no other choice, the grandfather said to his slaves, "Go home."

The slaves then filed joyously away and made their way to the house.

Afterward Ali came up to his grandfather, kissed him on the head, and left the square.

His grandfather was furious with him, but didn't let on in public.

When Ali arrived home that evening, he found his mother in tears. His grandfather came out in his nightclothes, his head uncustomarily bare. The minute he came up to him, he slapped him across the face, saying, "Get out of my house, you disobedient ingrate!"

His mother shrank away, while his grandmother tried to intervene.

As for Ali, he offered no resistance. "Yes, sir," he said to his grandfather. "I'm leaving."

There were tears in both their eyes.

Ali tried to kiss his grandfather's feet and apologize, but the gesture was rebuffed. Torn between the need to support her husband on the one hand, and her nurturing instincts on the other, Ali's grandmother blurted out to him. "Don't leave!" Turning to her husband, she said, "His place is here and nowhere else. If he leaves, I leave with him."

The response was swift and decisive: "Another word out of you, and you're divorced."

As for Fatima, who revered her father so much that she hadn't shown him her face since puberty, she couldn't argue with him, even if the matter had to do with her only son. Knowing what awaited him, she wordlessly gathered his things into a knapsack and, wrapping her arms around him at the entrance to the roofed enclosure, said, "Go to your uncle Sadeg's house until tempers have cooled."

Two days later Ali learned that his grandfather was sick in bed. He wanted to visit him, but Siddig advised him to postpone it. After all, his grandfather had fallen ill over what he'd done to him in the marketplace, and when Ali's paternal uncles had gone to see him he'd described Ali to them as "an ill-bred pipsqueak that still pees his pants." After the incident in the marketplace, Ali was forbidden to go to the shop where he'd worked with his uncle Muhammad. His grandfather took the keys away from him and entrusted them instead to Jaballah and Ali's uncle Amin. When Jaballah was away from the shop, Ali would sneak over to see him and get the latest news. He avoided Amin, who was a shameless, impudent man. Jaballah, on the other hand, was loyal and conscientious, and never turned his back on Ali.

After this, Ali's uncle Sadeg took him to work with him in the gold market. When his grandfather learned of it, he stopped passing by Sadeg's shop so that he wouldn't have to see him. Even so, Jaballah would just smile and say, "The old man's sore, but he loves you. I know, because he asks me about you. One time he said, 'Jaballah, go to the market and see what that pipsqueak's up to. And if his mother wants to see him, take her there in the wagon. But use the back gate, and go while I'm taking my afternoon nap to make it look as though nobody knows what she's doing.'"

About three months later Muhammad returned from Malta, worn out, wan, and thin. He showed up one day at the jewelry shop in the Zalam Market. Ali was learning gold engraving, a craft he was taking to little by little. As he sat engrossed in a piece he was working on, someone darkened the door. He looked up, and who should he see but Muhammad. Muhammad had looked for him both in the grain shop and at home, and when he found out what had happened, he'd come to find him in the gold market. The sight of his uncle was like glimpsing a beautiful moon on a pitch-black night.

"Hummayda!" he cried. "It was awful not having you around!"

"My dear Allaywi!"

In spite of himself, the boy fell into his uncle's arms and wept.

Passersby and vendors turned and stared at them curiously. After all, men weren't supposed to cry. In fact, no man ever cried even in this disease-ridden, poverty-racked city. He bucked up, resigned himself to the pain, and finally grew hardened. If he couldn't, he had to be prepared to endure people's hateful gossip. Consequently, for a man to cry was a rare occurrence, and if it did happen, it was kept hidden, like a sin committed in secret. So what earthshaking event had released these copious tears and heartfelt emotion within the hearing and sight of the city's marketgoers?

In his uncle's eyes, Ali glimpsed tears mingled with a look of fierce rage. And he heard him say, "If I don't repay them in double measure for what they've done, I'm not Muhammad Bin Shatwan."

The Fatal Omission

WHENEVER A LUNCH BANQUET was scheduled, the servants would begin preparing for it the day before. This way they could make sure everything was ready for cooking to begin straightaway on the day the guests were arriving. The most important element of the cooking operation was preparing the lamb meat, which was locally raised and considered of especially high quality. The meat had to be cut in such a way as to produce different pieces for different guests depending on how important they were and whether they were men or women.

An indispensable step in preparing the meat was to hang it from the kitchen's central pillar for it to dry in the open air. This was a task that had to be performed by one of the female servants before she went to bed, so that the meat wouldn't be devoured by the cats that roamed into the kitchen at night looking for food.

Three servant women worked until an especially late hour that night getting ready for the next day's feast. They divided the work among themselves and things went smoothly. Tawida would nurse her baby in the corner between his intermittent naps, and the women's chatting, joking, and occasional singing eased the work and made the hours pass more quickly.

Salem picked up the baby, who was just a few months old, in a cardboard box and placed him on the counter so that Tawida could keep an eye on him. Then he went to the market to shop for things they needed in the kitchen. Lalla Uwayshina would pass by every now and then, dressed to the hilt, to check on the progress of the work and spout instructions. Every time she came in, she would fiddle with the new hoop earrings she'd just added to her collection the day before and bark out more orders. On one visit she told them what to do with the usban, the couscous, the soup and the stuffed squash, and on another she told Salem to go to a well-known baker in the Hashish Market to order the kind of bread they needed for the banquet and to pass by the house of a woman famed for her holiday date-nut pastries.

As Salem came back with the things he'd been told to get at the market, Lalla Uwayshina was in the kitchen on one of her patrol rounds. She came up to the box where the baby lay and looked in on him. He had just nursed and fallen asleep.

"Glory be to God, what a little angel! May God protect him for you!" she said, addressing Tawida and Salem.

"Thank you, Auntie, and God bless you," Tawida replied dutifully.

Salem came in with his cargo and looked over at Lalla Uwayshina, who was scrutinizing the baby and thinking to herself: *If only Muhammad had a son like him. His wife keeps having one girl after another. Ugh!* As Salem put his bags down and came up to the box, she said, "He looks like you. Glory be to God the creator!"

A mosquito lit on the baby's nose. He opened his eyes and scrunched up his tiny legs. His irises were the color of almonds, his limbs were long, his hair lay down smoothly over his head, and he had no pug nose.

Smiling, Salem bent down and kissed the baby, cooing affectionately and playing with him. Salem never looked directly at the person addressing him, especially if it was a woman. He would always look at the floor or the ground. Only this time he had the baby boy to look at instead.

Tawida was the last person to leave the kitchen late that evening after washing all the pots, pans, and kitchen utensils, and putting everything in order. She was sleepy and her clothes were wet. Salem checked on her so that he could escort her back to the shack.

"Are you finished?" he asked in a low voice.

"Finally, thank God."

"Let's go, then. It's late, I'm tired, and tomorrow's going to be a long day. Here, I'll take the baby."

He picked up the baby in his cardboard box, she picked up the lantern, and they left the kitchen—the beehive of activity so central to the next day's celebration, which would be attended by the Ottoman wali's envoy, sheikhs of Sufi worship centers, and family chieftains in preparation to nominate those who would don the red burnoose.[1]

Tawida had worked long and hard. But she'd forgotten to hang up the meat!

---

1. "Those who would don the red burnoose" is a reference to the individuals appointed by the Ottoman ruler as tribal heads and elders for purposes of tax collection, military conscription, and the like.

Neither Muhammad nor Ali

SERVANTS ALWAYS ROSE much earlier than their masters. But if there was some special occasion in the offing, they hardly slept at all.

Tawida fell into bed exhausted beside her baby, and before long she was dead to the world. But little more than an hour after she'd closed her eyes, she heard an urgent knocking on the shack door, and Aida's voice calling her.

"Tawida! Tawida! Get up!"

Springing out of bed, she ran to open the door, alarmed at the urgency of her friend's voice.

"What's going on? Who died?" she asked in a stupor. "You scared me!"

"No, no, nobody's died," Aida said. "But the cats have eaten the meat!"

Only then did Tawida realize her mistake.

"Oh my God!" she wailed, striking her forehead with the heel of her hand. "Oh my God! I forgot!"

"So what do we do now?"

"We've got to take care of it. What do we do?"

Just then Salem showed up from somewhere and greeted the women. Then, noticing their jaundiced faces, he asked, "What's happened?"

Aida told him, and everybody was now in a state of dread over what would come next.

Right away Salem said, "We've got to get together enough money to buy another sheep now. Come on. Take a collection from the girls."

"I know everybody's situation," Aida said hopelessly. "There's no way we'll have enough."

"Quick! Who has a ring or something hidden away?"

Tawida collapsed in tears beside the cardboard box, whose little occupant woke up and wanted to nurse.

"Don't nurse him now," Aida said to her. "You're upset and your milk won't be good for him."

"But he's crying!"

"I'll give him some sugar water."

"He hasn't nursed since yesterday."

"It's all right. It's all right. I'll take care of him."

"What makes things even worse is that Muhammad isn't here, and neither is Ali."

"You've heard people speak of 'a day without either Muhammad or Ali'? Well, this is the kind of day they were talking about!"[1] Aida quipped ruefully.

When it was clear that the servant women wouldn't be able to come up with enough money to buy another sheep, Salem said, "I'll be right back." Then he took off in the direction from which he'd come. Running as fast as his legs would carry him, he kept going until he'd reached al-Figgi's house. He knocked gently on the reception room window.

"Who is it?" asked a voice from inside.

"It's Salem," he whispered. "Open up."

Hussein opened the window and, sounding surprised, asked, "Why are you back so soon? Did somebody see you?"

"No, no. But there's an emergency."

1. This is a local Libyan expression that hearkens back to the heroic figures of the Prophet Muhammad and his son-in-law, Ali Ibn Abi Talib, who once delivered the Prophet from mortal danger. When the Prophet got wind of the fact that his opponents from the tribe of Qureish were plotting to kill him, he fled by night, and Ali valiantly volunteered to sleep in the Prophet's bed to deceive the Prophet's enemies into thinking he was at home. A "day when neither Muhammad nor Ali comes" is thus an ill-fated day on which no protection is to be found.

Hussein opened the reception room door and Salem tiptoed inside. After closing the door behind him, the boy asked, "What's wrong, my little bird?"

"I need money to buy a sheep, and I need it right away."

"A sheep?!"

"Yeah. Tawida forgot to hang up the meat they were going to cook for a banquet today, and the cats ate it. Now we've got to buy another sheep before the masters wake up."

With a sudden twinge of jealousy, the boy asked, "And what do I care about Tawida?"

"Look. It isn't Tawida asking for your help. It's me. If they find out what happened, they'll torture her and take her baby away from her, and they might even sell him. I can't stand to see that happen to her."

Getting Salem's point, the boy fell into an apprehensive silence.

At last he said, "But I haven't got any money on me."

Sticking his face into Hussein's, Salem said sternly, "Get the money. Quick."

Hussein reached out and grasped Salem's shirt from behind.

"Are you angry with me? Calm down now! I'll borrow it from my dad."

"I haven't got much time. Now get us out of this mess."

Angry himself now, Hussein snapped, "What do you care about her, anyway? It was her mistake, not yours!"

"Hassouna, what's with you? Have you lost your mind? Don't make me repeat myself."

Grabbing Salem again, Hussein pleaded, "Don't be mad! I'll get some money from my mom. She's nicer than my dad, anyway. Wait for me at the end of the alley, and I'll meet you there."

The boy glanced up and down the street before Salem stepped out. When the coast was clear, he gestured for him to leave fast.

As Salem scurried out the door, Hussein hissed, "I swear, just knowing you is a mess!"

If the cooking for a luncheon banquet hadn't started by early in the morning, it meant either that the meat wasn't ready or that the cooks hadn't gotten up on time. On the morning of the luncheon, Lalla Uway-shina opened the window to her room and sniffed the air, expecting to smell something delicious simmering over a low flame, be it the usban, the soup, or the couscous with *tagliya*.[2] But her long, slightly hooked nose wasn't picking up anything. *The servants must have slept late,* she thought. *They need somebody to stand over them with a whip, damn it!*

She called Ahbara, her favorite servant, who came running, and asked her if the women were up. Ahbara told her they were all in the kitchen.

"So why don't I smell anything cooking?"

"I don't know," Ahbara replied with a shrug and a shake of the head.

Lifting her chin in the air, Lalla Uwayshina said, "Run down there and see what's happening."

Ahbara, who was well trained in spying out news and eavesdrop-ping on conversations in hard-to-get-to places, sneaked up on the dis-traught gathering in the kitchen. As Ahbara stood listening in the shadows, Aida rushed in carrying Tawida's baby and added something to the tense conversation. You could have read the entire situation in Tawida's terrified demeanor. She was clearly the culprit, and unless Salem came back with a solution, all she could do was wait for the punishment to descend.

Hussein kept Salem waiting for a long time at the corner, as he'd been through quite an ordeal with his mother in order to get the money. He'd told her scores of lies that he'd made up on the spot, only to replace them with other ones that were no less impromptu. In the end his mother had relented, not because his lies had been so persua-sive but because she was convinced that her son was keeping a certain thing hidden from her. She winked at him, as if to imply that she knew the kinds of fibs young men tell when they've hosted a prostitute in the

2. *Taqliya* is a Libyan stew served over couscous made with lamb meat, sautéed onions, steamed onions and chickpeas, cinnamon, allspice, tomato paste, salt, pep-per, and turmeric.

family's reception room. They might say, "I've got my buddy with me in the reception room, so could you serve us some supper?" For this reason, the roofed enclosure where the reception area was located was off-limits to the women of the household. The only person allowed to look in on the folks occupying that space—and then just once in the early evening—was the father. For purposes of camouflage, the door would usually be left ajar in those early evening hours, and the guest would be a man. Later, however, the situation would change.

As Hussein told his mother one tall tale after another, it hadn't occurred to him that she would be ready with a story of her own that served his purposes perfectly—namely, that a woman had shared her teenage son's supper and bed the night before, and that his urgent early morning request for cash was so that he could pay his lady friend's fees.

Hussein was surprised by his mother's fantasies, but he was happy to go along with them. It was in his interest for her to think some strange woman was to blame for wasting their money. After all, women were a convenient hat rack on which to hang all the world's ills. Promising to pay the money back, Hussein bolted out the door and ran down the street to catch up with Salem.

Salem was delayed at the butcher's, since all the butcher had on hand that day was an imported sheep and a billy goat from Malta, neither of which would work for a luncheon banquet. Finally, though, a ram was found and hurriedly butchered.

Salem went to work tearing into the meat alongside the butcher in order to finish the operation as quickly as possible. As he raced with the clock to stave off pending disaster, the sun continued its race with the night. Once he and the butcher had finished cutting the meat to the required specifications, Salem placed it in a cardboard box and hoisted it onto his head, perspiration dripping from his forehead into his eyes. Then he ran home with it as fast as his legs would carry him. His hands were dirty, and he reeked of a mixture of sweat and grease.

Despite his rapid sprint home, Salem's delay at the butcher's gave Ahbara time to gather enough information for her mistress's ears. Now that the news was out, everyone else in the master's household jumped out of bed and came rushing, curious, to the kitchen.

This is how the catastrophe unfolded: As Salem was racing down nearby alleyways, Master Imuhammad charged out of his room like an enraged bull, picked up his whip, and headed for the kitchen. As the lash approached, the servant women scattered out of its way. Those who didn't manage to escape plastered themselves against the wall like lizards. The exception was Tawida, who fell into the master's grip as she retreated into a corner, her arms raised in the air, begging for pardon.

But there was no escaping her fate.

"Forgive me, Master, forgive me!" she pleaded. "God curse the devil! I forgot. God keep you . . . no, no, no!"

As Salem drew nearer to the house, the whip drew nearer to Tawida. Then down it came: hard, hot, merciless. Her cry went up immediately and the last erstwhile defender vanished from the kitchen.

"Quick, close the door," Lalla Uwayshina ordered Ahbara. "People will hear the screaming and they'll know it's coming from our house." Ahbara did as her mistress had commanded.

Two of the female servants were so terrified they wet themselves as they hid next to a prickly pear hedge behind the kitchen. As she listened to Tawida's cries for help, Lalla Uwayshina paced the house's inner courtyard, at a loss as to how to salvage the banquet. It was an occasion of great moment for the notables who had been invited to it, and the family might not have the honor of arranging another one in the near future if the people currently occupying appointed positions in the Ottoman administration retained their titles.

When she heard Tawida's screams and pleas for mercy, Fatima jumped terrified out of bed. She came running from her room, gathering her hair into her headscarf as she went.

"What's going on in this house?" she asked her mother in alarm. "Why is Tawida screaming?"

"It's a disaster! A disaster!" cried Lalla Uwayshina, clapping her hands together and readjusting her earrings again. "That good-for-nothing servant didn't hang up the meat last night and the cats ate it all!"

"What!?"

Ahbara volunteered a detailed explanation without so much as a turn of the head from Fatima, who ran to the kitchen and, grabbing her father by the hand, tried in vain to make him stop the flogging. What good would it do, anyway?

"For the Prophet's sake, Baba, leave her be!" she pleaded on bended knee. "She's going to die! That's enough! She's a new mother!"

But the father's response to his daughter was a violent one. He pushed her away with such force that she went rolling across the kitchen floor and her face veil came off.

"Get away from me!" he roared. "Or I'll put you on top of her!"

Nothing would mitigate Tawida's fate.

Fatima fled from before her father, who grabbed Tawida by the hair and started dragging her toward the bathroom. With a forceful yank, he pulled down the clothes line to tie her up with it. Then he addressed Ahbara, who was crouching nearby.

"Quick, bring her son," he said, his breaths staccato.

At this point, Lalla Uwayshina intervened, afraid her husband might strangle either the servant or her baby.

"That's enough, Hajj," she murmured. "Don't dirty your hands with them."

Ahbara hurriedly brought the cardboard box that held the infant.

"Here he is, Master," she mumbled fearfully.

"Put him inside."

Ahbara watched Master Imuhammad as he bound a moaning, limp Tawida by the hands and hung her from the bathroom ceiling.

Oozing sweat and expletives, he growled, "If you're hung up yourself like a slaughtered animal, maybe you'll stop forgetting what job you're supposed to do. This isn't the first time, bitch!"

Then he locked her and her baby inside the small roofed enclosure that led to the bathroom and slipped the key into his pocket. "Anybody who tries to help her will end up in there with her!" he shouted menacingly.

Then he stormed off to his room in a fury, muttering, "That bitch is going to cause me a scandal."

Moments later, Salem sneaked in through the back door, panting, with the box full of meat. Finding no one in the kitchen, he lowered the box from on top of his head and looked around. There was no sign of anybody but Tawida. Her sash was on the floor, and a bead necklace she wore had broken and lay scattered all over the kitchen.

Shocked and alarmed, he looked around for answers to the questions in his mind. Then he took off toward their shack.

❧

Daybreak had descended all too quickly, bringing its hectic burdens with it. The kitchen servants would have to proceed with their work as if nothing had happened to their companion. They were expected to function normally despite the earthquake that had struck that morning, and Tawida's absence from the group as she endured her torturous punishment. They would have to prepare a feast for more than fifteen men, who would be gathering to decide on a matter that concerned their trade, their taxes, their life in the city, and their relationship with the Ottoman governor.

A pall of gloom settled over the kitchen help, and no one spoke. They scurried about like ants, without chatting, joking, or singing. The only sound accompanying their labor was that of Tawida's pitiful cries, which rang in their ears like a mournful slave hymn. She wept bitterly and cried out in pain, but there was no response.

Her baby was screaming to be fed, while she hung there helplessly, able to see and hear him, but unable to deliver him from his hunger and thirst.

"My little boy is hungry! He's thirsty! Please, somebody, untie me just so I can nurse him! Have mercy, people!"

Milk rained from her nipples and wet her torn dress, mingling with her blood and her sweat as her cries for help mingled with the sound of the call to the Friday noon prayer.

By this time the infant was pitifully thirsty, so she tried shaking the rope so as to come closer to him and let her milk drip onto his face. His face was contorted and his body convulsed, like someone choking and gasping for air.

Her strength spent, she cried out, "Aida, sister, save me! Salem with the kind heart, where are you? My son is dying before my very eyes!"

Wanting desperately to come to her friend's aid, Aida passed cautiously by the roofed enclosure outside the bathroom but she couldn't see any way to help. So she retreated again into the kitchen, fighting back the tears so as not to let Ahbara see her crying. When the tears fell in spite of her, she stood wiping them away with her shirtsleeve as she stirred the pot.

Fatima tried to get her mother to speak to her father, hoping she could persuade him to untie Tawida for the baby's sake at least. His screams had grown unbearable, and he obviously had nothing to do with his mother's transgression. But all her mother had to say was, "I can't. One more divorce pronouncement and I won't be married anymore. Don't bring ruin on my household, if you please."

Salem was in a terrible way himself. Head bowed and despondent, he stood in front of the large guest reception area listening to the screaming, which was so loud that it drowned out the call to prayer whenever he went in to get something.

Tawida was crying for help, her son was crying from hunger, and only God knew how long the incarceration would go on. In his mind's eye Salem conjured an image of the hungry child in his cardboard box. Then a voice inside him said: *He's hungry, Salem! Is it his fault that adults have made so many mistakes? Don't you love him enough to save him? He's a sinless little angel in this hellhole! So why are you standing here like a moron getting ready to feed a bunch of fools when an innocent soul is starving to death right next to you and you could do something to prevent it?*

Before long, all Salem could think about was the baby boy. So, even as one of the sheikhs invited to the banquet had his hands outstretched for Salem to wash them, he put down the washtub in his hand and left. Passing through the kitchen, he snatched a cleaver and headed for the place where Tawida and her son were imprisoned. Thrusting the cleaver angrily into the lock, he started pounding on it repeatedly in an attempt to jar the door open, his eyes bugging out and his heart weeping. Following her ears to the source of the racket,

Lalla Uwayshina rushed to the scene and tried to stop him. She knew that if Salem managed to rescue Tawida and the baby, the problem would just get bigger once word of it reached her husband. After all, Salem wasn't just breaking through a locked door. He was breaking the word of the master who had locked it.

"Stop! I swear the hajj will kill you!"

But he didn't stop.

Lalla Uwayshina started tugging at Salem's shirt from behind, but to no avail.

"Quick," she said to her daughter, "Call Amin and Abdussalam before things get completely out of hand."

Whenever she warned him of her husband's threat, Salem would say, "Let him kill me, then. I'd be better off. In fact, I wish he would."

When, at long last, the first piece of iron in the lock shattered, the men were coming back from the noon prayer in groups in preparation to eat lunch. Everything and everyone was ready and waiting for them with the exception of Salem, who had left his post in a wave of black fury. Lalla Uwayshina didn't know what to do about the guests, since it was obvious that the banging was coming from inside the house.

The hajj got wind of what was happening through his little boy, who said, "The slave's got the bouri, Baba."

Crazed at this show of insubordination, the master rushed inside in a rage. He picked up the whip again, poised to bring it down on Salem's back. Undeterred by the blows that began raining down on him from behind, Salem went on pounding on the lock with ever increasing speed and fury. The more viciously he was beaten and chastised, the more determined he became.

"You worthless slave! Do you dare disobey me? Seize him!"

Letting the whip fall from his hand, the master punched the slave in the face. However, Salem was prepared to stop at nothing until he'd accomplished his mission.

Aware of what was happening outside her dark prison, Tawida had grown quiet. The baby had grown quiet too, as though he'd nursed his fill.

The inevitable had happened.

While the women tried to get the master to stop, his sons Amin and Abdussalam joined him in his assault to avenge their father. As they pulled the slave in opposite directions by his arms, the master bloodied him in the face with a hoe.

Wanting to postpone Salem's punishment, at least until after the banquet, Lalla Uwayshina said, "You'll get all dirty and sweaty this way. Besides, you don't want to be in this state in front of your guests."

By this time the door had opened and Salem had been forced inside to join what everyone assumed to be his wife and son. After being dragged through his own blood, he was thrown into the corner of the bathroom in a pitiful, half-conscious state.

His eyes glinting with fury, the master bent over him and, gripping his jaw in his hand, growled, "You dare disobey me, you piece of filth?! You haven't seen anything yet!"

Battered, bloodied, and wheezing, Salem murmured in a voice that was barely audible, "The child that just died of hunger and thirst wasn't mine. He was yours. And there's an official birth certificate from al-Figgi to prove it."

The slave's words descended on the master with a force crueler than any lash or hoe. They stopped his heart and paralyzed his limbs, and his grip on the slave's jaw suddenly loosened. In a moment of panic in which he didn't believe his ears, he turned involuntarily toward the cardboard box. Looking strangely at the motionless infant, his eyes closed and his face spattered with his mother's milk and blood, the master reached out and shook him frantically. He shook him again, harder this time, but his body fell limp, a tiny mass of lifeless flesh. Leaping over to the bathroom pail, he scooped up the water in it with his right hand and sprinkled it on the baby's face. But there was no response. He had fallen asleep forever, never to waken.

The master exited the enclosure in a state far different from the one in which he had entered.

The price of a sheep that day was a baby in a cardboard box.

A Piece of You
Is outside of You

AT LAST Benghazi appeared on the horizon and the steamer made its way safely into the bay.

"Ha!" Muhammad exclaimed laughingly to Ali, "There's Benghazi, nephew! Now if that isn't a sight for sore eyes!"

It was the longest Ali had ever spent away from his hometown and, more importantly, from his mother.

As they came into port, Muhammad said, "So what now? We'll arrange to have the merchandise unloaded and then we'll go see our family."

"We made a profit," Ali said happily. "I bet Grandpa will be proud of us and host a dinner for his friends in our honor!"

Little did Ali know that since overseeing his infant grandson's washing and burial his grandfather had sunk into a deep depression, and that he spoke little, ate little, and spent little time with others. Not only had al-Figgi taken care of the entire funeral, he had even claimed responsibility for the deceased child, while the actual grandfather sat grief-stricken and dazed from the force of the shock.

After leading the congregation in the mid-afternoon prayer, al-Figgi invited worshipers to take part in the funeral prayer over his grandson, saying that his son Hussein had fathered the child with one of his slave women. Al-Figgi's presentation of the child in this way came as an added, and unanticipated, blow to the murderous grandfather. The sheikh had justified his decision as necessary to protect the actual grandfather by silencing people who might have heard a different story about how the child had died. This way, he would spare the culprit the ignominy and troubles that would have haunted him for years thereafter, not least of which would have been a loss of respect and prestige. Then there was the ill will of the qa'imaqam, who would have summoned him for interrogation. The qa'imaqam would first have tried to blackmail him, and if he had denied the charges and refused to pay him hush money, he would have found witnesses to testify against him and embroiled him in a labyrinthine case that he would never have found his way out of. Nor would the incident have ended there, since Hajj Imuhammad had rivals who stood prepared to exploit the issue as a way of bringing him down. His business competitors, for example, would have been all too happy to help Tawida lodge a complaint against him before the judge, knowing that even if, as was most likely, the complaint was dismissed, they would have succeeded in destroying him simply by publicizing the fact that he was suspected of wrongdoing.

He was in no need of all those crises. If, on the other hand, the deceased child was portrayed as the son of a slave woman by a man in the prime of his youth, no one would bother to ask about him. Many people had buried the children of slave women, and the matter had generally been forgotten as soon as people left the mosque or the cemetery, especially if the child's father was a mere adolescent who was feeling his way toward manhood.

Besides, al-Figgi had long been a steadfast friend and a trustworthy counselor who wouldn't have thought of sneaking into the graveyard to hide the corpse of a tiny baby who had been killed by his grandfather in a fit of rage. If he had, he would have been found out by the cemetery guard and the gravediggers, who knew the life stories of everyone in the cemetery and how they had died. They even knew the stories of the sorceresses who used to descend from the upper realms and fly around the cemetery. They would milk the moon into a black cup over one of the graves until it split open before them. Then the deceased person's hand would emerge from the grave and they would use it to make couscous. Once they'd finished, they would put the hand back in the grave and close it up again by pouring the moon's milk out of the cup.

Any cemetery guard who'd been able to determine the size and color of the cup in the legend could hardly have failed to notice a baby being hastily buried under cover of darkness by two of the town's respected dignitaries. By the next morning, the baby would have emerged from the grave as if by a miracle, and the cemetery guard would have shown him to the people of the village. The cemetery guard would have told the villagers that the grave had been dug up the night before by hungry wolves, and that if it weren't for his intervention the poor child would have been gobbled up. To whom, then—he would ask—did the freshly dug grave belong? And where were the family members whose duty it was to come and bury him again?

This was how gravediggers made their living when the town's notables weren't bringing them any new bodies to bury for wages that befit their families' station.

Attributing the dead child to Hussein would afford the grandfather full protection, while at the same time assuring the deceased a place in the ground that would remain undisturbed by wolves, dogs, and cemetery guards alike. Even if the slaves talked about the incident and the story came out, nobody would believe them. A slave's testimony was never taken seriously, and their account would be dismissed as some yarn they'd spun out of hearsay.

Al-Figgi hadn't taken these measures for his own sake. Rather, he had acted as he had out of devotion to a lifelong friend and companion who had never spared any effort to advise and help him however he could.

During the funeral prayer, the actual grandfather fought back tears of sorrow and regret, while al-Figgi maintained perfect composure. His head bowed, and supported on either side by two slaves, Hussein sat in silence near the tiny shrouded bundle, lifting his gaze just long enough to extend his hand to those offering their condolences. Wearing a long beard and the loose, flowing tunic of a Sufi adept, he looked like someone who'd died and been brought out of a tomb to act the part of the living.

Al-Figgi explained that his son was in shock over the loss of his beloved first child. Hardly had he discovered what it was like to be a father than the experience had been wrenched away from him. He'd been getting ready to announce himself as the child's father when death overtook him: the baby choked on his mother's milk while nursing one day and died.

Hussein kept to himself most of the time and wasn't known to many people. A homebody, he rarely frequented the marketplace or spent time in the streets. People close to the family knew him to be reticent and shy—traits he'd inherited from his mother. Consequently, he didn't fit the image of the man who ascends the city podium, still less of someone who intervenes in others' affairs and issues legal rulings on everything imaginable. As such, he was a mere shadow of his father.

What al-Figgi did had made things easier on Hajj Imuhammad in relation to other people. But when he was alone with himself, he was consumed with sorrow and remorse. How could such a thing have happened without his knowledge? Why had al-Figgi hidden the facts from him? If he'd only told him the truth, he wouldn't have killed his long-awaited grandson with his own hands. Now he might never have another male grandchild—that is, if Muhammad kept having girls, and if his family kept shying away from suggesting that he take a second wife for fear of causing a rupture with his in-laws.

Further, why didn't al-Figgi seem to be affected by the death of Muhammad's baby? Why wasn't he encouraging the bereaved grandfather to forget the matter and not blow it out of proportion? After all, he could have tried to make light of the incident, telling the grandfather that the dead child wasn't worth grieving over, since half of his genes had come from a slave woman.

"He was my grandson," Master Imuhammad lamented, "and I might never have another one!"

"Now now," al-Figgi said. "Why are you wailing over this like a woman? After all, you might have one through your other sons if God doesn't give Muhammad another male child."

"But Muhammad has a special place in the family."

"Bury the little one and bury the whole story with him. Then get rid of that good-for-nothing slave woman before your son comes back. If a mare is too much trouble, the best thing is to sell it and be rid of the bad luck it brings. The same goes for a slave."

"I've started to be afraid of her and the bad luck she might bring me."

"Leave her to me, then. I'll take of her."

On their way back from the cemetery, al-Figgi said, "Sell her to me. I'll relieve both you and your son of her in a single stroke. Then I'll deduct her price from the debt you owe me. There. What do you say?"

Master Imuhammad nodded, his thoughts somewhere else.

As for Muhammad, he hadn't seemed worried about whether he had a son or not, and had shown no interest in taking another wife. He'd never even spoken of the matter, and no one knew what he thought about it. His sister Fatima figured the reason for his lack of concern was the presence of Tawida and her son. Now that he was known to be the father of Tawida's child, the family understood why he had been reticent to speak: he had been waiting for the right time to announce his paternity.

The night the baby was buried was agony for his mother. She was inconsolable. For two days Jaballah and Aida plied her with date wine to numb her to her suffering. Jaballah would bring it, and Aida would have her drink it until she was knocked out. Then Aida would undress Tawida with the help of two other slave women, give her a bath, and put her to bed. On the third day, Lalla Uwayshina told Aida to gather Tawida's things into a bundle, since a wagon would be coming to take her somewhere else. The family had come to see her presence in the household as bad luck.

In tears, Aida cleaned Tawida up and, wanting to get her attention for a few moments, sat her upright. "Listen to me, Tawida." Aida said earnestly. "They're going to sell you."

But the only response Tawida gave was a repeated, "Aah! Aah! Aah!"

Not long thereafter Tawida left the house with a small bundle containing all her belongings and, in a highly secretive transaction, Lalla Uwayshina sold her to al-Figgi. He drew up a contract, according to which Tawida had bought her freedom from Lalla Uwayshina with the understanding that she would go to work for al-Figgi and that she would remain in his service until he had collected her price in full. She wouldn't be allowed to leave until she had paid off the debt, and if she fled she would be considered a fugitive slave who, if found, would have to be forcibly returned to her employer and flogged in a public square on orders from the judge of the Islamic court. The contract also stipulated that the police would be required to assist in hunting her down and bringing her back.

A free woman who asked to be divorced from her husband would be registered with the Islamic magistrate as "refractory," after which she would remain in a state of limbo for the rest of her life. Though legally bound to her husband, she would be neither married nor divorced, and no other man could ever touch her. So if this was what awaited a free woman who refused her husband, how much worse a fate would a slave woman endure?

There was also another agreement concerning Tawida of which Lalla Uwayshina knew nothing. This agreement stipulated that during the first quarter of the emancipation period, Tawida would be sold to Muhammad's brother-in-law—his wife Rugaya's brother—who was a merchant from Misrata. If al-Figgi agreed to it, this man would be Tawida's owner for the remainder of the time it took her to purchase her freedom. What this meant was that she would become free in Misrata, the city known to be the cruelest place a slave would ever have to work!

The agreement was thorny, convoluted, and riddled with legalese, the only simple thing about it being that with the price she got for Tawida, Lalla Uwayshina could complete her one-of-a-kind set of hoop earrings!

A slave driving a wagon arrived and waited for Tawida to be brought out. Jaballah carried her out in his arms, completely unconscious. Both he and Aida wept in silence, helpless to prevent the suffering that had been poured out on their friend. Meanwhile Fatima blamed her mother, reminding her that when her brother learned of the incident, he wouldn't let it go, no matter how carefully they tried to cover their tracks.

As Tawida was being taken away, Lalla Rugaya stood watching from her balcony. She whisked her fan unhurriedly back and forth, her features placid. Soon thereafter she removed two gold ornaments, each the size and shape of a date stone, from a necklace she owned, wrapped them in some cotton, and sent them in secret to al-Figgi as a token of her appreciation. She entrusted the ornaments to her private servant, with instructions to thank al-Figgi personally for his efforts toward banishing the servant woman.

As people bustled to and fro, anxious to be done with their day-to-day business, Tawida was being transported in a drunken stupor to a tranquil realm devoid of evil machinations. The only thing it contained was the image of a little cardboard box that had been lost forever, and the features of a beloved who might, or might not, come to her rescue.

> My wound is deep, it has no cure,
> I hide it, but the pain till death may endure.
>
> My wound is deep, hidden from view,
> Where is he whose love makes me ill?
> Faint, oh so faint, is my hope of rescue,
> When will the Almighty my hope fulfill?
>
> I have a wound that will not heal,
> It festers night and day.
> My heart pines for when he called my name,
> The beloved so far away.
>
> My wound is deep, it has no cure.
> I fear the pain till death will endure.

Pleading

THE SLAVES came into the house carrying the two men's suitcases and other things they had brought home with them. As soon as she heard of the travelers' safe return, Fatima let forth with a loud trill. It wasn't uncommon for ships to sink when exiting or entering the strait. Indeed, many a vessel had foundered on Benghazi's rugged coastline, causing untold loss of life and cargo.

Fatima's trills were followed by a shorter, softer trill by Lalla Uwayshina, who was engrossed in braiding her hair when one of the servants came and informed her of the two men's arrival.

Beneath the show of jubilance, however, the women were awkward and flustered, their hearts racing in dread of the moment when the returning son learned of his child's shocking death, and fearful of what would come in its wake.

Following the tragic incident, the baby's grandfather had given a lot of thought to what he was going to do. He had even considered sending his son into a kind of voluntary exile by having him stay in Malta on business. But here he was home again.

"Where's Tawida?" Muhammad asked his sister Fatima after hearing the news.

"She ran away after the incident."

"Where did she go?"

"Nobody knows."

"I don't believe you," Muhammad retorted. "You've agreed among yourselves not to talk, that's all!"

After a pause, he asked, "And where's Salem?"

"He's sick, God help the poor man."

"What's wrong with him? Or do you not know anything about him, either?"

"He's been bedridden ever since Baba beat him with the hoe. He doesn't move a muscle."

"Where is he?"

"In his corner. Other slaves are tending to him."

Gripped by a sudden rage, Muhammad headed for Salem's shack. His footsteps heavy on the ground, the fury in his voice was muted by suppressed tears. How could something so painful and tragic be real? The deaf slave woman, who had been sweeping in front of the shack as he approached, stopped and rested against the wall with her broom, stone-still except for her eyes as they darted fearfully back and forth.

He pushed the tinplate door open and went in. Freshly cleaned and swept, the place smelled of incense, and a tea kettle rested on the stove. The ailing man, asleep in the dark corner, lay beneath a pile of sheets and blankets. His face was swollen, and the hoe had left him with a fractured skull, a shattered nose, and a broken leg. When he sensed someone approaching, he opened his eyes a slit, thinking it was another servant, or Sakita, his favorite kitty. He was hardly eating, though he drank a lot.

He heard the visitor say, "Thank God you're still in one piece."

After some time, barely able to open his eyes, the slave murmured, "God bless you, Master."

"Salem . . ." Muhammad began, choking on his tears. Then, in an entirely unexpected gesture, he bent down and kissed Salem's hand, which hung limply off the bed. The slave quickly withdrew his hand and placed it on his master's head.

"Forgive me for wronging you! Forgive me!" Muhammad blurted out. "You're free now. Your writ of manumission will be in your hand this very day. And I'll have you taken to the hospital."

In reply, Salem murmured, "I'm a slave with nothing to give. I don't even own myself."

"On the contrary, I want you to forgive me the way a free man would forgive a slave. You're free now, but I'm not."

Salem said no more. He couldn't thank his master for a freedom that had come at the price of blood, agony, and the death of a baby boy. As tears flowed out of his closed eyes and down the sides of his face, he mumbled through parched lips, "What is there for me to forgive you for? The little one didn't make it."

"But you did your duty, and more."

Muhammad had a wagon readied to take Salem to the hospital. Then he sat down at the entrance to the slaves' quarters and sobbed audibly. He cried with a voice that wasn't ashamed to say: I may be a grown man in a world devoid of compassion that relegates tears to the realm of the feminine and reserves joy for the male of the species. But I still have the right to cry! I have the right to cry when I'm sad, and that's that.

He was my son, Lord! I entrusted him and his mother into your care when I went away. So why didn't you come to their defense? Why didn't you send your mercy down into my parents' hearts? Why did you give it to the weak and helpless and withhold it from those with the power to do what needed to be done? Why, Lord? Why??

As Salem was being trundled away, his white cat, Sakita, ran after him, and before the wagon turned off the long dirt road she managed to leap onto its back ledge and sit down at his head.

Standing on the Outside, Kneeling on the Inside

THOUGH IT WASN'T TIME for prayer, a woman came and asked to speak with al-Figgi in the zawiya attached to the mosque. Draped in a *farrashiya* and concealing her face, she greeted the sheikh and introduced herself as Rugaya Bint Zamzam.[1] Then, for purposes of more precise identification, she told him she was "the one who sent you the two gold pieces wrapped in cotton." As soon as she added this detail, he cordially returned her greeting and asked her to tell him what had brought her to see him, as women would sometimes come to him to inquire about religious matters.

"It's time to keep your promise, Sheikh," the woman said.

"I would, my daughter," al-Figgi replied, "but I've received a warning from above that I dare not ignore."

"What do you mean?" she asked, surprised.

Clearing his throat self-assuredly, he murmured, *"Bismillah ar-rahman ar-rahim"* (in the name of God, most merciful and compassionate) and *"subhan Allah"* (glory be to God).

---

1. A woman's garment particular to Libya, the *farrashiya* is a white, sheet-like wrap that covers its wearer from head to toe. It can be drawn across the face and eyes if one so wishes.

In reply to her question he said, "One Thursday morning after praying the dawn prayer, I lay down and dozed off for a little while. As I slept, I saw a venerable sheikh clad in pure white. He had wings that looked as huge as mountains. 'Open the door, Hamad. Open the door!' he said. When I heard him speak, I woke up and asked him, 'Which door, my liege?' He said, 'Open up! I am Gabriel, sent to you by Sidi Abdussalam Al Asmar.' Feeling afraid, I said, 'This thing is from the Almighty, Oh men of God!' The visitor told me not to be afraid, and said, 'Sidi Abdussalam has come to visit, not to destroy. And he wants you to release the slave woman.' 'I don't have a slave woman, my liege,' I told him. He said, 'I'm talking about the one you're holding. Then slaughter a black goat without a speck of white on it and distribute its meat, bones, intestines, and hide to the poor in the marketplace. Not a morsel of it is to enter your own mouth, not even its broth, its head, or its hooves.' So forgive me, my daughter, but I can't keep the promise I made to you. The sign from Heaven is clear—the only thing clearer would be the message of a prophet. If I were to keep her, it would be bad for me, my household, my wife, my son, and even people who come into my house. Your brother in Misrata has wealth, prestige, influence, and children. But if this slave woman were to enter his household, she would bring him affliction and disaster. May God protect both us and you!"

Clearing his throat, he continued, "You know how people gossip, and they'll say his sister had envied him and sent him an ill-fated slave woman that reversed his good fortunes. Remember, my daughter, that the greatest blessing lies in what God chooses. This is what I was told by the righteous saint who visited me. But if you think otherwise, I'll sell her to you and waive my ownership of her. As for the two gold pieces, I don't need them. As a man, I have no use for them, and they aren't enough to make a necklace for my wife. They've been in a jeweler's safekeeping since the day I received them, but I'll send someone for them now. If, on the other hand, you'd rather have cash, I can pay you for them."

He slipped his hand into his farmala pocket, but the woman jumped up and bowed down before him, kissing his hands, and reaching out shyly to stop him. "God forbid, Sheikh!" she remonstrated. "I didn't come to ask for them back, or even to talk about them. And I didn't come looking for money. I only came seeking your blessing and wise counsel!"

Reassured, al-Figgi said, "Whether she goes to Misrata or any-where else, the important thing is for you to be rid of her and her evil influence. That alone calls for a thanksgiving banquet."

"Of course, Sheikh," the young woman said, taking the hint. "We will be hosting a banquet and you'll be the guest of honor. We intend to do it as soon as my husband returns from the land of the Christians."

"God keep you, my daughter, and be well pleased with you."

"God bless you, Sheikh, and give you a long life. Ask God to grant me a boy and to guide my husband aright."

"Consider it done, my daughter. Consider it done."

The woman left feeling relieved, spiritually uplifted, and trium-phant. Al-Figgi had supplied her with a bottle of water into which he had recited special supplications and verses from the Qur'an. When she got home, she sprinkled some of the water on her bed, applied a few drops to her face, and spread some on her arms and her legs. Then she hid it under her bed, hoping it would help her to change her life and bring her the marital love she'd been deprived of for so long.

Before leaving the zawiya, al-Figgi instructed a slave to fill all the water bottles and tins in the mosque bathroom from the public spigot. No mosque or zawiya should ever be short on water. Not only this, but the water in such places wasn't just any old water. Rather, it was of a special kind because, when the sheikhs recited the Qur'an over it, dipping their fingers in it and breathing over it, its ordinary proper-ties were replaced with supernatural ones, including the ability to cure sicknesses of body and soul alike, both seen and unseen.

Muhammad, smitten with a black slave woman who had so taken over his soul that he'd been blinded to the beauty and charm of his lovely, fair-skinned young wife, was in need of a cure. The Qur'an would have to intervene and restore the common sense that had been stolen away by the delights of concubinage. Wherever pleasure resides, there resides Satan himself, who uses it to lure people into his snares. Once they've experienced it for the first time, they come back for more and more until they're hopelessly addicted, their reason and their will alike stripped away. Muhammad had been bewitched by this Negro woman. Everyone knew his infatuation was that of a madman, not that of someone in his right mind. But could any of them say he understood the difference between madness and sanity? If someone did claim to understand this, it might be because he'd never fallen in love himself. Does a sane person have the ability to fall in love whenever and however he wishes? Or can romantic love and volition only coexist in someone who's either crazy or bewitched?!

The Muhammad who belonged to the slave woman wasn't the Muhammad who related to his family and other people. That's what love will do to you. There are people who resent others who experience love because they don't experience it themselves, so they'll do everything in their power to keep it from coming into existence or, if it does come into existence, to make sure it doesn't last. One way they do this is by attributing it to sorcery. They convince themselves and everyone around them that love is nothing but a form of Satanic voodoo that afflicts the heart. Having done this, they can justify waging war on love by every means possible, including—irony of ironies—sorcery itself!

Be that as it may, Muhammad went on searching for his black beloved. Where could she possibly be? Where could she have been banished? He went looking for her in places where Negroes tended to congregate, thinking that she might have hidden among them under another name. He went to the city and asked slave traders about her, thinking that someone might have tried to sell her to them. He enticed them with money to find her for him. One day somebody sent a message to Muhammad, asking him to come to the bazaar. He rushed to the spot, in his mind's eye Tawida's face as he'd last seen it. He bounded up the stairs leading to an upper room where the merchant was waiting for him. When he got there, he was met by the sight of a beautiful young Negro woman whom the merchant thought was the one he'd been looking for. He went out to the roofed enclosure where slave girls were being displayed, hoping against hope to find his beloved among them. They had just recently been brought from the Sudan and still spoke its gibberish, whereas his beloved had been born locally to black parents who had themselves been third-generation slaves. Besides, she wasn't beautiful in the way the slave merchant would have expected her to be. After all, what white man would go to the trouble of looking for a runaway slave woman unless she was absolutely ravishing?

Tawida was a handsome woman, but not as beautiful as the Negro girls on display on the shop roofs: young girls dressed in special clothes designed to entice potential buyers, their arms and legs rubbed with olive oil to make their skin glisten, their lips drawn in black, their eyes enhanced and defined with a border of antimony.

It was a market for beauty of another hue in which Muhammad's beauty was nowhere to be found. So he left, dejected, and headed back to his own shop.

Where could she have gone?

Benghazi—the City of Salt—had no taste without her![2]

"Why don't you give up the search?" Ali asked him.

"No matter how hard I try, I can't forget her."

"You could get another one, couldn't you?"

"I'm not looking for a body. Every woman's got one, of course! I'm looking for a one-of-a-kind spirit that I've never found, and never will find, in anybody but her. What good would it do to be with another woman every day if she didn't have the spirit I love and long for?"

Where could you be, Tawida?!

Nobody knew where the unnamed slave on that strange wagon had carted her off to. Who had given her to whom? Who had sold her to whom? Who had bought her from whom?

Nobody could have cared less about a slave in that country unless he was a merchant or in love.

2. "City of Salt" or "Village of Salt" is an ancient name for Benghazi derived from its fame for salt extraction.

The Cloak and the Dervish

HUSSEIN SAT HUDDLED in a corner of the zawiya, his eyes closed like someone transported to another world, monotonously repeating the same verses of the Qur'an over and over again. His father, who had decided to try bringing Hussein out of one kind of isolation with another, had encouraged him to do a spiritual retreat. Hoping to turn his son into a real spiritual adept, he would come and check on him every now and then.

A wagon pulled up in front of the zawiya. Shortly thereafter, assisted by the slave who'd driven the wagon and supporting himself on a cane, Salem got out. He'd known where to find Hussein without asking anyone.

The Qur'an shook in Hussein's hand when he saw Salem come in. Then he buried his face in the book again and went on with his memorization.

Coming up to him, Salem said, "I want you to help me find a place to live and work. I'm free now, but I'm also homeless, with no job and no protection. I'm more scared than ever now in a country where you get eaten alive."

The boy nodded, leaning into the Qur'an he was holding, and said, "Believe me, nobody's free. There's no such thing as a free human being. There are just different kinds of prisoners, and different prisons. I can help you find a temporary refuge while your wounds heal. But I can't guarantee you anything beyond that."

Hussein went on, "There's no place for us in this bitter world, neither for slaves like you, nor for those who, like me, fall somewhere in the middle—half-slave, half-free. But we can find rest in voluntary isolation. There's nothing but either God the creator or people. I love God in spite of everything, but I hate people. At the same time, I'm ashamed of myself. God wouldn't want a Muslim like me."

Hussein's way of talking was new and strange, and Salem, whom life had shattered in every possible way, found it incomprehensible.

Neither of them said anything for a while, and Hussein went on rocking in front of the Qur'an. Then suddenly he stopped and, without looking up, asked Salem, "Are you happy to have your freedom?"

"I don't even know what it feels like to be happy," Salem admitted, hanging his head. "What I do feel is a kind of relief, mixed with a fear of the unknown."

"Maybe you could be a zawiya slave. You'd clean it, open and close it, and fill its water receptacles. You'd light the incense and paint its walls with lime. You'd prepare the ink for the students, arrange the books, and clean the sheikhs' feet. If we had guests, you'd slaughter and cook a sheep for them. But would you be able to push a wheelbarrow full of hot coals, firewood, and incense up and down the city streets when we celebrate the Prophet's birthday? Would you be able to heat the *bendirs* for the sheikhs, sling a drum over your back, and let a drummer beat on it from behind you?[1] Would you be willing to clean up after the adepts who lose control of their bowels as they wander around the zawiya chanting God's praises at the hadra? Could you guard this place against evil spirits and ritual impurity? Could you march behind your sheikh with a ram on your back all the way to a shrine without needing to stop and rest?"

"Of course," Salem murmured. "I've done things a lot harder than any of that."

1. Meaning "large hand frame drum" in Turkish, the term *bendir* refers to a traditional wooden percussion instrument that is used throughout North Africa as well as in Sufi ceremonies.

"You're sick, and too much moving around would hurt you. But if you join the zawiya, you'll be a great man who's close to God. It's completely different from the world of livestock you were living in before. Who knows? You might become an adept yourself someday. I'll ask my father to find you work either here or in some other zawiya. He's got lots of connections."

"Wouldn't you like to know how I got my freedom?"

"I already know how that happens. Slaves get their freedom either as a gift from their master for something good they did or because their master committed some sin that he wants to atone for. Slaves would never be allowed to advocate for their own freedom. That would be considered disobedience, and they'd be punished for it. But atonements and gifts are different, since they're initiated by the master, not the slave."

This said, Hussein went back to his recitation, his big writing tablet rocking back and forth before him. As he went into another trance-like state, tears welled up in his eyes, which were fixed on the verses of the Holy Qur'an.

Salem gave Hussein a bewildered stare, still wondering what had come over him.

As he turned to leave, he said, "You know, my little bird? You look handsome in that cloak."

"I don't recognize myself in it," the young man muttered.

Tracking the Spirit
of the One You Love

AFTER RETURNING FROM MALTA and learning of the baby's death, Muhammad avoided seeing his father. In fact, he didn't want to talk to anybody in his family. So he left the house and went to live in Tawida's shack, which came as a cruel blow to his parents and his wife. Fatima would bring him food and drink, and she and her son Ali would sit with him for hours as he cried and poured out his heart to her. All she could do was try to ease his pain with calming words.

Muhammad's refusal to have anything to do with his family frightened his mother, hurt his father, and broke his wife's heart. One day his father finally decided to go have a talk with him. Muhammad was lying on the bed when his father came in. He had expected the visitor to be Ali or Fatima, but who should walk in but the blustering old man, who jabbed him several times in the waist with his cane.

"Get up now, and stop being such a sissy. What's all this fuss over a slave woman with a split upper lip and hooves for feet? You've made us a laughingstock! It'll be a scandal to beat all scandals if your in-laws get wind of what you've been doing. You abandon your wife and your daughters to go grieve over a servant woman. Unbelievable! So which one's the slave—she, or you? Get up, damn you!"

"What pains me is the thought that my baby boy died of hunger and thirst under my own roof. Did it pain any of you?"

The old man was slightly rattled by his son's retort. But then, as if he hadn't heard a thing, he tapped the ground with his cane and bellowed, "Oh, so now he's your son whose death grieves you so! After he was born, you acted as if he didn't belong to you, and you were fine with letting him live in a cardboard box. You begrudged him even a cradle or clothes to wear. And now it occurs to you to weep and wail, 'My son, my son!'"

"So bring him back to me and let me acknowledge him as mine, circumcise him, and buy things for him the way fathers do for their sons without any interference from you all. Would you really have let me do that? I didn't get to choose my own wife, or even my daughters' names. So how much freedom would I have had to decide how to relate to a slave woman that you've assaulted along with me? But I'm to blame. All my life I've been a coward, scared of you and your anger. In relation to you, I'm not a man, and I've got no authority over anything."

"So you've found your tongue, have you?"

Lalla Uwayshina was nearby, listening in on the conversation and waiting for the right moment to come in and say something.

"God guide you, son," she said. "Your daughters ask about you. They say, 'What's wrong with our father?' And I don't know what to tell them. What fault is this of theirs, or your wife's? She hasn't done anything wrong, and she's been putting up patiently with your cold neglect. Do you think God's pleased with what you're doing to her? Curse Satan and get on with your life. If it's a matter of having a slave woman, you can go to the market and buy yourself a new one every day if you want to. All the men do it, son. But nobody would abandon his family for a slave girl."

Muhammad held his peace until they had both said all they had to say and left. Once they were gone, he bit his hand to keep himself from screaming. Then he burst into tears.

Nobody's willing to understand that I'm a human being and that you, my beloved, are my beloved!

⌇

Al-Figgi and his son left the zawiya after a tempestuous hadra in which the aromas of benzoin, gum ammoniac, and asafetida rent the heavens, hands burned from the beating of tambourines, and tongues waxed eloquent in praise of the Prophet and hymns to the Almighty. Singers, adepts, and seekers alike danced with their sheikhs until they fell to the floor in exhaustion, vying to reach the heights of ecstasy and rapture in which, divorced from the external world, they were filled with inner tranquility. When an adept had achieved this state, he was like a pure spirit soaring through heavenly realms with God and the noble members of the Prophet's family. The person wandering in the ecstasy of love, absent from this earthly realm, would be ushered into a higher world only accessible to a chosen elite: a supernatural world where hearing isn't mere hearing, nor seeing mere seeing, where the senses are vivid beyond description and vision is clear to perfection, where you can see the invisible, hear the inaudible, and touch the untouchable. It's a world merited only by those with the purest of souls and the sublimest of aspirations, by the reciters of the Qur'an and the knowers of its secrets who chant it day and night and believe unquestioningly in what it says about the outer appearances of things and their inner essences, by those whose spirits cling in love to God and His Prophet, who perceive the true causes underlying things and for whom the veil has been drawn back, who, step by step, ascend the ladder of spiritual illumination. These are the men of God, the praiseworthy helpers. Of these, the highest in rank is the sheikh of the hadra, who leads processions down the streets toward paths of light, knowledge, and the divine love.

Sustenance, sustenance, succor, succor.

After the religious gathering had dispersed, Muhammad waited on a side street that al-Figgi usually took on his way home. When al-Figgi and his son approached, Muhammad stepped out of the shadows and blocked their path. In his capacity as patriarch and sheikh of the hadra, al-Figgi was walking two steps ahead of his son, who trailed behind like a shadow, his collarbones visible through the neck opening in his mantle. With a downy-soft beard that lay flat over his cheeks and black circles around his wide eyes, he looked like a true dervish. At the same time, being a novice, he'd gotten dizzy from so much spinning and twirling, he had vomited repeatedly in the course of the hadra, and his spirit had nearly been wrested away in a state of spiritual ecstasy.

"Where have you taken Tawida?" Muhammad demanded.

"*Bismillah ar-rahman ar-rahim, a'udhu billahi min sharr ash-shaytan ar-rajim!*" al-Figgi muttered in alarm, calling on the Merciful to protect him from Satan and his evil forces.

"Where have you taken the poor woman?!"

"I have no idea where she is. What have I got to do with her and all your family problems?"

"So you're playing dumb, are you? You snake in the grass, you masterminded all the problems we've having in our household!"

Pushing Muhammad roughly out of his path, the sheikh retorted, "Get out of my way. It's enough what you did to me before."

Taking a few steps away, al-Figgi shouted at his son, who stood gawking into the other men's faces, "Come on, we're late!"

As the young man hurried to catch up with his father, Muhammad added, "We've still got plenty of scores to settle, Sheikh."

Brushing off the threat, al-Figgi retorted, "Do your worst. See if I care!"

The Cat's in the Bag

TAWIDA WAS BEING HELD in a brothel under the supervision of a woman who took her orders from al-Figgi.

After delivering Tawida to her, he instructed the woman, "Keep her as a trust. Don't use her."

He left her some money in return for Tawida's room and board, then disappeared. Tawida was placed in a dirty room in a large house under the strict management of the fiercest, most formidable of the slave women. She would bring Tawida her food without talking with her, or even asking her what had brought her there in such a miserable state. She would force her to drink an earthen jug full of *marisa*, a kind of locally made wine, and would stand guard over her, stiff and unfeeling, while she ate and bathed, as though she were a machine rather than a human being. When Tawida asked her, "Where am I?" she wouldn't reply, and when Tawida cried she would just tell her to be quiet. When Tawida blamed her and chided her for not doing anything to help her own kind—since the woman was also black—she slapped her across the face and bit her. One time she bit her on the shoulder and pinched her thighs until they bled.

Eventually, when Tawida heard the prostitutes' bawdy laughter and the loud ruckus they made with the clientele, she figured out what kind of a place she'd been brought to. So then: she'd ended up in the worst place in the world. The faces that peeked in and gawked at her belonged to the older, more seasoned whores, who went around all made up even when they weren't working, while the ones she saw out her window were the younger ones who walked the streets full-time. The brothel was populated by a mixture of blacks and whites, beautiful and homely, young and old. The place had a director, an administration, and a cadre of employees, each of whom had specific assigned duties. Some worked as hairdressers; others' job was to groom and depilate the other prostitutes; still others were responsible for makeup, hair dying, henna, oral hygiene, massages, and abortions. Each service had a certain fee and was governed by specific regulations.

The shushana who'd been assigned to oversee Tawida was a huge, extraordinarily cruel woman with bug eyes. She carried out orders down to the last detail and didn't appear to be moved by anything, not even by the tips or protection money she was paid.

As for the brothel owner, she was a short, thin, aging woman who acted and dressed younger than her age. She loved to chew gum, she wore lipstick all the time, and her hands and feet were always decorated with henna. She wore fancy silk dresses, beautifully embroidered vests, and loads of jewelry. She went around singing marskawi, and she got a kick out of calling her younger prostitutes bad names. She used to set a chair under a leafy bitter orange tree in the inner courtyard, and would sit there embroidering and smoking while she watched customers come and go.

One day the brothel owner came into Tawida's room and asked her why she cried all the time. Tawida told her that her baby had recently been killed before her very eyes, and that she felt wounded and hopeless. The woman said nothing, seemingly moved by what Tawida had said, and withdrew. A day or so later, she surprised Tawida by offering to help her forget her painful past and overcome her crisis. She pointed out that when we pay attention to all the things there are to worry about in the world, they can take over our lives. So, she said, Tawida needed to forget about her little boy, and about the white man who'd enjoyed her for a while and then gone his way. She needed to go on with her life, she said. She shouldn't hold onto anything or grieve anything's loss. After all, she added, Tawida was young and petty, and could still have a decent life if she took proper care of herself.

As for the baby boy, he would have been worthless to her as a black slave woman. He would only have brought her more suffering, since he would either have been taken from her and sold as a slave or, if his father had acknowledged him as his, he would have become a slave to his white brothers. When he grew up, he would have been conscripted by the Ottoman governor and forced to go fight somewhere for the caliphate state. The boy wouldn't have offered her any protection or provided her with a respected place in society.

She advised Tawida not to get her hopes up if she heard that this or that slave woman had gained her freedom based on the system known as *umm al-walad*, "mother of the son," which was supposed to guarantee that a slave woman who bore her master a son would be granted her freedom. That sort of thing only happened in fairy tales, she said. In reality, and for long centuries, slave caravans had brought more females than males. Every one of those slave women had become *umm al-walad*, but not one of them had received her freedom and a life of dignity. On the contrary, prostitution had spread and brothel babies were thrown in the street or left on mosque doorsteps.

After talking to her for an hour, the woman brought in a Bedouin man who'd come to the city to sell firewood, and who wanted a room to stay the night in so that he could sell the rest of his bundles the next day. He also wanted a Negro woman to keep him from getting cold and lonely.

But Tawida threw him out, filling the house with her screams. At the sound of the ruckus, the prostitutes came out of their rooms or checked out the bizarre spectacle through their windows. Some of them demanded that Tawida be shut up so that they could finish with their customers, while others made no comment. They figured this was her first time, and that she'd get used to it after a while.

"Be quiet, damn you!" the brothel owner barked. "You're causing us a scandal!"

The girls who'd come out into the hallway told her, "Don't make a big deal out of it. Pretty soon she'll get the hang of it and stop making such a racket."

As for the Bedouin, he said, "Let her scream. I like my women wild and unwilling! Leave her to me—I'll quiet her down. Here, take what I've got now and I'll give you some more tomorrow."

"That's not enough," retorted the brothel owner as she counted the money. "Don't you see how young and beautiful she is? No, no, that won't do!"

"Why not?"

"Her owner will punish me."

"I'll give you more, I swear—tomorrow, after I've sold the rest of my firewood."

A young prostitute who was assisting the brothel owner said to him, "But she screams. There are others who wouldn't be so loud."

"Shut up and go back to your work!" the brothel owner shot back.

Then, changing her mind about the agreement with the Bedouin, she said to him, "I'll give you another young pretty one. Don't bother yourself with this one. All she does is spout bouri."

"I want her young, mean, and clean."

"Damn the whole lot of you!" the brothel owner snapped, tying the hem of her dress at her waist. "You're ugly, filthy, and old, and you want girls that are young and clean!"

Shutting the door on Tawida, the eccentric shushana disappeared briefly, then came back carrying a sack. Then she took Tawida to the kitchen and set her to work crushing date pits to make fodder for their livestock. It was exhausting labor, especially with all the other chores she had to do now: cooking, washing the prostitutes' clothes, cleaning the house, foddering the donkeys belonging to customers who'd come from the outskirts of the city, and clearing the dung out of the place where they stayed in one corner of the house.

For several days, Tawida tagged along behind the shushana assigned to guard her and did all her work for her. Then suddenly the shushana asked Tawida to henna her hands and feet and put on lipstick and eyeliner. When Tawida asked her why, she replied curtly, "It's none of your business."

But Tawida would have none of it.

"No!" she objected vehemently. "I don't want to!"

Forced now to take extreme measures, the cruel shushana called on other women in the house, who tied Tawida's arms and legs to a chair, then started depilating her and decorating her hands and feet with henna to the sound of her loud shrieks. Accustomed to such situations, the shushana slapped Tawida, stripped her naked, and stuffed a piece of cloth into her mouth. When Tawida could hardly take any more, the shushana had her drink some locally brewed date wine known as *lagibi* to calm her down. Tawida downed the whole glass, hoping to God it would kill her and she could be done with it all. When Tawida's strength finally gave out, the shushana smeared lipstick on her mouth, plucked out her eyebrows, and drew them in with kohl.

By the time her guard had finished plying her with booze, Tawida was roaring drunk, and alternately singing and ranting incoherently. The massive shushana picked Tawida up, slung her onto her back, lugged her to the bathroom, and set her down in the washtub. She proceeded to scrub her like a filthy garment as Tawida cursed her and called her every name in the book. Undeterred, the shushana just pinched her or slapped her hands. Then she put Tawida's clothes back on, slung her onto her back again, and carried her to her room, by which time Tawida was too exhausted to put up a fight.

In a room redolent with incense, its sole window covered with a red curtain, a lantern flickered, and the man for whom all these preparations had been made sat expectantly on the edge of a canopy bed, incredulous that he had finally gotten to her.

The shushana came in, flung the object of his lust onto the bed, closed the door behind her, and left.

The brothel owner stood nearby, personally looking after the comfort of this special customer, while at the same time taking care to look just right in her newly acquired silk robe. She was pleased with the profit she'd made off this slave woman, who could fetch four times the price of some "baby zucchini," or inexperienced prostitute. She was also counting up the contents of the basket the night's distinguished guest had sent before coming. It contained a large quantity of food, for which she was grateful. So what could she say but "praise be to God" at the end of this day? After all, she'd been paid liberally, and she intended to give her brawny shushana a tip.

"This girl's a real money horse," she whispered to her shushana.

With a blank stare, the shushana nodded her head, repeating mechanically, "Yes, Auntie. Yes, Auntie."

As the shushana spoke, she was munching on something she had pilfered from the gift basket. When her mistress noticed, she cuffed her on the back of her neck.

"How dare you! Did you lick the jar of natural honey al-Figgi brought? Well, then, you're not getting a tip from me, damn you!"

With a mischievous gleam in her eye, the shushana said confidently, "I don't take money as tips."

"God damn you, you filthy dyke! Get away from me!"

The brothel owner rearranged her new silk robe and tied it more securely around her waist. Then, singing a tune under her breath, she did the rounds of her venerable establishment to check on the progress of the work.

> The one who comes to us when we call
> Approaches with a grace divine.
> Graceful as a gazelle, admired by all
> He comes clad in silk so fine.
>
> Oh how handsome, how handsome he is,
> Let us come to him when he calls.
> We want him with everything in us,
> The one who our hearts enthralls!

Tawida opened her eyes slightly, pondering her situation. *Why is this happening to me? What sin did I commit to deserve these never-ending punishments and curses?* She'd slept away a good bit of the time that weighed so heavily on her. But as soon as she woke up, she found herself in a vortex of black thoughts. First she'd lost her baby boy, and now she was being held prisoner in a whorehouse. If she stayed there, the brothel owner—the head whore—was sure to turn Tawida into a whore herself sooner or later. It seemed she really was a slave by divine decree. But Tawida wasn't a whore, and she never would be, no matter how much certain people wanted her to be. She'd been torn away from the man she loved and the household she'd known all her life. And now she could never go back to them. If she did manage to escape from the brothel, she wouldn't know where to go. Besides, al-Figgi would be sure to have her hunted down and brought back.

She recalled stories of slaves who had tried to escape before her. She remembered the man who'd been a slave at the Senussi zawiya. A sheep under his charge had been eaten by a wolf, so he'd fled for fear of being punished. After wandering for days in the desert, he thought he'd found his way to freedom. But the local authorities captured him and brought him back, and his hand was cut off. He'd run away to escape punishment, only to be punished a hundred times over!

She thought about a boy slave who had accidentally put out the eye of his owner's son while they were playing with sticks, so he'd run away for fear of being punished. When he was brought back, his master cut off his hand and kept him in his service. And as if that wasn't bad enough, three days later the master forced the boy to prepare his food for him with his other hand.

Then there was the slave woman who had run away from the brothels in Fezzan and gone to Benghazi, as she'd heard that being black in Benghazi wasn't as hard as it was in other places. She was raped repeatedly on the way, and by the time she finally found her way to freedom in Benghazi she'd contracted syphilis. She thought about others who had escaped from the farms in Jaghbub, Kafara, and Fezzan and made their way to the coast. But once they got there, no one was willing to employ them, and they ended up as beggars, forced laborers, prostitutes, and paramours. Worse than being slaves now, they were no more than human refuse.

Tawida thought about all sorts of people whose heart-wrenching stories she had heard. She had no desire to meet a similar fate.

So she closed her eyes and wept without a sound.

Tawida remembered Muhammad, hoping against hope that he would come looking for her and take her to wherever he was. She wanted to see him more than ever. She'd been in love with his very presence, which had equaled freedom, life, everything.

Glancing around in the darkness of the dank room, she called out softly to him.

"Come!" she whispered. "Please! Look for me the way I've been looking for you. Let me live inside you the way you've come to live inside me. Let me be with you and escape from all this sorrow! Are you even on this same earth, under the same sky? Do the same sun and moon shine down on us both? I don't eat, I don't drink. I'm a stranger to myself. I'm wounded through and through. I'm racked with pain, and I'm free game for anybody who wants to violate me. Beloved one deep inside me, between my spirit and my spirit, in the spaces between one moment and the next, I flee to you in my mind from this bizarre prison and the one who holds me here. I flee to you, knowing I won't survive wherever you aren't!"

> I weep over the days of my misfortune,
> Sorrow robs me of sense and sight,
> My tears flow without ceasing,
> My eyes are bereft of all light.
>
> Constant weeping leaves my mind in confusion,
> Bringing new sorrow every day,
> With no companion to offer me solace,
> And no guide to point the way.
>
> Copious tears have I shed in sorrow
> Over the loved ones from whom I didst part
> Can no one find me the longed-for cure,
> And bring health to my anguished heart?

In the evenings, the inner courtyard of the Arab-style house was transformed into a circle of merriment and affable exchange. Carpets were rolled out, coal stoves were lit, and incense was burned for the most refined of soirees. At times like this, the inside of the house bore no resemblance to its outside: elegant and cozy, it created a distance between itself and the external world that made it a center of gravity for minds and hearts.

It was the country's lost paradise.

The brothel owner thanked the black singer who had come with her small band to entertain the evening's gathering of elites. The musical strains made their way to where Tawida lay, her eyes alternately opening and closing. She craned her neck toward the window that opened out onto the courtyard, where delicate threads of candle light and the glow of a lamp flickering from beneath the bitter orange tree stole in to her lonely quarters.

The darabukkas were warmed up, and glass bottles and spoons were brought to be used as percussion instruments. Standing at the center of the gathering, the singer launched into a heartrending opening with her sweet, captivating voice:

> Aaaahhh! Wa ya la la la la la li! Ya li ya li ya laay!

> She asks not for a drop of water
> to wet her parched tongue.
> Though dying of thirst, she seeks no relief,
> To her dignity she has clung.

> To complain of your sorrows
> to any but the Almighty
> brings humiliation and disgrace.

> But in patience lies wisdom,
> and though privation now reigns,
> abundance will take its place.

> Oh, my aching heart!—Ah, ya 'ayni, ya daay!

At the sound of the music, Tawida crawled up to the window on her hands and knees. Drawn in by the singer's rich, melodious vocals, she took hold of the bars on the window, pulled herself up, and started to watch. In a perfectly rounded evening, the singer's voice proved the perfect vehicle for the mournful sounds of the marskawi. Every now and then the singer would take a swig of Nazli Durna from a glass that had been set in front of her before continuing with her rapturous musical production. Meanwhile, the rest of the band sang with her as the dancers took turns on the stage. Some of them covered their faces with long, gauze-like scarves; others tied sashes around their hips, performing the dances with a professional agility and grace.

After the first break in the program, Tawida burst into tears.

As for the second part of the performance, its lyrics spoke directly to her, baring the gaping wounds in her heart. She cried as though she were hearing the voice of her soul as it sang of her loneliness and insignificance:

They've taken my beloved away, and he's so far from me now!

Meanwhile, in another part of the city, on another side of its advancing night and velvet silence, Muhammad sat on his doorstep talking with his nephew Ali after a grueling work day.

"I'm not finding her, Ali," he said morosely, "no matter hard I look. If you know of some other way, or somewhere else I can look, help me out. I've sent out spies all over, and there's no sign of her. I'm afraid they might have carted her off to some far-away place outside Benghazi."

Where could you be, Tawida?

Ali gave an empathetic nod. "You'll find her one of these days," he reassured his uncle. "Let's do another search in the Slave Yards. We can also look in Al Birka, Al Kish, Ra's Ubayda, and Zurayri'iya. Pray they didn't give her to one of the Senussi brothers. If they did, we'll never get her back. The Senussis will fight to the death to hold onto their slave women, even the ones they don't use as concubines anymore."

"I'm lost, Ali. I'm done for."

A sense of defeat hung over him nearly all the time. Tawida had been the first attempt at rebellion by this traditionally raised young man. In his relationship with her, rebellion had mingled with the urge to experiment, and a decision to indulge the urge. It was a quest to please himself for once, to live his own life, and to shed an unquestioning subordination and dependence that had been passed down from one generation to the next. When he was with Tawida, he was freed from all the ways in which he resembled the society around him, and he'd discovered a unique individuality in himself that he approved of. Loving her had awakened a heart sated with mundanity and erased the boundaries between black and white, master and slave. It had brought about a rare realization of the soul's capacity to form itself anew. He liked who he was when he was with her. He was unearthing a personality that had been buried beneath that of his father, the family's effective ruler. He wanted to be himself, not what he was expected to be. With Tawida, Muhammad had found everything he lacked, and experienced what he had never been able to experience under the weight of his father's overbearing authority. The person he was in Tawida's presence was the Muhammad he loved: whole and complete. So with her sudden disappearance, he had disappeared too. He had been lost to himself.

When Tawida woke up, she shouted out her window to her guard, "I want some poison. I want to die! Get me out of here!"

As soon as she heard Tawida, the shushana came running. Then she closed the door behind her and proceeded to beat Tawida mercilessly all over with her thick, coarse hands. Dripping with sweat, she screamed, "Die, then! Die! Isn't that what you want? Take that!"

Her nose bloodied, Tawida fell to the floor, writhing beneath the shushana's blows. Instead of stopping, however, her tormentor started trampling her with her bare feet. Then, as though someone had reached out and stopped her, she stepped away from a half-dead Tawida and stood there without saying a word, her eyes glazed, her parched lips quivering. She pondered the corpse-like body before her, the thoughts in her head a confused jumble. She glanced out the window. All the rooms that opened out onto the inner courtyard had their windows closed and their red curtains drawn. It was still early in the day, and the brothel owner had gone to take care of some personal business in her private coach.

Unless the prisoner's heart really had stopped beating, this was her chance. She hurried to her room and knelt down in search of something under the bed. Then she brought out two bottles containing the remains of two types of locally brewed liquor—Nazli Durna and Wardi Mass. She hurriedly opened both bottles, took a swig from each one, and rushed them to Tawida's room. Once there, she hoisted Tawida over her shoulder. Tawida was breathing with difficulty through her mouth, her uvula clinging to her palate, blood streaming out of her nose. As the shushana forced her to drink from both bottles, the liquid ran down the sides of her mouth. But she kept pouring them down Tawida's gullet, wiping her mouth with her hands, saying, "Drink, drink! Never in your miserable life have you tasted anything like these! Didn't you ask for poison? Well, these are the best poisons around, little one. Drink up now!"

Between the two of them, they emptied both bottles. Then the shushana dragged Tawida's limp body to the door. After glancing outside to make sure the coast was clear, she hoisted Tawida onto her shoulder again, Tawida's head dangling over the shushana's buttocks and blood dripping from her nose as she whisked her to the bathroom. Once there, the shushana stripped Tawida naked, set her in the bathtub, and lit the burner under a large kettle of water. She stuffed Tawida's mouth full of chewing tobacco and sat watching and waiting, not taking her eyes off the wretched prisoner.

When the water had heated sufficiently, she got up and secured the door with the big wooden latch. With nothing to see by but the light that emanated from the burner, and from the eyes of a cat that lay on a stone bench built into the bathroom wall, the shushana began dipping water out of the kettle with a metal cup and pouring it over Tawida's head. Then, loofah and soap in hand, she went to work scrubbing off yesterday's filth and today's blood. In the course of several delirious rants, the inebriated Tawida told the shushana a jumble of things about Muhammad and her life in the livestock pens. She laughed and she cried, she ranted and she raved. Meanwhile, in a cloud of inscrutable calm, the shushana carried out her task to the rhythm of the splashing of the water and Tawida's spitting, gurgling, and loud guffaws. Then, like a sleeper stung by a scorpion, the woman suddenly stopped scrubbing Tawida's back and, in a series of rapid and unexpected moves, took off her caftan and trousers, and stuffed her voluminous torso into the tub with her.

Miftah Daqiq

IT WAS ONE OF MANY YEARS of drought and famine, and the Ottoman Empire had imposed forced conscription on the citizens of its vilayets, both Muslims and non-Muslims. The winters were bitter and cruel, and the task of getting firewood and coal for heating was an all-consuming preoccupation if one was to survive. The north wind blew mercilessly, skinning people alive and settling in their bones. With nothing to protect themselves against the elements, many starved or froze to death.

Like others, Tawida endured her share of the cold and privation. Al-Figgi, who had reserved her exclusively for himself, had to double the fee he paid the brothel owner to keep her under her roof without letting anyone else touch her. As a result, the basket of food that had preceded his arrival in easier times didn't always come. Tawida would then have to wait until he came to get something to eat. Otherwise, all she got would be the scraps and crumbs left after the others in the brothel had eaten. Because of the dampness in her room, she came down with a lung infection that made it hard for her to breathe. She coughed all the time, and would only drink water with frankincense to alleviate the pain. When al-Figgi asked her what she wanted him to bring her the next time he came, her reply would be "frankincense and lagibi."

Resignation to one's affliction has a way of inuring one to its effects. The things Tawida had once cried over no longer made her cry. The things she'd once been offended at no longer offended her. The things that had once filled her with sorrow had become nothing but daily routines like the five ritual prayers. Getting her drink mattered more to her than getting something to eat. All she wanted was to seclude herself as though she didn't even exist in this world.

Everything Tawida needed—be it food, drink, or anything else—was in the hands of the shushana who'd been assigned to keep guard over her. And nobody got anything for nothing. They would sit and drink together in the bathroom where the brothel owner couldn't see them. But each of them had her own reasons for imbibing. Tawida wanted to escape from where she was, to numb herself to the time that weighed so heavily upon her. The shushana, on the other hand, wanted to intensify her enjoyment of the place, and to make up for what she lacked there through Tawida. At the end of every drunken stupor, Tawida would weep over the beloved who hadn't come looking for her and over her thirsty baby boy, while the shushana munched on chewing tobacco and bit her as she wiped away her tears.

Within the confines of that dank room, Tawida had undergone abortion after abortion. She'd nearly bled to death on more than one occasion, only to come back to life. As her ordeal in the brothel dragged on, she felt like somebody who'd been delivered from death from one cause, only to die from another. Hoping to avoid more beatings and forced abortions, she carefully followed the instructions the shushana had given her for how to keep from getting pregnant. It was a way of making her life—or her death, as the case may be—a bit more peaceful, at least. As time went on she had grown quieter, more withdrawn, and so exhausted that she no longer had the energy to say yes to some things and no to others.

Then one cold, hungry morning, Tawida helped to deliver a young white girl who had conceived out of wedlock by a relative of hers. She did her best to persuade the brothel owner to leave the baby at the door of a local mosque instead of throwing him into the garbage bin, which was what they usually did with foundlings. This way someone would pick him up, and he would at least have a chance of surviving. She managed in the end to convince the brothel owner that if the baby died in a garbage bin, it would draw attention to the fact that somebody was not only disposing of newborn babies but, in all likelihood, performing secret abortions as well. If that happened, Tawida reasoned, somebody might report it to the police, who were sure to suspect the women in the brothel. Then the brothel owner would run the risk of prison, fines, and blackmail by the police. So why go knocking at hell's gates? As for the idea of leaving the baby on some distant mosque's doorstep, it would be both easier and less likely to get them in trouble, especially in view of the fact that nobody would want to get rid of a baby that was both white and male unless his mother was a free woman and his father was some well-known member of the community who was afraid of a scandal. So in the end, brothel owners were the ones who came under suspicion.

The old woman hesitated to let Tawida go on this mission, since the shushana assigned to guard her was out somewhere. On the other hand, they couldn't afford to keep the baby at the brothel for even so much as an hour after he was born. As a precaution, she sent another servant girl with Tawida, to show her the way and keep an eye on her. Whether the baby lived or died, the brothel owner wanted him off her hands without causing herself any problems. Her house was licensed only as a brothel, not as an abortion clinic. So if the inspector came around in response to some tip-off, she would go to jail. The house might even be seized and sold, and she would end up in the street.

After cleaning him off and nursing him, the baby's mother tied a thread from her dress around his wrist. Tawida picked him up tenderly as though he were her own son. In hopes of ensuring his survival, the mother had asked that he be left on some notable's doorstep. The brothel owner had agreed verbally to her request but, behind her back, she instructed her servant to put him in the garbage. Hearing this, Tawida intervened and suggested the mosque instead for fear that he would be devoured by hungry dogs, although she didn't mention this concern to the old woman. At his mother's request, Tawida wrapped the baby in a pink towel. This way, when people told stories later about where he'd been found, what he'd been wearing at the time, and what he'd been wrapped in, it would serve as a way of identifying him and locating him when he got older. Tawida laid him in a cardboard box, and the other servant picked him up. In the early dawn hours, before the darkness had dissipated to reveal a new day, the two women set off with the newborn down darkened streets and alleyways. They realized the seriousness of what they were doing, but they didn't let on how frightened they felt.

It was the first time in more than seven months that Tawida had walked down a street. She hadn't set foot outside the brothel, nor seen a face she recognized from her past. Yet now here she was, free all of a sudden, but her surroundings were completely unfamiliar to her. The other servant showed her the way to the mosque.

Much had happened during her confinement. Foundlings filled the streets, and there were so many beggars that they posed a threat to shop owners and street vendors, who had started appointing slaves to curse them, beat them, and chase them away. Forced conscription had spread on orders from the Ottoman state, so many people had fled with their sons to the desert, and it was a common practice for masters to offer their slaves as conscripts in place of their sons. Ali was called up for military service in the Balkans, but his grandfather paid a sizable bribe to the Ottoman military conscription officer, and then sent a slave in Ali's place.

After his emancipation Salem had settled at the zawiya, and Hussein had become a dervish. He would go into trances at Sufi worship gatherings and wander aimlessly about, careful to hide his hairless chest for fear that people would mock him for being girl-like. He would only take off his tattered cloak long enough to put on another one. His beard grew out and his chestnut hair got so long you could hardly see his face anymore. His father was pleased at his transformation into a spiritual adept. As for Salem, he became Hussein's personal servant. He would follow him from one hadra to the next, carry him home on his back if he fainted, and tend his wounds if he got hurt from being stabbed with swords, swallowing hot coals or chewing glass.

The beating Salem had endured with a hoe had left him with a limp, and he walked with difficulty. Nevertheless, he'd established a place for himself at the zawiya, where he was now a trusted servant.

One day Hussein came to him trembling with fright in the *khalwa*—the room where adepts would go for secluded time to meditate, pray, and recite the Qur'an. Hussein took Salem aside and whispered something in his ear. At first Salem had expected Hussein to tell him he had seen Abdel Qader Al Jilani in a dream,[1] or that he'd encountered one of the famed marabouts who would fly back and forth across the country, intervening invisibly to solve people's problems. Salem followed Hussein into the back room of the zawiya. When they came back out, Hussein picked up his wooden tablet and began reading Imam Malik's famous one-thousand-verse poem called "The Alfiya." As for Salem, he was in such shock over what he had just heard that he didn't know what to do at first. Then he gathered his wits, left the khalwa, and headed in the direction of the market without telling Hussein where he was going.

Stolid and determined, he trudged into a piercing wind that chilled him to the bone and exacerbated the pain in his leg. He passed shuttered shops whose owners had gone bankrupt, keeping an eye out for his old master's store. Would he find it open? Or had it met the fate of so many others whose businesses had been ruined by the crisis? Along the way he saw a gathering of men who, their cloaks wrapped about them for warmth, stood talking about hunger and about a steamer that was expected to bring wheat into port, while a number of slaves trundled carts of steaming chickpeas and broad beans up and down the streets to sell for people's breakfast. Preoccupied with the news he bore—news no less momentous than that of the steamer bringing flour into the Benghazi port—Salem counted the steps his crippled leg had left before he could deliver his tidings to the person for whom they were intended.

When at last he reached Muhammad's shop, Salem paused in the doorway. Muhammad was inside talking to a couple of merchants.

---

1. Abdel Qader Al Jilani (1078–1166) was a highly reputed Muslim theologian, orator, ascetic, and mystic.

When he saw Salem, Muhammad excused himself from his guests and came over to him, thinking he'd come to ask for some flour, coal, or grease. Instead of making a request, however, Salem simply greeted his former master and asked to speak with him in private.

As soon as they were out of ear range, he said urgently, "We've found Tawida, Master."

As though he'd been jolted by an electric shock, Muhammad suddenly grabbed Salem by the shirt. "What did you say?" he asked, a dazed look in his eyes.

"Yes, Master, we've found her," Salem affirmed. "She's not far from here, in the brothel."

"Who told you?"

"A little while ago, Hussein came to the khalwa and told me Tawida was being held against her will, and that al-Figgi was the one who'd taken her away."

"And who told Hussein?"

"There was a problem between his mother and father on account of al-Figgi's being out so much. His wife got suspicious and sent spies after him. Then she followed him to the brothel and found out what he was up to. Hussein heard them fighting, and he said his mother had threatened to expose his father and demand a divorce."

"Filthy bastard. Just wait till I get my hands on him!"

Taking Muhammad by the hand, Salem pleaded, "No, Master, please. For Hussein's sake. The poor kid's scared to death. He was shaking all over when he told me about it."

"I swear to God, I'll drink his blood."

"Please, Master, let's just work on rescuing Tawida for now, and leave al-Figgi's punishment to God."

"Do you know where the place is?"

"Yes, Master. Hussein told me."

"Come on, then, let's go."

Tawida had been wandering the city since the early dawn hours without a clear destination. When she and the other servant woman approached the mosque, all she'd been intending to do was wait until the prayer had started and the last worshiper had gone inside so that she could deposit the baby at the entrance and go back to where she'd come from. It was bitterly cold, and she'd been holding him close to keep him warm. Whenever she pulled back the blanket and peeked at his face, he was alert and placid-looking, his eyes twinkling in the darkness like a pair of distant stars.

The other servant had led Tawida down darkened streets and alleyways. They'd pulled their hoods close around their heads, both to shield themselves from the cold and to keep from being recognized as women. From a distance they looked like a couple of slightly built men who were either heading out early for a day in the salt flats or coming back from a night at the tavern. Tawida crept up to the mosque entrance where worshipers had left their shoes, looking for a spot that would be visible to those on their way out, but without being exposed to the bitter-cold wind. Only a handful of worshipers had come out for the dawn prayer that day. She saw them lining up in rows behind the imam and beginning the prayer. The little one was quiet as could be, gazing wide-eyed like a little kitten. After some hesitation, she set him down and moved away.

Before long she turned around and came back to secure the towel around his head so that he wouldn't get chilled, and to make sure it didn't cover his face and suffocate him. As she was rearranging the towel, he stuck an arm out and waved it back and forth like someone searching for something in the dark. It was the arm that had the string from his mother's dress tied around it. Moved with affection, Tawida thought about her own little boy. In fact, he'd been on her mind since the moment this little one had been born, especially when she learned that they were planning to bury him alive and, with him, the sin that had led to his conception. She had stepped up to the task in hopes of postponing his death. As for his fate beyond that point, it was in God's hands.

She kissed his little hand and tucked it back under the towel before joining her companion, who'd been checking to make sure the coast was clear and was getting irritated with Tawida for being so slow.

When Tawida finally caught up with the other servant girl, she herded her away from the mosque, berating her for taking so long.

When they got to the street corner, Tawida stopped up short and said, "I don't want to go back."

"Why not?" the other asked her, startled.

"I want to be free," she replied simply.

Grabbing her by the hand, the girl tried to force Tawida to go back with her. But Tawida pushed her to the ground and took off in the darkness, running as fast as her legs would carry her down the narrow alleyways. After getting a safe distance away from her escort, Tawida ran back to the mosque, her weary lungs wheezing, in a race with the worshipers who had just finished their prayer. Then she snatched the baby off the doorstep and disappeared in another direction.

One of the worshipers said, "I think I just saw a ghost grab something off the mosque doorstep."

"You must be imagining things," another mosquegoer insisted.

Still another quipped darkly, "Maybe some witch of the dawn swooped down to cast a spell on somebody's shoes. You all had better inspect your shoes before you leave. If you don't find anything in them, sprinkle them with water that's had Qur'an verses recited over it before you put them back on. The witch might want to piss in them to do some sort of black magic!"

"Beware of Satan," the imam cautioned darkly. "He'll whisper his evil suggestions to you whenever he gets the chance!"

Even a certain blind man in the group had to put in his two cents' worth. "Maybe she came to steal some shoes!" he suggested. "I mean, this year's cold will freeze your toes off."

Then the last of them, left with nothing else to suggest, offered, "Or maybe it was an afreet. I've heard stories about them that would send chills down your spine. Just ask the people who work in the salt marshes. They tell the weirdest tales about things they see in the early mornings."

As the men left for their houses, still speculating about the morning's apparition, the imam advised them, "Ask God's protection on your way, men, from evil women and sorceresses."

Tawida had no idea where she was taking either herself or the little one. All she knew was that she was running away from everything with the help of the darkness. When the wind howled, she would sidle up for protection to whatever she could find. If she heard a rustling sound or a dog barking, or imagined a ghost somewhere, she would shrink in place, holding him tightly to her chest. She made her way cautiously down lightless pathways, not knowing where they would lead her, until little by little the sun began to rise. Where should she go? Back to the household that had sold her in the first place? If not there, then where?

What if they discovered that she'd come back and Muhammad wasn't there? She'd be more of a prisoner than ever. This time she might be exiled to Benghazi's countryside and she'd never make it back. Exile was a fate she had to avoid at all costs.

So, then, where could she take herself and this white baby nobody wanted? She huddled with him in hiding from wild dogs rummaging through the garbage in search of something to eat.

"You and I have nobody in this world but God," she told him in a whisper. "I don't know where we can go. So we're just going to keep walking until God sends some good-hearted folks our way. He may not answer a whore's prayers, but he knows I didn't have any choice in the matter. Like you, I haven't decided anything for myself. I'm a black whore and you're a white bastard. At least that's how people will see us!"

The barking of dogs in the early morning hours was frightening, as was the sight of homeless drunks wandering through the streets, and the unknown to which she was headed with a newborn child.

Given her decision to take the child, her situation was more precarious than ever. She shouldn't have been so hasty. If she'd had her head about her, she wouldn't have done it. But she hadn't been thinking about anything, and had taken the brashest, most reckless step imaginable. Even making a dash for it on her own when she was halfway back to the brothel with the other servant had been a risky thing to do. Then all of a sudden she'd thought to herself, *What if I got the baby and took him back with me?* This thought had then turned into *what if I took the baby and didn't go back?* And that was what she'd ended up doing.

Who can we turn to, little friend? As she pondered her dilemma, she realized that she didn't know Benghazi as well as she'd thought she did. It was full of backstreets and bad places she hadn't known anything about. Even if she had decided to go back to the house she'd come from, she wouldn't have known how to get there from where she was. The first thing she would have to do, once it was light enough for her to see her way and people had started coming out into the streets, was to look for the Jarid Market. Then she could ask somebody to direct her to the slaves' quarters, and from there she could find her way to Aida.

Aha! So that's what we need to do, little guy! We've figured out a place we can go together other than the grave you would have ended up in, and the whorehouse I would have gone back to. Auntie Aida's! We'll put our heads together with her and Jaballah and find a solution. They're my family in God, and they're yours too. You're an innocent little baby, with no hand in the bad things big people do. I'll tell them your story, and they'll cry, and love you, and help you. But when they ask me your name, what will I tell them?

This is the morning of the day you were born. It's the first day of your life and you still haven't got a name or even any milk to drink. Well, there's no way you're going to spend the first day of your life with Tawida without getting yourself a name. We'll solve one problem at a time. First the name, then the milk. Don't worry, sweetheart. I'll dig into a rock with my bare hands if I have to, but I'm going to get you something to eat.

She studied him for a while, trying to think up a name that would fit a fair-skinned, blue-eyed baby that had just come from a filthy house in a famine-racked land where people waited in the bitter cold for a steamship laden with flour coming from Ottoman Istanbul.

"So, then, let your last name be Daqiq—'Flour!'—after the year you were born. That way we can use it to figure up how old you are."[2]

---

2. The "Year of Flour"—that is, the year in which the Ottoman State sent a shipload of flour to Libya in response to pleas for help due to the famine ravishing the land—is well-known among elderly Libyans, who sometimes date other events in the country's past in relation to that historic event.

Holding him up in the sunlight and looking skyward, she said, "Bear witness, you angels in the seven Heavens, that I have named him Miftah Daqiq! Let his arrival in this world bring good to him, to the country, and to its people. Pray for almighty God to grant him a happy life. After all, he's the one who holds our fates in his hands. From this day forth, little Miftah—'Key'!—will be a key in God's hand to open what's been closed."

Then she smiled at him and said, "Good morning, you good boy, you. Good morning, Miftah Daqiq! Thanks to your being with us, a window of blessing will open, God willing, and the daqiq will come into port!"

As they made their haphazard way to the Jarid Market, they happened upon a black woman begging in the streets. Seeing that the woman had a baby with her, Tawida asked her to nurse Miftah, since she didn't have any milk of her own. Looking at her pityingly, the woman told her she was hungry herself, and that she didn't have enough milk even for her own baby.

"Oh please, ma'am," Tawida pleaded. "He was just born earlier today and I've got no milk for him at all. If you could give him just a tiny bit! At least help him take hold of the nipple. He's hungry and thirsty and might die. I'll give you my shawl or my nose ring!"

Relenting in the face of Tawida's insistence, the woman gave the little one her breast. Heaving a sigh of relief, Tawida sat down beside her to rest for the first time after hours of walking. Frail, barefoot, and lost, she inhaled the cool, moist Benghazi air as if she were breathing for the first time. It was the air of freedom passing through her weary lungs.

She looked over at Miftah. As he burrowed into the woman's black chest in search of milk, she remembered the face of her own baby boy, who had left the world and on whose account she'd had to leave the household she'd grown up in.

How strange and sad life can be: she'd left home bereft of her own child and come back with somebody else's!

Take Refuge in the Distance

AN EARLY MORNING, an early rain, an early guest. That's how you could describe Tawida's reunion with Aida after their long separation. Aida hadn't expected ever to see Tawida again. She thought she must have been taken to some faraway place that she could never come back from. But here she was: sopping wet, exhausted, scrawny, and sick, holding a tiny white bundle of flesh wrapped in a pink towel.

It really was Tawida herself.

"Who's this you've got with you?" Aida asked. "Is he yours?"

"His name is Miftah Daqiq. He rescued me, and I rescued him."

"Here, I'll heat some milk for you. It'll warm you up. You're frozen stiff!"

"Are you all okay? We need to change the rags around the baby. He's wet himself. I'm afraid they're going to find out I'm here."

"Don't worry. It's safe here. Nobody spies on anybody. Ahbara's work is all internal now. She spies for Lalla Uwayshina on her daughter-in-law Lalla Rugaya and her daughter Halima, and Halima uses her to do the same thing to her sister-in-law Lalla Rugaya and her mother. She's busy with everybody against everybody. They all pay her to spy on everybody else, thinking she works just for them!"

After a pause, Aida resumed, "So, then, tell me what happened to you."

Tawida looked away absently for a moment, as though she didn't want to answer, or recall anything from the past: how she'd been taken to the brothel, what she'd been through there, the ugliness to which a crushed person can descend, the pleasure market, and the rules it operates under.

She wept, agitated.

"There's no time for tears now," Jaballah said gently. "Be strong. You've been through lots of hard times, but now you're free. You've got a new life to take hold of, so never go back to the past. A lot of runaway slaves hide in the Slave Yards under false names so that nobody can track them down. This is your chance to choose freedom over slavery. If they catch you, you'll go back to being a slave. If not, you're free forever. Folks in the Slave Yards look out for each other, so no matter how bad things get, you'll never have any reason to be afraid of the people around you. They help each other a lot more than slave families do. When you're a slave, you have to look out for yourself, and when you're scared, you might end up betraying some other slave or trying to get ahead at their expense. When you were here before, you weren't safe even among your own kind. Remember what Ahbara did to you?"

Tawida listened without comment.

"As for the little one, he'll either tie you down or give you wings. But I think you're lucky to have him. He'll make it easier for you to hide your identity. If, on the other hand, he poses a danger to you or if his family sends slaves out to look for him, you should get rid of him as fast as you can. But I doubt if they'd do that. I mean, who would let a bird fly away and then come looking for it again?"

Jaballah paused to collect his thoughts before continuing, "You'll need to change your name and come up with a story you'll tell people about yourself if they ask. And don't you dare forget it! Repeat it over and over to yourself so you won't mix up the details. You've got to get to the point where you've convinced yourself that this really is your story. And your name should indicate where you came from. The names of slaves that have fled from the West and South are different from the names of slaves from around here. So take advantage of the fact that you look like people who've come from faraway places. You can be a support to them, and they can do the same for you. I've got a trusted friend in the Slave Yards who can build you a shack there.

I'll introduce you to him as a newcomer from Fezzan or Tripoli. He's got a good heart, and he'll be happy to help you. But you've got to find work that won't take you into the city or put you in contact with people there. You need to stay in the Yards—beyond the wall."

Jaballah looked down pensively before adding, "You could do people's laundry, for example. Or bring water from the wells in Zurayri'iya. Or cook broad beans and chickpeas for the street vendors. Or wash floor mats, or sift sand. There are lots of things you could do there. But there are two jobs you should steer clear of: being a singer and dancer, and working for the prostitutes. In the end it's up to you, of course.

"Nobody but the baby's mother will come looking for him. If she remembers your face and your name, and if she goes to that mosque and verifies that nobody found a baby on its doorstep that day, she'll find you in the end. Then, if she's got a good heart, she'll do her best to keep the secret so as not to hurt either herself or you. Otherwise she might resort to nasty measures to take him away from you."

Getting up in preparation to go, Jaballah said, "I'll leave you two now. I've got to get the cart ready to take the master to market. Don't worry, Tawida. You're safe here. Just try to keep the baby from crying so people won't hear him. We'll talk more after I get back, and we'll find a solution for everything . . . Aida, milk the white goat for the little one. Its milk is good. And Tawida, we're thankful to have you back with us safe and sound."

Suddenly Tawida turned to her friend and, nudging her playfully, said, "So why have you still not gotten pregnant by this brave guy?"

"God hasn't opened the way yet. We've been thinking about making an agreement with our master that when he passes away, we and our children will be free. We'd have to come up with some money to pay him, though. Jaballah's been waiting for a chance to talk to the master and convince him. It looks like a long shot, but it's worth a try. Whenever I bring it up with him he says, 'Be patient for a little while longer. I'm waiting for the right time.' I don't want us to have children as long as we're still slaves. They'll just inherit our slavery, and that's the last thing we'd want for them. We'll see what God has in store for us."

"And Master Muhammad—how is he?"

The question came unexpectedly. Aida looked into her friend's troubled eyes. Then she looked down, not knowing what to say.

"Can you tell me how he is?"

Squeezing Tawida's hand, Aida said, "It's better for you to forget him. No white man around here would defend his love for a black woman no matter how attached he is to her. We just exist for their pleasure. If one of us leaves, there'll be others to replace her. Look around you. Have you ever seen an example of the opposite? From the poor man in the street, to the merchant, to the Sufi sheikh—they all take black women as concubines. Nobody gives a damn about a slave's heart and soul. Nobody."

Shifting in her seat, Aida went on, "Don't make yourself miserable on his account. He's just like any other man who's under his family's thumb and doesn't have the guts to stand up to them. When you first disappeared, he moved out to your shack. He ate and drank there. He slept there. He cried all the time. But after around a month of that, his family managed to bring him back into the fold. In his heart of hearts, he may really be in love with you. But he'd never sacrifice his wife—who's also his cousin, and the mother of his daughters—for the sake of a servant woman. He's no exception to the rule, Tawida. Traditions around here are set in stone. So, unless she's got some position in the family network, a woman will just be replaced by the one who comes after her as if nothing had happened—especially if she's a slave! I think they've convinced him that what attracted him to you wasn't really love, but the effects of some magic spell you'd cast on him . . ."

"What!!" Tawida burst out. "I swear to God I never did a thing to him and you know it! I just loved him, that's all!"

"I know, I know," Aida assured her. "But that's the way people are, Tawida. They outdo Satan himself when it comes to evil plots and machinations. In this rotten world, it's a rare person who's really good deep down. People like Muhammad's family don't believe that things happen because of the terrible things they do. If anything bad happens, they chalk it up to some kind of magic. Any development that's not to their liking, they assume it was caused by sorcery, and they'll do or say anything to reinforce this way of understanding it. The person they want to blame is turned into a wicked sorcerer that should be fought against. They complicate life like crazy, but trying to change the way they think is even more complicated. They accuse every black person of practicing magic, which makes us seem like weird, incomprehensible creatures. They make a tangled maze for us, and then they trap us in it. So instead of being able to demand our legitimate rights, we're always busy fighting off accusations.

"Don't forget that Muhammad isn't the first man who's fallen in love with a black woman. They've tried to convince him that what he's experiencing isn't love, but the result of a magic spell that will wear off over time with the right cure. He may have believed them, or at least have given the idea a chance. His sister Halima came all the way from Derna with specially treated water, incense, and all sorts of other anti-sorcery concoctions. Oh my God, is that woman ever nasty, and she packs a lot of clout too! She's got all sorts of tricks up her sleeve, and she's got venom running through her veins in place of blood. She even brought a sheikh with her from Derna. One night he came to the house and beat a bendir. Then he brought a bunch of enchanted knots and animal bones out of your shack. He said these were the things that had made Muhammad fall in love with you, and that you'd cast a spell on him to make him your slave!

"Jaballah and I were the ones serving them during the session, and we're sure it was the sheikh who planted them in your shack to convince Muhammad that they were yours. That way he could make him hate you. And I'm sure Muhammad's sister Halima paid that phony a pretty penny to do what he did. After he was gone, Halima stayed at her family's house for a while, claiming that she was protecting them from sorcerers' evil tricks. Actually, though, she's the one who's been practicing magic on him to make him change his attitude toward his wife. It's a way of protecting the family's commercial interests, since their in-laws are also their business partners. When his wife's relatives saw what bad shape she was in, they started pressuring Muhammad's family to pay back money they owed them. Don't forget that Halima stands to gain more than anybody else. She's concerned not to let family relations sour because she wants Lalla Rugaya's brother—Halima's cousin—to propose to her oldest daughter, Afifa. Little by little she's been winning Lalla Rugaya over to her side, so Rugaya's started trying to convince her brother to ask for pea-brained Afifa's hand.

"Men are really naïve in some ways. They believe all their family members' arguments and justifications. They don't think any of their blood relatives could hate them or wish them ill, and that only outsiders would want to hurt them. And Jaballah agrees with me about Halima. He says she's a witch and worse, that she's a demoness. She goes in secret to the Jarid Market and buys weird things from the herbalist and then comes back to use them in their house. He wants to warn Master Muhammad to open his eyes and see that the person who's working magic on him and hurting him isn't his concubine, but his own sister. Then again, how could Jaballah say a thing like that and be believed?

"Master Muhammad's been quiet for some time now. He lives his life normally and sleeps in his own bedroom. Beyond that, I don't know a thing. I haven't noticed any change in his relationship with Lalla Rugaya. Maybe his sister's magic has gotten to him. Maybe he's worried about hurting his business relations with his in-laws. Or maybe he's keeping his mouth shut while he makes other plans. God knows what's going through his head.

"I do think, though, that your having this white baby with you will complicate things between you if you get back together. Given all the nasty things his family has said to him about you, it won't be easy for him to believe that this baby isn't yours by some white man. And things will only get worse if he starts thinking the baby is al-Figgi's. Can you prove him wrong? I hate to say it, but I think you're going to be faced with a choice between him and the baby someday, between your heart and your humanity.

"One thing I do know for certain is that his relatives, and especially the women, want him to forget all about you. They're working on bringing him back into their circle and driving any strangers out of his life. If he has a son, they're determined to make sure the child's mother is a free woman, not a slave. So you need to start thinking about your life without taking him into account."

"But I love him. God knows my heart!"

Heaving a sigh, Aida remarked, "Like they say, 'Cordiality is a con.' Love is as true as a lie. Love started ruining your life the minute it walked in the door. After all, people don't like to have a love story grow up next to them if they're not a party to it. So they don't like to keep their mouths shut about it. If you want a life without a lot of hassles, you'll have to live based on common sense and throw your heart to the street cats."

Tawida cringed slightly.

Aida went on, "Love is considered immoral, something to be ashamed of. But not hate! When people around here openly express hatred, they don't feel ashamed at all, whereas love relationships are treated like something everybody should wage war on, and people do everything they can to discredit them. So what can we do?

"Think logically now. We live in a country that can't survive without racism and something to hate. So where do you think you could go and talk about love as something people can trust and approve of?

"As for the matter of the shushana at the brothel, don't tell anybody about her. Bury that story the way you buried your baby boy, and never think about it again. Remembering it just causes you pain. You know, Tawida, a lot of slave women have gone through this sort of thing, and worse, but when they tried to talk about it nobody sympathized with them. On the contrary, their lives just got that much harder, even among their own kind. When the body's violated, so is the soul. You don't need any more abuse than you've already suffered.

"So, for your own sake, and for the sake of this baby who's given you back your freedom and your life, put everything behind you. Bury even the old Tawida, and rise up as a new creation."

The Grudge

"SHE LEFT THE HOUSE AT DAWN. I swear to God, she's run away and we don't know where she is. You can search the rooms yourself if you want. I'm not a powerful woman, sir. I just make my living and don't go looking for problems. Al-Figgi brought her to me and told me to keep her here. And you know what al-Figgi can do. I couldn't say no to him. If he wanted to he could sick the qa'imaqam on me and send the chief of police to close the place down on any pretext. He's the one responsible for her. I'm just a nobody with no say in anything."

"And how did she escape?"

"She took off with her baby in the early morning while everybody was asleep. Even the shushana that guards her didn't wake up in time."

"She had a baby? So why would she have taken to the streets?"

"Sir, a leaky faucet will end up filling a huge clay jug and the gentlest breeze might break a huge branch. I wasn't hard on her, sir. I never did anything to hurt her. Like I said, somebody else had left her in my care, and it wasn't my place to do whatever I wanted. Otherwise I would have sent her back to you from the very start if I'd known you were her master. But I swear to God, nobody but al-Figgi came to visit her the whole time she was here."

"Show me where she was staying."

Scurrying ahead of him, the brothel owner opened the door to a musty, darkened room. He stuck his head in and looked around. It was nothing but some cheap whore's quarters. He didn't want to think of his beloved in a place like this with some other man, especially if she hadn't tried to bribe somebody to bring him word of her whereabouts. It pained him to think about that moment when the body numbs the voice of reason. He knew what that moment was like, since he'd experienced it himself with a certain black slave woman. His passion for her had emptied his life of all logic. Had Tawida surrendered to the tremor that had passed through al-Figgi's body and said nothing? Had her body, after the rush and the stillness, been too paralyzed to think of running away? She was, after all, a slave woman. And a slave woman's body doesn't rise up in protest. Rather, it's been conditioned to accept its lot. This is the mentality of submission on which concubinage is based, and it has molded slave women's temperaments down the centuries. When the body recognizes itself as enslaved, it doesn't resist the way a free person's body would. The free woman's body will refuse to act contrary to the convictions of her mind and, if she surrenders, her surrender will be as real on the level of the soul as it is on the level of the body.

Muhammad left the brothel in agony over what he'd heard and seen. It was too unbearable to contemplate. Al-Figgi had had intercourse with his beloved time after time in that squalid room, and not only that: She'd conceived and born a child! Why was all this happening to him? Why couldn't he find a single thing on earth that he didn't have to share with others? It seemed there wasn't anything he could really call his own—not his work, not the object of his passion, not even his baby's lifeless body. Why was it that no sooner had he found Tawida than he'd lost her again? Why was it that al-Figgi ended up being behind every ruinous thing that had ever happened to him? And why had it taken Tawida so log to rebel against her captor?

Muhammad's thoughts grew out of all sorts of unfounded assumptions. He seemed to suppose, for example, that even somebody who, like Tawida, had been born into slavery and had never imagined herself as anything but a slave, would suddenly rise up and claim her freedom. Selfish though it was of him—whether the selfishness of romantic love or of wanting to have somebody or something all to yourself—he seemed to be thinking: *It's all right for you to be my slave, but it isn't all right to be anyone else's!*

"Calm down," Salem said, as if he could read Muhammad's thoughts. "We'll find her!"

But Muhammad couldn't focus on what Salem was saying. He was too busy thinking about how he was going to get back at al-Figgi for what he'd done and what punishment would best quench his thirst for revenge. Muhammad's dispute with al-Figgi wasn't just over a slave woman anymore. It was a pitched battle against a man who had seized what belonged to him and treated it as a plaything. Al-Figgi had succeeded in luring Muhammad to the battlefield. So be it, then. Muhammad would duel with al-Figgi, and he would defeat him.

As the two men spoke, the old shushana was eavesdropping on them from the bathroom, where she sat surreptitiously taking snuff and, like Muhammad and Salem, sighing wistfully over Tawida's escape. After they'd left, she came out and asked her mistress reproachfully, "Why did you stir him up against al-Figgi that way?"

"This way maybe they'll get so busy fighting each other that they'll leave me in peace. If they want to feud over some slave woman, that's their business. But they should leave me out of it! Everybody's out to protect his own interests, and I've got nothing to gain from their cock fight. Besides, al-Figgi's gotten stingy lately. He doesn't bring us even a handful of flour anymore!"

"So that's it!" the shushana crowed. "If that's why you've got it out for him now, just say so!"

She guffawed so boisterously that her silver nose ring quivered.

"You shameless slut!" the brothel owner fumed.

When all the shushana did was cackle more loudly than ever, her mistress pelted her with the glass in her hand, shouting, "You haven't got a serious bone in your body, do you?"

Then she added, "Get up and take a bath. You're stinking up the whole place! Then go fix us something to eat."

Don't Knock on a Door
You've Got the Key To

SOMETIMES YOU DON'T KNOW when to say something you realize would be helpful for one person to know but not another.

As Muhammad and Salem were on their way to the brothel,
Tawida was approaching Aida's, and Master Imuhammad and Jaballah
were approaching the shop. When Master Imuhammad asked where
his son Muhammad had gone, a couple of merchants told him that
Salem had come and spoken with him in private and that the two of
them had left together.

What would have brought their former slave to the shop, and
where might the two men have gone?

His suspicions aroused, Master Imuhammad decided to investi-
gate the matter further as soon as he'd tended to some urgent business. His first concern that day had to do with a steamship about to set
off with a load of salt and slaves, and another ship, loaded with flour,
that was scheduled to arrive in Benghazi. The trade deal involving the
salt and the slaves hadn't yet fallen to anyone in Malta, and bids were
still coming in. Today was the day when the final market prices would
be set, and only then would he know who would be purchasing the
goods. He needed to make sure the gold merchants supported him at
that day's market session, since they were the ones who controlled the
prices, and in order for him to win the deal, his group and his partners, the Subaki Al Yunani group, would need to have an edge over

the Hammuda Al Garitli and Al Matuni group. That was all he could think about at the moment.

Meanwhile, in an atmosphere charged with intrigue, secrecy, and suppressed rage, Jaballah had come into possession of all the keys he needed to wrap up his own deal. He was now the one with the answer to every question. He was the one who'd been chosen to hold all the missing pieces, and he knew where and how to put them together. It was Jaballah's testimony that would redeem Muhammad in Tawida's eyes by disproving her belief that he hadn't looked for her or tried to rescue her. It was also his testimony that would disprove Muhammad's suspicions regarding Tawida and her relationship to Miftah.

In short, Jaballah held the connecting link between the lovers who had been lost to each other, since he was the one who knew where Tawida was and where Muhammad needed to go.

As he stood behind his master listening to the market talk and the commodity speculations, he reflected on himself, and on the various human "commodities" that were in the balance: *I mustn't let this opportunity slip out of my hands. I've got the key that will lead Muhammad to his long-lost love. But when I use it, I've got to propose my own reward. If I can exchange my freedom for this piece of information, then the moment I've dreamed of is about to come. As for that stingy old man,* he thought, casting a sideways glance at Master Imuhammad, *he wouldn't grant me my freedom no matter what I did! In fact, he'd try to get even more out of me. He'd want my children to be slaves to his children. He'd demand that his kin inherit mine!*

I've got to make a new start for my children and my grandchildren. I've got no business dragging anybody into a life like mine. So even if it means consigning myself to a kind of living death, I won't have any children as long as I'm a slave. This is my way of revolting for their sakes, so that they can have lives that are better than the one I've lived.

Every storm has to bring good to somebody somewhere. And now, Jaballah, you'll be able to father a son who's free, a son who's yours and not somebody else's, and who's answerable to himself, not his master. Some things happen for the sake of something else that seems to be completely unrelated to them. And this is the kind of situation you're looking at today.

Who would ever have imagined that, in the Divine Providence, you and Aida would finally be free because Tawida had been trapped in a brothel and then run away? But it's true. If it weren't for her situation, this wouldn't be happening to you. This is life's mysterious game.

Closing his eyes, Jaballah thought back on his trek from Al Jufra to Benghazi. He'd been just a little boy, who cried from having to walk barefoot through the hot sands, and who survived by eating grass along the path.

The Virtue of Truth,
the Vice of Silence

ALI CONTINUED, "My grandmother tried over and over again to get rid of the slave woman her son had gotten so attached to. I heard about many of the attempts she made, and I'm sure there were plenty more I never heard about. But once I'd grown up enough to understand life better, I didn't trust her silence about the issue. My grandmother always went with the crowd. She would bow to other people's opinions, and was afraid of being gossiped about. So, the fact that she didn't talk about certain things didn't mean they weren't happening. My mother used tell me about things that went on in the house when I wasn't around. Like me, she was crazy about her brother. She had huge respect for him too, and did everything she could to make his life happier and more comfortable. At the same time, she didn't want to make her mother angry over a servant that her brother happened to prefer over his wife, who also happened to be his maternal cousin.

"To be honest, women's world is complicated, and it's exhausting to try to get inside it, still less figure it out! In any case, sometimes my mother would tell me things, but most of the time she didn't tell me anything at all. As a young widow living with her parents, who helped her take care of her orphaned son, the main thing my mother cared about was protecting my interests, even if it meant living in the shadow for my sake. I have a feeling her perspective on everything was colored by her concern for me. Apart from this, she had more contact with her sewing machine than she did with people. She spent more time being silent than she did talking. And although she might not have felt very hopeful, she put up with a lot without complaining.

"She was more attached to me and her brother Muhammad than she was to all the rest of her family put together.

"Once when we were on our way to Mecca for the hajj, she talked to me about the slaves in our household, and she mentioned Tawida. I'd been just a little boy when a kind of 'mass abortion' was performed on a number of slave women who'd been taken as concubines. The wives of the men concerned had decided to abort the slave women to keep them from giving birth to children who could share in their children's inheritances. Everybody was looking after number one, as they say. When you choose to wrong somebody else to keep from being wronged yourself, that's the human ego at its ugliest. In any case, these women had agreed on a day when they'd all take their slave women to the public bath. The day before this, my mother saw my grandmother giving Tawida a concoction that had been prepared for the occasion. After drinking the stuff twice in the same day, her face was drawn and her lips were all dried out. When my grandma tried to get her to drink it a third time, she refused. By this time, she'd started getting mysterious pains in her stomach, she was dizzy, and she couldn't control her movements. When she saw what was happening, my mother tried to intervene, and she asked my grandmother to stop. Tawida was exhausted. In fact, she looked as though she might die any minute. But my grandmother just said that if she died, it would be better for her and everybody else.

"Even though she couldn't say so directly, my mother sympathized with Tawida and took her to our section of the house. Her strength was giving out and she couldn't even walk anymore. She'd also started vomiting, and she cried nonstop, though all you could hear was the sound of her occasional labored breathing. My mother had Tawida lie down on the carpet. Then she put cool rags on her forehead and over her legs. She'd expected her brother's baby to be aborted that night. As it turned out, however, it didn't happen till another night, when my grandmother came to see what had happened. When she found out that my mother had been taking care of Tawida, she started an argument with her.

"My grandmother's fellow conspirator was Hajja Manani. The two of them were always performing abortions on slave girls without letting the men know about it. The only people who knew what was going on were the slaves themselves. But if any of them dared opened their mouths, they'd end up being exiled to the countryside, where life was truly unbearable.

"Exile was such a frightful punishment that after a while the slaves started turning a blind eye to what was happening. Voluntarily deaf and blind, they stopped talking about abortion as a bad thing to do. Their silence became second nature to them, and slave women's fetuses were aborted nearly as fast as they were conceived.

"The next morning, poor Tawida was led away with slave women from other households to the public bathhouse, where they were subjected to still further ordeals that completed the process. According to my mother, a certain place in the bathhouse was so bloody, it looked like a sacrificial altar, and the cats that hung around the entranceways sat waiting for placentas the way a fasting person waits for Ramadan to end.

"As the faint pregnant girls lay prostrate in the steamy room, hefty-framed slave women massaged their bellies and had them inhale herbs that were being burned as a kind of medicinal incense. The poor young women were sweating so profusely that their veins had nearly shriveled up. Then the blood began gushing out in torrents from below, signaling that the near-lethal process was about to end.

"This is how Muhammad and Tawida's first child died. My mother says it was fully formed, as the pregnancy had been quite advanced. I asked my mother if there had been other babies and other abortions. But she doesn't like to say bad things about my grandmother, and she wouldn't tell me any more. All she said was, 'When you've got that many slaves, you don't count, son. Otherwise, you won't have enough to feed them all. Lord have mercy on people's souls.'

"This is why my mother had me take her on the hajj to Mecca not just once, but twice. The first one was for herself; the second was for her mother, in the hope that God would forgive them for the things they'd done . . . The more we give in to our destructive impulses, the more tyrannical they become."

Ali and Atiga sat there for a while without saying a word. At length he continued, "We live our lives thinking we've learned all there is to learn, and that we know all there is to know. Then there comes a time when we discover that we've missed the simplest things. We see that we were so concerned about other things that we neglected or ignored the ones right under our noses.

"When I learned goldsmithing from my uncle Sadeg, I fell in love with the work, and I started traveling often to Misrata, Tripoli, Tunis, and Alexandria. The fact is, Tawida was one of the reasons behind that shift in my life. It was because of her that I was kicked out of my grandfather's house and forbidden to go back to my job at the grain shop, which is why I went to work for Uncle Sadeg. I slept in his guest room for a month during the time when my grandfather wouldn't talk to me. Well, one day as I was picking up some jewelry from Uncle Sadeg at the entrance to the roofed enclosure at the front of his house, I happened to catch a glimpse of his middle daughter, Maryam, as she walked past the open door. From that day on I couldn't get her out of my mind. All I could think of was that I wanted her in my life.

"I went directly to my uncle to ask for her hand, which was a disastrous thing to do in those days. Even though we were relatives, it was a violation of tradition. I swear, I thought he was going to kill me, he was so furious! When I first asked him the question, he went dead silent. Then finally he said, 'The proposal has to go through your grandfather.'

"'All right,' I told him. 'I'll speak to my mother about it. Then I'll go ask my grandfather's forgiveness, and whether he'd be willing to ask for her hand on my behalf.'

"But then he told me he had daughters who were older than Maryam, and that it wouldn't be proper for him to let her get married before they did.

"I said, 'I know the proper thing to do would be to wait until her older sisters are married. However, I've got her dowry ready, and my mother is keeping it for me.'

"Offended all over again, he smacked me on the back of the neck. He said I was a hardheaded boy and that I should just patch things up with my grandfather.

"So one day when my grandfather was sitting in his inner courtyard, I went in to see him unannounced. I hadn't planned it out ahead of time, since I was afraid I might not go through with it. I just picked myself up and went over there. I walked into the courtyard and knelt at his feet. Then I kissed his hands, asking him to overlook what I'd done. I started to cry, and told him I loved him and couldn't stand having him angry with me. Then he started to cry too, and put his arms around me and forgave me. I was so happy and relieved, I kissed his head over and over.

"At lunch later that day, I broached the subject of marriage. When he looked over at me, I got scared, and lowered my gaze. But finally he said approvingly, 'You're a fine man, son. You don't wait for others to do your duty for you. Don't worry, now. I'll make sure your uncle Sadeg gives you his daughter in marriage.'

"Suddenly alarmed, I blurted out, 'You do mean Maryam, don't you, Grandpa? Don't you mix things up the way you did with my uncle Amin! You asked about the sister of the one he was interested in, and he ended up marrying the wrong girl by mistake!'

"What I said made my grandpa so mad, he bopped me with his cane, and I thought he was going to throw me out all over again! But thank God, I got to marry Maryam after all, and we had a family that took up all my time. She and I were both young, but we had a good life together. She supported me in my work, and after a while I managed to buy a house in Misrata—the city of my ancestors. When we moved there, I took my mother with us.

"Later on both my grandparents passed away. First my grandpa died of a hereditary heart condition. Then my grandmother fell in the bathroom and hit her head during a diabetic fit. She held on for a day and a night, and passed away the following evening. After that my mother-in-law died of some mysterious illness and my father-in-law remarried. We were worried that my father-in-law wouldn't be happy with his new wife, or that she wouldn't be good to his children, so we took in my wife's younger brothers and sisters. As a result, I was weighed down with responsibilities, and the very social ties I valued so much turned into shackles.

"After my grandparents were gone, their house went to my uncles Amin and Abdussalam. As expected, this was followed by a dispute over the estate between these two uncles, Uncle Muhammad, and Aunt Halima. In fact, one reason I brought my mother to live with us in our new house was that I wanted to get her away from that ugly inheritance battle, and since I had enough to take care of her, I had her waive her share of the inheritance.

"Around that time Muhammad had been getting more and more adventurous on the market, and was speculating in a number of commodities. He seemed to be doing it as a way of distancing himself from his brothers, or even competing with them. I worried about him, and I used to warn him against being so reckless. The same daring that was a strength in some areas of his life was, in others, his biggest weakness. He suffered huge losses, though on numerous occasions he managed to recover them. Meanwhile, he went into the wholesale trade and never stayed in Benghazi for very long anymore. He couldn't sit still. During our occasional brief times together, he would tell me that he felt pained, and that part of his pain was related to his family.

"He would send for Tawida when he needed her. But he'd changed. He was a different man now, and hard to understand. Sometimes he was happy, but other times he was miserable and depressed. His moods had taken a turn for the worse because of his inability to conceive a male child. In his quest for a son, he'd fathered one daughter after another. The one male child he'd ever fathered then died of hunger under his very own roof. After that, he turned into another person. Sometimes I would catch him crying alone. Other times he would get drunk and call his parents murderers. He'd accuse them of having killed everything in him that had once been alive. Then finally he started disappearing from the house entirely, and from all of Benghazi. He would go off on business just to get away from the family.

"In our society, it's not an easy thing to break free from your family if they're the source of your problems. In a case like this, you might resort to going on long journeys, and only come back on short visits when you've got no other choice. I think this was the solution Muhammad finally settled on for himself. He started taking long leaves of absence in Malta and Venice. He also started drinking too much. But he still remembered Tawida and the way—as he saw it, at least—she had abandoned him. During his drunken rants he would say she was nothing but some cocky woman who'd gotten her back up and run away to spite him.

"He'd been told all sorts of obnoxious things about Tawida, of course. People said she'd run away and prostituted herself with other men, or that she'd gone to slave shamans to have them cast spells on him. Meanwhile, in reality, she was paying the price of freedom: she'd taken on a new identity in the Slave Yards and was busy earning her own keep. She'd even concealed the fact that you were her daughter for fear of harm coming to you if people knew the truth."

"Even though she was essentially free by this point," Ali continued, "she still lived in fear for the most part. Like many others, she was indebted for her freedom to the arrival of a new master who had wrested control from a previous one. When the Italians drove the Ottomans out of Libya in 1912, they required all Libyan slaveholders either to register their slaves under their own names or to grant them their freedom so that they could register themselves. Italy was one of a number of colonial powers that had replaced the enslavement of human beings with the enslavement of entire countries, and that were setting their new houses in order based on their own customs and laws. As a consequence, Libya's system of slavery was toppled at one fell swoop, and Tawida and others were officially emancipated. No one could force anyone back into slavery without violating the law of the land. When this happened, Tawida demanded that Muhammad provide her with a written acknowledgment that he was your father, though she didn't ask anything for herself.

"During Tawida's imprisonment in the brothel, Muhammad had been desperate and furious. He'd looked for her in all the places where he knew slaves congregated. When he finally found her, however, it was only because Jaballah had told him where she was. And that was when their quarrels started."

"You didn't come looking for me or try to rescue me!"

"You slept with al-Figgi and other men in the brothel, and I can never forget that."

"You didn't do anything to protect our baby boy because he was the son of a black slave woman. Instead you went and took a second wife. You're a slave to your family and a doormat to your mother and your sister!"

"Miftah is your son, and don't you deny it!"

"You're just jealous and selfish. You think you own me as if I were a thing. Well, I'm not a thing, and I don't belong to you!"

"I've never heard of a slave woman saying such things to her master."

"I'm not your slave woman, you cipher!"

"You're the one who wants me."

"You're the one who sends your coachman to the Yards to have him bring me here. What does a man with money and status want with a poor Negro woman?"

"Say you still want me."

"I don't want anything from you. I don't want your money, and I don't want your property, no matter how much you've got. Whether you acknowledge your daughter or not, she's still your child before God. If you don't, I'll register her in my name the way they do with slaves, and I'll never give her up to you, since you can't protect her. All you are is my lover."

"On the contrary, I'm your husband in reality and truth."

"I'm not your wife! A wife has rights, but in relation to you, I've got nothing. All we do is give each other pleasure. I'm your concubine, who enjoys you the way you enjoy her."

"Don't you love me?"

"Yes, I do: the way a concubine loves the one who gives her pleasure. That's got to be a kind of love."

"This is the kind of battle you emerged out of. You came into being once upon a truce. Tawida would blow hot and cold. Muhammad would fight her, then make up with her. He would abandon her, and then come back to her. Hate her, then love her. Forget her, then remember her. Give her the cold shoulder, then pine for her. Leave her for Malta, then come back to Benghazi to be with her.

"Tawida never recovered from the brothel year either. She went on guzzling marisa to forget her pain. Sometimes, in a fit of mad rage, she'd spit on Muhammad and call him every name in the book. Sometimes she'd refuse to go with the servant he'd sent to bring her, and threaten to sleep with somebody else if he didn't stop harping at her about al-Figgi.

"She wore him down by alternately coming to him and staying away, and by refusing the things he gave her. She would give herself to him heart and soul, but reject his gifts. Being treated this way by a former slave really killed him.

"So, then, you were the offspring of these contradictory, overlapping moments. You were conceived out of a union between a white madness and a black madness that fought tooth and nail, pulling each other in two different directions, between two hearts joined by love and kept apart by other people.

"One time after a big falling out between them, she went looking for him. That evening she found him asleep beside his son's grave. He told me she was constantly reminding him of the part he'd played in their baby's death.

"Now that Tawida had her freedom, she refused to return to Muhammad as a mere servant. In response to her insistent pressure, he promised her time and time again that as soon as he'd taken care of certain matters relating to his business, he would officially recognize you as their daughter. But although he meant what he said, she didn't believe him. I remember him telling me that when he got back to Libya after an upcoming business trip to Malta, he planned to go straight to the mosque and announce that he was your father. But destiny had other plans—cruel plans that tore my life apart and plunged me into the depths of despair. One morning before he was to leave Malta, he was found dead in his bed. Even with all his grief and despair, he'd still been young, exuberant, driven. When he died, a part of me died with him—the part of me that took joy in life. I felt as though fate was playing a sick joke on me. I had to face life's troubles alone now, and I hated Benghazi without him.

"See, here's the last photo I have of him. It was taken in the city square during the winter of the year when World War I started. He was so handsome.

"Now, does he look sick to you?"

Tears filling her eyes, Atiga drew the picture closer for a better look. She gazed at the face of the stranger in the photo. Then she kissed it, saying, "He does look sick, actually, because he's sad."

There's More to a Person Than Meets the Eye

AFTER A LONG TALK over lunch at Atiga's house, the two went to the Sabri beach and stood side by side in the sand. In the course of their conversation, Ali had touched on the subject of Atiga's inheritance rights. He told her that after a battle with Muhammad's other heirs, he'd managed to prove that she was legally entitled to inherit from him too. When Ali first started talking about the inheritance, Atiga clammed up and stared into the distance as if she were trying to think of a way to change the subject. Every time he brought it up, she managed to get onto some other topic. Once she talked about how happy she was that Yousef had painted the window frames blue, which was one of her favorite colors. Another time she started talking about the planters filled with basil, calamint, flowers, and mint that she'd been growing at home and at the clinic. Still another time, she went on about the arrangements she was making for the danga season and her plan to visit Sidi Dawud's shrine with her children, Muhammad and Tawida. In still another attempt to avoid the topic, she showed Ali around the Slave Yards, where she'd grown up. She told him she wanted to give him a guided tour through the place before he went back to Benghazi and got ready to travel the next day to Misrata.

As they walked along, he struggled to suppress one cough after another. She suggested that he go to the clinic, but he wouldn't hear of it.

There were moments when neither of them said anything, when they were both engrossed in private conversations with themselves. As they walked through the Slave Yards, Ali had to fight off torrents of grief that gushed out at him from Atiga's childhood haunts, while Atiga proudly concealed the pain of her memories. In a moment of distraction, their eyes met and Atiga broke the silence, saying, "So, this is the Yards. It's home to me: a huge, empty-looking expanse of sand, water, wild plants, and endless open sky."

Looking upward, she went on, "Somebody who looks at this place might think there's nothing here. But to me, it's everything."

She bent down and picked up a handful of sand. "I know its boundaries from those boulders over there. They haven't changed a bit even after all these years. You see that one that juts out into the water more than the others? That's where I used to sit and dry off after I took a bath . . ."

As she spoke, Ali broke in suddenly, saying, "Come here."

"W . . . w . . . why?" she stammered, taken by surprise.

Without replying, he lifted his arms and pulled off his jard over his head.

"Come here," he said again. "Let me put it on you."

"But I'm not cold," she said, still perplexed.

"I know. But it belonged to your father. When he died, I kept all his things, including his clothes. It's got his name embroidered onto it in Ottoman script. Look."

Atiga burst into tears. Anything she might have been planning to say suddenly escaped her mind.

"Please don't cry, Atiga. Your tears burn me."

He came over to her and raised the garment's knotted opening over her head. She leaned forward and raised her arms, allowing it to descend over her head and shoulders. Grasping its embroidered edge, Ali held it up between them and said, "I went to the best tailor in the Jarid Market and had him sew your name on it with the same color thread. This is the jard your father would put on when he wanted to dress up. I'm sure he must have met your mother in it on more than one occasion. And you're the person who should have it now."

Tearing up, Atiga took the edge of the jard in her hands and kissed it. Then suddenly she burst out, "God have mercy on your spirit, Baba. God have mercy on your spirit!"

Small fishing boats glided over the water's placid surface as gentle waves lapped up in succession, leaving the shore a different color as they washed back out to sea.

After a brief silence in which she drank in the air with her nostrils, Atiga mused, "I wonder if these are the same waves that used to wash up to me when I was a little girl, and whether this is the same sand I used to play in. We'd come out here and build flimsy little houses that would get blown over by the wind and washed away by the tide. The houses we lived in weren't much sturdier!

"The houses in the Yards used to be scattered every which way, but now it's a regular neighborhood with streets and street names, and with houses arranged in neat rows on either side. You and other people who left Benghazi weren't around to see all the changes. But the Yards is an actual part of the city now rather than being separated from it by a wall like before. It's got electricity and light poles, running water, and networks of streets that would put an ant colony to shame. You hardly see horse-drawn carriages or earthen water jugs anymore, and gone are the days when the dead were carried on donkey back. When I was growing up, the isolation here was deadly, it was pitch black at night, and people had nothing to fend off the long, cruel winters. Cats, dogs, and chickens would roam the beaches, picking through the sand and the debris for whatever they needed and, as time went by, I put down my roots there deeper and deeper.

"I tripped and fell in its sands as a toddler, and I played there as a little girl. If it hadn't been burned down on account of the plague, I would never have left it. It's where I washed my clothes and took baths. It's where I learned to swim the way all the other kids did. I don't know how or when we learned—we just did, as if we'd been born underwater. It's also where I met Yousef, the man of my life.

"The Slave Yards is my living birth certificate, you might say, one that could never be lost. And then there's my secret birth certificate, the one my mother hid before she died trying to protect me from the treacheries of time. Here in this soil is where Tawida lies with Muhammad's jard, and the piece of paper he gave her recognizing me as his daughter. I don't know the exact location of the shack whose dirt floor my mother used to bury things under. But wherever I step into this huge expanse, I feel her calling me. 'I'm here!' she says. 'I see you and know you even if you don't see or recognize me!' Under this salty, nostalgic piece of Benghazi live my roots, and here my secret lies hidden.

"Wherever I go, I'll find comfort in wrapping myself in my father's jard with his name embroidered on it in silk thread. I'm even comforted by the memory of my mother's black body, which was violated, degraded, and tortured before it carried me. The place I lived in, and live in still, is all the documentation I need in this universe. I embody Muhammad, the white man who sought refuge in a black love, and in the black woman who sought her own refuge in marisa and lagibi. I'm slavery's final way station, where slave caravans stopped to rest for the last time, where 'white' and 'black' blood circulate and mingle in my veins. I was formed out of everything: out of slavery and freedom, water and salt, degradation and dignity, humiliation and honor, sun and soil, hunger and satiety. I came out of Benghazi's cleanliness and her filth, her coldness and her warmth, her tears and her playfulness, her grape trellises and her fig groves, her shamelessness and her pride, her salt marshes and her red clay, her date palms and their fronds, her sands and her sea. I'm everything from her coquettish lilt to her voice of majesty, from her stern order to her dizzying disarray, from the soulful marskawi and Baghdadi poetry sung at weddings and parties to the reverent hymns sung in gatherings for worship, from her mosques proclaiming God's greatness to her church bells ringing, from the domes of saints' shrines glinting in the sun to slaves' tambourines being beaten in anguish and hope. Here is where my story began and spread. So am I Benghazi's daughter, or is she mine? It's all the same, actually. Each of us is the other's birth certificate, and in her I was able to form myself out of the nothingness of the places where she cast me.

"This is the Benghazi of the immortal Muhammad and Tawida, and I am the seed of love they planted. It's the Benghazi of the little

Miftah, who went from being lost in city streets and on a mosque's doorstep to clinging to the hem of our mother Tawida's dress. Each of us was, to the other, a lighthouse for a ship lost at sea. Like the Akhribish lighthouse, we can only shine the way we're meant to if we're surrounded by darkness."[1]

After listening attentively to Atiga's reminiscences, Ali launched into what he felt was a needed explanation of other aspects of Atiga's history. He said, "Your father was bitter about the way the women in his family had been treated. 'Listen, Ali,' he said to me once, 'my uncles on my mother's side are a bunch of bullies and tyrants. When my grandparents died, they looted the inheritance that was due my mother and her sisters. They wouldn't let them have it on the pretext that when they got married, the money would go to outsiders—meaning, their husbands. They fooled them—and other women in those days—into thinking that women can't inherit under Islamic law. If any woman had the audacity to request her inheritance—still less demand it—she'd be shamed, and lose her brothers' support for the rest of her life. My mother and other women of the family were afraid they might need their brothers someday. What if, for example, their husbands weren't good to them and they needed somebody to come to their defense? But if a woman came out in public asking for her inheritance, she could be sure her brothers would never stand with her again. The mere words *I want my inheritance* would be enough to spark a family feud whose fires would never die out.

"'Like they say, *You can't spit in a well and then go on drinking from it.* It might seem that women give up their inheritances to their brothers of their own free will. But in fact, it's the fear of what the future might bring that keeps them from speaking up.

"'My uncles started up their businesses with the inheritance money that should have gone to your grandmother and her sisters. Then they expanded their trade and registered us as their partners to

1. Akhribish is a well-known historical district of Benghazi.

make sure no outsider would be able to turn against them or betray them. They're just biding their time until they have sons of their own who can manage the trade for them. Once that happens, they'll quietly and politely dispense with our services and cut us out of the business.

"'In this way we're turned into slaves of a different sort: invisible slaves who run somebody else's business and live on whatever crumbs our masters decide to throw us. But they would never acknowledge us as their equals.

"'My father's too weak to stand up to them, and he's no match for them on the market. As far as they're concerned, he's nothing but a rich laborer on hire by folks richer than he is. He taught me how to be a merchant, but he didn't teach me how to be my own man. So now's my chance to break free from all of them. I want to strike out on my own and enter the market as their competitor. I'm ready to butt heads with them. The market is a battlefield. Blood ties and sentimentality have no place there. If they approach me in any other context, I'll welcome them. I'll honor them. I'll treat them like royalty. But if they approach me on the market, I'll compete with them just the way I would with anybody else. Then whoever profits, profits, and whoever loses, loses. But I won't let them bring their business into my bed with their sister to manage things however they like.'"

Ali went on, saying, "Muhammad invited me to go in with him on his venture. He said, 'If you want to go in with me, Ali, I'm ready to shake your hand. Dictate your terms, and we'll move forward with everything out in the open. But if you decide not to, I won't hold it against you.' He promised to love me just the way he always had, and to stand by me no matter what. But he was serious about wanting to be free from the other men in his family, and he didn't want anybody else to share in his money and possessions.

"This scared me a little, if you want to know the truth. 'Now hold on, Uncle,' I said to him. 'You're so angry about all that's happened, maybe you're going a little too far.'

"'Well,' he said, 'everything has its time, and I'm not going to put this off any longer. I plan to have my revenge on everybody who's wronged me, whether they're relatives or outsiders. They're going to find out that beneath this calm exterior of mine there's a storm, that behind my silence there are words, that beyond my seeming helplessness there's power. I'll hurt them just as much as they've hurt me.'

"'First,' he said, 'I'm going to free Jaballah and Aida, my mother's favorite slaves, for what she did to my concubine in my absence. They don't deserve to be her victims too. Then I'm going to take a second wife. This way, Rugaya will know that her selling Tawida won't keep me away from other women. I'll bring her a cowife who's free like her, who enjoys the same social status, and my excuse will be that she hasn't given me any sons. As for Halima, God damn her, I'm going to ban her from my house for as long as I live. And I'm going to burn al-Figgi the way he burned me when he assaulted the concubine I love and used her to crush me. I'll get so drunk that I won't be able to imagine him on top of her anymore. That's the only way I can be with her as the Tawida that belongs to me.'

"As you can see," Ali commented, "Your father had a compassionate side, and he had a side that was as tough as nails. He would hide his suffering out of pride, act as if his wounds didn't hurt. And even though he was young, he was ready to do battle to make sure nobody lorded it over him. In this country it's been hard even for men to assert their freedom. But he did everything he said he would. He started his plan with al-Figgi. One morning when al-Figgi was on his way home from the dawn prayer, Muhammad blocked his path on a narrow alley. He'd brought along some slaves he'd hired to tie him up and muzzle him. Then he took him to some far-off place where a fire was waiting for him. He burned al-Figgi's private parts, then threw him onto a desert road. He knew Bedouins would find him and take him captive, and that he'd be forced to live with them from then on without being able to say anything about what had happened to him.

"The fulfillment of the rest of the promises came in turn. He freed Jaballah and Aida at Jaballah's request, his only condition being that they go live in the Slave Yards near Tawida. He married the daughter of the sheikh of a major tribe in Barqa. He rented a big house and, the day after his wedding, he moved Rugaya and his new wife there so that they could start fighting it out.

"Aunt Halima sent him one notable after another to mediate for her, hoping to end the feud that everybody had been gossiping about. But he rebuffed all her overtures. He even told our family sheikh, 'If I die, I don't want her at my funeral,' which I think was going too far. It was almost as if he'd predicted that he'd die without a funeral because, when he did die, he was buried in one place and his funeral was in another. He died alone and a stranger on a distant shore."

⬥

Ali coughed, covering his mouth with the handkerchief.

"Ali," Atiga said anxiously, "tell me the truth now. What's wrong? That cough of yours sounds downright scary."

"Oh, it's nothing to worry about!" he insisted lamely.

"Show me the handkerchief."

"It's nothing."

"Why are you hiding it from me, then? Come on now. Let's go to the doctor. Bardoushumu is a friend of mine. You can stay at his house and he'll take care of you."

"Let's go see Miftah."

"No, let's go see Bardoushumu."

"I want to see Miftah. Please take me to him. I feel like listening to that kindhearted man. I miss sitting with him in front of his shop downtown. We smoke together and talk, and I like to laugh at the funny stories he tells about life and people. I miss the hot sifiniz he makes with local honey. I love his calm demeanor and the way his kids run out and hug me, saying, 'Uncle Ali! Uncle Ali!' People like him are a balm to the soul, a safe haven. You feel better just knowing they're in the lives of the people you care about."

"Let's go see him now, then," Atiga said, relenting.

"Might I ask you a favor?" Ali asked her suddenly.

Atiga felt his eyes boring a hole in her, and she could tell he was hesitant to say what was on his mind.

"What is it, Ali?" she pressed. "Is something wrong?"

"Smile! I have a present for you," he said to her in his heart. But what came out of his mouth was, "No, it's nothing at all. Let's be going now."

There's More to a Person Than Meets the Eye •

From the first time he met Atiga, Ali's vest pocket had held a set of hoop earrings that his grandmother had completed with the money she made selling Tawida to al-Figgi.

He couldn't return any part of her mother to her, not even the price that had been paid for her on the day she was sold. Every time he saw Atiga, he would think to himself: *No, not yet, Ali. Go easy on her. She's been through so much already, she must be totally worn down. However fit an apology this might seem to you, it would be cruel. Leave it till some other day.*

Najwa Bin Shatwan is a Libyan academic and novelist. She is the author of several short story collections, plays, and three novels, including *The Horses' Hair* and *Orange Content*. She was chosen as one of the thirty-nine best Arab authors under the age of forty by the Beirut39 project of the Hay Festival. She has also been awarded the 2019 ArabLit Short Story Prize for "The Sharp Bend at Bakur."

Nancy Roberts is a freelance Arabic-to-English translator. Her literary translations include Salwa Bakr's *The Man from Bashmour* and Ibrahim Nasrallah's *Gaza Weddings*, *Time of White Horses*, and *The Lanterns of the King of Galilee*, for which she was awarded the 2018 Sheikh Hamad Prize for Translation and International Understanding.